Before It's Too Late

EastCoastPinay

Some lines were taken from the following:

Copyright Registration Number:
TX0009454254

Songs:
Before It Sinks in
By Moira Dela Torre
What If I Never Get Over You
By Ryan Hurd
I'm Never Getting Over You
By Gone West
Take Her to the Moon
By Moira Dela Torre

Quotes/Poetry Lines By:
Shefali Dang
S.L. Gray
Beau Taplin
Sabina Laura Poetry
Rhiannon Janae
Leezajaydepoetry
Lonely Penguin Poetry
Ram Chilhate
Shahrukh Khan
F.D. Roosevelt

Movie Lines Used/Quoted:
Movie Title:
Before We Go
Love Happens
Anatomy of a Scandal

This book is for all who felt how it was to be heartbroken.
For all who believed that it wasn't the ending, who bravely walked away before it
was too late, slowly picked up the pieces, and took the chance to love again.

You are not alone.

You were never alone.

And will never be.

Table of Contents

Author's Note

It's human nature that when we love, we hope and dream of a happily ever after. But in love, we don't always get a happy ending. This story may seem an ordinary love story, but it's one of the real ones, from finding love, experiencing how it is to love and be loved, getting hurt, and choosing whether to endure or step away.

I felt the pain as I slowly found Avery's voice. It was a hard battle between expectation and reality, when Avery chooses a very important life decision in the end. But through this journey I learned some of love's great lessons.

I hope that as you enter Avery's world, may you also see that there is love in letting go. When in a relationship, one must never sacrifice LOVE FOR ONESELF. Just like Avery, may you have the courage to believe that someone you love can only continuously hurt you if you give that person the power to do so.

Believe that when loving breaks one's heart, it shouldn't be the ending. Be brave to pick up the pieces, however slow and long it may take. Only when you step away will you get the chance to find the new meaning of love and, hopefully, the one that your heart genuinely deserves.

Live. Fight. Love.

Chapter 1

B: *Hon, what are you doing right now?*
Missing you so much. I love you!

AVERY JACKSON COULDN'T FIND the words to describe the mixed emotions she felt when she read the message that popped on her boyfriend, David's, phone. She didn't know if her eyes were fast enough to have read it before the notification faded or if the heavens wanted her to read it. Her body froze, her heart stopped, and a heavy and painful pounding dominated her chest. She gasped for air. Her whole body stiffened. It was like any second, her head would explode. Every inch of her body trembled. Her stomach flipped with nausea. She covered her mouth with her hand to stop the vomit. When she heard the bathroom door unlock, she immediately returned the phone to where David had left it before he took a shower.

"Are you okay, babe? What's wrong?" David asked her. "You're trembling." His eyes widened.

"Ah… um. I need to go to the bathroom. I think I have diarrhea." She bolted for the bathroom.

She locked the bathroom door and sat on the cold tiled floor, leaning her trembling body against the wall. Her eyes welled up with tears.

She didn't know what to do. Should she confront him? Since when has this been happening? Who is she? How? Where? Why?

An intense piercing and poking sensation burned like hell in her head. Her brain asked all the different questions but failed to find answers to any of them. She pressed her chest slowly and hard, hoping her hand could lessen the pain when she heard David from outside the door.

"Babe, are you okay? How are you feeling? Do you need medicine?"

"I'm okay," she answered softly, hiding her silent cries.

"Do you want me to buy you an energy drink or something?"

"Yes, please… Thank you." Her voice crackled.

She burst into tears when she heard their main door shut. She shook her head multiple times, denying that David had cheated on her. Even though she knew in her heart it wasn't true, she hoped the message wasn't for him.

She quickly left the bathroom. David's phone wasn't where she had placed it a while ago.She tapped her forehead several times. *Stupid Ave! No cheating bastard would leave his phone behind.* Her feet started pacing. She had to think of something. Confronting him could be good or bad. How would she do it? Reality hit her. Her woman's instinct was activated. Were there signs? She had either been so dumb, so trusting, or so in love.

How would she have known the signs?

There was no manual or a guide for her to know if he was cheating on her.

Maybe David is good at hiding, she thought to herself. She started going back to the past days, weeks, and months. Then, on cue, her tears fell again. The heaviness and poking in her chest intensified. But she had to brave the pains to find answers. Someone other than David might know.

Who else knows?

Self-pity struck her. Did people in the firm know? Was she the last one to know? These were just a few of the questions that popped into her mind. The unexplainable pain sucked all the strength in her. She wanted to confront him but was afraid she might be wrong. She felt the urge to call and ask, especially those in his inner circle. But she doubted they would tell her. If people who knew about it wanted her to know, at least someone should have mentioned it to her already.

"Oh, God! I'm so naïve and stupid! David is their boss. Their loyalty is with him, of course," she exclaimed.

She felt alone and pitiful. In times like this, she always ran to her family. But this time, she wouldn't because she still wanted to protect David. Stupid as it may seem, she wanted him to be on her family's good side.

What was she thinking? She suddenly remembered when Shelly, her best friend, caught her fiancé giving his secretary a "mouth-to-mouth" resuscitation inside his office. She'd wanted to smack Shelly when she lied to her parents to protect the guy's "respectable" image. Was *she* being Shelly right now? What should she do? She started doing personality analyses of each woman in the firm mentally. She couldn't seem to match anyone, any lady employee in particular. For years, she had been working in the firm; most of the ladies there were not the type to flirt still. Their relationship was an open book in their workplace. Only a marriage certificate was missing to confirm how deep they were into it.

David had come into her life unexpectedly. He was someone who had been around for almost three years. A guy she knew, a colleague she had never noticed before. He was that someone she saw every day but never thought about. But after their unexpected lunch together, she realized the reason behind it. She knew then that he had a long-time girlfriend. Though he attracted most of the ladies around the firm, Avery never joined the "fan club," knowing he was "taken."

Avery had experienced many different firsts after meeting David. On their first lunch together, he told her, *If your boyfriend doesn't come and look for you, he doesn't know what he's missing!* It was the first time a guy had told her there was something in her. Her heart had skipped a beat. How he gazed at her in all their times together made her heart flutter. No one had ever made her feel that way.

"Babe, are you okay now?" David asked her.

"Better, I guess."

She realized he was already back. She watched him as he opened the bottle of energy drink. Then, she focused on the cell phone he had placed on the bedside table. Even without going near it, she could tell it was in silent mode judging by the number of times the notifications lit upon the screen.

"Here, drink it, babe. Make sure you don't get dehydrated. Do you need anything else?" What she needed was for him to be honest with her.

"Nothing, thanks."

She gulped the drink without taking her sight off David. He was grinning as he grabbed his cell phone from the side table. She watched him as he sat in bed. He was so engrossed in what he was reading he didn't notice her eyes glued to him. A lump formed in her stomach. He had the same excitement and the sweetest smile on his face now that he'd had the morning he'd asked her to be his girlfriend. Except for this time, Avery was sure it wasn't for her. When her body started trembling again, she placed her hand over her heart.

She couldn't seem to breathe. Her breathing was becoming loud. It was so loud that she had to cover her ears with her hands. Then she couldn't seem to hear her heartbeat. She felt as if her heart had stopped beating. She started pressing into her chest—everything around her blurred. Then, there was total darkness and silence.

Chapter 2

"BABE, AVERY! WAKE UP!"

David's loud voice awakened her. His arms were wrapped around her restless body. His eyes were wide, and his brows furrowed. But Avery couldn't find the strength to say anything. Instead, she looked into his eyes and silently asked the questions herself. The questions she couldn't dare ask him.

She wanted to know why.

"What happened to you?" David touched her forehead. "Do you want me to take you to the hospital?"

Avery shook her head. She was fine. She needed to be. "I'll get you water. Stay in bed for now," he told her.

Saying nothing, Avery stood up and shuffled to the bed. She saw his cell phone on top of his pillow. The phone screen was lit up with silent call notifications. She grabbed the phone. The contact calling was the same person who'd sent him the message. Fifteen missed calls, all from the same caller. She heard footsteps coming near the bedroom door, but there wasn't time to put the phone back. Their eyes locked, and then David focused on the phone in her hand.

"Your phone." Avery reached out the phone to him. "Someone's been calling you fifteen times now."

Avery's eyes never left him, but his eyes looked away. David snatched the phone from her hand. His eyes flickered as his hands started wiping the sweat from his forehead. But he still didn't look at her.

"It's Jonathan. He's been calling me regarding our recent case." David handed her the glass of water. "So, take a rest for now, babe. I'll call Jonathan. Stay here. I'll be back."

She nodded and watched him as he rushed out of their room. The adrenaline and jealousy gave her body the strength to move and run for the door. Quietly, she watched him from the small opening.

His gestures were familiar. Bright smile. Sparkling eyes.

But she knew one thing for sure. They were not for her this time.

Avery was always confident. On top of her class, from grade school to her master's class days. She always received praise for being intelligent and was regarded as one of the most eloquent speakers in the law firm. She knew how to hold an audience of lawyers. She was a quick thinker and a problem solver. But at that exact moment, she felt like nothing. Worthless. Hopeless. Dumb. Numb.

Her mind was overflowing with silent questions.What did she do wrong? What did she fail to do? Did she lack something?Was she too much?

All the *whats* and *whys*. Her thoughts made her doubt herself and question her worth.

The sound of approaching footsteps awakened her from her thoughts. Finally, she went to bed and rested against the headboard.

David paced at the end of their bed. He tousled his hair and took a deep breath. "Babe, will you be alright if I meet with Jonathan for an hour or two?" He bit his lower lip. "We badly need to discuss our plan for tomorrow's court hearing."

She looked him in the eye and balled her left hand into a fist. She wanted to know why he had to lie. "Do you have to meet Jonathan at this hour?" She cleared her throat. *Where was he really going?* "Can't you guys meet early tomorrow instead?"

David stretched his neck, avoiding her gaze. "You know how Jonathan is, babe. He wouldn't stop calling and texting unless I meet up with him. A nervous wreck and a workaholic rolled into one!"

Who was he really meeting? All she could say was, "Okay."

Avery was still in disbelief. The David lying to her face now was the same who promised her forever. The David she thought for an angel had turned into a lying monster in front of her, but she was too weak and so afraid. Too weak to confront him and so scared to get an answer she might not want to hear.

"I have to go, babe. I'll be back as soon as I can."

Like in a dream, everything floated and blurred. Then Avery realized David had already left after hearing his car revving away from their garage.

Her mouth opened, but no sound could come out. What was happening? It was just six months after they got engaged. They'd confirmed a schedule to meet with the wedding planner only yesterday. She stood fast, took her phone, searched her contacts, and pressed the call button.

"Jonathan speaking."

"Hey, Jonathan! It's Avery." Her voice croaked. "I want to ask what case you and David scheduled for tomorrow?"

"Ave! We don't have any cases right now. The last time we worked together was before your engagement. I wished we had a case together. Working on a case with your man is much easier."

"Oh! I know." A lump formed in her throat. "How's Izzy and the kids?"

"Well, Izzy is with her mom in the province. I'm on leave for three days babysitting. Daddy duties!"

"Sorry to have bothered you, Jonathan. Kiss the kids for me and tell Izzy I said hi."

"I will. Send my regards to your man! Goodnight."

"Goodnight, Jonathan."

Avery leaned back against the bed and gave in to the silent tears that cascaded down her face and onto the bed sheets. Everything in her body ached. Her heart pierced and broke into a million pieces. Her imagination was running wild. David was driving fast, excited to meet his "Jonathan." An image came into her mind of their engagement picture. She couldn't help but remember that day as she held the heart-shaped frame. Her heart was full of happiness and love. They both looked so in love. Their eyes sparkled. David was holding her hand, showing the engagement ring, an heirloom passed down from his grandmother to his mother and David for her.

"You said you love me!" she shouted her heart out.

"You promised me forever!" she yelled like there was no tomorrow.

"You said you want to spend the rest of your life with me!" She cried until she couldn't take it anymore. She threw the picture frame with all the strength left in her, and the glass shattered around her.

Between sniffles and heavy breathing, she pressed 1 on her phone. "Hello. Are you at Jonathan's already?"

"Hey, babe. Yeah, I'm here now. Izzy says hi!"

Avery pressed her chest and bit her lower lip. "Okay, I just want to make sure you arrived safely."

"Don't wait for me, babe. It might take longer than I thought. Sleep well. Goodnight, babe."

"Goodnight."

That night, David gave her another first. The first time in their relationship that she cried herself to sleep. The first time she slept alone in their bed, her heart broke into a million pieces, like the shattered glass on the floor.

Chapter 3

AVERY WOKE UP, FEELING the cell phone in her hand. Her eyelids were feeling heavy and swollen. Seeing the pieces of broken glass on the floor started the waterworks. The time on her phone said 3 a.m. David hadn't come back since last night.

No text or even a missed call. Her chest heaved deep, followed by uncontrollable sobbing. Another first for her. The David she knew would never let the clock strike midnight without texting or calling her. The David she fell in love with would never leave her alone at night. He would never leave her side, especially when she wasn't feeling well, even with just a sign of a simple cold.

Three a.m. turned to 5 a.m. Two hours had passed with her comparing what the David she knew would do and what this new David was now doing. Then, before her tears started falling again, Avery heard his car parking in the garage. The shattered glass on the floor came to mind.

"Shit!" She didn't have time to clean up. Immediately, she pulled the duvet towards her body and pretended to be asleep. David entered the room quietly. He didn't see her watching him since he didn't glance in her direction. When he went for the light switch, Avery closed her eyes.

"What the hell? Bloody shit!" David's voice echoed in the room.

He stepped on the floor where the pieces of broken glass were. Avery was lying deadly still, pretending to be sleeping deeply.

David's face was scowling; he was clearly in pain as he removed a few pieces of glass from his foot. At that moment, Avery felt the fragments of broken glass stung on David's skin where the pieces of her broken heart were. Each piece tried to fight back against the person, causing her terrible pain.

"What the fuck happened here? Why was this broken?" David cursed and complained in a whisper.

When Avery felt him slowly getting into his side of the bed, she prayed for restraint and strength. David must have believed Avery was asleep. He must have been unaware she had been observing him all along. He'd cleaned the broken glass in fifteen minutes, sneaked in a shower, and placed his clothes in the washer.

She was so tempted to confront him and wanted so much to get answers. But she couldn't seem to find the courage. Her mind had been telling her to go for it, but her heart was too afraid, too weak. So, though David's body was next to hers, it was the first time in their relationship that Avery felt alone.

She couldn't help but remember how and when their story started. She'd treasured their happy moments together over the last year, but now they were in danger of becoming just memories. She still couldn't believe she was in the same bed with someone she trusted her heart to be married to, who, in less than twenty-four hours, seemed like a stranger. She tried hard to sleep again by assuring herself that David was beside her. But was he really with her? A question she felt was worth millions. Though her mind was fighting the urge to go into a deep slumber,her body gave in.

"Ave, are you okay, babe? You've been pale and quiet since you blacked out last week."

"I'm good. I just easily get tired these days," Avery replied as the corner of her eyes crinkled. She couldn't understand how he could act so normally.

David scanned her expression. "Don't you think you need to go to the doctor?"

She shook her head. "Don't worry about me. I'll visit Shelly this week. I'm sure she can do a routine check-up on me if I can't get a schedule with my primary."

David nodded. "How's Shelly, by the way? How's their wedding prep going on?"

"I think she's having second thoughts." Avery watched as David slowly sipped his coffee. "I can't blame her. She caught Art cheating again."

David's eyes widened as he clasped his hands on the mug, and he almost spat out his coffee. She silently apologized to her best friend. Avery couldn't think of any better answer to David's question. She didn't say it to jinx her best friend's wedding preparations. She'd only wanted to get David's reaction.

"What do you mean? Did she confirm it?" He focused his eyes on her.

"We haven't talked about the details. I'll update you once I get the juicy part!"

"Don't you think Shelly wasn't fully trusting Art because of what he'd done before? She needs to move past it so they can move on, especially now that they're getting married soon. What do you think, babe?"

"Maybe. I hope it's just a misunderstanding. It's hard to break one's trust. Especially since Shelly forgave him before. But I don't know what I could have done if I was Shelly. I would never want to share you with another woman." Avery stared at David as she held her bread knife. "I might kill her, or I might kill you."

"Um… Babe. We're talking about Shelly here. It isn't about us." The color drained from David's face as he watched Avery stab her pancake multiple times.

He gulped the glass of juice and a bottle of water in less than ten seconds. His Adam's apple bobbed up and down, wanting to pop out of his throat. Avery chewed her pancake without removing her glare from David.

"Did I get you there?" Avery crackled. "I was joking! I know you wouldn't even get a chance to think of doing such a thing." She reached for David's hand on the table and squeezed it hard. "You wouldn't give me any reason to doubt you. All the more to kill someone!"

"Uh… ah, of course, babe," David answered as little sweats formed on his forehead.

"Speaking of…" Avery pointed to her phone. "Shelly is ringing me now." She stood up. "Let me talk to her while you finish your breakfast. Then I'll wait for you in the car." She winked at David and walked toward the door.

David nodded; his face flustered. He looked like he was about to choke. He took a deep breath when Avery started walking. But her loud voice echoed.

"Shells! How are you? Are you going to kill someone this time? Who? I suggest you just cut Art's dick and balls into pieces!"

Chapter 4

"DAVID, WHAT? ARE YOU fucking kidding me right now, Ave?" Her best friend's eyes blazed with anger.

"I wish I were, Shells." Avery looked away as she tried to fight back her tears.

"Oh, Ave! I'm so sorry to hear about this. Why didn't you call me right away?" Shelly, her best friend, moved toward her side of the table. She wrapped Avery in her arms and gave her the most genuine embrace she had ever thought she needed since that painful night of David's text shenanigans.

"It's been killing me. I don't know why and how it happened. I can't even ask him. Since then, I've been walking crazy."

The tears and sobs she'd been trying so hard for the past days to keep inside erupted. She could show all her emotions in front of Shelly. Shelly was the only person who could understand her right now.

"Stop crying, Ave! That bastard doesn't deserve your tears!"

"What should I do? My mind has been all over the place ever since."

"Oh, I'm sure. Trust me, I know. But we're smarter now. Guys like David wouldn't admit it unless we caught them in the act. You can't confront him without receipts!" Shelly's eyebrows raised.

Avery's eyes bored into Shelly's. "What do you mean? I wanted so much to confront him. But I'm unsure if I'm ready to hear his answer."

Shelly's jaw clenched. "He thinks he can play you with his cheating game. Let him think you don't have any idea. Play dumb as you make the smart moves to catch him."

Avery didn't have any idea what Shelly was trying to say. But there was no one else she could trust and depend on. She didn't even know what she wanted to do. Since that night, she'd been floating, going with the flow of things around her. She was still in disbelief at what was happening between her and David.

Sadness clouded her face. "Shells, I just want to know why."

"Trust me, Ave. What's important right now is to confirm that David is cheating on you before we can get him to answer all your whys and hows."

After hearing what Shelly said, Avery decided confirming the truth should be her priority.But how she'd do it was another million-dollar question. Having experienced the same with her now fiancé, her best friend sounded like an expert in giving advice.

"I'm telling you, there are different ways. But you have to make sure that you're ready for it," Shelly sighed.

Avery looked Shelly in the eye. "I just want to know the truth, Shells."

"Well, knowing and confirming the truth will only be the start. Be careful what you wish for! In situations like this, we might open Pandora's box with a can of worms." Shelly tapped her fisted hand on top of the table. "What do you plan to do if you confirm David's cheating? Knowing is just half the battle, Ave."

Avery's face paled. She couldn't think of any. Avery Jackson, the most organized person in the world, didn't have a plan. Thinking about it just gave her piles of questions. Would she confront him? Would she forgive him? Would she stay or leave? But, though she didn't have answers to all her questions, she was sure of one thing: she wouldn't be in David's game without a fight.

"Ave! Avery!" Shelly snapped her fingers in front of her.

Avery tapped both of her cheeks with her hands. "What were you saying?"

Shelly shook her head. "There's one important question you should be ready to answer once you confirm David's cheating. Are you still going to marry him?"

Avery's eyes glistened. "I love him. Our families are so into each other. The whole of Boston knows we're engaged." Tears ran down her cheeks. "It's not like I can switch my heart off so it can stop from feeling anything for him in an instant. How can I not marry him?"

"Oh, Ave! I'm sorry that you're going through this right now. I am." Avery felt a squeeze in her hand.

Shelly was saddened to see how devastated Avery was right at that moment. But she didn't lie when she said she understood her feelings. Shelly had been there and done that. Learning from her experience, she could never leave Avery alone in her battle. Together, they would uncover the truth about David. Though she could give her all the advice in the world, Avery would still be the one to make the ultimate decision: it was her love life. But Shelly was sure of one thing: it would not be easy.

Weeks had passed since Avery asked for Shelly's help. She hadn't gotten the chance to put to the test the "mission" Shelly had given her. Her best friend had sworn it was a tried and tested strategy.

"Remember, you need to do this so we can have the chance to know David's whereabouts," Shelly had told her.

Shelly's words kept playing in her mind. When she saw David's phone while he was in the shower, it gave Avery the idea it was her best chance to do what Shelly had taught her. She added his phone number to the locator app she installed on hers. Her heart stopped beating as she waited for the confirmation message to appear on his phone. It needed to be accepted on David's phone while he was still in the shower. The mission was to activate the tracker on his phone without him knowing.

She begged the phone to work quickly. She needed the confirmation message before he got out of the shower.

It seemed forever as she waited for the confirmation to pop up on David's phone. As soon as it showed, she clicked agree. Immediately, she hid the tracker app icon in a hidden folder. Shelly had reminded her multiple times that David could never know about it. Finally, she'd promised that she wouldn't admit anything to David, whatever happened.

"What are you doing with my phone, babe?"David's voice startled her.

Avery scratched her head. "I was trying to check if my call can get through on your phone. Trying to call Shelly has been taking me forever, but it doesn't go through. I texted her and she said she didn't get a call from me."

David lifted a brow and gave her a once-over as he took his phone from her. He checked his messages and call log. Avery took a deep breath when he noticed nothing.

"Try it now. Call my number." When his phone rang, he smiled at Avery.

Avery clapped. "Yey! It's working on yours. It must be Shelly's line that has an issue."

David kissed her forehead. "I think so too. I'll be in the office. There are documents I brought home with me."

Avery nodded as she watched David walk toward his small office in their apartment. She pressed her chest to calm her fast-beating heart when he entered the room. In a second, she sent Shelly a message.

Ave: *MISSION ACCOMPLISHED.*

Shells: *TRY IT NOW!!!*

Chapter 5

AVERY'S BODY WAS SHAKING as she read Shelly's reply. Her hands trembled as she opened the locator app on her phone. She told herself there would be no turning back as she confirmed her tracking request. As the instructions said, it would only take a minute or two for the results to arrive.

Her heart skipped the moment her phone chimed. Her cell phone got heavier, and she felt her hand weaken. She knew she had this. She told herself to relax and breathe. Opening the message gave her hope and anxiety at the same time. Avery hoped that if tracking was a success, it would surely help her in finding the truth. But she knew she would forever be anxious and guilty since she had to do it behind David's back.

"You are just playing smart on the game David started!" Shelly's words echoed in her mind. They assured her that what she was doing was right. After a deep sigh, she opened the message.

LOCATE ME APP: *David is at HOME.*

She couldn't believe it was accurate. But she didn't know what to do next. She began having another round of crazy thoughts. Likely scenarios here and there confirming David's cheating. Since that night, her imagination had gone wild. So wild she started imagining David with different employees of the firm. All to analyze mentally who might play the cheating game with her fiancé. But since she didn't have *receipts*, as Shelly called it, she could only imagine things.

Now she could have all the receipts in the world!

The notification sound of a message woke her from her thoughts. Before she could reply, Shelly was already calling her.

"How was it, Ave? Can't wait to know!"

"It's amazingly accurate."

"Very good! Now we can start. We must have a code!"

"What code? What do you mean?"

"Ave! Like in the movies, anything can happen. We have to make sure we cover our bases. Don't you watch movies?"

"I do. But not the spy or action movies."

"If you watch sad romances like the ones with love triangles and betrayal, that's how they do it. First, change his name on your tracker app. So even if someone else sees the tracking result, his name will not show up."

"Oh, okay, I got it."

"We have to give him another name so we can talk about him whenever we need to, even in front of other people."

"I should use the same name on the tracker. What do you think?"

"That's a great idea! Just text me details about the code."

"But when do I use it?"

"From this moment. Anytime that bastard's ass leaves your apartment, the mission starts."

Avery's voice croaked. "Shells… are you sure we're doing the right thing?"

"Of course!" Shelly's loud sigh followed. "Unless you have another idea?"

There was complete silence from Avery's end. Since she seemed to have lost her quick-thinking skills, she could not concentrate on anything. Instead, her hormones had been making her dreamy and emotional. As a result, every song she heard sounded sad and heartbreaking. She had gone crazy. Music or a movie could easily make her cry and laugh simultaneously. Even a pillow commercial made her cry.

But, of course, her excuse for crying was that she remembered David had gifted the same pillow to her when he asked her to move in with him.

"Avery! I guess you don't have any idea with that long silence."

"Sorry, what were you saying?"

"Ave! Don't tell me you zoned out in the last three minutes?! Focus!"

"I know. I think it still hasn't sunk in. We were just so happy after we got engaged. And we just confirmed a schedule with my dream wedding planner. But then this shit happened!"

"Stop the fucking sobbing, Ave! Cheaters don't have a sense of time or day. Wherever, whenever they feel shit, they strike!" Loud breathing from Shelly's end overpowered the sobbing from Avery's line. "You'll get over this! I promise you, whether you want to leave David or fight for what you two have, you have me all the way! Understand that?"

Avery nodded continuously. "I know, Shells. Thank you so much. I'm sorry…"

"I love you, Ave." Shelly took one deep breath. "I know it's easier to say confront and leave him. But who am I to preach? I'm to marry a guy who did the same thing to me. Be strong. You have a battle ahead of you."

"Thanks. I need to hang up before David returns from the other room."

"Okay, you can text or call me anytime. Don't forget the code name. Love you. Bye!"

"Bye, Shells, love you!"

The silence that followed mirrored Avery's weak mind and body. Ever since that night, she'd dreaded being alone in their apartment, especially in their bedroom. Every corner reinded her of David and everything they had together. She thought Shelly was right. The easiest way was to confront him and leave. But it would be easier said than done.

Avery didn't want to cry, knowing that David was just in the other room, but her eyes had their own mind. When she looked around and saw their engagement picture in a replaced frame, the sobbing became a powerful force she couldn't fight anymore. She wished one could easily replace broken trust, like when one replaces a broken frame with a new one.

"What's wrong, babe? Why are you crying?"

Chapter 6

AVERY FROZE. DAVID'S SCENT filled her nostrils. The warmth from his body radiated behind her. She knew her tears would betray her if he saw her face and she saw his. She hoped David would leave her and not insist on getting an answer. But she hoped that maybe, just maybe, everything was just a misunderstanding and David was still the same man she had fallen in love with. The man who promised to love her forever. The one whom she still loved despite everything.

The crying she was trying so hard to keep to herself turned into loud and continuous sobbing. Finally, Avery couldn't control her emotions anymore. When David put his arms around her and made her slowly face him, she lost it all.

"Babe, what's happening? Why are you crying? Did something happen?"

David's concerned expression made her forget she was looking at the person who had been hurting her for weeks. She wrapped her arms around him and cried harder.

"I'm in so much pain right now," she uttered, her voice croaking.

"Tell me, babe, what's going on? What is hurting? Why?" David pulled his body away from hers and inspected her face down to her body.

"My heart is hurting… in so much pain for weeks now." Avery's body was shaking between sobs and tears.

As David wiped her tears with his fingers, he kept asking her questions. He was unaware of what she was about to say. "Is there something wrong with your heart? Did the doctor find something?"

Avery shook her head. "No… but I discovered something. It has been causing me tremendous pain, killing me every day."

"You're making me worried now, babe. Tell me, please." He motioned toward the bench at the end of their bed. As they sat together, he clasped his hand with hers.

Avery felt hopeful. She thought it might be the chance she needed to confront him. It was now or never. "We need to talk."

David nodded. "Okay, talk to me. Tell me everything."

Avery removed her hand from his. She looked him in the eye. "Who is she?"

"Who?" David asked with his brows furrowed. His hand cupped Avery's face. "What do you mean, who is she?"

Avery straightened her body, not taking her eyes off David. "Please be honest with me. Who is the woman you are cheating on me with?"

David's face fell. His breathing turned heavier and louder. The warmth from his hands turned ice cold. Slowly, he removed his hand from hers and immediately brushed it through his hair as his eyes looked down at the floor. Dead silence enveloped the room. Avery knew it was the chance to lay everything down. As painful as it may be, the only way to know the truth was to get answers from him.

"I knew it from the night I blacked out." She didn't ask him a question this time. "I accidentally read the message she sent you that night. You didn't meet Jonathan. You didn't have any reason to meet him at all."

"Ave, babe. You know I can't lie to you." Though he looked her in the eye, his gaze moved fast away.

"But you did. You lied to me." Avery sniffled. "You've been lying to me all this time."

If there was one thing Avery learned as a paralegal, it was to interrogate without asking. "I called Jonathan right after you left. He didn't have any clue. Izzy was in her parents' province;no way for her to tell you to say hi to me."

"Babe, I'm sorry." David clasped his hands together. Then, slowly, he traced Avery's lips and looked directly into her eyes. She didn't look away. Her tears and sobbing stopped. She felt braver, empowered seeing his sorry, guilty face.

"Who is she? Tell me! What did I do wrong?" Her eyes darted to his. "What did I not do?" Then she removed his hands from her face.

David started massaging his forehead. "There's nothing wrong with you. It wasn't you; it was me. I was stupid! I'm sorry, babe." He lowered his head.

"Ave. I'm sorry."

David said the three words she didn't want to hear. She had been agonizing for weeks, knowing the truth. She didn't realize that hearing the truth from him would be a thousand times more painful than how she had been feeling all along.

Avery confirmed that the truth hurts. She had valued honesty all her life, but at that moment, she wished David could have just lied to her face again. Hurt wouldn't give justice to how she felt when he gave her the confirmation she had been longing to get from him. It wounded her heart. It cut, it stabbed, and it pained her already bleeding heart.

"Ave, babe, I'm sorry. I know there is no excuse for what I did."She took a deep breath. "Who is she? Since when?"

"You don't know her. She was a client's assistant. We met a little over two months ago, and it was a random hook-up." David tried to hold her hand, but she pulled away. "I swear I didn't plan or think of it. I never thought in a million years of cheating on you. It just happened."

"Two months? You've been making a fool out of me for fucking two months?" Avery's chest rose and fell with rapid breathing.

"No, babe. I met her the night I told you I would meet Jonathan. I ended everything with her. Please believe me!" David's hands brushed his hair in insanely fast succession.

The memory of that night flashed back to Avery. David's sweet gestures, bright smile, and the sparks in his eyes. She wouldn't forget the image of him reading messages on his phone. He may lie to her face, but her heart felt the other way. His face then hadn't shown an inch of a man about to end everything with the woman whose messages he was reading excitedly.

Avery's mind told her not to believe him. To not forgive David would be the most reasonable decision. But her heart reminded her how sorry his face was. His asking for forgiveness should put her at ease. Just like any other sinner, David deserved a second chance.

"After you confirm David is cheating, what do you plan to do?" Shelly's voice echoed as if her best friend was beside her.

"Ave, please say something. Please forgive me. Please."

His words woke her from her thoughts. She stared at his face. She didn't know what to do with him.

Avery felt too weak even to say a word. Her eyes were locked on his. If only her eyes had sharp arrows flying out of them, they would have surely hit his body bulls-eye. Slowly but fiercely. She remembered what she had told herself: She wouldn't be in this game without a fight.

"Ave, tell me what I need to do for you to forgive me, please."

With precision, she wiped the remaining tears on her face with her fingers. Then she held her chin up. "I want you to tell her everything is over between you two… in front of me."

Chapter 7

DAVID MASSAGED THE BACK of his head as he felt a rising tide of fear in his whole body. "Don't you believe me? I ended everything with her."

Avery rose from her seat. "Make me believe you!" Her scream pierced the air. "Through your actions, not just with words." She walked toward the bathroom and locked herself inside.

David slouched and pounded his fist on his right side. The sound of his fist pounding and Avery's sobbing inside the bathroom replaced the laughter and giggles that usually filled the room. Avery wondered whether they could navigate their way through such a challenging situation.

David: *Please, babe, talk to me. I'm begging you. Let us meet our wedding planner as scheduled.*

Avery's eyes were glued to her phone, her mind trying to grasp the words. She didn't notice Shelly taking the seat in front of her. It had been a week since she last spoke to David. They stayed in the apartment together, but she moved to the guest room and didn't speak to him.

That cheating monster! She shook her head, remembering their last conversation, the confrontation, and David's admission.

David: *"I'll leave for a few days to let everything cool down."*

Her eyes had blazed at him.

Avery: *"No, you're not leaving! Stay here and bear how I'm going to be around you! That's the least you can do for making me a fool all these months!"*

David: *"I won't go to her. I ended things between us. Please believe me. I can stay with my parents."*

Cheating bastard!

"Earth to Ave! Are you sure you're okay? What's going on?" Shelly asked.

"David sent me a message. I don't know how to answer him." She started huffing and puffing.

Shelly sighed, "What lie is he weaving now?"

Avery glanced at her phone and threw it between them on the cafe's table. "He's begging me to be with him and meet our wedding planner as scheduled."

Shelly sipped her coffee, her eyes lingering on her best friend's face. "What does your heart tell you?"

Avery's lips trembled, and tears bobbled down her cheeks. Shelly wrapped Avery in a warm embrace. Having Shelly around helped to ease the heaviness in Avery's heart.

"Cry it out, Ave. It's okay to feel and show your pain. I'm always here for you."

"I don't know what to do. I don't know what to feel anymore," Avery whispered in her croaking voice. She let go of the hug and straightened her body.

Shelly straightened her shoulders then cupped her face. "Look at me. My opinion doesn't count here. Nobody's opinion does. Forget about other people. Ask yourself the most important questions."

Avery's eyes didn't leave Shelly's. "What questions?"

"Can you let go of David? If not, can you forgive him and move past his cheating? Will you be able to trust him again?"

Avery's face dimmed. She twisted the engagement ring on her finger. "How can I unlove him? Since we met, my days have revolved around him. There isn't a place here in Boston that doesn't remind me of him, our times together." She bit her lip. Her face trembled.

Shelly took the chair beside her. "If I knew another way, I would have told you without asking. You don't have to punish yourself. You don't need to unlove him if you don't want to. Whatever will make you happy. I will not judge you if you still want to continue loving him and marrying him. I want your happiness, Ave."

"Thank you. You're the only one keeping me sane these days." She exhaled and wrapped her arms around her best friend.

"I'm your ride or die, Ave! Whatever your decision will be, I'm always on your side." Shelly clasped her friend's hands in hers. "Right now, you have to decide whether you like it."

Avery nodded. Her eyes wandered around the corners of their favorite cafe. Then, finally, they darted to the board, where there was a picture of her and David showing off the engagement ring on her finger. She drew a long breath, held her phone, and texted her reply.

Avery: *Let's talk in the apartment tonight.*

She gasped when her phone chimed less than fifteen seconds after.

David: *I'm here. I've been waiting for you. I love you, Ave, only you.*

David was waiting in the living room when Avery arrived at their apartment. He gazed at her as she walked toward the couch opposite him. She crossed her arms over her chest, her expression dulled. He drew in a long breath and straightened his shoulder. His eyes were wide with fear.

"I know I've been an asshole. You may blame me and be angry with me. I know I fucked up!" He moved in front of her and kneeled. "I don't deserve your forgiveness, but I'm begging you to please give me another chance. My life is nothing without you, Ave!"

Avery's face flushed. Her mouth fell open; she couldn't believe he was begging her while on his knees. But tears shimmered in her eyes. She gazed at his face; lips tied. How could she not forgive him?

He lifted her chin and pressed his left hand to her cheek, using the other to wipe her tears. "Please say something, Ave. I'm sorry."

She stayed quiet. She didn't know how to make her heart unlove him in an instant. "I love you, Ave, only you." He squeezed her hand softly.

David's face was flushed; his eyes were red, and his lower lip quivered. At that moment, she realized that her love for him was beyond all the pain he had caused her. She felt in her heart the willingness to forgive and trust again. She would never let him go. She ran her hand through his hair and lifted his chin. His eyes lit up, and his lips curved with a smile. Then, without saying a thing, in silence, their eyes spoke. Their hearts beat in sync as they softly kissed.

That night, she and David had another first, making up and making love after their first couple fight. A relationship challenge every couple would wish not to experience. A phase in a relationship one can only hope to survive. But for Avery, it was a nightmare she never wanted to relive again. A thing of the past she would forget so she and David could start again. It would always be a reminder that she had to forgive to trust again.

Chapter 8

"HOW WAS IT?" SHELLY was grinning as she took a bite of Avery's cinnamon roll. "Yikes! That's cold." Her upper lip curled, and her nose wrinkled. "How long have you been staring at that poor roll?"

Avery just looked at Shelly, asking a question but saying nothing. Shelly quietly stared at her. They'd formed a sister bond as children, and Shelly could tell what she was thinking just from the expressions on her face and the movement of her body.

"What's going on? How was your meeting with your dream wedding planner yesterday?" Shelly batted her lashes as she mentioned 'dream planner' because they shared the same.

A choice they'd both made when they were still in high school.

Avery nibbed her bottom lip, and her mouth curved into a half-smile. Her eyes glinted, and she looked away. It had been a month since she and David talked. The night when the begging, forgiving, and make-up sex happened. That night, they both put their relationship nightmare to rest. David asked for another chance, and she agreed. She told Shelly everybody deserves a second chance, especially in love.

"I won't judge you," was Shelly's only reply.

Avery had been assuring herself she had done the right thing. She would regret not trying. She could have blamed herself for causing both their family's pain if they'd canceled the wedding just because she couldn't try working things out between them. But who was she to judge him? People make mistakes. She wasn't a saint in whatever happened between them! She wondered if she maybe lacked something.

Shelly tapped her hands on the table. "Ave!"

Her eyes blinked. Her best friend's loud voice zoned her back to the present. She loved him. She did the right thing.

Avery needed someone to assure her. But something was niggling at her, a feeling that something wasn't quite right. She couldn't put her finger on it. Even though everything had gone back to normal in their relationship, her instinct was saying otherwise.

Not bothered by her best friend's yelling in her face, she asked, "Is this normal?"

"What?" Shelly asked, her eyes widening.

"After you forgave Art, did you still feel the same warning signs? Like your woman's instinct was trying to tell you something else?"

"Did something happen?" Shelly asked as she rested her chin on top of her clasped hands.

Avery shook her head. "Nothing happened… not yet. Maybe I'm just paranoid." Shelly tsked and shook her head. "Did he do anything? Tell me what's bothering you."Avery crunched her lips. "Was it the same with you, then?"

"What, what? Give me specifics so I can understand!" Shelly tugged her hair.

"Ouch!" Avery pretended to slap Shelly's hand. "I'm not complaining. David has been the best since we agreed to move past his cheating. It's just I've got a feeling that something is still wrong."

Shelly nodded. "Is the locator app still active on his phone?"

"Yes… why?"

"Don't beat yourself up too much. Smart women like us feel more guarded and suspicious after getting cheated on because we don't want to make the same mistake."

"Did you feel the same before? Whenever David tells me something, like an auto-pilot, I always look him in the eye and feel in my heart if it's the truth or a lie." Avery closed her eyes.

Shelly paused. She had been in the same situation and wanted to ensure that every word she said would be less hurtful, if not comforting, for her best friend. Though they were best friends, Shelly kept some things to herself because she felt she had been a burden to Avery while experiencing her relationship shit show. Keeping some things to herself saved a little of her dignity.

But she wondered how she would tell Avery that the most fucked up role in a cheating game was being cheated on? First, you get hurt and betrayed. Second, you get to make the hardest decision—to forgive or not? Then, when you forgive, have the bravest face, the determined mind, and the strongest heart.

"Ave, that's normal. It will take time for you to feel at ease. But it doesn't mean that you must disregard the signs all the time."

Avery nodded. "It's been a month since we had that talk. David has been the absolute best. I can't see any chance for him to see whoever that woman was or any other woman again. He's been spending most of his time with me."

"Then stop the paranoia! The make-up sex glued you to each other." Avery shushed Shelly as she looked around the cafe. Shelly continued talking, clearly not minding if other customers could hear her. "Sometimes it annoys me when he calls asking your whereabouts whenever you're not with him."

"Really? You think?" Avery giggled.

Shelly took a deep breath. "It's going to be hard at first." She squeezed Avery's hand. "It might take months, years, or even a lifetime. Forgiving is easy. To trust the person who betrayed you even once is harder."

"I'm sure I forgave him. Trust him?" Avery sighed aloud. "I'm trying. I want so much to trust him. Same as before everything happened. I feel guilty sometimes because I see how he's been trying so hard to make me feel better, but he feels I still have doubts."

"Well, fuck him! That's the price he has to pay! Nothing compared to what he did to you!" Shelly whispered with her nostrils flaring.

Avery shoved her hair away from her face, straightened her body, and pouted her lips. "It's his karma for cheating on a smart, gorgeous, one-man-woman like me!"

"You got it right, girl!" Shelly gave her a high-five like the mean girl she pretended to be when they were little girls. "Now tell me what happened at your meeting."

This time, it was Avery's turn to roll her eyes. She raised her hands in front of Shelly's face. "Okay, okay! You're my maid of honor! I know that's what you're curious to know."

Shelly gave a lopsided grin. "That's a given! I couldn't forgive you if you didn't make me. That'll be the worst cheating in all relationships there is!"

"You're crazy, Shells!" Avery smirked at her best friend.

"Have you chosen a date? Just make sure it's months after mine." Shelly winked at Avery. "You're also my maid of honor, remember?"

"We haven't chosen a date, but David wants it soon. I think long preparation is better. So, I guess we don't need to rush."

"But how long is long?" Shelly stared at Avery's face as if she spoke Greek.

Avery's lips curved into a small smile, and she sighed. Shelly knew Avery was trying to say something between the lines. But Avery knew she would keep it to herself. She wouldn't want to add fuel to the fire. No judgments.

They may have swept the issue under the rug for the time being, but they could read each other like a book.

"I'm always available for you, Ave. Don't forget that!"

"I know, Shells. I love you so much!"

"Me too! And Art knows." Shelly formed a heart with her hands. "You both are in my heart!"

Avery gave back a finger heart. "I know. And I'm thankful."

Shelly took a long breath and held Avery's hand. "But seriously, the locator app is on your phone for a purpose. There's no harm in using it sometimes. When a woman's instinct is strong, it can be a sign. You should listen to it."

Chapter 9

DAYS FLEW BY SO FAST. It had been months since both sets of parents met and agreed on their wedding date. David didn't listen to Avery when she told him they should schedule anything related to their preparations after Shelly and Art's wedding. Instead, he insisted they set up a dinner with their parents to get their input in choosing their wedding date. Avery's excitement at preparing for her dream event was still there, but she couldn't deny her woman's instinct was getting stronger each day.

But if one good thing happened after they moved past their relationship dilemma, David became more considerate, affectionate, and open in communicating everything to Avery. So, when he consulted her on an out-of-state transfer for a promotion the firm offered him, it was a first.

"Babe, whatever you decide is my decision." David's voice was in submission. She wondered if it was a chance for her to assure him she was also trying to get everything back the way it was between them.

When she looked at his face, his body was like an offering to her in atonement. She could see he was trying his best. She would have to trust him.

Avery smiled as she traced the corners of his lips. "You should accept the transfer."

David pulled her body to his. "I'm not sure if I can stand to be away from you four to five days a week." His voice choked.

Avery clasped her hands around his neck and whispered, "We need to. Remember, this is a promotion." She lifted her chin to face him. "Besides, it's not permanent, right?"

She looked him in the eye. It was a habit she had developed since that unfortunate night. Whenever she asked him a question, her eyes automatically darted to his, wanting to ensure she read the truth in whatever answer he gave her. She kept telling herself she had to trust him, but her heart was still apprehensive. She had to remind herself that he was doing the best he could. But her instinct kept giving a negative vibe. How long would she live with her doubting mind?

"I hope not!" David shook his head. "The contract says five to six months.

Besides, I promise to come home for the weekends."

Avery placed a soft kiss on his cheek. "Or I can always visit you and spend some weekends with you there."

David nodded, then looked away. Deep inside, something had been bothering him. But he wanted to keep it to himself. If there were anyone he wouldn't want to hurt again, it was Avery. He would be forever sorry he caused her pain by cheating on her.

The night he admitted everything was his most regretful one. How could he have cheated on the most important woman in his life? Though he admitted everything and told her it was a fucked-up mistake, he knew it wasn't just a mistake. It was the most hurtful and regretful choice he had made.

With everything happening, all the cover-ups he'd had to create for that one choice had dug him into a deep hole of piled up lies. There were nights when he wanted to blame his efficient skill as a lawyer on how he faced the events that passed. But it was too late to backdown now; he was just hoping for the best. He prayed that his latest plan would solve the mess he had created. The top of his list was to protect Avery and ensure she didn't get hurt again.

Everything would work out fine, he thought. *One day at a time.* These were the exact words of assurance he'd been telling himself lately.

He only had one goal: to make Avery his wife. And he needed to make it happen soon. Despite the unfortunate events both known and unknown to Avery, he realized one important thing. He had never felt such great love for anyone other than her. And if hiding the truth from her was the only way he could protect her, lying was what he would have to do. Until such time he had taken care of everything.

The first month after David transferred went by fast. But before his transfer, he made sure they set up everything for their wedding, from the date, venue, and reception to the honeymoon. He was with Avery every step of the way. They completed all the needed meetings with their wedding planner. The only thing left for them to look forward to would be the last two meetings with the planner two weeks before their big day. In agreement with their parents, they set the date a month after his six-month out-of-state contract.

Three months passed, with David returning to Boston every weekend to be with Avery. Though it was the first time they'd been apart from each other most days in a week, he exerted extra effort to make her feel his presence every day. He called her every morning before they both went to work. Lunch breaks, dinners, and bedtimes wouldn't pass without them talking and seeing each other through video calls.

Because of their all-planned honeymoon schedule, Avery's paralegal tasks had tripled since David's re-assignment. If David was working his ass out of state for his promotion, Avery ensured she finished all her tasks within six months. They both filed for three months' leave from work, starting once David returned from his assignment. It ensured they would get a month free before the wedding and another month after their honeymoon in the Maldives.

In the fourth month of what they called their not-so-long-distance relationship, David was overwhelmed with his paperwork, unable to come home for the weekend for the first time. Avery accepted his never-ending apology. Though it was unbearable for him, knowing he wouldn't see her beyond five days, his workload would make the weekend pass by in a breeze. But, saying nothing to each other, they both had their battles going on inside them. David's fears and Avery's doubts.

"A penny for your thought," Shelly whispered in Avery's ear.

They screamed as they hugged each other. The people in their favorite cafe were all eyes on them. Some were smiling, enjoying seeing two best friends who had missed each other. Others looked unimpressed at the two for breaking their peace while savoring and sipping their favorite coffee.

As expected, the two ladies were unstoppable. They didn't care about their surroundings. It had been a month since they last saw each other. Shelly had just returned from her month-long honeymoon in Greece, so they had a lot of catching up. Though Avery missed Shelly's company for a month, she was happy to see the newlywed with a spark in her eyes, coupled with her giggles here and there. Her best friend was one lovesick puppy.

"God, I'm so happy to see you, Shells!" Avery took both of Shelly's hands. "I missed you so much!"

"Me too, my girlfriend!" Their eyes were on each other as they held hands.

Shelly's eyes widened. "What did I miss? You were zoned out. You didn't even notice me coming in a while ago."

"Not much." Avery pouted. "I was thinking about how I'm going to spend my weekend alone for the first time in months."

"What do you mean?" Shelly's brows raised. "Is David not coming for the weekend?"

"No, he's swamped with paperwork. He has to stay to ensure he completes everything before the six months are over."

"It shouldn't be a problem. If David can't come to you, go to him." Shelly rolled her eyes and smiled mischievously. "I don't think David would mind a surprise paralegal secretary who can give him countless orgasms for the weekend."

"Shells!" Avery's cheeks reddened. "You naughty girl!""Hush! That's what surprises are made for!"

Avery nodded, laughing. "Not a bad idea! But what happened to you? Are you a love guru now?"

Shelly winked. "Let's not waste time. We have shopping to do. We will buy the sexiest and kinkiest lingerie for David's lifetime surprise!"

Chapter 10

THE TWO DIDN'T WASTE any time and went to the nearest lingerie outlet in town. Shelly's honeymoon hangover gave them the motivation they needed. Avery felt bold and excited by her best friend's encouragement and approval.

She tried the five best-selling designs that Victoria's Secret was offering. Shelly's relentless prodding made her buy one set in all five designs. She realized David deserved a pleasant surprise when she remembered how he'd tried his best to regain her trust. From the lingerie and emergency leave from work, she decided it was time to embrace David back into her life wholeheartedly. *No ifs and no buts!*

Shelly's words hit her. "It's time to let go of your doubts, Ave. Let David back in your heart fully."

"I can't thank you enough, Shells!" She was in the clouds. "I've never felt this relieved and excited for him and me."

"You've got this!" Shelly's eyes blinked multiple times. "There are times you must be bold to spice up your romantic life. Make impulsive, kinky decisions!"

Avery couldn't help but grin when Shelly gave her a final seductive wink. It paid that she rarely asked for emergency leave from work. Instead, Avery got the fastest approval via a phone call from her immediate boss and HR. She couldn't imagine how surprised David would be when he saw her inside his apartment. Even though she had only been to his unit once, she was confident she could get to its location. It was in the same building as the legal office branch David was assigned.

"I've never been this excited in my life." Her footsteps were floating as she walked around the shop.

"I told you it pays to be impulsive sometimes!" Shelly bit her lower lip. "Men love excitement!"

After Shelly dropped her off, she packed everything she thought would suffice for the five days she planned to stay in LA. She smiled and giggled in front of the bathroom mirror as she did her night routine.

She knew that David deserved this. He had shown regret and proven she could trust him again.

"Do you have the lingerie sets inside your luggage?"

"Yes," Avery sighed aloud.

"Did you do all the preps last night? Waxing…"

"I got it, Shells!" Avery rolled her eyes. "Don't you trust me?"

"I'm just making sure. It's your first time doing a random act concerning David."

"I know," Avery groaned. "And I thank you very much."

Shelly giggled, "I feel like a mom sending her daughter, who's about to lose her virginity, on a prom night."

"Well, thanks, Mom!" Avery crackled. "I have to hang up now. I need to go. My flight just got called for boarding."

"Take care, Ave! Good luck, slut! Call me when you get into his apartment. Also, call me anytime you need kinky advice, okay?" Shelly blew her a kiss on her phone screen.

Avery did the same. "I'll surely do it! Bye! Love you, Shells!"

She walked toward her boarding gate, unable to believe she was doing something so spontaneous. Though she knew David wouldn't mind having her come unexpectedly, she still couldn't deny the anxiety she felt imagining herself knocking on his apartment door. In her mind,she had been practicing lines to say to him once he opened the door for her, maybe because it was the first time she was carrying out such an impulsive act.

After putting her luggage in the bin, she readied herself for at least two to three hours of sleep. The flight time from Boston to LA was six hours and fifteen minutes. She expected to be in David's unit between 1130 - 1145 AM. However, she could be inside as he came up for his lunch break. He usually called her around 12 NN.

Perfect timing. Avery couldn't wait. Her body synced when the plane took off, and her eyes dozed off.

Avery couldn't describe the somersault in her stomach as she waited for her turn in the taxi bay outside the LAX. The temptation to message David was strong, but on cue, she received a text message from Shelly reminding her not to even think about ruining the surprise.

She wondered whether Shelly had psychic powers. How could she message her even before she could type a message to David?

Her lips curved into a smile as she entered the cab with her carry-on. Her best friend knew her so well. Before she got a call, she replied to Shelly, assuring her she wouldn't ruin the surprise.

The ride from the airport took her thirty minutes despite the usual lunch-hour traffic. Trueenough, her estimate was on point. She was in front of the building concierge at exactly 1125 AM. As she approached the lady at the front desk, she already had her HQ Paralegal ID in her hand. To ensure everything went according to plan, she introduced herself as someone from the HQ with approval to use one room in the penthouse suite. Her boss didn't fail her. As promised, the central office had already called her name. They granted her entry to the building and access to the penthouse instantly.

Avery's heart pounded as she rode the elevator to the penthouse. She needed to be inside before David came up for his lunch break. She took a deep breath once inside the suite. Her watch showed 1150 AM. She'd made it just in time.

She brought in her luggage and stayed inside the room beside David's. The plan was to hide while waiting, expecting him to enter in a few minutes. When she checked herself in the bathroom mirror, her cheeks were pink, and her grin was the biggest she had seen on her face as she remembered the black underwear under her clothing.

She couldn't believe she was doing this right now. What had Shelly done to her?

Chapter 11

THE TIME WAS FIVE minutes before 12 NN, so Avery put her cell phone into silent mode. David had been calling to check on her daily as he ate his lunch. She remembered how he'd exerted so much effort to make her feel loved and special every day. Her day started with his wake-up call, reminding her to eat breakfast before going to work. Then, he sent messages between breaks to ask how her day was going. Finally, he video-called her at lunchtime while devouring his lunch in the penthouse dining.

Her stomach growling made Avery realize it had been an hour since she expected David to come inside the suite and call her. But she didn't hear any sound from outside. She wondered if he'd maybe eaten lunch out. She checked her phone to see if she had missed any messages or calls from him—no text or call.

Confused and her angry intestines gurgling, she sent David a message.

Ave: *Are you done with lunch?*

Five minutes passed, and her message was still unread. She wondered how busy David must be that he could not even check his phone. Checking over her call logs, it surprised her he hadn't called or even shot her a message since morning. Something seemed odd. David hadn't missed a day sending her a message or calling her since the HQ transferred him out of state.

She debated whether to call his phone or call his office phone. He might get an idea if she called the office. After a deep breath, her fingers pushed the call button for his number. Several rings and her call got transferred to voicemail. She assumed he must be swamped with work. She'd have to reschedule her surprise after office hours.

Avery discreetly went downstairs, aiming for the small coffee shop she saw across the building when she descended from the cab this morning. Her stomach badly needed a refill. Especially now that her plan A had failed. As if on cue, the moment she sat in a hidden booth in the cafe, her phone rang.

"Hey, Avery! You might be so horny right now, but you could have sent me a message saying that you have arrived safely!" Shelly yelled from the other line.

Avery chuckled. "I'm sorry I forgot to send you a message. Thanks for your concern, Mom!"

"I called after giving you two hours, tops. Your quickie lunch is now over since David has to return to work." Shelly's giggling was loud. "Tell me, are you still in bed? For sure, David was late after the lunch break."

"I'm sorry to disappoint you. But unfortunately, David hasn't come to the penthouse yet." A long sigh followed Avery's declaration.

"What the freaking hell! He doesn't know yet that you're there?"

"You got it right! He surprised me instead!"

"What a busy man, huh? Didn't you tell him when he called you during his break?" Shelly's voice echoed in her ears.

"That's the thing. I didn't get a call or even a message from him today. So, I sent him a message asking about lunch." She took out her phone from her bag and checked the message she had sent David from the bedroom. "It's still unread."

"Don't be a Debbie Downer. I'm sure he has a reason. He better have!"

"I'm just worried. Maybe I should have called to tell him that I'm coming today."

"Well, it's not the time for regrets now, Ave. Even if he is busy now, he will come up tonight, however late it is. He will still sleep; I'm sure of that!" Avery laughed at the annoyance she heard in Shelly's voice.

"You're right! But we forgot to prepare a Plan B..." Avery's voice croaked. Her body stiffened. The once piercing, burning, and choking sensation she felt in her chest was back. But unfortunately, it was too late for her to avoid the scene that was playing in front of her. So, she sat in that hidden space on the right side of the cafe. Her reason was to hide from people and occupy a seat facing the parking lot.

"We should make your Plan B now. I suggest you take a bath before the end of office hours. Change your lingerie..." Before Shelly could finish, Avery stopped her.

"I think that will be the least of my problems now. I'll have to call you back. Bye!" Her hands shaking and her chest beating fast, she aimed her cell phone toward the parking lot. She had an unobstructed view between the half-open blinds covering the glass wall that separated her from the outside, and she pressed the record button on her phone.

She told herself she could do this.

The moment she pressed the record button, it felt like she was in a trance, hypnotized by the scenes unfolding. Suddenly, the big cafe caged her body in a box-like atmosphere. Avery couldn't breathe. She couldn't feel anything, numbness occupying all of her. It was like all her senses had shut down except her sense of sight. So, she glued her eyes to the scenes she thought only happened in the movies, except this was real life. And it was Avery's life.

Once the scene ended, she typed a message for David. Her hands may have stopped shaking, but her tears just started falling. She didn't bother checking the time. The rapidly typed sentences mirrored her combined anger, hate, and self-pity.

Ave: WHERE ARE YOU RIGHT NOW? READ YOUR FUCKING MESSAGES! REPLY NOW!

Even without him replying, Avery was sure David got her message. She watched as he looked over his cell phone several times and immediately scanned the area. He took a deep breath and exhaled. Then he placed his phone back in his pants pocket and, to Avery's surprise, he got inside a car and drove away.

She wanted very much to confront him. But her mind overpowered her heart. Her best friend's never-ending reminders played back in her ears.

Play dumb to outsmart him. The more receipts you get, the better.

She wrapped her arms around herself. Her body badly needed a hug of comfort. But she cringed as her shoulders slumped. Her silent tears turned into soft sobs. Sobs she tried so hard to control. She told herself that the bastard didn't deserve her tears. The locator app had a purpose. She knew she shouldn't ignore her instincts.

Remembering the locator app she downloaded on David's cell phone gave her an idea. She opened the app on her phone and confirmed the request. Then, her fingers started tapping on the table. Mentally, she was counting the seconds when her phone chimed.

Chapter 12

LOCATE ME APP: D is in the vicinity of Cedars-Sinai Medical Center.

♫ Far beyond my reach
Is the future you promised ♫
♫ Now, what I never even had,
I have every reason to miss ♫

Avery was at a loss for words. Her mind floated. Everything around her seemed to pause. She couldn't hear anything except her heart's fast and loud thud. She pressed her hands to her cheeks, trying to feel anything. Since the moment David had driven away, her whole body had stiffened. With tears running down her cheeks, she kept questioning herself.

What had she done wrong? What had she not done?

David's words kept playing back in her ears. *"There's nothing wrong with you, babe. It wasn't you. It was me."* How she wished the problem was just her. Maybe the pain wouldn't be as intense as it was now. But, though her heart wanted so much to wallow in self-pity, her mind insisted on the other. She needed to act. She needed to think smart.

She wiped her tears. She raised her chin; her hands tightened into fists. After placing her things inside her bag, she rose from her seat. With a determined mind, she strode in the penthouse's direction. Once inside, she took her luggage and moved into David's room. Her eyes caught the frame with their engagement picture. She was fighting back her tears. She had to be strong. She decided she needed to make a choice. She didn't need Plan B. What she needed was a perfect plan.

Without hesitation, she dialed David's office phone number and sat on the edge of the bed. She needed more information. All the receipts she could get, she would take.

"Attorney David Thomas' office, how can I help you?"

"Hi! Avery Jackson, a paralegal from the main office. May I speak to

Attorney Thomas, please?"

"Good afternoon, Miss Jackson. I'm sorry, but Attorney Thomas is out of the office for the day because of personal reasons. He will be back tomorrow. Is there anything I can assist you with?"

"It's fine. I'll call back tomorrow. Thank you."

As she hung up the phone, she'd confirmed one thing: David was not in the office the whole day. Her instincts were right the entire time. If David could play his game, he was up to the biggest surprise of his life. She typed another message.

Ave: *What time will you finish work? I have a surprise for you at the penthouse.*

David: *I'm out of the office, babe. With a client right now. I'll call you once I'm back.*

A jolt of anger caused prickly sensations throughout her body. Her muscles tensed. "Screw you, David!" Each corner of the penthouse heard her pain and felt her wrath. Immediately, she opened her office laptop and logged into the lawyers' master schedule. Since she was one of the senior paralegal secretaries in the main office, she had access to the schedule master list. David's itinerary for the day was marked as Emergency Leave for Personal Reasons. After taking a screenshot, she reviewed the list of clients handled by his office. Unfortunately, the list didn't show any female clients.

She rubbed her temples. Remembering David's message telling her that he was out with a client made her laugh bitterly. *Who was he kidding?* She pressed the videos tab on her phone and played the one she had taken in the cafe. Her hands started shaking. David walked to a parked car and helped a pregnant woman exit the driver's seat. They hugged and kissed on the lips. For a moment, David rubbed the woman's belly. Afterward, he assisted the woman in the front passenger's seat. She would never forget his face after reading her message. David looked around and took a deep breath. And just like nothing, he got into the driver's seat and drove away. The suffocating pain awakened her.

Avery thought about how cruel life's mysterious ways were. It took her almost six months to get over David's cheating. Over twenty-four hours to prepare for the surprise trip. Then, when she let go of her doubts and trusted him again, a less than five-minute scene shattered everything. With tears in her eyes, she twisted the engagement ring on her finger. Why was this happening to her?

Slowly, she leaned her whole body on the bed. She tried to relax, but her body shook and wilted as she crouched into a pillow beside her.

"What did I do to deserve this?" she whispered.

If she followed Shelly's words, she already had all the receipts. What should she do now? Trying to analyze the situation, she couldn't help but compare, which was more painful. Was it the first or this time around? No betrayal is less painful, she told herself. The hurt that she felt before and now broke her the same way. What pained her more was knowing that the same man had broken her trust. The same man betrayed her again.

How could she face him without telling him she knew everything?

Lying in bed, she looked up at the ceiling with her hands crossed over her chest. She started thinking about what went wrong between her and David. It would be a puzzle if he meant that what caused him to cheat was on him and had nothing to do with her. She thought they were off to start fresh the night they confronted the issue. What about the care and romantic gestures he showered her with over the past months? Had it all been a lie?

Many questions were popping into her mind. Unable to think of an answer, she decided she must have been the devil in her previous life, to be betrayed not only once but twice by the same man, the man she loved and trusted. The life she envisioned with David as her husband dimmed. The future they promised each other seemed to fall further away.

Her eyes glistened. She sniffled quietly. She couldn't help but contemplate if her love for David could endure the second time. Was their relationship worth saving? She needed her best friend. Shelly's voice was all she wanted to hear right now. Before she could dial Shelly's number, her phone started ringing. She felt a congested pain in her chest, seeing David's name. She immediately moved from the bed and started pacing in the room. The ringing sound got louder and nearer as the doorknob moved from outside.

Before any plan could come to mind, she found herself face-to-face with David. Both stared at each other, unable to find words to say.

To say that David looked shocked would not do it justice. His face was as white as Casper's as his mouth opened. All his body froze except his chest racing, heaving high and low. He struggled to control his loud breathing—the only sound in the room.

"Babe… what are you doing here?"

48

Chapter 13

DAVID'S FACE COULD PASS for one that had just seen a ghost with flying colors.

"Surprise! Is that how you greet your fiancé, who flew from Boston to LA to see you?"

David raked his fingers through his hair. The rising and falling of his chest, accompanied by rapid breaths, didn't escape Avery's eyes. Instead, she plastered on a smile, representing the opposite of what she felt inside. Finally, David threw his phone on the bed and jolted toward her with arms wide open. He gave her the tightest hug, followed by his signature soft and small kisses on her forehead, nose, and lips.

It stunned her—a devil's kiss.

With her face on his shoulder and his arms still hugging her, she remembered the scenes in the parking lot. Her body trembled. The tears she tried so hard to hold in fell. Her mind was too weak to fight her emotions. All the pain, anger, blame, and self-pity she had felt in the past hours turned her into a sobbing mess.

David slowly removed his arms around her and lifted her chin. "Why are you crying?" he asked with his fingers softly brushing her tears away.

"I'm just so happy I'm here with you. I miss you."

"Oh, babe! Sorry, I didn't get the chance to call you today. I miss you too!" She looked him in the eye. How could he do this to her?

"Have you eaten? What time did you arrive? Why didn't you tell me? I should have picked you up from the airport." His voice was upbeat.

"Slow down, babe! We have all the time for your questions. I prank message you, remember?" Her gaze was sharp. His eyes avoided hers.

"I thought you wrongly sent it."

"When I didn't get a reply, I called your office."

He frowned, his face turning pale. "You called the office? When? What time?"

"I talked to Sue. She said you were out. It was when I landed and decided whether to get a cab. But since you texted, you are out with a client..." She touched his jaw, moved her face toward his ear, and whispered, "I put things in my own hands. I don't want to disturb my busy fiancé."

David's anxiety was overflowing. If there was one thing he didn't see coming in all his plans, it was Avery's surprise appearance. It relieved him, thinking she hadn't arrived earlier. Little did he know she saw it all. Whatever his reasons were, the same reasoning would cause him to lose in the dangerous game he was playing—a possibility he hadn't considered from the start.

"I'm so glad you are here, babe. What do you want for dinner?" His trembling body couldn't seem to hide his emotional state. He pulled her outside toward the suite's living area. Avery knew she got on his nerves with his hands shaking and his forehead creasing with sweat.

"Why don't we go for just coffee and pastries? I saw a cafe just across this building when I came today."

His eyes widened, and his chest heaved past and high. "Yes, the coffee shop… in front. Are you sure you want coffee?"

"I'm sure, babe." She flashed her grinning smile. "Besides, I want to have you alone for myself. When I saw the cafe, I thought it seemed hidden and peaceful."

David looked at Avery's face as though he was trying to find anything in her expression.

Her smile was the only thing he would see. "Sure, babe. Let's go."

Since they had a go-to cafe in Boston, David offered to make the order. While placing their order, Avery found the perfect spot for them. When he came to their table with their food, he found her opening the blinds which revealed the parking lot only divided by the cafe's glass walls.

"Is it heavy? Your hands are shaking." Avery took the tray from his hands.

David shook his head. "I'm just tired and hungry. Are there no other booths available?" His breathing was extended as he looked around the inside of the cafe.

Avery smiled. "I guess this is perfect! We have the view of the parking lot for ourselves."

He looked confused, his brow furrowing. "Take your seat."

She saw his eyes glued to her as she served him his coffee and pastries.

Avery made sure her face and actions weren't showing anything. But, instead, she was her usual jolly and charming self. He watched her serving his food first.

Avery was the same woman he fell in love with. Sweet, caring, charming, jolly, and innocent. She always made him feel he was the priority. Today was no exception. Maybe he wouldn't have wanted to be surprised by the surrounding circumstances. But her coming to see him despite her busy schedule and distance proved to him how much of a fucking asshole he was.

David realized how dangerous and complicated his situation was. Unconsciously, he raked his messy hair with both hands, elbows on the table.

"Are you okay? What's going on?" Avery lifted his chin, and worry was on her face.

He held her hand as the other touched her face. "Nothing's wrong. I guess I'm just exhausted." He placed her hand on his lips with his eyes gazing at her face. He didn't want to lose her.

"Look at you. You looked tired and worried. What can I do to help? You can have me as your extra personal secretary while I'm here." She winked at him. Two could play this game.

"What did I do to deserve you, Ave?" She wasn't sure if it was the sadness she saw on his face. Her heart spoke volumes, but her mind knew better.

"Let me think… you have been the absolute fiancé! You are loving, passionate about your work, and most importantly, honest!" Her eyes didn't leave his face. He gasped for air as his face turned pale white again.

When his phone rang, Avery saw a B flashing on the screen. She gave him her sweetest smile, pretending not to mind. His face froze. With his eyes on his phone, he was undecided about whether to answer the call.

"Are you not going to answer your call?"

David shook his head multiple times. "It's my client from today. I always tell them not to call me beyond office hours."

"It must be important, then. Just answer it."

"Are you sure you don't mind?"

Avery's lips curved into a smile that reached her ears.

Chapter 14

"WHY DON'T YOU ANSWER your call? Here… in front of me."

"If it's important, they should have messaged me already." In a flash, David declined the call and sipped his coffee. His hands were shaking as sweat showed slowly on his forehead while the cool temperature inside the cafe was at its best.

"I thought I could take notes for you while you talk to your client here."

David tried so hard to read Avery's statement between the lines. He couldn't see any, but he felt something different about her. It felt like he was about to lose his sanity, trying to gauge what was happening inside her mind. Seeing her gaze at him while telling funny stories about Shelly made him conclude he was overthinking the situation.

"I guess I have Shelly to thank for this pleasant surprise." His hand gently touched Avery's face.

"That or you might curse her! Good thing you're just really busy with work. Imagine my reaction when she told me I should also take this chance to check on you. Crazy Shelly!"

He didn't say a word. But his eyes said it all. In less than two hours they had been together, Avery learned how to get on his nerves. She slowly removed his hand from her face, remembering how he had used the same hand to touch the woman's pregnant belly hours ago.

Silence separated them. Both stared at each other, trying to read whatever was running through each other's minds. David was eager to comprehend what Avery knew. Since they were together, he could not see beyond her for the first time. Avery was fighting the urge to confront him. A perfect plan would only succeed if she did everything right. One thing was for sure—the ball wasn't in David's court right now. She had the ball in her hands and needed to ensure that the game would not end without her giving a fight.

While they quietly stared at each other, David's phone rang again. His mouth twitched; shoulder sagged. His actions gave it all away. Avery knew who was calling. With a smile, she told him to answer his phone while she went to the restroom. While she was walking away, she heard him say hello. She reminded herself to be calm and keep walking toward the restroom area.

After ensuring she was out of David's sight, she secretly peeped in his direction. He looked tired and weary. Avery lost count of the number of times his forehead creased. Finally, he stood up and started pacing around their table. The strong-willed, confident, and in-control David she knew seemed to have vanished. He slowly sat, face shocked and mouth opened. Though she felt so much anger and pain, her instinct told her to run toward him. Avery couldn't explain it.

"What did your client say?"

David was speechless. He couldn't find the strength to think about how to get through his situation with Avery. The fear of losing her consumed him as he tried to tell her everything. He couldn't stop. His plans were near completion. Nothing would go wrong, not this time.

"Are you okay? What was the call about?" Avery asked as she shuffled his already messy hair.

He didn't want to lie to her. But at the moment, he thought he was doing the right thing again. Or at least that was what he wanted to believe. He couldn't hurt her again. He didn't want to take the risk of losing her. But he had to do one thing.

"Babe, my client's wife is having an emergency. She can't contact him. I need to go find my client."

Avery fought the urge to get emotional in front of him. Instead, she reminded herself that she had a role in this game. Pretending clueless would put her ahead in the game David had started. As painful as it may have been, this was one of those times she needed to be stronger, braver, and bolder.

"I can come with you." Avery started picking up her phone. "Anyway, we are done here."

"No, babe. Don't worry about it. It'll be quick. Let me take you back to the penthouse so you can rest. And I'll return as soon as I get hold of my client."

"This must be a VIP." She looked at him straight before taking her bag from their table and walking toward the cafe door.

"Something like that. The company can't afford to lose them both." David's heart was battering while his mind convinced him he was doing the most reasonable thing.

He was clueless about what woman Avery had become in the past hours. His plan was fool-proof. Nothing could go wrong, not tonight. He expected everything to fall into place.

Avery acted as naive as she could to make David believe he had got her in the palm of his hands. Everything going on was to his liking. Never would he have expected that her mind was already steps ahead.

Once they got inside the suite, he paced again. Avery watched him in disbelief. How could a top-notch attorney believe he could hide all his lies forever? Was that how weak and stupid he saw her? She rubbed her chest—the familiar pain and numbness were getting into her.

"If I didn't know that you were leaving to meet a client, I would take from your facial expressions and body gestures you are about to sin. Like a terrible and unforgivable sin, babe."

David's Adam's apple bobbled, his eyes darting around the room. He froze in front of her. Avery knew she was pushing his buttons. She wished he would just come clean and admit everything to her now. Maybe it would be easier for both of them. Less painful for her already grieving heart.

"But I know I can trust you, babe." *You have been a big lie all along.* "There is no way that you will even think of hurting me. Not again." *But you kept on doing it.* "I'm sure you will keep your promise."

He was restless. Unable to think of the right words to say. Eyes closed; he sat on the couch with his hands covering his face.

"I'll go to the room. If you change your mind, knock on the door. I'll go with you." Avery walked away from where David was sitting. But instead of going to the bedroom, she watched him from the kitchen counter. The scene tore her heart. She bit her lip, preventing her eyes from tearing up. Yet, she couldn't deny she also felt bad for him. She saw how he was struggling.

How did they get to this? Was there still a way for them to get through this?

His phone rang. Hands shaking, he answered the call without realizing Avery was nearby. "Hello… yes, it's me. How long is the interval? I'll be there."

Chapter 15

AVERY SAW IT ALL. David turned his back, shut the door, and left without a word. She couldn't believe how she kept her composure and remained silent as she watched him go. The moment the door shut, tears fell down her cheeks. She closed her eyes and bit her lower lip. There were no words to describe her intense pain and hate.

She had no one; she was desolate. The day that had started with excitement and joy was ending with hate and sorrow. She didn't think twice; she returned to the afternoon video she had recorded and forwarded to Shelly. A while back, she told herself that the pain of deception she'd experienced both the first time and today had the same intensity. After what had just occurred, she concluded that betrayal by the same person twice and being left behind was a lethal combination.

Before she burst into tears again, her phone rang. Her caller ID showed Shelly's name. She was so lucky to have a great best friend. She may not have been fortunate in the romance department, but having Shelly was a blessing. When a complicated situation occurred, Shelly either called or came for her.

"Where is that bastard right now? Where are you, Ave?"

"Shells… I'm here at the penthouse. He left a few minutes ago."

"Find him now! Use the locator app, and I will give that asshole a dose of his own medicine!"

"How will you do that? I'm so alone. I have no one." Avery's sobbing developed into a full-on wailing. "Coming here was a mistake. I shouldn't have come here!"

"Stop blaming yourself! And you are not alone. I won't let that happen. Come down to the lobby now. I sent someone for you."

Like a little girl crying, abandoned in unfamiliar territory, she didn't ask Shelly questions. Whoever showed up for her in the lobby, she'd take it. She didn't want to be alone. Getting left behind and being alone with a broken heart would be her death.

After grabbing her phone and bag, she ran for the elevator. While waiting for the lift to stop in the lobby, she sent a command for the locator app to search for David. Even without getting a response, she knew where he might have gone.

Her phone chimed when the lift door opened in the lobby. Before she could check her phone, she saw Shelly standing at the front desk. Her eyes welled as they ran toward each other. They didn't say a word. Shelly's tight embrace gave her all the comfort she needed.

"How are you here? You do not know how happy you've made me!"

"I told you I'm your ride or die, Ave!"

"Thank you, Shells! But how did you do it?"

"I knew something was wrong when you told me he didn't show up for lunch. It was confirmed when you hung up on me when I called you. You didn't reply to my messages after, so I booked the next available flight. Art is outside waiting for us in the rented car."

Avery couldn't believe what her best friend had done. Shelly had come with her husband to be with her. First, she wiped Avery's tears and fixed her hair. Then, when she saw the cell phone in her hand, Shelly remembered David. "Did you find him?"

Avery nodded as she checked her phone. Her chest grew heavy. She felt embarrassed to disclose David's location to her best friend. But she knew Shelly would not let the day end without fighting her war. She would even die for her if she needed to.

"What did the locator app say?" Shelly asked.

Avery shook her head, worried about what her best friend might do. "It's okay, Shells." Her voice cracked. "I don't want to complicate the situation even more."

"Are you crazy? There's nothing more complicated than this. Complicated is not even the right term to describe what a jerk of an asshole your fiancé is!" Shelly shook her head. "No! I will not allow you to let him disrespect you again. If someone should be afraid to face the situation head-on, it should be him, not you."

Avery nodded. "Locator says he is in Cedar Sinai Hospital right now." She sobbed again. "Oh, Ave! We should show that bastard that you're not stupid and that you know what an asshole he is. Enough with his lies!"

To say Shelly was furious was an understatement. But, if there was one consolation Avery got from the situation, it was confirmation that she was lucky to have a great friend in Shelly—flying to LA without her asking, feeling the need to be beside her at the moment. Shelly was one hell of a best friend. She was the only reason Avery was still standing with all the agony David had caused her.

"I won't take no for an answer, Ave. We are going to the hospital now. That asshole needs to stop making a fool out of my best friend. I will ensure that this is one case he will never win!"

Avery didn't decline when Shelly started leading her outside the building. But when they reached the car, she felt worthless seeing the pity on Art's face when he greeted her. Embarrassment made her unable to find the words to express her gratitude. "I'm sorry to have dragged you into my drama, guys. You didn't have to come here, you two." There was no response from the couple.

The silence inside the car was deafening. Shelly's heavy and long breathing was the only sound they heard on their drive to the hospital. Finally, after one loud, deep breath, Shelly broke the silence. "Well, we wanted to come here for you so we could put some sense into your brain. And to show that asshole he didn't just mess up with you. He hurt you, he hurt us!"

"Relax, sweetheart. Keep your cool. Let Avery handle David once we get to the hospital, okay?"

Shelly glared at her husband. Art looked like he regretted saying anything. Avery was silent. She couldn't think how she would face David. Avery wanted to know why David couldn't be like Art. Why'd he risk his second chance?

Drowning in her thoughts of David, Avery didn't notice that Shelly had already ushered her toward the hospital's information desk. So, she just went with the flow. It was like a dream, watching Shelly and herself going through the elevator and reaching the Obstetrics/Maternity department. The next thing she realized; they were both standing in front of the nurses' station. Shelly was already talking to a nurse.

"Hi! We are here for Baby Thomas." Avery felt a soft squeeze in her hand after Shelly said the last two words. She replied with a nod, telling Shelly it was okay.

"May I know how you are related to Baby Thomas?" the nurse asked, glancing at both of their faces. Before Shelly could give her annoyed response, Art came running toward them, holding a balloon bouquet.

"We are family," Art replied. He gave the nurse a wink.

"You guys came in time. Baby boy Thomas is now with his dad in their private room. As we speak, the mom is still in the recovery room. The room is to your right at the end of this hallway—606. We don't want those balloons delayed." The nurse glanced at Art and gave him her sweetest smile.

"What the F was that, Art?" Shelly's face was red as they walked to the end of the hallway.

"I'm just trying to help, sweetheart. I didn't want you to get into a fight," Art stuttered.

"Be thankful it worked." Her eyes darted between Art and the balloons in his hand. "I give you an A for the props!"

Reaching the end of the hallway, Avery stopped. "I'm scared, Shells."

Shelly held her hand and looked at her face. "I know. But you should let your anger overpower your scared heart. We are not backing down. There is no better time than now."

"I hate to say this, but Shelly is right. Calmly talk sense to David. I have made the same mistake in the past, but I learned from it. But David." Art shook his head. "After asking for your forgiveness, I can't find any logical explanation for why he'd make this happen. Why didn't he lay all his cards when you confronted him before? He should have been honest about everything."

"We will be right behind you. We won't leave you alone with David. I promise." Shelly embraced her tightly.

"You deserve to know the truth, Ave. David has to end this double life." Art gave her a sad smile and walked ahead of them toward the room. Shelly took her hand and slowly led her toward the door marked as 606. Before they could reach the front where Art stood, his action stunned them. After peaking through the glassed portion, he took a deep breath and punched the sidewall.

Shelly ran and held Art's hand, which reddened from the punch. Avery looked through the exact spot where Art had looked a minute ago. She gasped as she covered her mouth. She felt a huge and heavy lump on her chest. Inside was David, seated on the bed, gazing at a newborn in his arms. A sudden, powerful jolt of pain hit Avery from her throat down to her chest. She gasped for air, unable to breathe. Total darkness followed. The last thing she heard was Shelly's voice calling her name.

Chapter 16

"AVE! OH, GOD! PLEASE wake up!"

The last thing she remembered was hearing Shelly's voice. She felt a hand squeezing hers. Even without opening her eyes, she was sure she was lying on a bed. With her eyes shut, the recent image of David holding a newborn in his arms flashed back to her. She didn't feel like waking up. The courage to open her eyes diminished, thinking David was possibly near her. She couldn't imagine sharing the same room with the person inflicting her sorrow. She didn't want to see him. Not in her current state. How could she have fainted when she was supposed to slap his face as she confronted him about his big fat lies? Avery wished Shelly felt her dilemma. Or she would have to pretend to be asleep until she could confirm David was not in the same room. But, like most of the time, Shelly may have heard her thoughts.

"Art, make sure that asshole won't get the chance to enter this room. I don't care how you do it. I don't want him near Ave."

"Sweetheart, you can't decide for Avery. When she wakes up, talking to David is her decision to make."

"I know, but as her friend, the only thing I can do to protect her is to get him away from her. Can you blame me?" Shelly's voice croaked. "She doesn't deserve any of this shit!"

Art cleared his throat. "What about her parents? Shouldn't we call them to tell them she is in the hospital?"

"And say what? That their asshole son-in-law-to-be caused all of this to their precious daughter?" Shelly's sobbing followed.

"Calm down, sweetheart. Let's wait for Ave to wake up and be the support that she needs. I don't want you to be stressed out and get sick, too."

After hearing the couple's conversation, Avery couldn't help but cry. She realized her plight had been affecting the people she cared for. She wished there was a way to turn back time and not come here to surprise David. Perhaps things would have been better. Shelly and Art would be at peace enjoying their newlywed life in Boston. She wouldn't be in misery. But would she choose to be blindsided by David's continuous betrayal of her?

"Ave, how are you feeling?" She felt Shelly's hand wiped the tears from her face. When she opened her eyes, Shelly gave her a clenched half-smile. She was seated on the right side of her bed while Art stood behind her, giving a deep sigh. Avery cringed with humiliation; she felt guilty and sad.

"Where am I?"

Shelly tried to stand up from her seat. Art placed his hands on her shoulders to stop her.

He motioned for his wife to calm down.

Shelly sighed aloud. "We're still in Cedar-Sinai. You collapsed when we were about to open the door to room 606."

There was hesitation in Shelly's last words. Avery knew her best friend didn't want to remind her about David. Maybe Shelly thought Avery hadn't seen David with the baby before she'd fainted at the door.

"Does he know that I'm here?" Avery looked at the couple's faces.

Both nodded in unison. She bit her lip and fisted her hands. She couldn't cry. It would only add to the worry her friends were feeling for her. However, she didn't deserve to be where she was right now. Shelly and Art didn't deserve to get dragged into her life's tragedy. Before she could say another word, Shelly beat her to it.

"He was insisting on being here beside you. He said he wanted to explain."

Art couldn't help but add, "When I asked him if the baby was his, he tried to talk me out of it. When eventually he said yes, I couldn't help it. I punched his face!"

"That's nothing compared to what he had done to you, Ave! Art may have smashed his jaw, but David broke your heart! He crushed your soul!"

Avery's tears started falling again. David had broken her. She'd believed all his lies.

Her body started shaking as she fought so hard not to make a sounding cry. Finally, Shelly stood up from her chair and embraced her tightly.

She patted Avery's back gently. "It's okay to cry it out, Ave. Let it all out. I hate to tell you this, but Art was right. You need to talk to David. Remember that you're not alone. We are here for you. We will stay."

Art nodded. "I told him to wait until you're ready. Then, anytime you feel okay with seeing him, I will call him for you. Shelly and I will stay outside this room when you guys talk."

"Did he say anything?" Avery looked at Art, expecting that both guys had already discussed things.

"He did. But I told him to his face that he fucked up. He may have his reasons, but it's his story to tell."

"How long do I have to stay here?" she asked Shelly, looking at the IV drip still attached to her wrist.

"You've been out for a couple of hours. And the doctor decided to keep you for twenty-four hours for observation. You're dehydrated and stressed, Ave. They ran some tests on you."

Without asking, she knew David had signed for her in the hospital. He was her emergency contact, and when they got engaged, he added her to his medical insurance, one thing she was now regretting. The last thing she wanted was to depend on David. But who would have expected that there would be a part two of his cheating game?

"I need to talk to him soon. I have to."

"Are you sure? You don't have to do it right now. You, Art, and I can all return to Boston after you get discharged. David can follow us to Boston to have your talk."

Avery shook her head. "The more I delay our conversation, the longer the situation will torture me. Please, Art, tell him to come here after twenty minutes. I need to freshen up."

Art nodded. "I'll go tell him while you guys do your thing here. I'll bring him up in twenty minutes."

"Thanks, Art. I owe you guys, big time!"

"Don't worry about it. I know you would do the same for Shelly."

Shelly's eyes grew at what Art said. Immediately, Art understood the gravity of what he had just said. "Not that I'm going to do what David did. I meant that any time, you would be the first one to come for her when Shelly is in need. You are practically sisters!"

"Good save, hon. Now go get that fuckhead," Shelly said as she pushed him towards the door.

When Shelly helped her settle back on the bed after giving her time to freshen up, the doctor and two nurses came inside the room. Since they were in LA, neither knew the doctor or any of the nurses personally—one reason Avery wanted to leave the hospital soon.

As one nurse fixed her IV and the other readied a pen and her chart, the doctor started with his usual round of questions.

"I'm glad you're awake now, Avery. I'm Dr. Germain. How are you feeling?"

"Better, I guess, Doc. How long do I have to stay here?"

"I instruct you to complete the drip so we can check off dehydration from the list. And twenty-four hours of rest will be a big help."

Before the doctor could continue, Art arrived, followed by David, who displayed a swollen jaw. Shelly held Avery's hand and squeezed it. An awkward stillness engulfed the room. No one amongst the four of them wanted to say a word. Finally, unaware of the drama, Dr. Germain resumed the conversation and looked at the two men.

"Hello, gentlemen. I assume that one of you here is the father, yes?"

Avery looked at Shelly with brows crooked as Art glared at David. Then, speechless, all four looked at Dr. Germain's chuckling face.

Like a quartet, they asked the same question. "What father, Doc?"

Chapter 17

THE FOUR OF THEM were in shock. Then, finally, it was Art who dared ask the question. "What did you say, Doc?"

"Avery is two months pregnant. I believe congratulations are in order. I referred her to an OB. She must have prescriptions and diet advice to avoid the same situation, especially with the baby."

They could have heard a pin drop in the room's silence. Even after the doctor and nurses left, they still stood staring at each other, no one knowing what to say. There was a long pause before Shelly said the first word.

"Do you want to have that talk with him now?" After getting a nod from Avery, Shelly held Art's hand and dragged him towards the door. "We will just be outside waiting." As they passed by David, Shelly scowled at him.

David quietly sat on the chair beside Avery's bed when the door shut. He tried to take her hand, but she pulled away. She made him talk without asking questions. David was the one who had all the explaining to do.

"Ave, babe… I'm sorry. Please let me explain." His head bowed. Avery didn't even glance at him. When he lifted his head and looked at her face, he saw stiffness and anger. But the suffering he felt emanating from her body made him feel more guilty. When Avery unconsciously placed her hand on her stomach, they lost it.

Avery's eyes welled with tears as her chest heaved fast and deep. David's tears fell on his cheeks. For ten minutes, they said no words. They just let all their tears explode.

As she wiped her tears, Avery glanced at David. His eyes were closed, tears falling. His hands froze on his messy hair. How did they get to this? What happened to them? She thought he'd already answered the same questions when she first confronted him. How easy it could have been if his answer had solved everything. "It's not you; it's me." But, instead, their situation made her realize it wasn't just a simple *not her, but his* reasoning. All his lies and betrayals had brought them where they are right now.

Avery understood everything that had happened was no longer a question that needed answers. Instead, their situation now required action. A solution that would not just be about them.

She remembered the precious one inside her body as she placed her hand on her belly. The baby was more important than her feelings. It was her priority now.

"You should have been honest with me. Telling me you want out is better than this! How could you lie so well?" Avery asked in a whisper. Immediately, David lifted his head and looked her in the eye.

With tears flowing down his cheeks, he gazed at her face. "There are no words to explain what I did. Babe, I'm sorry. I'm sorry for not telling you everything. But please don't doubt my love for you. I thought I was doing the right thing. I didn't want to hurt you."

Before he could touch her hand, Avery snatched it from his reach. Though brimming with tears, her eyes shot angrily at him.

"Which part of what you did didn't hurt me? I wasn't just hurt; you broke me. Not only once. I can't even count the times you tore my heart into pieces. Did I doubt your feelings for me? What a statement that was coming from you! I guess you have a different definition of love."

Avery's long and loud breathing echoed in the room. She felt nauseous remembering that David's baby with another woman had just been born a few hours ago. She fought the urge to throw up as events in the cafe parking lot flashed back. Her eyes squinted, and carefully, she patted her stomach. David seemed to notice her discomfort. He stood up and placed his hand on her belly.

"How are you feeling? Are you okay, babe?"

In between tears, Avery answered. "I'm not okay. How can you expect me to be? Being here is not how I envisioned my pregnancy news to be. I trusted you! I forgave you! How could you do this to me?"

David put his arms around her and accepted Avery's pushing and punching on his chest. He knew he deserved it all and even more. If her beating him black and blue could make up for all he had done, he would gladly offer every inch of his body for her to hit. It numbed his body from the pain, knowing that the hurt he caused was incomparable to what she'd been going through. He couldn't think of anything that could measure or heal her from all his betrayal and lies.

"What did I do wrong to deserve this?" Avery whimpered. Her hands slowly stopped punching David's chest. The sorrow and frustration were evident in her voice and trembling hands. He embraced her tighter, not wanting to let go. He wished Avery could feel his overflowing regrets and never-ending love through his arms tight around her shaking body.

With Avery's face in his chest and eyes welling, David mustered the courage to say the things running through his mind. "Please listen to what I wanted to say. Believe it or not, I never stopped loving you. I was a douche for making a wrong choice at the moment that led us here. You were never the reason or the problem. You are perfect in my eyes. The reason I fell in love with you. The same reason I'm so messed up knowing that despite you being you, I still made that one jackass choice that I will regret for the rest of my life."

"You said you ended it! Then, when you begged me for forgiveness, you promised to make things right. You swore you would never hurt me again."

David lifted Avery's chin slowly and cupped her face. Then, straight in the eye, he continued talking. "I ended it. But when she came back a month after telling me about the pregnancy, it scared me to tell you. She told me she had no one. I may be a schmuck, but the baby is still my responsibility. I told her it's you I love, and you're the only one I will marry. So, the baby wouldn't change anything between us."

Avery couldn't believe what David said. Her eyes shot daggers at him as she distanced her body from his arms. "How could you say the baby wouldn't change anything between us? What were you thinking? How long did you plan to keep the truth? Were you planning to set up baby play dates before you admitted everything?"

"I didn't think right. My decision to hide it was an action based on impulse. I knew I had to take responsibility as the father. But I can only give my heart to you, Ave. I only want a family with you, with our baby. Please believe me."

"I had been a fool for believing you. Look where it brought me. I have only wanted to be enough for you since I had you. Even after discovering you were cheating, I trusted every word you said. How stupid of you to think that you can keep hiding this? You never stopped loving me? But you kept hurting me repeatedly. We don't deliberately hurt the ones we love, David."

David gradually sat back in the chair. His eyes were begging for her forgiveness. All his secrets came back right at him. HARD. It was crazy difficult not knowing what was going on in Avery's mind. The complexity of their situation was overwhelming. It was like a court case he couldn't find any way to win over.

Meanwhile, Avery's mind and heart were at war. Her heart couldn't deny she still had feelings for him. She could easily say how she hated him, but it was torture knowing that hating him didn't make her unlove him instantly. But her mind was like an alarm that kept sounding, reminding her of all the lies. She was torn between following her mind and following her heart. To forgive and forget again? For whose sake? Would it be for the baby?

She took a deep breath. She needed to decide. "Let's call off the wedding."

David's face lost all color. He stood up and paced inside the room. He was speechless. After walking several times, he sat back and reached for Avery's hand. He clasped his hand in hers. Avery sat on the bed, looking beyond the hospital wall before her.

"I can't live without you, babe. I love you so much that the thought of losing you is killing me." David buried his face in the bed's side in their clasped hands. Avery fought the urge to look at him even after she felt his tears in her hand. Instead, his uncontrollable sobbing echoed in the four corners of the room.

"But you can't continue living while I'm dying in your lies." Avery's voice was quivering.

David lifted his head and clasped Avery's hand with both of his. "Ave, babe… I can't. I won't. My life is nothing without you. Please…"

Chapter 18

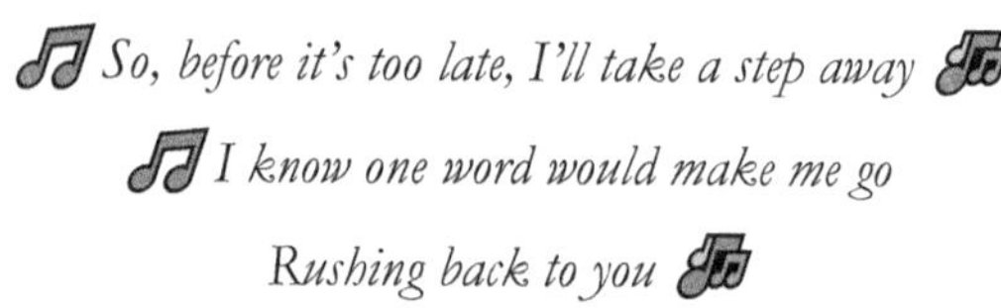

"LET'S CALL OFF THE wedding. I can't marry you."

Avery's voice was calm yet ear-splitting. She sat up straight against the headboard in the bed. She didn't spare even a glance for David. She was crying but kept her eyes focused beyond the hospital wall fronting her.

David felt defeated. The calmness in Avery's voice was like arrows piercing every inch of his body. Intense and excruciating. It wounded him beyond what he could imagine. This time, he couldn't hide. He found himself on a dead end. His trembling body shuddered, followed by a deep and uncontrollable sobbing.

"Ave… babe… I can't. My life is nothing without you. Please…"

His voice was lined with desperation. When he lifted his head and stared at her, he remembered their first face-to-face conversation in the office dining room. The feeling of butterflies and flurries she caused in his stomach, the echoes of her naive yet charming laughter that were always music to his ears. He felt everything all over again. Just this time, the gorgeous smile on Avery's face was gone.

He doesn't know what he's missing if he won't look for you. He told Avery these words when she mentioned that her then-boyfriend might have broken up with her. *Before I cheated on you, I should have thought I could lose you.* The words kept echoing in his mind. But the irony of it all was that both of their actions were bound by one thing—time.

Because of his actions, David was too late to realize he was losing the only woman he promised to love. Because of her inaction, Avery worried about losing herself if she kept allowing the only man she adored to stay in her life.

Outside the hospital room, Shelly was in tears. Her heart was bleeding for Avery. She heard everything. Though in the last few minutes, no words had been said between the two inside. For Shelly, the silence, the cries, and the sobbing from both spoke volumes.

When Art clasped his hand with hers and wiped her tears with the other, Shelly gazed at her husband's face. She was thankful for the man he had become, continuously proving that he deserved her forgiveness. But Shelly wouldn't say it, not yet. She wanted Art to learn from Avery and David's story.

"It sucks, you know. Sometimes a man only realizes what a woman brings to the table when that woman packs up her shit, or worse if she finds another table to bring it to." Shelly gasped as she remembered how Avery went through hell upon discovering David's betrayal. The struggles her best friend had to overcome to trust again. In the end, Avery suffered for nothing but to get hurt again.

Art sighed. Shelly was right. He was one lucky prick. It wasn't too late when he realized Shelly's importance. He got the time to rise above his mistakes before he could have gotten too deep, like where David was now. But, on the other hand, maybe David took Avery's silence on it all for granted. Another lesson learned; Art told himself. Never mistake a woman's silence for her weakness or innocence.

Sometimes fate has its own game; we can only wonder. In the same space, only divided by the hospital walls, four lives had experienced the same, but each saw the importance of time from different perspectives.

Shelly valued the chance for her husband to have witnessed what David had gotten himself into because of his poor life choices. Art felt gratitude, realizing on time how important having Shelly in her life as his wife was. David drowned with regrets for overestimating Avery's love for him. And Avery hoped that her decision wouldn't be too late or wrong.

Why do they still choose to do so despite knowing they could lose someone they love by hurting them? Why is it always too late before one realizes the importance of someone in their life? These were the questions that Avery was asking herself. Suppose she would reference David's answers. Why cheat on her? She wasn't the reason, and it just happened. When asked about hiding the pregnancy, he said it scared him to tell her. In his thinking, lying, and hiding things that would hurt her was protecting Avery.

"Babe… Ave. Please." David's voice was lined with remorse. His grip on Avery's hand tightened. "You're the only woman in my heart. The only one I will ever love."

In tears, Avery poured her heart out. "Maybe our love for each other was never enough. I believe you love me. I feel the same for you. But sometimes, even when we love each other, letting go of each other is the best option."

"No! Babe, no." David's tears were unstoppable. His whole body trembled as his lips peppered Avery's hand with tiny kisses. "I can't!"

Avery started brushing his hair with her other hand. "We have to. We need to. While we still have love left for each other."

Like a child, David clung more to Avery. "Never will I abandon my son. The baby's mother knew it all along. We agreed I would only take responsibility for my child. It was my fault for not telling you about it immediately. I was so scared that you wouldn't understand since you forgiving and trusting me again was already too much. I thought it would be easier for you to accept once we were married."

"David, look at me." Avery removed her hand from his clasp and cupped his face, making him look her in the eye. "That's what I'm trying for you to see. Your intention, perhaps, was not to hurt me. But since you got into a relationship with another woman, everything, and I mean everything that you did from then on, was based on lies. And in the end, it hurt me more."

"But I promise... no more secrets... I'll be honest, babe. Give me one last chance."

Avery smiled at him; eyes welled with tears. She touched his cheek, down to his jaw and his lips. "How I wish this time was as easy as the first. When I discovered you were cheating, I believed I was at fault. That's why I kept giving and exerted more effort to make us work. I thought forgiving you would change things."

"It changed me. I realized then that I only needed you. I ended everything when I told you I ended it. So please, think about our baby."

"The baby will be fine. I'll take care of our baby. I need time for myself. You also need time with your newborn. Being a husband may not be for you right now. But please be a decent man. Be a good father."

David took Avery's hand from his face and interlocked his hands with hers. "We don't need to cancel the wedding. You can have the remaining two months before the wedding for yourself. Just take a break, please, Ave."

Before Avery could say something, Shelly entered the room with a phone in her hand. "Ave, your mom is on the line. She wants to talk to you."

Their silence and anxious faces reflected Avery and David's unreadiness in getting a call from the person Shelly had just mentioned.

"Hello, Mom."

"Hi, Muffin! I'm with your mother-in-law right now. We just got your wedding invites from the planner. You'll surely love it! The design came out so pretty! And don't forget our dinner this weekend. We can't wait to help you with the invites and the guest list. Kiss David for me. Bye! Love you!"

Chapter 19

AVERY DIDN'T GET TO say goodbye to her mom on the other line. It was the happiest she'd ever heard her mom. But it made her heart cringe. Her head ached, thinking that David wouldn't submit to her decision. She knew she had to think of the best way to break the news to their parents.

David squeezed her hand, pulling her out of her reverie. They both realized their parents played significant roles in their wedding preparations. It reminded them of their scheduled once-a-month dinner for both families. Fear showed on their faces.

David shook his head. "We can't tell them. It will break their hearts."

"We need to tell them," Avery answered.

"We're just taking a break, babe. Let's spare them the…"

"Looks like you're ready to be discharged, Avery. I'm Doctor Jamison, OB." The cheerful voice of the doctor interrupted their exchange. Shelly saw that the doctor looked confused; she would have seen David with his newborn baby in the other room.

"It's a surprise to see you here, Mr. Thomas. I just introduced Baby Thomas's pediatrician to your…"

"Well, fuck our lives! It's a small world, after all!" Shelly facepalmed herself in an exasperated voice that caused the doctor to pause.

Avery realized the situation and diverted the doctor's attention to her. "Nice to meet you, Doctor. I hope you can give me a clearance immediately."

"I just ordered an ultrasound to check on the baby, and then we can process the discharge. I assumed you would do the rest of your prenatal in Boston, right?"

Avery bit her lip and nodded. "I can't wait to be back in Boston."

"Thank you, Doctor. We will leave as soon as Avery finishes with the ultrasound. We were just here for a surprise visit." First, everybody in the room heard the sarcasm in Shelly's voice. Then, her glaring eyes focused on David's.

Everything that happened after the OB visit went by quickly. First, Avery felt her body floating around like a feather, weightless. Then her mind drifted off, unable to hear anything around her. The last thing she remembered while in the hospital was Shelly's voice commanding Art.

"I don't care, hon. Make him. I will not let him fly with us."

Art didn't contest what his wife said. Instead, he tapped David's shoulder and motioned for him to follow outside. Avery felt like she had gone into a deep slumber, unable to decipher the following events. When she came around, she realized the three of them were already seated on the plane going to Boston.

"Do you need anything?" Shelly asked worriedly.

"I'm good. How long have we been here?"

"Oh, God, Ave!" Shelly embraced her tightly; how long had Avery been out of it? Art's face was in disbelief, mouth opened. Then, with only their eyes talking, the couple inferred the upsetting events had zoned out Avery from the hospital to the airport.

"I'm okay, you guys. Don't worry about me too much. I'm just tired, that's all." Avery gradually removed herself from Shelly's embrace. Then, with her eyes closed, she pressed her body towards her reclined seat and drooped. She wished everything that happened in LA was a memory she could also zone out of.

Exhausted wouldn't describe even half of Avery's physical and mental state. Her mind was empty of thoughts, yet it felt like it would explode any minute. Her body was numb, though she had rested in the hospital bed for twenty-four hours. She felt weak, physically unable, and mentally unwilling to move. The food Shelly forced her to eat didn't satisfy her palate.

The only reason she was still breathing was because of the precious life inside her. Each time Shelly asked her to do something, whether to drink, eat, or stop crying, she reminded her of the baby. "Ave, drink for the baby. Please eat, the baby needs food. Stop crying, Ave; the baby will feel your sadness." She knew the baby was the only motivation she'd been holding onto.

When they landed in Boston, Art's voice pulled Avery back to reality. "Hon, let me take the luggage. Just guide Ave towards the waiting area as I bring the car to the front." Avery felt Shelly's arm on her shoulders. Quietly, they walked towards the chairs near the exit of the arrival lounge. As they sat in the chairs, she squeezed Shelly's hand.

"Ave… stay in our house for tonight… please," Shelly said. She really didn't think Avery should be alone after suffering such a huge shock.

Before Shelly could finish, Avery squeezed her hand again. "Thank you, Shells. Thanks to you and Art. I could never imagine how I would have survived LA if it weren't for you guys."

"That's what friends are for Ave. We are a family. You are my sister. I'm your ride-or-die!" Shelly's voice croaked, then she bit her lower lip.

"I love you, guys!" Avery wrapped her arms around Shelly. "I'll stay in your house tonight, but only because I know you wouldn't take no for an answer."

"You bet! I don't plan on having a headache and heart attack thinking about how you're doing alone in your apartment." Shelly placed a kiss on her forehead. "And I love you too!"

After sharing a warm embrace, they looked at each other's faces and grinned. "Let's have a cookout! Art got a new grill." They nodded with their mean smiles. It was the first time since LA that Shelly saw Avery smile. Her worry lessened, but she knew that spending their time together away from David's drama was just a quick fix to her best friend's suffering. But she would do anything to give Avery just a few seconds to be free from it all.

When Shelly's phone rang and she saw Art's name on the screen, she looked outside. "Let's go. Our Uber is waiting." They chuckled and walked towards Art's parked car.

"Art is your amazing Uber, Shells! One hell of a guy you got!"

Once they were inside the car and Shelly sat beside her husband, she pecked Art's lips. "Thank you, hon!"

Art flashed a smile in wonder. "Anything for you, my lady!"

"That's for keeping up with me and my tantrums while we were in LA!" Before she buckled up, Shelly gave him one more kiss. "And that is for the grilling you will do later!"

They filled the car with their laughter. The two ladies giggled at Art's funny antics and stories on their way to the couple's house. All three looked forward to a random cookout. They had only one goal: to escape the memories of their last twenty-four hours, even for a short time.

In silence, Avery lay in the bed, eyes glaring wide at the ceiling, even when the lights were out. In just a few minutes, more than a year's worth of her life shared with David flashed in her mind—starting from their unexpected lunch. She remembered very well how she became smitten with his charm. He had a smile at the times she was sad. His words were heartwarming in the bitter moments of her life.

How could she not have fallen for him? The charismatic and sweet David always knew the right words: *"I promise God and myself that I will never hurt you. Every day of my life I will only spend with you. Your happiness will always be my priority."* She believed him and fell for him hard. Did he love her? She couldn't tell the truth from a lie after everything that had happened. She felt the only truth existing was the life inside her body.

Affectionately, slowly, and softly, she touched her belly. "Never doubt that we love you, my little bean. Whatever happens between your dad and me, remember we conceived you out of love. Nobody can take away all the care and happiness you deserve."

No tears fell. But it didn't stop Avery from wondering about how love works. Did it always need to hurt? Was there an easy way to let go?

Wanting an answer, she called the one person who she knew would never stop loving her. "Hello, Muffin. Why are you still awake? Is everything alright?"

"I miss you, Dad."

Chapter 20

"I MISS YOU TOO. Are you okay? Where are you?"

"I'm spending the night here at Shelly's." Avery's voice cracked. "I wanted to hear your voice."

"I'm glad you called." Her dad paused. "Do you want me to pick you up? Or maybe have a brunch date with me tomorrow?"

"I'd love to have brunch with you tomorrow, Dad."

"I'll pick you up at ten tomorrow. Can't wait to see you, my Muffin."

"Me too, Dad. I love you."

"I love you more, my Muffin. Goodnight."

Avery didn't mention her situation, but her dad knew her very well. There was her dad before there were the boys in her elementary and high school days. Always ready to listen to her stories. Before there were guys in college, her dad had been a shoulder to cry on. And before David promised her forever, her dad was, and would always be, there to hold her hand.

As always, Avery's dad didn't disappoint. He came in time to pick her up for their brunch. They enjoyed their usual panini and clam chowder at Abigail's Tea Room, Avery's favorite restaurant since she could remember. She would never forget how her dad religiously spent a special day with her once every month from when she was a little girl. They called it their brunch date. Their schedule was always the same until she graduated from college.

The schedule of once a month turned into once every two months. Avery's time with her family had lessened since she moved into her apartment and started working in the firm. When she began dating, their brunch became an invitational and rare occasion. But when she had her first heartbreak, her dad was the first person to comfort her. When David came into her life, her dad was the objective critic, and her mom was her cheerleader.

She had always been a daddy's girl. Though she also had a close relationship with her mom, her dad had always been her voice of reason. The three of them never kept secrets from each other. So, it was a first that she kept everything to herself when she started having issues with David. When Avery thought about it, she realized she didn't dare to tell her parents because she wanted to prove that she could make things better. That hers and David's forever would be like her parents'. But maybe their forever also had an expiration date.

Avery sighed with exasperation. She didn't notice her dad when he sat beside her on the park bench. It disrupted her inattentiveness when he handed her their favorite strawberry ice cream cone. It was their routine after every brunch date. They always sat down together in the park for dessert.

"I miss this so much! The last time we had our date was the day after David proposed to you, right?" Her dad directed his stare at her.

Avery looked away. "Yeah, that was the last. You don't know how I miss this too, Dad."

Her dad gently touched her hair. "I think I have an idea now, Muffin."

Silence descended between father and daughter. All they could hear were birds chirping, the footsteps of people walking, and children's laughter from the carousel.

"Whenever I see a park or pass by one, I always see you, my little Muffin, happily eating your favorite strawberry ice cream. I haven't told you, but those times we had together were when I felt great and proud as your father."

Avery felt a soft kiss on her head. She moved toward her dad's seat and gazed at his face. "Why is that? You've always been a good father to me."

"Maybe because those are the times I see you the happiest. A father only wants his child to be happy." Her dad cleared his throat. "But I guess right now is the first time I might be failing."

"Dad…"

Avery could not control the first tear breaking. The moment she felt her dad's warm and tight embrace, her unbroken river of tears followed. The soft yet many strokes of her dad's hand on her hair would describe the pain only a father could feel for a daughter. Her dad's silent warmth allowed her to break free from the heaviness she had been carrying. As her tears soaked through his shirt, her dad's fist clenched for not knowing what or who had caused her daughter's anguishing state.

"Cry it all out, Muffin. Dad is here for you. You can tell me everything."

In between sobs, she broke the news. "We need to call off the wedding.

I'm sorry, Dad. I can't marry David."

Her dad slowly wiped her tears when she pulled away from his embrace. She looked him in the eye. There was no judgment, no question, just plain sadness. One that comforted her, knowing that he was with her. Just being a dad ready to listen and understand, not to ask questions.

"He cheated on me. We kissed and made up. I thought it was all in the past and we were moving on. But the woman he cheated on me with just gave birth to his baby," Avery whimpered.

Her dad hugged her. "Oh, Muffin! Why didn't you tell us? It must have been hard for you."

"I'm sorry, Dad. I didn't want to disappoint you and Mom, but..."

Her dad stopped her. Instead, he fixed her hair and kissed her on the forehead. "Muffin, you don't owe us an apology. You could never disappoint us." When her dad placed his arm around her shoulder, Avery leaned her head on his chest.

"I tried to understand and accept things as they are, but..."

"You reached your limit. David crossed a line," her dad responded. Avery nodded. "I know the feeling, Muffin. I've been there."

Her dad's words surprised her. She couldn't remember a time when her parents had any issues whatsoever. Yet, despite the confusion on Avery's face, her dad continued talking.

"No, I'm not talking about your mom and me. Remember when you came home crying because your first boyfriend broke up with you? We spoke here at the same spot over ice cream. I told you that bastard may be your first love, but you haven't met your true or even your greatest love."

Avery nodded. "Yes, I remember that. You told me Mom wasn't your first love, but she's your one true love."

"Yeah. Before your mom, I had a girlfriend for five years. We lived together for two years before I gave up."

"What happened?"

"Cheating happened. The woman cheated on me. I discovered the night I planned to propose. But because of the long time we had been together, I thought holding on was the right thing to do. So, at night, I slept next to her, yet I felt alone. It kept me wondering why she wouldn't treat me right. I even blamed myself, believing it was my fault."

"Oh, Dad. I didn't know." Avery squeezed her dad's hand.

"It's all good now, Muffin. If it didn't happen, I wouldn't have met your mom. You wouldn't be here to complete the happiness in our family. What I'm trying to say is you shouldn't regret things that happened beyond your control. Learn from it."

Avery cackled as she wiped her tears. "I will surely learn so much from this. But thinking now, I regret one thing. I allowed him to let me fall asleep at night while I wondered why I wasn't good enough."

"You are enough, Muffin. That asshole was just greedy!"

"I've decided, but I'm worried. There's this feeling that I can't let David go. Yet I'm also apprehensive about holding on to him."

"This is the time you'll have to let go of a man you don't want to let go of to create space for the man you truly deserve. We will be beside you. We won't let go of your hand, whatever your situation is."

"Thank you, Dad. I love you and Mom so much!"

"We love you more. Your mom and I will never stop loving you." Her dad pulled her into another embrace.

"Dad, there's one more important thing I need to tell you," Avery whispered.

"Is there anything worse that asshole could make happen? Don't tell me he impregnated another woman?"

Chapter 21

HER DAD'S EYES GREW bigger. Avery cleared her throat. "Dad, I'm pregnant. You and Mom are going to be grandparents."

"That disgusting piece of shit! Oh, my Muffin!" Tears slowly filled her dad's face. He seemed to be wavering between devastation and happiness, his jaw quivering.

Avery gently wiped her dad's tears. Though her lips curved her signature muffin smile, inside, her heart was grieving. The tears that fell from her dad's eyes shot like daggers to her heart. She felt insensitive, spilling the complicated stories of her life in one enormous blow.

"I'm so sorry, Dad. I didn't mean to overwhelm you this one time. But…"

"My Muffin, stop apologizing. You have nothing to be sorry about." This time, her dad wiped the tears that slowly fell on her cheeks.

"I know my situation is such a complicated mess. I don't even know how I'm going to tell Mom. First, about the wedding not pushing through and me having a baby alone." Avery started sobbing, like when she was a little girl, and her dad would cup her face in his hands.

He lifted her chin and tucked the strands of hair behind her ears. "Look at me. We are going to tell Mom everything together. Like the best dad–daughter team we'd been. There's nothing you should worry about. Mom loves you most in this world. We both love you, and nothing can change that."

"Thank you, Dad." They shared a tight embrace.

"I love you and that little munchkin in your tummy. Mom and I will ensure you and the baby will be fine."

While Avery and her dad were preparing to leave the park, her cell phone rang. Her fingers automatically canceled the call when she saw it was the name of the last person she wanted to see or hear from. But, just by the look on her face, her dad knew who was calling her.

Once they buckled up in the car, Avery's phone chimed multiple times. She and her dad looked at each other. Then, before she could open the messages, her dad sighed aloud.

"Go ahead. Read what that son of a bitch has to say!"

With her hands shaking, Avery opened the messages she dreaded reading. She knew that as much as she would want to avoid David, the time would come when she wouldn't have a choice but to face him again.

David: *Babe, where are you? I just arrived at our apartment. Please let us talk before our family dinner tomorrow.*

David: *Ave, babe, I love you. Only you.*

David: *Babe, tell me where you are, and I'll come to pick you up.*

Lost for words, emotionless, she slid her phone inside her bag. Even without glancing at her dad on the driver's side, Avery was sure he was all eyes on her. Her eyes wandered for a moment to see nature in front of them. Birds chirped in chorus in a straight line on a tree branch. Leaves danced gracefully with the soft blow of the park wind. There was a calmness in the faces of the people enjoying the cool air breeze on that fine early afternoon. It was such a perfect moment.

Except that to Avery, it wasn't a perfect moment. Nevertheless, she felt that telling her dad everything would be the start. After reading David's messages, she imagined what would transpire during their families' dinner tomorrow.

"Muffin, let's go home to Mom." Her dad's voice awakened her.

"Mom is so invested in the wedding preparations, just like David's mom. You think they can handle the news?" Avery asked without removing her gaze in front of her.

"They both should. It's not your concern. Mom and I will talk to his parents like the mature and reasonable adults we should be. So check it off your list of concerns," her dad declared.

Avery took a deep breath. "David wants us to talk before tomorrow's dinner."

"What's there to talk about? Tell him to talk to my fist! And I'll have my knuckles kiss his face!"

"Dad…" Avery faced her dad. "You understand that eventually, I'll have to talk to him, right?"

"I know." Her dad nodded. "That asshole infuriates me. I wouldn't want him anywhere near you if it were only me. And the second you told me about the baby, I already fell in love with my little munchkin, but it doesn't change the fact that the asshole knocked you up, knowing his other woman was pregnant with his child."

Avery felt a sharp pain in her heart. She couldn't say which caused the pain. The hurt she saw in her dad's eyes or the truth he spoke of. Whatever the reason, David didn't mind getting her pregnant while his "Jonathan" was about to pop.

Slowly, the pain she felt transformed into anger. David was one selfish bastard! She probably lived in a transparent hole where she didn't see who the real David was. Avery trusted him so much. It bubbled her world with only David in it when she fell for him. It felt sickening that everything between them might have been a big lie.

"Dad, what have I done? Why didn't I see the signs?"

"Muffin, stop blaming yourself. Don't blame yourself for that asshole's infidelity. Believe me. You can never know. Most of the time, the person cheated on is the last to know."

Avery shook her head. "I shouldn't have forgiven him when I found out. I could have left earlier."

"Listen to me, Muffin. There's a perfect quote to explain that. We all know we deserve so much more, but we still settle for less because we fear the unknown that comes after letting go."

Avery held back her tears. It had already caused enough pain for her dad. Maybe what her dad quoted was right. She didn't realize it then. The thought of losing David, her love for him, and the idea of not wanting to disappoint or hurt their parents. She may have kept their relationship and held on to her feelings for David. But she also started losing herself.

"You don't have to talk to David on his terms. You can take your time if you're not ready. At tomorrow's dinner, you don't even have to come. We can take it as our chance to talk to his parents about canceling the wedding. We weren't there for you when you needed us, Muffin. I promise you we got your back. This time, we will do what parents should to protect their daughter."

"Thank you, Dad. I love you so much." Her dad replied by squeezing her hand. Then, when they started driving away from the park, Avery did what she thought she needed to do.

Avery: *Talk to your parents first and be honest with them. Spare them a heart attack. I'll talk to you when I want to. Not now.*

83

Chapter 22

David: *Babe, where are you? I just arrived at our apartment. Please let us talk before the family dinner tomorrow.*

READ

David: *Ave. babe, I love you. Only you.*

READ

David: *Babe, tell me where you are, and I'll come to pick you up.*

READ

Avery: *Talk to your parents first and be honest with them. Spare them a heart attack. I'll talk to you when I want to. Not now.*

DAVID READ AVERY'S REPLY over ten times since her message came. Amidst all the chaos that had happened in LA, the last thing he wanted to do was sit down with his parents. Not that he didn't care about them. But he only had one mission, flying back to Boston. To make Avery accept his plea for the last chance.

To everyone, he might be the sickest and most disgusting asshole of all assholes. But ever since he laid his eyes on Avery, he knew she was the one. He could never imagine his life without her. But the intelligent and reasonable man, the David everyone looked up to, fucked up once. Just once, but it was a one-time big-time.

"Why did you do it, dude? Didn't you learn from me?" Art's disbelief had echoed in his ears since that night in LA. Art had almost broken his jaw, but David didn't feel the pain nor got upset with Art for hitting him. He'd deserved it. If only they knew his agony, the sleepless nights, and the guilt that claimed every cell of his body.

Why did he do it? He had been asking himself this question for months now. The night that started as an accidental encounter between him and his newfound colleagues at a conference in LA began it all.

"Attorney David Thomas! Who'd have thought that the elusive bachelor is now engaged!" exclaimed a paralegal whom he had met at another conference a few years back.

"This is a perfect time and place for you to enjoy your remaining bachelor days, David," a new colleague shouted against the loud sounds inside the bar.

"Welcome to the club! I bet you haven't experienced the greatest challenge for an engaged man. But remember, what happens in LA stays in LA!" said the most senior colleague in the group.

It was the last night after the conference. He didn't listen to his inner voice when the group invited him for that night out. Before he left Boston for that once-a-year conference, his senior partner reminded him: *"David, don't ever make the mistake of joining the Big Five on their nights out. Nothing good will come out of it."*

But he didn't listen. He'd believed they'd caught him in the wrong place and time. He was supposed to fly back to Boston that same night, but the weather caused his flight to be rescheduled for the next day. So, when he went for a drink in the bar, he didn't expect the Big Five to be there. Finally, after multiple shots of tequila and relentless prodding from the group, he caved in.

Each one of them, with a woman attendee from the same event, got a room in the same hotel where they'd stayed for the conference. David barely remembered how they'd got back to the hotel from the bar. He just realized what happened that night when he woke up in a bed beside a brunette he couldn't remember meeting.

He immediately gathered his clothes scattered on the floor. There was nothing he wanted to do but get out of that hotel room. Without saying a word, he rushed out of the bathroom, ran to the hotel exit, and took the first cab to the airport. When he reached their apartment in Boston, he first took a bath and picked up Avery from the firm.

That was the first time he couldn't look Avery in the eye. Whenever she looked at him, he felt she could see beyond him. At that moment, he promised himself he would never let the same thing happen again. David loved Avery with all his heart. He wanted a future with her. What happened in LA would stay in LA. It was a nightmare he intended to keep to himself until he died. So, he thought.

But a few months later, he bumped into the same group at another conference in Boston. He'd wanted so much to avoid them, but it was too late. When they saw him with Avery, David reluctantly introduced them. Again, he felt his stomach flip, seeing the guys from LA with the same group of women.

"Who do we have here? Attorney Thomas and the fiancée," the senior in the group said.

All the while, Avery was genuinely happy to have met them. David was fidgety and felt twists all over his body. After all the introductions, he wanted to avoid them very much. But as his senior partner warned him, nothing good could come out once he'd joined them.

"Avery, I hope you wouldn't mind if we borrow David for a night to cap our Boston experience. We took care of him in LA, and he promised to return the favor once we're here. And you are free to join us."

"I wouldn't mind, not at all. But unfortunately, I can't join you guys. It's my best friend's birthday. We've already made plans for the night. But I'm sure David here will be happy to join you. Right, babe?" Avery was clueless.

David wanted to tell Avery he'd go with her, but he had no choice, as he made himself believe. That night, what happened in LA happened in Boston. He didn't realize the first time might have been a mistake, but the second time was a choice he would regret forever.

Avery didn't notice that David hadn't come home that night. Every year, she and Shelly celebrate a day before each other's birthday overnight together. They call it their BFF night. So, she didn't know David had dug a deeper hole for himself that night.

Before David could leave the hotel room where he and the same brunette spent the night together, he got a shocking proposal.

"I enjoy what's going on between us, David. No strings attached. I think we can be a wonderful team."

"What? This shouldn't have happened," David exclaimed.

"We can always do it the same way. What happened between us stays between us. What happened in this room stays in this room. It's not like I'm asking you to marry me," said the brunette.

Silently, David put on his clothes and took off. The events in LA and that night in Boston slowly consumed him. He promised himself again that it would be the last. But it seemed like fate had planned a temptation challenge for him. The following corporate case assigned to him was a collaboration with the senior lawyer of the Big Five, who had the same brunette as his junior associate. And the rest, as they say, was history.

When Avery confronted him, he didn't lie when he said that he had already ended things between him and the woman. However, it was the situation that caused its end. The case they were both on was finished. The collaborating firm's representatives moved back to its LA office. David thought it was for the best. He'd tried to bury everything that had happened over the last two months. When he'd learned Avery knew about it, he made sure whatever happened in those two months was something he wouldn't want to revisit in his life ever.

He valued the forgiveness Avery granted him. She was the only woman for him, the one he would spend the rest of his life with. Then, just as he thought his nightmare had ended, the last woman he'd wanted to see appeared in front of him. Several months after they last saw each other in Boston, the brunette associate disguised herself as a client for consultation. When she dropped the pregnancy bomb on him, he realized that his worst nightmare had just begun. He wanted her out of his life, but the once no-strings-attached woman gave him only two options: be with her for the duration of the pregnancy or deny her, and she would tell Avery about it.

For the endth time, he made another wrong judgment. Instead of telling Avery about his situation, he hid it. Then, when he could no longer keep everything to himself, he poured his heart out to his senior partner.

"You did what? David, you didn't just dig your hole; you dug your grave deep!"

"I know, and I regret everything. Avery just started trusting me again. If she knew about this, it would be my end." David sighed as he raked his hair with his hands.

"But you have to tell her. Better to tell her the truth than hide. I'm warning you—if you give in to what that woman is asking now, she will have you wrapped around her fingers. No one can keep secrets forever!"

Chapter 23

DAVID COULDN'T SHAKE HIS senior partner's words in his mind. *"You can't keep a secret forever!"*

Guilt and fear had beaten him up since then. Pressure had been eating at him. Then, like a bad omen, his senior partner's words struck. Every decision he had made from then on turned from bad to worse and worse. Hiding the truth from Avery had become his daily goal. All for his idea of not wanting to hurt her. While his lies piled up, he did everything possible to make Avery agree to the quickest wedding preparation. Everything that happened, he made himself believe, was for his love for Avery. He didn't realize what he was doing was what would also cause him to lose her.

When he couldn't bear all the mixed emotions that were haunting him, he made another lapse in judgment. The lies he put himself into were blinding him. Little did he know that what he thought was his last action to end it all would be the start of his end. But, unfortunately, the plan that aimed to protect his relationship with Avery was the same that destroyed everything they had.

"You sure hadn't stopped. I warned you before, and I'm saying it again. There's no better way to end this than you tell Avery everything." His senior partner was beyond disbelief.

"I can't... not now. Just give me the LA reassignment, and I promise after the baby is born, after our wedding, I will come clean to her."

"I'm worried for you, man. Giving birth in LA and having you reassigned before the wedding... But I don't think that's what will solve all this mess!"

"Please, I'm begging you. She promised me after birth, she would leave the baby to me. And she will be away from us forever." His fast and heavy breathing was drowning him.

"I don't know... How sure are you that she will do as she promised after the baby is born? I will sign your transfer because I know you are perfect for the job. Other than that reason, I'm out."

"Thank you. I owe you!" David gasped as if his senior partner had thrown him a life jacket.

"David, take my last advice as a friend. I care for you and Avery. I hope you'll

reconsider your decision. Nothing is more important in a relationship than being honest with your partner. Sometimes, things we consider a solution are what could break us. Please, think twice."

Still, David didn't listen. He made himself believe he was doing the right thing. That everything he was doing was to avoid hurting Avery. Deep inside, he knew the truth. He calculated everything, hiding in the shadow of his love for her. What he thought was a perfect plan destroyed him perfectly. It was too late. Even if he would have liked to come clean, it wouldn't have made any difference.

"Dude, why did you ask me to come here?" Art's voice broke the eerie silence inside his and Avery's apartment, enough to bring him back from memory lane.

"I need your help." David looked Art in the eye as he gulped the red.

Art shook his head. "You do not forget I'm not on your side, right? Besides, I'd rather die than be on the nasty side of Shelly!"

"Please ask Shelly where Avery is right now. I need to see her. I've been trying to call her, but she's been declining my calls."

"She stayed with us last night, but she left this morning. I don't think you would want to know where she is right now, dude." Art's words challenged him.

"I'll go wherever she is. If I have to get down on my knees and beg her, I'll do it. Just tell me where she is, please."

Art scratched his head abruptly. "You should expect that aside from my wife, other people close to Ave are out for your blood now, dude."

David nodded. After emptying his second glass of red, he desperately bowed his head over the table, his hands gripping his hair. "I just want to see her… and talk to her," he said in a high-pitched tone. His shoulders started shaking. He breathed in and out in quick succession, hard and fast. Soon, he was wailing.

Art was taken aback as he stood on the right side of the dining table. "Dude, you need to calm yourself. If you want Avery to talk to you, you must give her time. After all that happened, I guess the only thing you can do is wait. I hate to say this to you, but I think whatever is about to happen will now be all on Avery's terms. You can only wait."

"Art, please tell me where she is. Maybe she will go back to your house?"

David asked as he reached for Art's hands.

"I'm not sure. But let her be for now. Her dad picked her up this morning. I'm sure her parents know by now what happened between you two."

David's shoulders slumped as he buried his face in his hands. He felt defeated hearing that Avery was with her dad. When Avery moved in with him, her dad had been the most challenging and terrifying hurdle he'd ever had to overcome. Avery being an only child and a daddy's girl hadn't made it any easier. Before he'd proposed to her, he'd begged her dad countless times for approval and blessings.

"I'm so stupid for hurting her… I'm a big asshole!"

Art could only nod in agreement. He'd been an asshole too, but he'd lived up to his promise of not committing the same mistake once Shelly forgave him. He wasn't as eloquent and popular as David, but he knew when to man up. Whenever temptation came his way now, he fought it hard, ensuring he lived up to and was still living up to his promise not to hurt his wife again.

"I can only confirm that. You're one big asshole! I'm not as smart as you, dude, but you fucked up stupidly!" Art shouted.

"I should have known better," David whispered.

"Yeah, you're right there. Why haven't you learned? You could have just told her the truth from the start. For all you know, she already had an idea. Women's instincts are powerful. I learned from Shelly. If she asks about it, she knows about it. So don't lie about it."

David seemed not to hear what Art was saying. He straightened in his chair. "You think she is with her parents now? I should go there."

"Tsk. Tsk. Possibly." Art tapped him on the shoulder. "But if I were you, I wouldn't dare go there. If my wife could kill you, imagine what Ave's dad would do to you if he saw you now!"

David knew Art was right. Avery's parents would be in so much pain on behalf of their daughter. He would need to take the risk to prove his sincerity in getting the ultimate chance he was aiming for. There was nothing he could think of but to speak to her in any way possible. Maybe he should listen to Art. He should do things according to Avery's terms.

Chapter 24

"YOU SON OF…!" David's face numbed, and he was sure it swelled when his father's knuckles slammed into his jaw. Still in shock, his mother stood on the side, watching the scenes unfold. It was the first time his father had ever hit him. And he was sure by the redness and fierceness in his father's eyes that he wanted to hit him even more.

The scene froze when he immediately kneeled in front of his father. Head bowed down, he tried to grasp his father's hands, but pulled away. His mother came to stand between them.

"I'm sorry, Dad… Mom." David's voice croaked.

"Sorry, just won't cut it, asshole! What were you thinking? Did your dick grow bigger than your brain?" exclaimed his father.

"Stop that language! Let us talk about this calmly. What happened? Can someone tell me what this is all about?" His mother's plea echoed in their living room.

David knew the time would come. So, when Art left him last night, he visited his parents. He wanted to follow Avery's previous message and admit the situation to his parents before they meet Avery's parents for dinner. But hard knuckles greeted his face when his father came from an early morning golf session. It reminded him that Friday mornings were golf days for the older men in their families. But he was late in breaking the news. His father already knew.

"Yeah, why don't you tell your mother what a sickening monster you are, David!" His father tried to punch him again, but his mother blocked his action.

"What the hell is going on? You are both making me sick! Please, someone, tell me now!" his mother started sobbing.

"You're right! This asshole of a son we have will be the death of us. I just talked to Avery's dad. There will be no wedding! They're calling it off. Heard that, David?" His father's voice was full of spite.

His mother's gaze darted between David's and his father's faces. "Why? What happened? Did something happen to Avery? What did you do?" His mother lifted his head to make him face her.

"I'm sorry, Mom. It's my fault. But I promise I'll beg Avery to forgive me and marry me still."

His father was shaking his head. "This asshole cheated on Avery! Then even after the poor girl had forgiven him and still agreed to marry him, he couldn't keep his dick zipped, and he impregnated another woman."

His mother's knees weakened after hearing her husband's words. Before his mother could fall to the ground, his father instantly caught her and guided her to a seat. Silently, David followed. His action was not only causing Avery pain but also his parents. His mother's disappointed and sad gaze never left him.

Silence erupted in their living room. No one dared to speak, even after everyone got seated. His mother's crying followed.

"How could you do that? What happened to the son we raised? Did we not teach you to be a decent man?" his mother asked in between sobs.

"Mom, please don't blame yourself. This is all on me. But unfortunately, I gave in to the temptation."

"Temptation, my ass!" his father shouted. "I thought you were smart. Where did all my dollars paid for your Harvard law school go? Did you not know why your brain and heart are on top of your body? To remind you that those two have more power than your dick!"

"Stop, you two!" His mother's face was full of tears, brows crinkled. "How is Avery?"

"What do you expect? After witnessing this dickhead's other woman give birth, she learned a few hours after that she's also pregnant," his father scowled at him.

"Oh, my God!" his mother gasped in shock as she covered her mouth with her hand.

"Mom... Dad... I'm sorry for ruining your reputation. For causing this embarrassment to the family."

His father couldn't hide his disbelief. "You turned into a dickhead! Do you think this is about reputation? This is about you turning into a disgusting devil, impregnating a random woman while you're engaged to your fiancée, whom you selfishly got pregnant while living in your web of lies!"

"We must make sure we meet them for dinner later so we can talk to them. I want to ensure Avery is okay," his mother declared.

"I will come with you guys. I want to see Avery. I need to talk to the Jacksons," David said.

"You are not going anywhere near the Jacksons, the more Avery. Stay still in your apartment, or better, go to hell! I don't care! Her dad has said he doesn't want to see even the tip of your hair. You don't know what a father could do to an asshole who broke his only daughter's heart. Just be thankful they still want to talk to us, given the mess you've created," his father commanded.

"I'm so disappointed in you, David. How are you sure you're the father of that random woman's child?" asked his mother.

"Yeah, how sure are you? I wonder how you get recognized as one of the top lawyers in this state. Leaving Avery behind here, going after a random woman in LA. Uh! I can't take your stupidity! All your lies and actions made me feel sick to my stomach!" yelled his father.

"What did we do wrong for you to do these things?" His mother was devastated; her eyes were full of pity and regret.

"It's not your fault, Mom. Nobody is to blame but myself. I thought I was doing the right thing in protecting Avery, avoiding her getting hurt again."

"Have you not watched any films on cheating and its after-effects? You idiot!" His father's words were nasty but true.

"You both, please stop!" his mother shouted. She turned to face David. "You stay here and wait for your father and me to return from the Jacksons. Our conversation doesn't end here."

Though David was a few months shy of twenty-eight, his mother still held power over him and his father whenever their family argued. He realized in his fucked-up situation that he didn't need more people opposite his corner, especially his family. His parents loved Avery. It was a bonus that both their parents had clicked immediately.

He remembered their family's extraordinary times, vacations, dinners, and holidays. His heart ached. How did he not consider or think of it all before he brought his and Avery's perfect lives into a deep mess? The feeling of heaviness and pounding sound engulfed his head. Reality hit him. Hard. Painful. He didn't hurt Avery. He broke her and the hearts of everyone who'd been part of their relationship. Avery's parents and his. It wasn't just Avery that he'd betrayed. He'd also undermined the bond their families had formed from their being together.

How could he ever fix this?

Before he could get over the painful thoughts in his mind, the chime from his phone woke him.

B: *What gives? You don't expect me to discharge myself from this hospital alone with an infant out from my vagina just twenty-four hours later?*

Chapter 25

DAVID'S VISION SPUN. EACH day that passed by, he noticed how different Avery was. She never demanded from him, even if she had the right to. Instead, she'd always given her way when he needed to choose his work over their plans. Since they'd been together, she was always soft-spoken, sweet, and humble. She was always his number-one cheerleader. Even more, he couldn't find any reason at all to justify his unfaithfulness.

If only he could turn back time. He was thinking about all the decisions that led to his situation. It made him question himself. Did he hide the pregnancy to protect Avery from getting hurt? Was everything he did for Avery? If it was, why was she hurting the most?

Despite knowing how much he loved her, he still lied to her. He disrespected her for not fulfilling his promise. Instead of honestly admitting the situation, he manipulated her. He acted in the situation for selfish reasons. He realized all the things he did to cover the truth were not to save Avery from the hurt. It was to save himself.

He was a coward. For the first time, David admitted this to himself. Of all the days since he had been a fucked-up mess, it was the time he felt the most shivering goosebumps of fear. How did he let things come this far?

As cliche as it may seem, at first, he thought it happened because the opportunity had presented itself. He was in the same bar in LA while the group was there. Though he couldn't deny he should have left that drunken evening that had evolved into a one-night stand. It was supposed to have been a one-time mistake, but it had turned out to be something so much worse than that.

When he had faced the same opportunity in Boston, he'd felt fleeting fear and remorse. He became anxious about Avery finding out about the affair. But when the supposed mistake repeatedly happened, as monstrous as it may have seemed, there were times he lived through those moments guilt-free. He saw the cheating as a needed stimulant for change or, as the Big Five senior often said, *"Something that just happened."*

There was always regret after, he kept telling himself. Then, remembering the events that had transpired in those two months, he realized how he had spent so long trying to cover up and shy away from uncomfortable emotions.

It was like getting high, but as soon as he was done getting high, guilt, shame, and remorse followed. He was sure he was feeling guilty. But if someone had asked him then, he might have answered no. Because every time the opportunity presented itself, he realized he wasn't in touch with most of his feelings.

Whenever his senior partner got the chance, he kept reminding him: *"David, repetition doesn't transform a lie into truth. Don't you remember Franklin Roosevelt's words? I don't think you're seeing the danger in which you've put yours and Avery's relationship."* His senior partner was right. It felt as if the repeated instances of cheating had transformed his feelings of guilt and shame into something like a daily routine. Sometimes, it was like a challenge that pumped his adrenaline to survive.

Although he was already feeling contrition when Avery confronted him, he got the chance to take a step toward getting over the guilt and shame when he admitted to it—allowing Avery to react made him feel how badly he did. It was much bigger than it was in his mind before his admission. Avery confronting him made him realize what he wanted. He wanted to marry her, only her.

But when the pregnancy news slapped him, he didn't live up to his promise again. Instead of revealing the situation, he focused on saving his face; he covered the truth with piles of lies disguised as not wanting to hurt her.

Knowing he was in deep trouble, all the reminders and warnings he'd got before came back at him. Truth had revealed itself. This time, it wasn't just between him and Avery. Every time someone else learned of their predicament, that one person was like a wall getting in between them. He felt Avery getting further and further away. As Art had told him, more people were now out for his blood. People who cared for Avery, including his parents.

With all the events unfolding, Avery leaving him and wanting to cancel the wedding, their parents learning the truth, and the unexpected demands from the woman with whom he wished to undo all connections, everything was a list of recipes for disaster. But through it all, there was only one thing he could wish for: Avery and their child.

Fear and regret had been consuming him. He'd been trying to reassure himself that he could still convince Avery to give him the last chance he'd been begging for. He would be willing to give up everything if there was at least one sure way to get such, together with the lifetime vow to never break her trust and heart again.

He begged God to help him just this once. What should he do? David uttered his prayer. Deep within his heart, a pang of worry kept creeping in. The idea of Avery not wanting him back started to kill him. He couldn't visualize a life without her. More a future not spent with their child. He should have told her the truth instead of hiding it. Visions of the future without Avery and their child beside him were suffocating.

He couldn't let it happen. It was time he admitted he needed help from people close to Avery. But who would he run to? All the people close to her who were aware of the situation by now would surely want him dead. He could only imagine how those people would even be willing to kill him for her if possible. Even his parents were not on his side. Why would they be? He broke her, and what he did shattered the relationships of all their families and close friends.

But he didn't have a choice. He'd take the risk. Anything that could help him, from anyone. Slowly, he stepped toward his parents' room. He took a deep, long breath and knocked. When he heard his mom's voice say, "Come in," he opened the door with his hands shaking.

His mother bit her lip, glanced at him, and immediately looked away. She didn't have to say anything. He got the message loud and clear. He slowly held her hand as he sat beside her at the foot of the bed. He was thankful his mother didn't pull away. But she also didn't move at all. She just looked at him with a questioning face.

"I'm sorry, Mom. I'm so sorry."

"What are you sorry for? Make me understand." Tears slowly fell on his mother's cheeks.

Then, with his trembling hand, David gradually wiped the tears from her eyes.

"I'm sorry for everything. All the unacceptable things I've done. All the hurt I've caused, Avery, the disappointments I brought upon you and Dad. I deserve nothing good after all the bad I've done." His mother cupped his face. "Please help me, Mom. I can't lose Avery. I need her and our child in my life." Then, with his voice trembling and hands shaking, he covered his mother's hands.

"As a mother, I know that sadness can come in many forms. It breaks my heart because I didn't expect one of its forms to resemble your face right now." His mother sobbed as she wiped the tears that glistened from his eyes.

"I don't know what to do, Mom. What should I do?" His eyes begged for answers.

His mother's warm arms hugged David. "I wish I could tell you the right answer. How I wish this time were like the old times. Like when you were still a little boy, my warm embrace could comfort you whenever you were sad."

"Mom, please tell me everything's going to be fine."

Chapter 26

DAVID'S WORDS WERE LINED with desperation. He remembered a few memories of what his mother had said. He longed for the simpler times of his childhood when her warm embrace and soothing voice were enough to ease his sadness. He wished the current situation was just a nightmare and he could wake up to a life with only himself and Avery.

Scared was a simple word compared to the complex emotions that stirred up anxiety in his body. With each passing second, the probability of him losing Avery seemed to increase. Even though he tried not to entertain the thought, after several days with no communication or sight of Avery, his worst nightmare appeared to be coming true.

"Son, my heart will not stop loving you as your mother. But I cannot condone or accept your actions towards Avery."

David was speechless for the first time since he presented himself as one of Boston's young and eloquent defensive court lawyers. Hearing those words from his mother was like getting a losing verdict from a judge during a trial.

The shock on his face was evident as he uttered, "Mom…" He had hoped that she could be the one to help him earn Avery's forgiveness.

"Your father and I are meeting the Jacksons for dinner in a few hours. I understand that you wish me to persuade Avery to reconsider, but our priority is apologizing for the situation and ensuring her well-being. We must listen to her and respect her decision regarding your relationship. Please keep an open mind." His mother's gaze shifted toward him as she spoke.

David held his mother's hand, and she clasped him with both hands. Despite his pleading, his mother remained firm and gazed at him with determined eyes. "Son, please listen to me," she said. Consider how you would react if Avery were in your situation, and you were in your father's or my position. If Avery was the one who cheated, how would you feel? Would you want her parents to influence your decision after all you've been through?"

He was in denial and struggling to understand his mother's message. His gaze was fixed on her face, pleading for clarity. Before he could speak, his father interrupted the conversation from the bathroom, where he had overheard everything.

"Let's not waste our words. We're not meeting with the Jacksons to beg on your behalf. Our goal is to demonstrate that we're decent human beings who have respect for their family." His father spoke firmly and pointed at David and himself, explaining that they are an example of how children can differ from their parents.

David's mother pleaded with his father to stop talking. "Please, let's talk about this after dinner and after we speak with the Jacksons. I'll feel much better if you wait here for us to return," she croaked. David had no choice but to nod in agreement with his mother's request.

David felt that time had frozen since his parents left to meet Avery's family. The sharp wit and brilliant intellect he had displayed for years seemed to have disappeared, causing him to miss Avery even more. He remembered how she'd always lift his spirits with her inspiring words and comforting gestures, which helped to soothe him whenever he felt stressed from work. Since he met her, his life had never been as lonely or challenging. However, he destroyed the best relationship he could have had and broke the heart of the only woman who loved him unconditionally.

He couldn't just stay at home and wait. There might be some other way to get to Avery. So, he took to his phone and sent a message.

David: *Art, please tell me Shelly is with you right now. I need to talk to her. Can I please see you guys? Shelly is my last chance to get through to Ave. Please, man!*

Art: *I don't know, man. We are at home. But I'm not sure if it's wise for you to come here. Shelly hates you more than Ave does. You know that.*

David: *I know. Just please let me come to your house. I'll accept whatever Shelly decides when she sees me.*

Art: *Okay, but please don't tell me I didn't warn you. I'll have to tell Shelly that you are coming. I don't want to hide our conversation from her.*

David: *Thank you, man!*

David's hands were trembling as he felt Shelly's intense stare at him. Although he had been seated on the couple's living room sofa for five minutes, Shelly had remained silent. Despite this, he was grateful to be allowed to enter their home, as Avery's best friend seemed to be silently murdering him.

"Well, man, you look… like shit!" Art remarked, trying to break the silence in the room.

David replied, running his fingers through his messy hair, "I also feel like shit."

"Well, you're a shithead. What would you expect?" Shelly reacted.

The room was tense as Art gestured for David to speak with his wife. Art wanted the conversation to be over and done with.

David nodded and cleared his throat. "I didn't come here to fight with you, Shells. But I wanted to apologize for everything I've done. I know I've hurt you as much as I did Ave. So, please talk to me, and hopefully, you can help me make things right with Ave."

"You don't have any idea what you've done to Ave! Hurt is not even the right word to describe what you made her suffer. I can't believe you got the nerve to talk to me here. Of all people!" Shelly's voice was calm but firm. Her whole body was shaking.

"I know. Believe me, Shells. And I will forever hate myself and regret what I have done to Ave. I need your help, please. I'm begging you!"

"You know why I allowed Art to let you come here? I have something to say. Avery is too kind to say the things I want to say. I pray you realize how good she was to you. I hope it will always remind you how much she cared about you. That your heart fucking breaks every time you remember she loved you more than anybody ever will." Shelly poked his chest multiple times. "I hope you remember all the nights she cried over you, the nights you made her go to sleep feeling worthless. I'm happy you feel like shit right now! You finally feel what she felt when you ripped her apart. You deserve to feel the fucking pain she felt for you!"

Art pulled Shelly toward him. In her husband's arms, Shelly cried. David was at a loss for words. Everything that Shelly said was true. The truth hurt. It pierced him, causing a painful sting he couldn't explain. He was happy Avery found a friend in Shelly. But he was also sad. In his heart and mind were only regrets and sorrow.

"Shells, thank you for being a good friend to Ave. Sincerely, I thank you for being there for her in LA and for always having her back. Also, I want to tell you that I will never take it against you. All you have said and done for Ave. I deserve it."

Shelly felt David meant what he said. Having said her piece, she pulled away from Art's embrace. She stood up and motioned for David to get up for a hug. After all, they were also friends. Having seen David's state and hearing his words, the guy was in deep, deep shit. He reminded him of Art when he had nowhere and no one to go to. It surprised David, but he thankfully accepted the hug.

"Asshole, this doesn't change the fact that I still hate you!" Shelly pulled away from the hug and slapped him on the shoulder hard. "I wouldn't stand between you and Ave. But I wouldn't back you up, either. I will respect whatever decision she makes. You can't expect her to be the same person she was before. You took advantage of the trust she had in you. Yet she forgave you for hurting her. You drained the fuck out of her, David. You lied to her and continued hurting her. It made her question her worth. It won't shock me if she doesn't want you back."

"I'm only asking for one favor, Shells. Please tell her I wanted to see her and talk to her." David put his hands together as though he were in prayer.

"That's the only thing I would do for you. I won't ask her to see you. Instead, I'll relay your request." Shelly pointed her finger at both men. "You asshats should remember this: a woman treats you how she wants to be treated first. Then she treats you how you treat her."

Art covered his chest with both hands. "Hon, why me? I did nothing. It's just him." He pointed at David, who nodded in acceptance.

As David was bidding the couple his goodbye, his phone chimed.

Mom: *Come home. We need to talk.*

Chapter 27

"I'M SORRY, SON. YOU should give Avery the time and space she needs. Her parents want you to respect their daughter's decision. She wants us to tell you not to worry about her and the baby. And she talked to your father about the baby in LA."

David felt trapped inside their family's living room, struggling to breathe as he received news he had been dreading. As he glanced at his parents seated on the left side of the sofa, he noticed his mother's eyes were still red from tears, and his father's face was flushed with emotion.

He was feeling devastated. This emotion overwhelmed him, overpowering all the mixed emotions that were churning inside him.

Avery refused to see him and declined to have a conversation with him.

"I made some calls in LA because Avery begged me. Bless her heart! Right now, a paternity test is being conducted at Cedar Sinai. I've sent someone to take care of everything there," said his father calmly. "Why did you leave LA without handling everything? Just look at yourself! Avery was correct. You're an enormous mess!" His father's voice expressed frustration as he got up and walked towards the kitchen.

As David massaged his forehead, his mother's hand ran through his hair. This act conveyed her love and concern, causing David to surrender to her embrace like a young boy, as tears streamed down his face.

"It's admirable how Avery continues to show love and concern for you despite the past events. I respect her for that. When the woman who gave birth in LA couldn't reach you, she immediately called her. Despite any negative emotions she may have felt, her first thought was for the baby's well-being. She will make a wonderful mother."

David's body quivered as his mother began to pat his back. He had never felt more remorseful than he did in that moment.

"The mother in me wanted to beg her to accept you back. But the woman in me felt compassion for someone broken and hurting. Respecting what she wants is the least we can do. Avery will always be the daughter I never had."

As David gazed at his mother, he saw only compassion and sincere worry etched on her face. He longed to understand the depth of her emotions, to feel the sorrow that only a mother can experience for her child. Yet, despite his grievous error, she held onto the hope that her beloved son could overcome any obstacle he faced.

"You must give Avery the time and space she requires. She has decided, and you must now concentrate on making things right with the baby. Your father, her parents, and I have decided to contact the wedding planner and hold all preparations. There is no need to inform the guests now, as the invitations have not been sent out yet," his mother's voice crackled.

"I wanted to talk to her... beg her to forgive me."

His mother pulled him away from her arms. She lifted his chin as she wiped his tears. "She already forgave you. But she couldn't make herself see or talk to you right now. You need to pick yourself up. Use the time to show her how sorry you are. Not by forcing her to see you. Talk to your dad. Settle things in LA so you can take care of the baby. He already made arrangements there."

David couldn't think of any better decision than to follow his mother. Even if it meant he couldn't see Avery for a while. He didn't have anyone but his parents. He accepted the fact that he badly needed their help. His brain couldn't seem to function. This time, he needed the right people around him.

"Talk to your father. And, please, don't allow your situation to break your relationship with him. You need us. Your son needs you. Your parents can only help if you allow us to."

David silently rose from his seat and walked towards the dining area where his father was. Upon reaching the door, he saw his father pouring their favorite red from the minibar. As he was beside him, the latter swiftly poured another glass of red for him. After ensuring that the amount was appropriate, his father handed it over. The two of them enjoyed the wine in serene silence.

Sitting beside each other, David remembered things he and his father shared when he turned eighteen. He learned everything about wine in the same spot from the man he always looked up to. His father was always the objective one. So, their conversation when he turned eighteen was one for the books. His father got him on the first pour.

"David, turning eighteen is not just a legal permit for you to drink. It's a gateway to a world of responsibilities you'll face. Some of these responsibilities will be exciting, while others will be challenging. You'll have to deal with having a girlfriend, sharing intimate moments, going to college, earning a degree, getting a job, receiving promotions, finding the woman of

your dreams, and getting married. There will be times when you'll have to face these responsibilities simultaneously, which can be overwhelming. If things get tough, take a step back. Listen to your heart and remember what your mother and I taught you. When everything around you gets too loud, and challenges make you feel lost, stepping back is okay. You'll always have a home here with us. Everyone may give up on you, but your father and mother never will. You only have to ask."

"Avery is one hell of a girl! You fucked up on that one." His father's voice was firm yet soft. Almost the same as when they last had a serious conversation when he was eighteen.

"I did, Dad. And I'm so afraid it's too late for me to make things right. I don't know what to do."

"Sometimes you must do things that won't make sense initially. But one day, you'll look back and thank yourself for doing those things, just like I did about LA. I've told myself I wouldn't lift a finger since you made a fool of yourself. But Avery made me see things from a different perspective. She made me understand that I should hate your actions, not you, the person."

"I'm lost, Dad. Please help me. I feel like I'll want to die if Avery won't be a part of my life anymore."

"Once the result is out, and it confirms the baby is yours, your life will not just be yours. Stand up and be a father. Learn to be selfless. How you raise your son will guide Avery in deciding whether she can allow you to be present in her baby's life."

"You think Avery will still find it in her heart to give me another chance?"

His father sighed. He poured another glass and gulped the liquid all at once. When he looked into David's eyes, his father saw how lost he was. He placed his hand on top of David's.

"Son, from here on, it's not about you and Avery anymore. That ship had already sailed. Avery presents the last chance you've been asking for but through the baby. So, make it happen that your sorry ass gets proven through your son's life. Be a better man by being a good father. I assure you everything will fall into place. Use this chance to change for the better. You wouldn't like to have the same conversation we're having now with your kid someday, right?"

Before David could say another word, his phone chimed multiple times.

B: *Smart move, Atty. Thomas! You can't make your ass come here to discuss things with me and instead send Daddy's pool of lawyers to make me sign all these ridiculous papers. LOSER!*

*

SR. PARTNER: *Where are you? What happened? I got a copy of Avery's irrevocable resignation today.*

*

ART: *My wife wants me to relay a message to you. Avery declined to see or talk to you. Sorry, man! Shelly won't text you because she feels she is betraying Ave by sending you a message.*

Chapter 28

Shells: *How are you? I did what you asked me to. I talked to your shithead ex-fiancé to rebuild the bridge. (If it were me, I'd rather keep the bridge burned.) He asked to see and speak to you. Call me when you can.* ♥

Ave: *Thank you, Shells.* ♥ *you too! Please tell him, sorry, but I don't want to see or talk to him.I will call you soon.*

Shells: *I'll be glad to pass on your message!* 😍

*

David: *Ave, babe. Please talk to me.*

*

Mama T: *We just talked to David. He and his dad are having their talk alone. Thank you for that.Please remember what I told you; you will always be family, my daughter. We will always be here for you and the baby, no matter what. Take care.*

"HAVE YOU STARTED PACKING? Do you need help?"

Avery slid her phone inside her pants pocket and nodded. She smiled at her mom standing at her bedroom door.

"Yeah, I guess I need to start packing."

Her mom tried to move her lips, but her eyebrows lowered and pulled close together. No words were spoken when she came home with her dad after their brunch date. Just looking at her and her dad's faces, her mom knew something was off. Immediately, she welcomed Avery with a warm embrace. She felt at home when her dad enclosed them in his arms.

If there were someone invested in her relationship with David since day one, that would be her mom. If her dad was her voice of reason, her mom was her romantic guru—hopeless romantic and all in between. She got the cheerfulness and understanding heart from her mom. Though they hadn't spoken about David, she was the best mom she could ever have. The dinner with David's parents went well because of her mother's lead. She was a champ at not showing any negative emotion when they discussed calling off the wedding. Her parents were terrific toward the situation in front of the

107

Thomas couple, though Avery knew deep inside they were hurting.

Seeing how her parents survived the night with David's parents gave Avery the strength to brave that dinner, too. It wasn't easy, but she had to. She was firm and calm during the entire dinner and discussed things that needed to be done. Even when she talked to David's father, she exuded class, politeness, and strength. Again, she exceeded her expectations of herself.

When Mama T asked to talk to her alone, she felt torn. One of the many reasons she felt so profoundly for David was his family, his mother the most. Had anyone asked Avery to choose another woman best fit to be her mom other than her own, it would be David's. From the second David introduced them, they saw eye to eye. They connected and formed a special bond. A bond that sometimes made David giddily jealous. *"My mom loves and believes you more than me now,"* he'd always tell her.

The talk Avery almost declined turned out to be the moment she would forever cherish with Mama T. Her heart got broken tenfold after hearing what David's mother had said. It was liberating and saddening at the same time. Letting go meant breaking away from the relationships formed between families. Telling David's mother her decision was like repeatedly going over the breakup. It was sadder because the second mother she almost had, whose heart was breaking, was nothing but very loving toward her.

"When David brought you into our lives, it was one of my happiest moments as a mother. He was his happiest and liveliest. It breaks my heart knowing he'd made the biggest mistake of hurting you. As his mother, I felt you should partly blame me for not knowing when my son lost his way. But then I told myself, as his parents, we guide and love him. It was he who made that choice. It saddens me you may not be a part of us like we would want it to be. But hearing your side of the story and feeling all the pains you've been suffering; I wouldn't be selfish to beg you to stay. Walk away even if it hurts, even if it breaks your heart. Because you deserve to be happy and shouldn't stay where your heart isn't cared for."

"Are you okay, Muffin?" Her mom's voice zoned Avery back in. She felt her mom's hand caressing her hair. Not wanting her mom to worry, she blinked her tears away.

"I'm okay, Mom. I just remembered Mama T. I will surely miss her."

Her mom sighed, "I know. I'll miss our random lunches and shopping. But T and I got closer because of you and Dav..."

Her mom paused before mentioning David's name entirely. Though she wanted to talk about her daughter's situation, she gave her the time she needed.

She would wait until her daughter felt comfortable to open up freely. When her husband told her about the situation in secrecy, she cried out all the tears a mother can cry. She promised to be a solace and pillar of strength when her daughter decided to confide in her.

"It's okay, Mom. We can talk about him now." Avery motioned for her mom to sit beside her on the bed.

"There's nothing in this world I want but your happiness and peace. Yours and the baby. Your dad and I love you both." Her mom's sincerity radiated from the warmth of her hand as she tucked stray strands of hair behind Avery's ear.

"I know, Mom. I love you and Dad more for that."

"We are grateful you decided to keep the baby. From now on, we will be with you a hundred percent whatever you wish to do. I want you to know you don't have to leave Boston if you don't want to…"

Avery held her mom's hand. "I want to do this. I need to… for myself."

"I know, Muffin. I know. God knows how much I wish whatever pain you have could be transferred to me instead. But I promise you… sometimes, loving yourself gets hard. Harder than anything you can imagine. But it's a million times better than wasting your efforts on someone who does not value them."

Avery nodded. "I'm just scared, wondering whether I'll be able to do everything without him. But I won't know until I try. And I feel the first thing I need to do is to be away from here. Away from everything that reminds me of him."

Her mom gently touched her cheek. "It's normal to be scared. Just remember, Dad and I are with you."

Avery placed her hand on top of her mom's. "You and Dad need not leave. You guys should stay. I don't want you to leave the life you built here to be with me."

"You are our life. We go where you go, especially now we have our little munchkin to look forward to."

Avery felt her mom's excitement as she slowly moved her hand from her cheek to her belly. Amidst all the unpleasant events happening, all the hurts and disappointments, one good thing that came out of it was her little bean, her parents' munchkin. Both immediately declared their retirement when she told her parents about her decision to move to her grandparents' retirement home in Florida. She tried to talk them out of it; she felt guilty dragging them with her. But her parents had made up their minds. The next day, her dad filed his retirement in the consulting firm he was working for and sent feelers to his contacts in Florida for freelance consulting jobs. And her mom discussed their Boston house with their family's real estate broker.

In the morning, before David's parents came for dinner, Avery and her parents had already planned their new life in Florida. But they mentioned nothing about their decision to move. The three of them felt it best to keep their decision to themselves. Avery planned to tell Shelly only a few days before their flight. Not that she didn't trust her, but she wanted to ensure David would not get any ideas from Art. Maybe she didn't trust herself or didn't want to be around when the paternity test results came out.

Once her mom called it a night and left her room, she rested on her bed. She stared at the ceiling, her hands resting on her belly. Quietly, she let her tears come. She could lie to everyone, but she couldn't lie to herself. Every night, she still cried herself to sleep. Even if she didn't want to, tears just came out. She believed she'd made the right decision. This time, she had to do it for herself.

Someday, David would understand what it took for her to walk away, with every part of her wanting that 'one last time.'

Just as Avery had turned off the light on her bedside table, her phone chimed.

Shells: *Art relayed your message to David. He replied, telling him the paternity test result was out. That was fast! Money talks! I told Art to reply tell it to the Marines, or he can shove it to his ass!* 😠

Chapter 29

***"THE PATERNITY TEST RESULT** is out."*

Shelly's message was longer, but it was the only sentence that stayed and kept flashing in Avery's mind. Her eyes were closed as she lay in bed, but the information she received kept her awake. Since she came home to her parents, there hadn't been a night she hadn't cried. Everybody had been telling her it was time to love herself first. Give herself a break from all the pain. She could do better by moving on. But nobody ever told her how.

How could she unlove him?

How could she give herself a break when she was beyond broken?

How could she move on when the ending was not as easy as when she'd started loving?

Avery knew she was trying hard. However painful, she kept trying every day. She wanted to get over David. Get over the hurts. Every time she closed her eyes, she still saw their moments together. It's said time is the best friend of a broken heart. What if time won't do what it was supposed to do? Weeks, months, or even years may pass. Her little bean would always remind her of David.

She kept on assuring herself everything would be better with her alone, just her and the baby. Yet, deep inside, she knew how big a space her fears were occupying. It was she who begged David's father to help him. Have a paternity test done, and if the results confirmed the baby as Thomas, she made his father promise to guide David in securing the baby's future. She knew how David was in a wrecked state. Avery would only be at peace leaving Boston if she knew David's parents were behind him.

The paternity test result is out. It would reveal another truth soon. She'd ask his father to do it. She felt as if she wanted to turn back time. Not that she regretted asking, because she would like someone to do the same thing if it were her child. It was the fear of not knowing how she could handle the result. Would it break her heart again?

Since she discovered David's cheating, she realized nothing could ever prepare someone to face the ugly truth. At first, she told Shelly she just wanted to confirm it. But, when David admitted it to her face, she felt an unbearable pain she could never compare. In LA, she went to the hospital, needing to see things with her own eyes. But when she witnessed David holding a newborn, it shut her senses down. Whatever the result, she knew it would surely hurt. It was supposed to hurt since it would break her heart either way.

As if her hands had minds of their own, they automatically patted her belly gently. Since she learned about her pregnancy, it'd been giving her the comforting idea that she would never be alone. Her little bean had been her source of everything that kept her sane.

Days passed in an instant. David kept reminding Avery of his existence through his daily text messages, begging her to see and talk to him. Avery fought so hard at the urge to reply to any of his messages. Her fear of hearing another truth from him scared her. She knew she would eventually need to meet and talk to him but couldn't face it now.

Though it was ideal to know the truth about anything, for Avery, getting the truth from David's mouth had been nothing but the source of her devastating pain. A misery she'd never dreamed of for herself, but fate had made it her reality.

"Are you going somewhere, Muffin?" Her dad's voice came from the main door behind where she was standing. She got lost in her thoughts while taking the amazing neighborhood view from their porch.

"Shucks, Dad, you startled me!"

"Did Grandpa startle my Munchkin too?" Her dad looked at her tummy as if he could see the baby inside her. "Are you contemplating going out or asking Daddy for a ride?"

Avery shook her head. "I'm waiting for Shelly. She's picking me up. We'll get a referral from my OB here, then hang out in their house."

"Are you telling her about Florida today? We only have three days left." Her dad's eyes fixated on hers.

"I know, Dad. I'm telling her today. You know I wouldn't do that to Shelly. I wouldn't leave her without saying goodbye."

Avery slowly approached her dad for a hug. In return, he gently patted her back.

"When your mom and I said to keep our moving low-key, you didn't take it as though we're going to be thieves in the night and disappear on the face of the earth with no one knowing, right?"

Avery put a distance between them and looked at her dad's face. "What do you mean, Dad?"

"Tell David. Maybe not all the details, but as the baby's father, he deserves to know that you are leaving with his child."

Avery was speechless. Her eyebrows squinted, and her forehead wrinkled when she looked at her dad, wondering why he would tell her this.

"Muffin, you know we are and will always be on your side. And I know David was the shittiest man for doing what he had done. But he deserves to know. His parents deserve cordiality. They've been the nicest people to us and mostly to you."

"Dad…" Avery felt her hand squeezed softly. "Promise me you'll at least think about it."

Before Avery could say something, the loud voice of Shelly blasted into their entire neighborhood. Her dad kissed her on the forehead, and the ever-cheerful Shelly had her buckled up in her car in record time. She was physically with her best friend, but her dad's statement mentally dawned on her.

After she picked up the document from her OB in Mass Gen, they drove to Shelly's house, where Art was already busy grilling. Again, she felt the love the couple had for her. They remembered how much she'd enjoyed the last time they had a BBQ together, so they prepared a feast for her.

Once the three finished cleaning up after their meal, Avery decided it was time to let Shelly know about Florida. She suggested they watch their all-time favorite hangout movie, *Notting Hill,* in the entertainment room. When they got inside the room, Shelly excitedly prepared everything. Avery felt guilty about having to break the news last minute. But most of all, she felt sad, realizing that spending time with her best friend was one of the greatest things she would miss about Boston.

"Earth to Avery! What's happening in that sexy brain of yours, my girlfriend?"

"Promise me you won't get mad, Shells. There's something I need to tell you." Shelly's eyes widened. Immediately, she rushed and sat beside Avery.

"Cross my heart, Ave! I won't be mad. But if you don't tell me in five minutes, I might. Spill!"

"Me, Dad, and Mom are going to Florida in three days. I'll surely miss you, Shells!"

"Oh! Well, we can take a week or a month away from each other. If only I didn't use all my work offs for the honeymoon, I would love to join you guys. Like when we were cute little girls, vacationing together."

Avery started crying when she remembered the numerous girls' trips they'd had together in grade school. They were practically sisters. There was never a summer they didn't spend together. When they both got boyfriends, it became like a double summer date. Shelly was the sister she'd never had. The best friend anyone could ever ask for. And just like she always told her, Shelly is her ride-or-die.

Confused, Shelly watched Avery shed tears. Then, since they knew each other too well, she realized why her best friend was crying. "Shut the front door! Are you guys moving to Florida?"

Avery couldn't say a word and nodded, tears falling down her face. Shelly's shoulders sagged. Her hand covered her mouth as she let her tears fall. She could never be mad at Avery, her precious Ave. Then, realizing it might be their last time hanging out in Boston, she pulled her towards her, and they shared the tightest and warmest embrace.

"You know I can never be mad at you. But you can never stop me from getting emotional right now. We have been best friends since we were in second grade." Shelly started wiping Avery's tears.

"I'm sorry for not telling you earlier. I will surely miss you, but you are always welcome to come and stay with us—you and Art. I really need to do it. I need to be away for now. It's harder if I stay."

"I know, I know Ave. Don't be sorry. Don't worry, and I'll surely take your offer to go there and stay with you. You know how I hate too much snow! So, we can have a no-snow Christmas for a change."

Avery nodded. "Yeah, we would love to have you guys anytime." "Does he know? David? What did he say?"

Avery looked into Shelly's eyes. "He doesn't know, Shells. I wasn't planning to tell, but Dad asked me to think about it."

"I get it." Shelly nodded. "David fucked up! But think about it, Ave."

"I know. Let me think about it. But, for now, I want to move away and forget."

"Isn't it sad? Sometimes, the people we want to forget are those who once made us the happiest?"

"Why are you so smart, Shells?" Avery started tickling Shelly on her side. Shelly tried running around as their giggles filled the room. Art opened the door and rushed inside.

"Hey! What is not clear with 'only girls hanging out'?" Shelly exclaimed.

Art motioned for them to be quiet. "Shush… David is on the back porch waiting for you, Hon."

"What the F? Why did you invite him? Do you want me to divorce you now?"

Art shook his head. "I didn't invite him. He just came. I didn't say you guys were here. He said he wanted to talk to you about her." Art pointed at Avery. "Ave, he wanted you to be the first to know about the paternity test result."

"God! How am I gonna lie when you are here?" Shelly started pacing.

"Gosh! My bag! I left it on top of the table on the back porch." Avery's eyes pulled up as her mouth stretched.

It stupefied the three of them when Art's phone sounded. "Oh shit! Triple shit!" Art said.

David: *Man, is Ave here? Is she inside? Please let me talk to her.*

116

Chapter 30

"OH SHIT! TRIPLE SHIT! What do I tell him?" Art asked, his eyes darting between Avery and Shelly.

Avery's face paled while Shelly kept pacing behind her. She'd thought about what her dad told her, but getting cornered by David wasn't on her itinerary. She would talk to him and tell him what she thought he deserved to know, but it should be on her terms at her own time. Her stomach roiled with irritation.

"What is he doing here? What should we do?" she asked Shelly and Art.

Shelly stood still and looked Avery in the eye. "Tell me what is on your mind, Ave. I will go out and tell him whatever you want me to tell him. I can't lie to his face and tell him you're not here…" Shelly pointed at her. "Well, because you are here."

"That's a good point, Hon." Art nodded in agreement.

"I wouldn't want you to lie for me, too, Shells. Besides, I'm sure he got the idea that I'm here with you. He probably had seen my bag."

Art nodded again. "True! That's why his text was asking if you're here. I should have locked him in the garage."

While the three stood silent, waiting for Avery to say something, Art's phone chimed again. It bewildered all three faces hearing the sound.

David: *Ave, babe. I know you are inside. I want to be the one to tell you the important news. Please talk to me.*

Avery wanted to ease the couple's minds, so she decided.

"Art, please tell him to come to my parents' house tomorrow anytime from 10 AM. I'll see him there. Not here, not now."

The grandfather clock in their family living room struck 6 AM, as Avery confirmed on her phone. Though she came home yesterday before dinner exhausted from all the giggling, singing, and picture takings she and Shelly shared, she couldn't sleep immediately. When she went to bed at 9 PM, it took her an hour to fall into a deep slumber, only to wake around 3 AM.

She knew why: David would come today. He confirmed with Art yesterday before he left. During dinner, she casually informed her parents that David would be coming. Her father sighed deeply while her mother repeatedly asked her if she was sure about it. Then, before she said goodnight to her parents, she assured both that she thought her decision well.

Would she be okay?

Avery couldn't lie to herself. Knowing she'd be seeing and talking to David face to face after LA had awakened all the stress-causing veins in her body. Maybe because she'd wanted their first conversation after that hospital meltdown to be in her lead; she knew how intimidating and intense David could be, being a defense attorney.

She was never good at confrontations. She always used a bigger person's excuse if she faced an argumentative situation. She was soft-spoken versus a persuasive orator during her school days. Her motto was always better to be one to understand than the one who needs to be understood. As Shelly always said, she was too kind to utter a word that would hurt even a fly.

That was why talking to Boston's eloquent and undefeated defense attorney had her stressed since yesterday. She wanted to be a different Avery in front of David. Someone who could speak her mind without shedding a single tear. A changed woman who could decide for herself and her baby. A woman who was firm with her decision.

Was she just stressed or afraid? In a whisper, she answered her question. She wasn't stressed or scared. There was one thing she could confirm: she felt stressed recognizing all her fears. Aside from reminding herself, the first confrontation she and David had in their apartment finished in a different direction. Deciding to have their much-awaited talk at her parents' house deserved her a pat on the back. She praised herself for doing a good job selecting a neutral ground, or much so, a place to her advantage.

Whatever happened, or if things worsened, Avery felt comfort knowing her dad would be around. Accepting that sleep was not her best friend at the moment, she decided to make use of her time.

Suddenly, Avery felt pumped. Her years of experience as a reliable paralegal secretary came in handy. She began logging her arguments in bullet points mentally. Canceling the wedding was non-negotiable. She needed new surroundings, a reason for moving without hinting permanently. She could go through with the pregnancy with the guidance and care of her parents.

In Shelly's fashion: I DON'T NEED YOU, AND I DON'T WANT TO SEE YOUR FACE!

She couldn't help but smile, imagining her best friend saying it. How she wished she was as bold and brave as her best friend.

Maybe in another life, she might transform into AVERY 2.0! Realization sunk into her. Was her lack of boldness and bravery the reason David cheated on her? Of course, but in his words, nothing was wrong with her. It just happened. The same reasoning is cut out from usual infidelity-themed movies. Which, up to now, Avery found unfair. Because if the tables were turned, and God forbid she was the cheater, she would have a definite reason for doing such a thing. One fucking good reason, most probably. And as Miss Organized, she would have served David her bullet points of justifications on a silver platter.

Fuck, David! You don't just impregnate a random woman, move to where she is while awaiting her delivery, and end up in the hospital bed, cradling a newborn. All because there's apparently nothing wrong with your fiancée; everything just happened, and despite all those messes, you still love your fiancée and can't live without her?

How stupid did he think she was?

Her alone time had added to her inability to sleep, causing Avery's adrenaline rush. After eating breakfast, she felt more energized. She took a shower and opted to wear the same dress she had on when she accepted David's marriage proposal. It was to give a statement. What started with her yes ends with her no. She sprayed on a perfume different from what David liked her wearing. She curled her long, straight hair for the first time. She made sure she looked the part she was aiming for—a different Avery.

After checking herself in the mirror, their doorbell rang just a few minutes later. The time on Avery's cell phone said 9:35 AM. "Sorry, Atty. Thomas, but the showtime starts at 10 AM!" Avery whispered to herself.

When their housekeeper knocked on her bedroom door to inform her of David's arrival, she instructed him to wait. This would be happening in her own time.

Exactly five minutes before 10 AM, Avery descended the stairs. As she took her steps toward the living room, she saw David seated on the couch. It surprised her that he was also wearing the long-sleeved shirt he had worn when he proposed. David had lost weight since she last saw him. He had bags under his eyes and longer hair; she could tell he was nervous. Avery knew very well because David was cracking his knuckles. She always placed the same knuckles between her hands and kissed them to appease him whenever his nerves were killing him.

As she got nearer, she uttered, "God, please help me. Please give me strength."

It seemed to take him a few minutes to recognize Avery. Though she seemed different, she still mesmerized him. Then, a sudden jolt of fear hit him. Avery was doing okay without him. An idea he refused to entertain.

Immediately, David stood up and approached Avery. He aimed to kiss her and wrap his arms around her. God knew how much he missed her, but it disappointed him when Avery turned away from him. Instead, she power-walked toward the couch and motioned for him to sit again.

"Hi! How are you, babe?" David asked, handing her a bouquet of pink and red carnations. "This is for you."

"I'm excellent. Thank you."

David noticed that Avery didn't look at the flowers and just placed them on the center table. It was unusual because before, when he gave her flowers, she would take the time to smell them and ask about their meaning, especially if they were other than roses. How David wished she could have asked him. He would have been glad to tell her that the pink ones signified how unforgettable she was. Yet, at the same time, the red one symbolized his admiration and longing for her.

Like before, he wanted to touch her hand, caress her face, and smell her hair, but Avery seemed emotionless. He had no idea what was going on in her mind or how she felt about seeing him. Everything about her had changed. Though her eyes were on his face, there was no spark, only sadness and pain—the pain he had inflicted.

"What do you want to talk about?" asked Avery.

"I want to fulfill the promise I made. That I'll be honest, and no more secrets. I want you to be the first one to know about the paternity test result. I want you to hear it from me." David brought out a folded envelope from his pants pocket. Avery nodded but raised her right hand for David to stop handing her the envelope.

"Let me say first what I needed to say."

"Babe… Ave, please let me explain everything."

"No. Before you show me what's written on that paper, I need to say what I have to say." Avery was unyielding.

David had no choice but to keep the envelope in his right hand. His breathing was deep and long. His eyes didn't leave Avery's face. He felt his heart constricting. Slowly, he glided his trembling left hand on his leg. Fear engulfed him, and he did not want to hear what Avery had to say.

"My parents and I are going away in the meantime… out of state." Avery's eyes were on David.

"What do you mean?" David stood up. "When? How long?"

"Maybe the whole duration of my pregnancy. We're leaving in two days."

"Ave, babe. Why? Let's talk about this. I know I can't change your mind about the wedding for now, but I'm working on myself. I learned my lesson. Everything you asked me, I'm doing it." He started pacing in front of her.

"It's for me. I wanted to be away from all of Boston for now. I promise to keep you updated about the baby. I'll take care of the both of us." Avery caressed her belly slowly.

David shook his head. "No, Ave. Please don't do this to me. Not seeing or hearing your voice for weeks… it's been killing me. Thinking you're away from here will be the death of me."

"Sometimes we need to die to be alive again. Thinking about it, I have died several times already." Avery's face was blank.

"Babe, don't you love me anymore? Please… let's fix us." Tears ran down David's cheeks.

Avery's eyes glinted with sadness as she faced him. "If I still do, I can love you quietly from a distance."

David's mouth fell open. He moved toward Avery and dropped to his knees in front of her. She didn't move when he held her hand. "Ave, please look at the pain in my eyes, not the words I say." He touched her cheek, her jaw, and her lips. He lifted her chin so she could look him in the face. "I can't stop you from leaving… if this is what you want. But I can't stop loving you. I'll be waiting for however long it may take. Anytime you need me, text or call me, and I will come to you, wherever that is."

Avery's lower lip trembled. Tears shimmered in her eyes. She took a deep breath. She moved David's hair back away from his face. Slowly, she wiped the tears from his face. She let him be when David placed his other hand on her lips.

"I regret that we ended up this way. We were leaving one another with pain, with wounds. It seemed as if everything we shared was wasted time," Avery said as she touched his jaw.

David grasped both of Avery's hands and clasped them inside his. "If I have to wait forever for you to come back to me, I will. Please don't say it's our end. I'm sorry, Ave. I really am. Regret will forever be in me. For all the things I've done that hurt you. And all the times I made you cry."

"I wanted it to be you. I so badly wanted it to be you until I understood. Unfortunately, our situation didn't want it to be me," Avery stammered.

David stood up and lifted Avery from her seat. He pulled her toward his chest and wrapped her in his embrace. Both were in tears. He whispered for Avery to take care of herself and the baby. "I won't stop loving you, Ave. You're the best thing that ever happened to me. I'll always be waiting for you. I love you."

Before David left, he handed her the envelope. In return, she gave him a copy of the picture of her latest ultrasound. Avery didn't decline when he kissed her on the lips to bid her goodbye. Instead, when she saw her parents looking at her as she walked toward the stairs to her room, she smiled at them. Once inside her room, she opened the envelope.

Whatever was written inside didn't matter anymore.

D21S11	2.36	28	29	29	
D18S51	22.53	11	15	11	16
D7S441	8.74	11	13	10	11
D19S433	2.48	13	15	13	15
TH01	8.82	6	9.3	8	9.3
FGA	2.63	21		19	21
D22S1045	1.42	16		11	16
D5S818	1.37	11	12	11	12
D13S317	3.89	11	13	11	13
D7S820	0.93	10	12	9	10
SE33	7.14	23.2	30.2	18	23.2
D10S1248	2.89	15		14	15
D1S1656	4.55	13	16.3	12	16.3
D2S1338	6.26	16	25	16	20
Amelogenin		X		X	Y

Interpretation:

Combined Paternity Index **830,244,467**   Probability of Paternity **99.9999998%**

The alleged father is not excluded as the biological father of the tested child. Based on testing results obtained from analyses of the DNA loci listed, the probability of paternity is 99.9999998%. This probability of paternity is calculated by

Chapter 31

AVERY'S EYES SWAM WITH tears. Her shoulders tensed. Slowly, she laid down on her left side, her face sinking into her pillow. She pressed her fingers into her lips. *Whatever was written inside didn't matter anymore.* She thought it wouldn't matter, but she was wrong. The truth made her realize that what she said was a lie. Truth did matter.

It mattered. All her pain came back. She died again.

One piece of paper brought back all the pain. Reading the confirmation of David's paternity turned a switch on. It showed all the agonizing events since the night she discovered everything. It felt like getting hurt all over again. The painful truth cut through whatever thread of hope remained for her and David. The truth was the murder weapon. She died again.

Avery realized she had cried herself to sleep an hour later. She heard whispers behind her door. When she checked her cellphone, she found several missed calls and messages from her parents and Shelly. Minutes later, she heard a knock on her door, and her best friend came with a food tray.

"Hey, your mom said you missed lunch. So, I brought you food." Shelly placed the tray on the other side of her bed.

"Thanks, Shells! I'm glad to see you here."

"Eat now. You and the baby need to be fed on time. I'm staying so we can hang out here in your room."

Quietly, Avery started eating. Even without Shelly saying anything, she knew her best friend had come for a reason. Avery felt glad and relieved that she'd have someone to talk to. Once she finished her food, she broke the news to Shelly, who was checking her face in the vanity.

"David is the father… I was hoping he wasn't. But truth cannot be uglier. And it hurts," Avery's voice croaked.

"Oh, Ave!" Shelly sprinted and put her arms around her. "I came here as soon as Art told me you got the result. Then, right after I learned the result, I slapped him in the face. If that will make you feel a little better."

"How?" Avery's forehead wrinkled. She pulled away from Shelly and looked at her face. "After talking to you, he went straight to our house. He told

Art everything you guys talked about and the result. Then he asked me to come here and stay with you. I told him I was coming without him telling me. That piece of shit," Shelly growled with anger.

"Our conversation ended well; I think. David insisted we get back together initially, but eventually, he gave in. I didn't tell him many details about our move. Instead, I gave him pictures of my latest ultrasound. He gave me a copy of the paternity test result…" Avery sniffled.

"That fucktard! Maybe he thought you were exchanging gifts. You gave him Christmas, but he gave you a death note in return!" Shelly's fingers started combing through Avery's hair. "Ave, I can't tell you to stop crying. I know tears just come out. I'm here for you and your parents. We're all here for you. You're not alone. You have all our love. So much love you wouldn't need any from that fuckhead! Though I credit him for asking me to be with you this time."

Avery nodded. "Good thing he went to you and Art. Our conversation must have overwhelmed him."

Shelly facepalmed. "What am I going to do with you, Avery Jackson? Stop worrying about him. You should at least be mad at him!"

"I know, Shells. But my heart says otherwise. I felt he meant it when he said he still loved me. It's not that easy to unlove someone. Though I already accepted the fact. Maybe we're just two people who love each other, but we're not meant to be together."

"You're the strongest woman I've known, Ave. I can only imagine what I could have done if I were in your shoes. Either I have skinned the whore, or I chopped David's penis into pieces!"

Avery gave a half-smile and slowly touched her belly. Shelly kneeled and whispered in her stomach. "Sorry for my language, my dear godchild. Please forgive your pretty godmother!"

"Godmother?! That I'll need to think about," Avery snorted. Shelly laughed hard.

"But seriously, Ave. If there's any consolation to you finding out, it's closing *Chapter David*. What do you say?"

Shelly stood up and motioned for Avery to give her space on the bed. She got inside the sheet beside her. Just like old times, they both remembered. Sitting beside each other on either one's bed means a long and serious girl talk.

Avery didn't decline; she always felt comfortable telling Shelly everything inside her heart. The more when she wanted to spare her parents' hearts from breaking again.

"Even without confirming the result, I've already decided." Avery placed her hand on top of her heart and laughed. "Though this heart of mine can't seem to move on yet, my brain's working wonderfully this time."

"It'll take time, for sure. Better to do it under the amazing Florida sun in your bikini." Shelly pointed to the curves of her body.

"I thought it wouldn't matter. I was hoping I had already cried it all. It was funny how a piece of paper, or a series of numbers—99.99—crushed my soul today." Avery kept shaking her head.

"What about we change it to a 100? Like, I'm 100 percent sure someone is waiting for you somewhere. Or someone is getting ready for you, Ave."

"I don't know. I'm not thinking about those, Shells. Anyway, I have my little bean to focus on. But in all seriousness, how come no one told me it would be this painful?" Avery asked, massaging her chest.

Shelly lifted her chin and cupped her face. "I think the heavens sent my love story as a reminder. Art's mistake was a warning sign, but David was too fucked up to learn from it."

"Where am I in that equation, then?" Avery smirked.

"You, my best friend, are getting prepared for something bigger, somewhere better, and someone best for you!"

"Oh, Shelly! Stop with your hopeless romantic lines! Who'd ever want someone like me?"

"Hey! Look at me! Don't you ever underestimate yourself! You deserve someone better. When you go to Florida, live your life!"

"I will surely miss you, Shells!" Avery pinched her best friend's cheeks. "What will I do without you?" She started sobbing.

"You fool! I'm just a plane ride away. Anytime you ask me to come, I'll be there with Art in tow." Shelly's eyes glistened with tears.

In between tears and sobs, the two hugged each other tightly. They would surely miss being near each other, but the bond founded by genuine friendship wouldn't change a thing between them. They were each other's ride-or-die. In silence and hugs, they vowed to keep it that way.

True to her promise, Shelly stayed with Avery for the night while Art kept David company. They may have had different views on the circumstances between Avery and David, but genuine friendship kept them together.

After Shelly left the following day, Avery realized she still had the engagement ring. She thought long and hard. How would she give it back? Nobody else came to mind. So, to return the ring and say goodbye, she sent a message.

Avery waited inside the coffee shop David had proposed to her a year ago. She sat in their favorite spot. Her eyes wandered the corners of their favorite place until they reached their engagement picture posted on the cafe's wall. She circled her thumb around the diamond engagement ring on her finger. It was an heirloom from David's mother's side of the family. She smiled as she remembered the happiness and overwhelming emotions she felt when her dream guy expressed his love for her in a way she would never forget.

She closed her eyes as memories of her and David flashed back. Today was her last day in Boston. How ironic that when he promised forever, it started in the same spot where she was currently savoring the end of all their memories together. As she touched the ring on her finger, she whispered, "What started here ends here."

"Have you been waiting long? I'm sorry if I made you wait." The voice awakened Avery.

Avery opened her eyes and smiled. "No, not at all. You're just in time."

"Thank you for asking me to meet you. You don't know how happy you made me when I read your message."

Chapter 32

AVERY STOOD UP AND hugged Mama T. "I'm sorry for the short notice. Thank you for coming," she whispered to her.

"I told you; you will always be family. Whatever happens."

"I need to give you something. And I wanted to see you too," Avery stammered.

"David told us about your leaving for a while. I so wanted to see you. I'm happy you gave me a chance."

"Oh, my Mama T!" Avery placed her face on the woman's shoulder. "I'm sorry for telling you just now."

Mama T's eyes glittered with tears as she embraced Avery tighter. Then, when a server approached their table, both women separated and took the chairs facing each other.

"When David and I talked last time, I forgot to return something. I don't want to overwhelm him more. Other than him, there's no one else I thought I should return this to but you." Slowly, Avery removed the ring from her finger. She grasped Mama T's hand and placed the ring on her palm.

Mama T clasped the ring in her hand. She bit her lower lip and let her tears fall. The tears only a mother could cry for the genuine love her child had just lost. Subsequently, she wiped her tears with another hand and smiled at Avery.

"I'm sorry, Mama T. I need to be away from here. From everything that will remind me of him. I need time for myself."

"I perfectly understand how you're feeling. Please promise to update us about the baby. I hope you allow us even the smallest space in the baby's life. Anytime you want us around, we will be happy to come."

"I surely will. Mom and Dad would want that, too."

"I'll keep this ring to myself for now. I hope you understand a mother's heart. David resigned from the firm. He signed up for a six-month volunteer mission in Africa with Lawyers Without Borders. He decided after your talk. Hope it'll do him good."

"I hope so, too. I'll pray for him," Avery beamed.

"Just to let you know, the woman in LA asked our lawyer for $500,000 in exchange for her releasing all her rights to the baby. So David and his dad assigned someone to take care of the baby while everything legal was in the works. Right now, we are in the waiting phase."

"I hope the baby gets the chance to be with you soon. Before David leaves for Africa."

"That's what we're aiming for." Mama T squeezed her hand. "I wanted to assure you that we feel the same care and love for your baby. We look forward to seeing and holding our grandchild in the future."

"I know, Mama T. I promise." Avery bit her lip and looked at the ceiling as she fought her tears. "The baby will know you and David. You'll all be a part of the baby's life."

"Thank you, Avery. Sorry for all the pain my son caused you. But please don't doubt the good and happy times you two shared. He truly loved you, and he still does."

Avery nodded. "I know. I guess some things are not meant to be." Avery bowed down.

Mama T stood from her chair, moved toward Avery, and put her arms around her. "My dear Ave, our lives will never be the same without you. Seasons may change, and times may pass, but the hole you leave in my son's heart will be his life's greatest regret."

Avery succumbed to the warmth of the woman she considered mother next to her own. Her dad was right. Leaving Boston behind secretly and without a trace would have been unfair to David and his parents, who had accepted and embraced her as their own.

At that moment, a warm embrace and gentle touch were exchanged between two women who shared nothing but love for the one man, David. A mother's never-ending affection for her only son was tested by fate. And a woman's genuine love for the one man she trusted and adored was challenged by destiny.

On her last night in the bedroom where she spent her childhood, Avery felt sadness, fear, and hope.

Sadness because after everything she went through, the sacrifices and the agony, David's and her story still didn't have a happy ending. It made her question if she would still find her happily ever after.

Fear of the unknown was what her dad said. But her fears are multitudes. What was in store for her and her child in Florida? Was she doing the right thing? What if she couldn't get over David? Would someone comparable to him still come?

But amidst the sadness and the fear, she was hopeful. Whatever transpired in Boston would give her the strength to overcome life's challenges in the future. Courage would empower her to live life the best way she could. Her family's love would inspire her to love herself. Then, hopefully, when the right time came, she would be ready to open her heart again.

"Ready, Muffin?" Her dad's voice interrupted her phone conversation.

"Shells, I have to go. They're now calling our flight for boarding. Love you!" Avery immediately got up from her seat and followed her parents as they walked toward their gate.

While in line, she looked around Boston Logan. She felt her chest tighten. It was really goodbye.

Once seated, she checked her phone before turning it off. She had message notifications from Shelly, Mama T, and David. She decided not to read any of them and turned off her phone. She closed her eyes and dozed off.

"Dad, I'll make a quick bathroom break. Then I'll see you and Mom in the cafe."

"It's okay. We still have a forty-five-minute layover, anyway. We'll go ahead and wait for you there."

On her way to the airport bathroom, Avery remembered their family's travels when her grandparents retired to Palm Coast. They always spent their layover time in Charlotte in the same cafe where they enjoyed its signature cinnamon roll.

She washed her hands and applied lip balm, seeing her pale face in the bathroom mirror. A smiling, chubby-cheeked little girl waved at her when she passed through the door. Avery smiled and waved back.

After walking a few steps away from the bathroom, she felt someone tugging her jacket from behind. When she stopped to look, the same chubby-cheeked girl was holding her jacket hem. Her button-like eyes were smiling brightly at Avery.

"Are you lost?" Avery asked as she kneeled in front of the little girl.

"You're so pretty." The little girl smiled as she blinked her eyes.

Avery smiled and looked around. "What's your name? Where is your mom? How old are you?"

"I'm seven," the little girl answered as she tried showing seven fingers to Avery.

"I think you're lost, Cutie. We have to find your parents. What's your name?" Avery asked again.

"ELLA!" A loud, frantic voice echoed inside the airport lobby.

The little girl touched Avery's cheek and looked toward where the loud voice was coming from.

"That's my name!"

Chapter 33

A WOMAN IN HER mid-forties came running toward Avery and the little girl. She immediately checked the little girl and looked at Avery.

"I'm her nanny." The woman gasped for air as she massaged her chest. "God! Ella, you gave me a coronary!"

Avery stood up and introduced herself. Ella clasped her tiny little hand to Avery's.

"Why would you do that, Ella? I told you to wait for me. I was washing my hands." The woman paused and took a deep breath. "Your dad would have killed me."

Avery patted the nanny's shoulder. "I think she followed me when I came out of the bathroom."

"She's pretty and nice," Ella told her nanny, giggling, hand still clasped on Avery's.

"So sorry, Miss Avery. Good thing she followed you and not some creep. This is the first time she did this, though."

"It's alright. I thought this cutie was lost. I'm glad you found her."

When Avery saw her parents approaching, she fixed Ella's hair. "It was nice meeting you, Ella. Don't leave your nanny again. Promise?"

Ella removed their clasped hands and motioned for Avery to do a pinky promise sign with her. Afterward, she hugged Avery tight. Then Avery cupped her cute little face and kissed her forehead.

"Take care, Ella."

"Bye, Miss Pretty," Ella answered, waving goodbye as her nanny ushered her in the other direction.

When Avery stood up, she touched her belly and wished her little bean would be as cute as Ella.

Their flight from Charlotte to Daytona was uneventful. The caretaker in her grandparents' home picked them up at the airport. Along the way, the bright afternoon sun reminded Avery of what she wished for in coming to Florida—a fresh and bright start in life.

Their first few weeks in Palm Coast consisted of daily morning walks on Flagler Beach and trips to several restaurants they had missed for years of not visiting. Since the death of her grandparents, their visits to the retirement home had stopped. Now more than ever, she was thankful that her grandparents left the house to her as part of her inheritance.

After weeks of comparing three different OB/Gynecologists from the list she got from Boston, Avery went for the one with the nearest clinic to her location.

"If only we didn't schedule your dad's annual general check-up today, we would love to come with you," said her mom.

"Don't worry about it, Mom. This check-up is just the first of more to come. Just drop me off at the clinic, please." Her mom nodded with a pout.

After much convincing, Avery's parents agreed to drop her off outside the clinic of the OB she had chosen. While waiting for her turn, she filled up the usual paperwork. The doctor seemed to be popular, for the line for her day's appointment was a blockbuster. Avery was thankful they accepted her at the time she requested.

Realizing it might take her over thirty minutes to wait, she scrolled over her text messages. Unfortunately, since they flew to Florida, she only replied to Shelly's messages.

David: *Thinking of you and our baby. Please be safe. I will always love you.*

Mama T: *Hope you guys have a safe flight. We're always here for you. Take care.*

While debating whether to reply to Mama T, she heard her name called inside. A nurse assistant took her temperature, blood pressure, and her weight. Once the nurse assistant had written all her data in the chart folder, she ushered Avery inside an inner cubicle.

A petite blonde woman in a white coat welcomed her. She extended her hand and gave a genuine smile that made Avery feel at ease.

"Have a seat, Avery. I'm Doctor James… Stella James."

"Thank you, Doctor." The doctor's eyes, which seemed familiar, captured her attention.

"Your OB in Boston was a classmate of mine in medical school. The files she forwarded to me look great! We'll do another ultrasound like last time, then discuss your prenatal meds and vitamins."

Avery nodded and bowed her head. She felt a lump in her throat, thinking Doctor Stella already knew about her marital status. The other patients in the waiting area had glanced at her, being the only one who came with no companion, making her feel even more self-conscious. She caressed her belly as if assuring her little bean that it didn't matter if it was only the two of them.

As if the good doctor could see through her, she gave Avery a reassuring smile and led her toward the ultrasound area. The doctor enumerated all the good things about her pregnancy. It made her relax and focus on the little bean she saw on the ultrasound monitor.

Before she left the clinic, Doctor Stella got her attention. "Avery, please let me know if you need anything. I know you just moved here, and I'll gladly help you in any way I can. We'll keep you and the baby healthy."

Avery felt the sincerity in Doctor Stella's words. She felt as if Shelly was in front of her. She felt affirmed and encouraged, and unable to remember where she saw a familiar gaze that warmed her heart when she looked into the doctor's eyes.

She left the clinic calm and assured. She made the right decision in choosing Doctor Stella. The doctor's parting words, "I'll be glad to be your friend, Ave," touched her heart. They said their goodbyes and promised to meet outside the clinic for a meal sometime.

"Live your life! Meet new friends," Avery whispered to herself.

Grinning, she walked into the park just outside the clinic building. She felt inspired, free, and refreshed. The Florida sun indeed gave her a distinct feeling. Gently, she stroked her belly. She was going to be okay.

Suddenly, Avery felt like her surroundings had changed. She started hearing the birds chirping, seeing the trees swaying, and feeling the happiness of the kids giggling in the nearby play area. Then, when she saw a park bench, she stopped and sat as she closed her eyes for a moment, wanting to inhale the Zen-like vibe around her. This was their new life together. She wanted to make it their happy place. They would create new memories together.

While her eyes were closed, Avery heard tiny footsteps walking toward her, followed by a set of bigger ones running after the little ones. Then, before she could open her eyes, a small, soft hand touched her cheek gently. It startled her.

When Avery opened her eyes, the familiar bright buttoned-like eyes were gazing at her.

"Ella! What are you doing here?" Avery asked, relieved to see the little girl's nanny standing behind her.

"Surprise! Is this your park, Miss Pretty?" Ella grinned and immediately clasped her little hand to Avery's as she sat beside her.

"This isn't my park. I was around the area. Do you live nearby?" Avery's eyes turned to Ella's nanny.

"No, Miss Avery. Her dad asked us to wait here. We're going to their family dinner from here."

"I see," she smiled and caressed Ella's chubby cheeks. "It's lovely seeing you again, Cutie Pie."

Ella started squeezing Avery's hand. They exchanged hugs from time to time. She seemed to have smitten the little girl. After a while, she showed her what was inside her pink backpack. When Avery saw her hairpin collection, she offered to fix Ella's hair. The little girl agreed with loud clapping.

As the new friends enjoyed each other's company, time passed unnoticed. In return, Ella also placed her butterfly clips in Avery's hair.

"Ella! Princess!"

Chapter 34

UPON HEARING THE VOICE that called her name, Ella stopped what she was doing. She stood and ran towards the man walking.

"Daddy!" Ella shouted and burst into giggles.

From a distance, Avery felt the father-daughter bond between the two. It brought back the memory of the warmth and love she felt around her dad when she was the same age as Ella. It pierced her heart a little. How could she be enough for her little bean, knowing there would be no constant father in the picture?

Guilt for her baby slowly disturbed her. In a swift motion, she gathered Ella's stuff and placed it back inside the backpack. When she turned around to hand it to the nanny, it surprised her to stand face to face with the man holding a smiling Ella on his arm.

One. Hotness. Of. A. Man. In his mid-thirties, he had bristly eyebrows, defined cheekbones, a well-chiseled jaw, masculine tanned skin, and endowed with the most enchanting smile of the male species Avery had ever seen. Taking from what Ella's very hot dad was wearing, from head to toe, he was one hotshot. No wonder Ella's stuff, her clothes and shoes, and a nanny in tow spoke of such wealth.

Avery felt intimidated. The hot dad in front of her made carrying a seven-year-old girl in his left arm look like a GQ magazine cover sold out within seconds of its release. She felt uneasy standing with only Ella's tiny legs and arms in between them. Uneasiness turned into embarrassment when, without warning, Ella took her hand and clamped it with her dad's right hand.

The little girl's action stunned Avery. For a moment, it deterred her brain cells. She felt a tingling sensation on her skin that turned into small butterflies inside her stomach, which ended in an erratic pounding in her chest. Her eyes gawked at her hand, sandwiched between the hot dad's and Ella's tiny one. She tensed. Astonished. Muted. Her eyes sauntered between their three hands, Ella's blinking eyes, and the mesmerizing gaze of the captivating man in front of her.

Though Ella's innocent act amazed her dad, Avery's obvious discomfort concerned him more. He didn't want to ruffle the nerves of the fascinating presence standing before him.

"Ethan… Ella's dad." Slowly, he shook the same hand clasped into his.

"Princess! I'm your princess, Dad!" Ella corrected with a pout, making both adults laugh.

Avery's laugh turned into a chuckle, watching the still-pouting little girl. "Avery Jackson."

"She is Miss Pretty, Dad!" Ella butted in as she nuzzled Avery's cheek gently.

Ethan's eyes grew with awe, gazing into Avery's eyes. He wanted to savor the chance of knowing every detail of Avery's face. Ever since his daughter mentioned finding her Miss Pretty, he had been curious. What did the only woman who had smitten his choosy daughter look like? How did she charm a seven-year-old and make her never forget about her? Now that he was gazing at her, he only had two words for Avery. ***Bewitchingly Beautiful.***

He chuckled, seeing hairpins in multiple spots on top of Avery's brown hair. Her almond-shaped eyes sparked in confusion. Though her smile was beyond gorgeous, sadness and uncertainty mirrored in the depths of her light hazel eyes, one important thing that didn't escape Ethan's sight.

He gradually removed the first hairpin he could reach to disregard the sudden jolt of emotions he could not define. But his action worsened when Avery panicked and immediately grabbed his hand. Their abrupt skin-to-skin contact caused both of them to stare into each other's eyes. Unspoken words confused them both. There was a deafening stillness.

"Ella!" a familiar voice broke the silence.

"Mama Ste! You're here!" Ella gestured for her to be released from her dad's arm. Then, happily, she walked toward the woman she called Mama Ste, the same Doctor Stella Avery had met hours ago.

Everything clicked into place. Reality sunk in. She let go of Ethan's hand. His wedding band now flashed at her. Envy pinched Avery's heart when Ethan greeted Ella's Mama Ste with a soft peck on the forehead.

When her eyes met the doctor's, Avery wished the ground would open up and swallow her. Her face was burning. Unable to think how she could get away from the family reunion in front of her, she sat back on the bench.

Her facial color and movement got Ethan's attention. "Are you okay?" he asked.

Avery bowed her head to hide her embarrassment. Immediately, Doctor Stella was beside her. "How are you feeling, Ave?" The doctor started checking her pulse, eyes focused on her face.

"I'm alright. Just got a little dizzy, I guess."

Ethan's eyes seemed to inquire the doctor in silence, but the doctor just smiled.

Ella, who was watching them, endearingly touched Avery's cheek. "Are you okay, Miss Pretty?" she asked.

"It seemed you found a new friend, Ella. She's my new friend too," Doctor Stella declared as she peppered the little girl's face with kisses.

Ella's eyes twinkled. "Yey! We have the same friend!"

"Should we go now? Our dinner reservation is in twenty minutes," Ethan asked.

Realizing she'd been intruding on the reunion and not wanting to delay the family; Avery removed the remaining hairpins on her and handed them to the nanny.

"Would you like to join us for dinner, Avery?" Ethan's question stunned her. The willingness on Doctor Stella's face confused her. Ella's anticipation of her response was priceless.

"Oh, no!" Avery shook her head multiple times. "Thank you for the invitation, though. You guys should go and enjoy your family dinner," she replied.

"We would love to have you," Doctor Stella tried to persuade her.

Avery declined again despite Ella's pouting. She knew her boundaries and felt her presence at the joyous family reunion had taken longer than it should.

"You go, guys. My ride is on the way to pick me up, too."

"Promise me we'll have time for lunch or dinner next time, okay?" Doctor Stella squeezed her shoulder.

"Sure, next time, Doctor. Nice meeting you both." She smiled at Doctor Stella and nodded at Ethan.

Before Ethan started walking, he pulled out a name card from his wallet and handed it to Avery. Once accepted, he took Ella's hand while Doctor Stella held the other. Then, together, the three walked hand in hand away from the park bench where Avery was sitting.

Once the car that Ella and her family got in had left, she exhaled aloud. She closed her eyes, trying to rewind what had just happened in her mind. Instead of recalling the events, the bristly eyebrows, defined cheekbones, well-chiseled jaw, masculine tanned skin, and Ethan's enchanting smile flashed back at her. She opened her eyes, trying to get rid of the face that had captivated her.

It was a strange feeling for Avery. The last time she felt the same was when David asked her to be his girlfriend. No other man had fascinated her since David. Not to forget that her ex-fiancé was in his birthday suit then, when Ella's dad was in full clothing.

She told herself to get a grip. Mr. Hot Dad was obviously off-limits!

When she called for her ride, she remembered the name card Ethan had handed her. Her nerves bounced with excitement to find out information about Mr. Hotshot. She felt brain-sick reading what was written on it.

ETHAN JAMES, M.D.
PRESIDENT/CEO MAYO CLINIC
Rochester, MN 507-437-5467

Ethan James. Stella James. Doctors. Wedding band. Same eyes. Ella.
Avery did the math. All parts of the equation resulted in one thing.
ONE HELLUVA OF A HOT MAN WITH A BIG X MARK!

Chapter 35

AVERY STARTED MENTALLY LISTING the flaws of a man like Ethan James. It reminded her of one of her fears. Would there ever be someone better than David? Caressing her belly assured her once more. Her little bean would be better than anyone else. They would be better together. When her ride arrived, she looked around the park before walking toward the parking area. She might as well avoid the park. But how would she avoid Doctor Stella James?

Stella James would always remind her of one person. *Ethan... no, Ella.*

Ethan... Avery shook her head multiple times. *No, Ella.*

She whispered the two names to herself. It had been a few weeks since her embarrassing experience in the park. Every time she checked the fetal development chart in her baby book, she saw the face of Doctor Stella. Who then reminded her of the father and daughter. As if Shelly had heard her thoughts, her phone started ringing. She didn't answer immediately. Instead, she video-called her best friend once she was inside her bedroom.

"Hello, stranger! I dreamt of you!" Shelly screamed. "Good or bad dream?" Avery asked.

"It depends on how you're going to take it. But important announcement first!" Shelly's screaming was louder.

"You broke your orgasm record? Or you're pregnant too?" teased Avery.

"OMG, Avery! Where are thou, my meek and innocent friend? Since when you have been crude?"

Avery pouted. "I'm just stating the obvious! Your face is screaming; you just got fuck!"

Shelly brushed her fingers on her hair. "It's called making love!" Avery rolled her eyes at her. "Hold your breath for my announcement. Art and I are coming to Florida! We're attending a Dermatology Expo."

"That's triple OMG!" Avery exclaimed.

"I know, right?" Shelly nodded. "We will surely come and visit you guys.

I'm taking your offer about us being welcome in your Palm Coast home anytime."

"Always! You guys are family." Avery covered her mouth. "I'm so excited!"

Shelly waved her hand at her. "Shush! Now, about my dream. It's about your destiny. I time-traveled to your future. I saw you meet your destiny in Florida, my dear Ave!" Shelly dramatically pointed her index fingers at her temples.

Avery laughed, watching her best friend doing her funny antic in front of her phone camera. They'd been best friends since grade school and could read each other like a book. Both had mastered the skill of reading between the lines. Aside from "Shelly the Intrusive" between them, Shelly was also the mind reader.

Shelly stopped. Her eyes grew like they were going to pop out. "Avery Jackson, spill! I know that look! What happened?"

"I met a girl, Ella. In the airport and at a park outside my OB's clinic."

Shelly's mouth twitched, and her eyes sparkled teasingly at Avery. "Go on."

"I met her dad, too. He was nice." Avery looked away from the phone camera.

"And the dad was hot! So hot, he made your panty wet?! His heart's arrow hit yours." Shelly feigned an arrow striking her chest.

"Now you sound like a perv! Hot? Yes. Nice? Yes. Available? NO! So, stop thinking like that!" Avery rolled her eyes.

"Thinking like what?" Avery's flushed face magnified Shelly's curiosity. She put her laptop on her arm. "What's his name?" Her fingers were on her keyboard, ready to type.

"Shells! No name! Stop your stalker mind! This isn't high school!" Avery yelled while grinning.

Shelly shook her head. "Er, NO! After what David did, I promised myself we would do what we should have done when you met that fuckhead the first time."

"And what would that be?" she asked.

"Vetting the ass of any man who will come your way! And I mean it!" Shelly exclaimed.

"Sorry to disappoint, but there's no reason to vet Ethan since he isn't available. Never in the world will I be like David's LA whore!" Avery shook her head.

Shelly's eyes grew bigger. "So, Ella's dad has a name." She typed on her laptop. "E-T-H-A-N, Palm Coast Florida."

Avery's face burned. "Shells, give up! You won't find him with just his first name. I could only imagine how many Ethans there are online." Avery found her best friend's curiosity unbelievably funny.

"Have you forgotten my greatest quality, Ave? I won't give up without a fight!" Shelly moved toward a table and placed her laptop on top of it. She grabbed a chair and sat with her legs placed on another chair. Her eyes and fingers never left the laptop keyboard.

"You won't give up, will you?" asked Avery.

"Nope! Now be an obedient girl and tell me Ethan's last name." She gave Avery puppy eyes with her hands in prayer. "Ave, please! I want to see his face. Promise!"

"Okay! Only to see his face, nothing else?"

Shelly nodded with a grin while Avery kept shaking her head. "He's married, Shells. He had a wedding band on his finger."

"Did he confirm it? Did you meet his wife? Did Ella say she has a mom?" Shelly's questions were in rapid succession.

"I think it's my OB. They have the same last name. Ella has her eyes. All their names rhyme. I saw them walk away going to their family dinner," Avery's voice quivered.

Shelly paused, eyes on her best friend. She felt sadness, envy, and disappointment in Avery's voice. If she could give her the world, then she would. She cleared her throat. "Well, Ethan or any other men you're going to meet, married or not, wouldn't matter. It's not a sin to admire hot men, desirable men. They add spice to women's lives. It's not like you would tempt them if they're in a relationship. It's just like when we were in high school. We stalk good-looking guys and admire them from afar."

Avery nodded. "I guess you're right. It's not like I will see him again, anyway."

"Honestly, Ave, hearing you find a man other than David attractive and hot is a joy to my ears. I'm ecstatic you can now see other people and admire other men."

"Yeah, I find it amusing too. I guess the Florida air is doing me good." Avery smiled.

"You're doing better. Believe me. Everything will be better for you and the baby."

"With you always behind me, I'm sure it will be, Shells. Love you!"

"Love you back, Ave!" She blew Avery kisses. "I need to go. I have a patient in an hour. I'll call you once we have our final travel details. By the way, what's your OB's name?"

"Um… Stella James." Avery's forehead was crinkled. "Why?"

"No reason. I need to go. Bye!" Shelly wrote on a piece of paper and hung up.

Avery was dumbfounded. Just like that, Shelly got the information from her, no sweat. Knowing her best friend's intrusiveness and Art's IT knacks, finding everything about Ethan would now become the couple's major project.

She wouldn't be surprised if Shelly called her back in a day or two with Ethan's portfolio. Knowing that Doctor Stella was married to Ethan dampened her mood. Of all the OB/Gyn names on her list, why did she choose her? She felt anxious, realizing she would see the doctor for another prenatal visit in a week.

Had it not been for Ella's captivating hot dad, Avery thought Doctor Stella could have been her Shelly, Florida version. The doctor was so warm, welcoming, and sincere. She'd made an awkward scene in the park. Would the doctor still want to be her friend after that? Her gaze at Ethan, the touch, and her crimson face. How would she face the doctor again?

It wasn't like she'd made a pass on her husband… had she?

Suddenly, Avery felt embarrassed imagining what had transpired in the park. She hid her face under her pillow. She felt blameworthy, thinking Doctor Stella might have seen her gaze at Ethan while gripping his hand.

She was reminded of David and the woman in LA. Didn't they feel guilty while doing what they did? Did the lady feel remorseful after knowing she existed in David's life? If Shelly could hear her questions, she would get a resounding NO.

Heck, no! After everything that happened, why would she even ask questions with obvious answers? When would she stop thinking about David?

As though telepathic, on cue, her phone chimed. David's name flashed with a text message. *Speaking of the devil.*

David: *My Ave, I'm leaving for Africa today. I love you and our baby. I always will. Whatever you need, please let me know anytime. I made changes in my will. Whatever happens to me, everything I have is yours. Take care of yourself and our baby. I will always be here for you both. I pray that one day, you'll find it in your heart to forgive me. Always yours, D.*

Avery read the message over and over. Her tears fell. In her mind, she believed she had already forgiven David. But her heart felt different. Deep inside, she was in pain, grieving. Uncertainty was still clouding her. She was trying so hard to let go so she can move on. Letting go hurts, and moving on was the hardest part. Would she ever get over him?

She wiped her tears while contemplating if she should reply to him.

Shells: *I sent you a zip file. Please check your email.* ♥

Chapter 36

AVERY'S ATTENTION SHIFTED TO Shelly's message. It had been less than an hour since they'd had their video call. *So, what zip file was she saying?* She was curious to know what her best friend found out so quickly.

From: Shelly. MD

Subject: Your Destiny.zip

To: Jackson. Avery

📁

Destiny.zip

Ave,

See attached.

BTW, you're welcome! 🤩

Shells 🖤

Avery muted, seeing how Shelly named the file. Her curiosity turned into nervousness. What if she wouldn't like what was inside the file? Should she open it or answer David's message?

Quick thinking, it would seem easy for her to decide. Read the file or reply to David? But the battle going inside her mind was like a sign. She knew choosing between the two could signify the path she might take.

What did she want? It was like choosing between a known hell or possibly an unknown heaven. Was there still heaven for her? Uncertainty clouded her mind. It reminded her of what her dad said about letting go vs. fear of the unknown.

She remembered the goal she set for herself when she took the plane from Boston to Florida—leaving all memories of David behind. Letting go of everything, David. Though she knew it would be the challenge of a lifetime with her little bean. She still had question after question. Every night before she slept. Every time she was alone. Whenever she thought of what future she could give her child.

On her phone, she could see the names of Shelly and David, reminding her of both messages. If she replied to David's, it would not live up to her promise of no contact after Boston. He might misunderstand her response. It might give him false hope. So she reminded herself of the first step: *letting go*.

The questions that still bombarded her at night, whenever loneliness struck, every time she doubted her capability of raising a child alone loomed. Was she making the right decision? What if she was unable to move on after letting go?

It had been months, yet her fears still haunted her. Everybody knew everyone had an opinion, and each one cared. Each time her fears hit her; Avery wished someone could instruct her on ways to end them. It would be convenient if there was a manual or a TikTok video for letting go and moving on.

"Everything alright, Muffin?"

Her dad's voice ended her reverie.

She looked at him standing by her door, watching her. "I don't feel like I'm okay now, Dad."

Slowly, her dad walked toward her and gestured, asking if sitting on the other side of the bed was okay. Avery nodded. She badly needed a wise man's advice.

"What's going on? You know you can always tell me."

"David texted me. Today, he leaves for Africa. He put me in his will. He said he won't give up on me." She held back her tears and leaned her head on her dad's shoulder.

"How do you feel about it?"

"Mixed emotions… sad, worried and doubtful… of myself."

Slowly, she felt her dad's arms covering her in a warm embrace. "Why are you sad? Do you miss him?"

Avery's silent tears turned into soft sobs. "I still do, Dad. But my mind had overpowered my heart. It's just sad that even though I'm trying hard to let go, there are days I still see him when I wake up in the morning. And now that he's leaving, going far away, I guess it's now letting go in the real sense."

"Oh, Muffin! Letting go hurts. Goodbye is never easy with the ones we love. But then, genuine love knows when to say goodbye. In doing so, you learn to love yourself again."

Avery nodded between tears and sobs. "My fears still worry me. What if I'm being selfish? Just thinking of myself and not of the baby's future. Will I be enough for my child? Am I capable of raising a child without a father?"

"Muffin, accept that love is imperfect. We will never be enough." Her dad squeezed her hand. "You think if your mom and I were perfect, we would allow you to get hurt like now? We can try to be as we love."

"How come even after I let go, I still remember everything… about him… us together?"

"Because it's a process. We let go so the new one could come in. But moving on is the hardest part. You may have to grieve or cry buckets for days or months. Then, you give yourself time to heal. Afterward, you start and try again."

"Oh, Dad! You always know when to say the right things." She felt her dad's gentle kiss on her hair.

"No, Muffin, it's living life. We are here to guide and love you unconditionally. But seriously, you're doing great in making your first step. Congratulations! On having the courage to move on. Allow the process, however slow or long it will take. Let destiny take its course." Her dad left, seeing a smile on her face.

Let destiny take its course. Her dad's last statement made Avery smile. It reminded her of the file Shelly sent. Should she open it? She decided there was no need to rush. Destiny might want her to slow down, to take her time.

As much as Avery would have liked to take her time and slow down, the days passed instantly. Then, finally, the day she was dreading arrived. She wondered why her parents didn't offer to accompany her to her prenatal appointment. Instead, both just gave her a ride and didn't even say anything about picking her up after. She felt equally relieved and disappointed when a different OB welcomed her into Doctor Stella's clinic. The doctor informed her that Doctor Stella had a family event, which was why she was absent. She thought of changing her OB. It might be better for her nerves and her sanity. But she reminded herself of her new mantra: *let destiny take its course.*

Her check-up went smoothly. Little Bean's heartbeat was strong, and its development aced all the checklists. When she left the clinic and saw the park, she missed Ella. Knowing that Doctor Stella wasn't around, she knew none of the James family was there, so she decided to go in. With a smile on her face, she patted her belly.

Unconsciously, Avery reminisced about her moments with Ella and how she missed her button-like eyes and cute, chubby cheeks. She couldn't deny the little girl had grown on her in such little time. She smiled, feeling the warmth of her tiny hands. Spending another day in the park with Ella would have been nice.

Don't you miss her hot hotshot dad, too? Her lips curved into a bigger smile. *Destiny yourself, Shells!* As if talking to her best friend, she kept on mentally listing the reasons Ethan James was off-limits. Then, she started seeing Mr. Hotshot's face everywhere in the park. *OMG! What's happening? Yeah, I met Ethan James. That's it. Charge to experience!*

Suddenly, the urge to check the destiny file sent by Shelly made her anxious. First, she looked around to ensure no one was looking at her. Then, slowly, she sat on the nearest park bench. She looked for Shelly's email among her unread messages. Surely her best friend knew by now that she hadn't opened it. It was unusual for Shelly not to call and nag her, especially since it had been a week.

How could she open and read the file without Shelly knowing? Although embarrassed to make it known she got curious and gave in to her best friend's craziness. Finally, she planned to read it fast and mark it unread after.

Just as she was about to open the message, her phone rang. It startled her to see Shelly's name on the caller ID. *WTF!*

"Shells, how are you?"

"I'm good! Why do I feel you are about to do something life-changing?" Shelly chuckled on the other line.

"Life-changing my foot, Shells! When are you coming here? I miss my best friend!"

"I miss you too! So much that if you turn to your right, you will see me waving at you!"

Still holding the phone, she turned to her right and saw Shelly waving at her from the car lot. Avery couldn't believe it. Before she could get up from the bench, Shelly came running to her. Like when they were young girls, they hugged each other with giggles and happy tears.

"I can't believe you're here! Now I know why Mom and Dad pretended not to care."

"I wanted to surprise you! Look at you and your tiny baby bump! I miss you so much, my Ave!" Shelly kissed her on both cheeks.

"I miss you too, Shells! God, I'm so happy! When did you arrive?"

"We arrived last night, but so much with the interrogation. We're going somewhere. Art is waiting in the car."

"Where are we going?" Avery's brows lifted.

"To a birthday party." Shelly paused, gave her a once over, and winked at her. "You're ready. As always, you're as charming as ever!"

In Shelly's fashion, she ushered Avery into the car. Avery had no idea where and whose birthday party they were going to. She was so happy being with her best friend she set aside her confusion and questions. Listening to the couple's funny stories and bickering made her realize how she missed the company of two of the most important people in her life. Smiling, she whispered to herself; *they are my ride-or-die!*

Avery was so entertained listening to Art's antics that she ignored her surroundings while on the road. Only when Art stopped the car in front of a guardhouse and got permission to proceed did she realize they were entering an exclusive gated community.

From the community entrance to all the houses—she should say mansions—her eyes could see from left to right. It seemed like they'd just come into a homeowner's haven. It surprised her that Shelly or Art hadn't mentioned knowing someone from this part of Palm Coast.

"Where are we exactly?" Avery's widened eyes looked at Shelly.

"Island Estates Community. Gorgeous homes they have here!" Shelly turned her face away.

When they got out of the car, all three of them paused. They were speechless at the lavish spectacle in front of them. Her eyes gaped in front of a one-of-a-kind stunning estate home on an intra-coastal waterway. Once they got closer to the main entrance, the magnificent home didn't disappoint. It looked like it came to life from the cover of an Architectural Digest magazine.

"I didn't know you knew someone from here." Avery's eyes darted at Art.

"Friend? Relative?" she inquired.

Art looked heavenward. His nose wrinkled when he faced Shelly and bowed his head when he met Avery's gaze. "I plead the fifth. I'm just a driver here."

Shelly frowned at her husband. "An old schoolmate lives here. Let's get in. The party is about to start." The pink gift box in her hands distracted Avery, but Shelly's stammering didn't stop her from wondering.

Upon entering the main door, a party arc of pink, silver, and white balloons accentuated with gold ones molded in significant number 8s welcomed them. It gave Avery the idea it was a girl's eighth birthday party. Getting inside confirmed how exceptional the home was. It had premium appointments such as natural wood, marble, travertine flooring, cathedral ceilings, Swarovski crystal chandeliers, fine granite, quartz, and wood finishes. Richness and extravagance rolled into one.

Avery felt lost, not knowing who owned the house or whose party she was attending. Before she could ask Shelly another question, a familiar button-eyed chubby-cheeked girl came running toward her. *Ella.* She was wearing an eye-catching pink princess dress with a tiara and a glittering sash with the word *Princess* written on it. Running after her was her nanny, holding another sash with the word Queen.

Stunned wouldn't describe the surprise on Avery's face. Her eyes immediately looked for Shelly.

"Sorry, not sorry!" Shelly uttered softly, giving her a peace sign.

Everything happened quickly. Ella hugged Avery tight as she placed the Queen sash on her. She didn't get any chance to inquire why or to decline. It was overwhelming to see how happy Ella was. The little girl was all smiles, saying she couldn't believe Avery had come. It warmed Avery's heart. But coldness immediately replaced the warmth she felt when she saw Ethan walking toward them. The hot hotshot glued Avery to her place. Her body trembled with embarrassment, realizing Ethan was also wearing a sash with the word *King.* She panicked, wanting to remove her sash, when she saw Doctor Stella following behind.

Chapter 37

ETHAN, THE HOT DAD of Ella—one hotshot of a man—walked toward them in all his glory, wearing casual, comfy black jeans, and a cream cotton shirt. Oozing with charm, he looked delectable even with a glittering king sash.

Avery blinked to ensure she read the word on Ethan's sash correctly. Her cheeks reddened as her mouth snapped shut. Triple OMG! Why did Ella put the Queen sash on her? She was glued to the spot. Her mind tried to convince her that Ella's hot dad hadn't mesmerized her for the second time, but her body didn't agree with her.

She couldn't read what was going on in Ethan's mind. He coolly walked toward them with the same gaze as when they were in the park. Shelly and Art were there for the free show. The couple couldn't take their eyes off Ethan and Avery. Art was focusing more on analyzing Ethan, man to man. Shelly couldn't decide. Would she play cupid for the two who were undeniably smitten? Or would she keep her mission of being the best friend slash inspector slash guardian angel slash Vetter slash protector?

The shift in the atmosphere was evident. Shelly, Art, and the nanny all had their eyes on Ethan and Avery. They felt a significant connection between the two. Ella, innocent as she should be, also knew something special was happening. She was too young to understand what was happening around her, but she knew one thing: Miss Pretty and her dad together always made her happy. In her eight-year-old mind, they were her mission.

"Daddy! Miss Pretty is here. Look!" Ella pointed at the sash she put on Avery. "I found our queen. We're complete now." The little girl's eyes were twinkling.

Avery nearly choked hearing what Ella said. Art's eyes bored into Ethan. The nanny was grinning. Shelly was ecstatic in silence. She looked between her best friend's deep red face and Ella's hot dad.

"Are we going to play Cupid now? I feel bad for David," Art whispered to Shelly.

Shelly gave Art a dreadful look. "Stop patronizing that dickhead! Go get us popcorn!"

From where Shelly was standing, she witnessed a raw but special moment. Ethan, Avery, and Ella were in their bubble. Ethan was clearly bewitched by Avery, who was captivated by his piping-hot charms. Both were unaware of the powerful effect that incited happiness on young Ella's face. She was right. *Could this be Avery's destiny unfolding in front of me?* Shelly thought to herself.

Avery's attention was diverted to Doctor Stella, who was approaching them. Shelly noticed her discomfort. Avery's hands were clamped onto her queen sash. Shelly recognized the panic on her best friend's face. She knew Avery wanted to remove the sash to prevent Ste from seeing her wearing it.

Shelly smirked. *Poor Ave! You should have read the file. It would have saved you from anxiety!*

Before Avery could remove the sash, she saw Shelly run toward Doctor Stella. She was speechless. The two hugged each other. She stared at the two, talking and laughing together. Was she missing something?

While Avery and Ethan focused on the joyful reunion between Doctor Stella and Shelly, Ella took advantage of the situation to fulfil her mission. Ethan amused at Avery's expression, watched the exchange of pleasantries between the two ladies in front of them. He memorized the face that had been popping into his mind since that afternoon in the park. Avery was on the verge of having an anxiety attack. Her dilemma was turning weak in front of Ethan and being embarrassed facing Doctor Stella.

Shelly has lots of explaining to do! Avery told herself. Even without looking, she could feel the eyes of the desirable creature gaping at her. It made her knees weak. She decided not to look at him for as long as she could. Without a doubt, her body would betray her once their eyes met.

You're truly a beauty, Avery, Ethan whispered to himself. He used the moment to immerse himself in her shy and mysterious grace. How he wished he'd get a more extended time to cherish everything.

Little did both know the two ladies laughing and babbling were talking about them. They were concocting the greatest project of their lives. Who would have thought Shelly and Doctor Stella knew each other from way back? They were active Dermatology Interest Group (DIG) members while attending Med School at Yale.

Once Shelly got Doctor Stella's name from Avery, it only took her ten minutes to contact the OB/Gyn and rekindle their long-lost connection. After remembering each other through the video call Shelly started, they found they had a mutual dream: to bring happiness to the two people they loved. Shelly knew her best friend wouldn't read Ethan's file.

In the same way, Doctor Stella knew Ethan wouldn't have the courage to make the first move toward Avery. It motivated them to plan what began at Ella's party. Before they could further discuss what to do next, Ella's loud voice and giggling snatched their attention.

"Now, the king and the queen will never be apart!" Ella was clapping, grinning at her masterpiece.

Ethan and Avery's faces were both crimson. Pink handcuffs linked their hands. The nanny was nodding her head continuously.

Ella's action amused Art. Shelly and Doctor Stella winked at each other. "Thank Heavens!" both whispered as they approached the two in handcuffs.

"Ella! Princess, please give Daddy the key," Ethan asked.

Ella shook her head and pouted. "There's no key."

Avery's chagrin was beyond what she could imagine, especially since Doctor Stella and Ethan were in front of her. If only she could make herself invisible. *Oh, Shelly, that grin of yours!* She promised she would make her best friend pay.

"Ella, can you please give Mama Ste the key?" the doctor begged calmly.

"It doesn't have a key. Jamie gifted it to me, but she left the key in their house," explained Ella.

"Can we call Jamie then?" asked Avery.

"Yes, call Jamie," Ethan directed the nanny.

But to their surprise, the nanny cracked up hard instead of obeying. "Jamie just dropped off her gift and left an hour ago."

Everyone was focused on Ethan and Avery. Then, as if someone gave them all a signal, they laughed aloud. The boisterous laughter of people around them earned chuckles from the two in handcuffs.

Doctor Stella had to sever the fun when she remembered the cake. "Ella, it's time for you to make your wish and blow out the candles on your cake."

"Yey!" Ella cheered. "Come, Daddy, Miss Pretty. Let's all go together!"

Avery looked at Ethan, then at Shelly. "Can we do something about these handcuffs first?"

"We can work it out after the cake. Let's go, guys." Doctor Stella motioned them toward the cake.

Ella held the other hand of her dad. Then, while walking, Ethan whispered to Avery, "I guarantee you I'll take care of these after." Avery had no choice but to nod.

While all the singing and candle-blowing were happening, Shelly couldn't help but snicker as she watched Ethan, Avery, and Ella together. Ella's smile was up to her ears. Ethan's face was beaming as his gaze focused only on his daughter's joy and Avery's presence. Avery's glow was radiating in the room. Her gape was centered on both the father and daughter.

When the cake ceremony concluded and the guests went to different parts of the mansion, Shelly stood beside Avery. When Shelly handed her a tissue, Avery frowned, and her brows raised.

"You're drooling at Mr. Hotshot," Shelly whispered to her best friend and rolled her eyes.

As Ethan had promised when most of the guests had left, he brought Avery inside his man cave. While inside, he gave her a tour explaining the massive room's multifunction. Library, entertainment/bar, and storage for his do-it-yourself tools. When they were done removing the handcuffs, he guided Avery toward the minibar.

"Would you like red or white?" he asked.

Avery shook her head. "I'll pass. Um, I can't. I'm…" She pointed to her tiny bump. Ethan's eyes narrowed.

"You're pregnant?" his voice was taut.

Chapter 38

"YOU'RE PREGNANT?" ETHAN REPEATED his question with his head low.

Avery nodded without taking her eyes off him. The look on his face puzzled her. She couldn't explain why his gaze of devotion abruptly superseded gloom, setback, and confusion.

"Doctor Stella is my OB."

Ethan nodded. It felt like the massive room was shrinking. Avery's confirmation of her pregnancy brought him back to before Ella was born—the period when Ella's mom was preparing him. Not just for their daughter's arrival, but in the end, he realized she also prepared him for their ending. *Oh, Patty, you're so unfair! You didn't even ask what I wanted.*

"Are you okay?" Avery's shaky voice snapped Ethan back to the present.

He gulped the white he poured into a glass. The cool Ethan changed into an anxious Ethan. He stroked his hair with his hand a few times and took a deep breath. "How far along are you?" He looked Avery in the eye and scanned her baby bump.

"Going on my fifteenth week," Avery shyly answered. She caressed her bump and muttered little Bean's name to herself.

"I didn't notice when we met in the park. But I wondered how you and Ste knew each other. I guess the connection slipped my mind." Ethan slowly shook his head.

"Oh… Doctor Stella is one trustworthy and law-abiding doctor," Avery stammered.

Ethan lifted his head and placed his hand on his chin. His intent gaze prompted Avery to explain.

"I meant knowing your relation and her checking on me in the park… I expected she would have told you about our doctor-patient connection when you left." She felt her nerves.

"We both are. We follow doctor-patient confidentiality unless Ste needs my expert advice or a second opinion." Ethan poured another glass and drank it fast. "I assume your pregnancy is going well?" His stare started at Avery's face and ended on her bump.

"My little Bean…" She smiled and placed both hands on her stomach. "That's what I call my baby. He or she aced all there is on the developmental checklist. I'm just one of the few who show a slight bump."

"I see." Ethan nodded. "How about you?" He directed his gaze to her eyes.

Suddenly, Avery felt like their conversation had turned into an interrogation. She felt awkward. "I'm fine, I guess. So far, so good." She looked at the door. "We should head out. We don't want Shelly sending a search team." She chuckled but halted, seeing Ethan's expression up close.

Ethan led her toward the door without a word, and they walked to Shelly and Doctor Stella's group. "You and Doctor Stella raised your daughter mighty fine. Ella is the sweetest and the cutest!" Avery's eyes glowed.

Ethan's eyebrows waggled. "Oh, Ste isn't Ella's mom. She's my older sister, but she's been a great help in raising Ella. She even shifted from Dermatology Medicine to Obstetrics and Development Pediatrics after Ella was born. I'm so lucky to have a sister like her."

Avery paused. She was stupefied. *Good heavens!* Shelly noticed Avery's shocked state from a distance. Immediately, her best friend/protector instinct made her run toward her.

"Are you okay, Ave? How are you feeling?" Shelly asked.

"I'm good." Avery touched her forehead and feigned a headache, embarrassed everyone's eyes were on her.

Ethan ushered her swiftly to the nearest couch. "Ste, please check on her quickly!"

Avery signaled for Doctor Stella to disregard what her brother said, "It's all good. I just got a little nauseous."

Doctor Stella nodded, smirking that in a flash, her brother left and came back with a glass of milk for Avery. "Drink this. It's warm, and it'll be good for you," he said.

Shelly fake coughed after winking at Doctor Stella. "That was one hell of an Usain Bolt move, but appreciated, right, Ave?" She pouted her lip, signaling for Avery to say something to Ethan.

"You didn't have to but, thank you." Avery took the glass of milk from Ethan's hand. She didn't take her eyes off him. She watched as he strode toward Doctor Stella. *His sister.* Why didn't she think of it?

Ethan and Doctor Stella started arguing, their voices in whispers. Shelly tapped Avery's shoulder to get her attention. "What's going on between you and Ella's hot dad?"

"What? Oh, no, Shells! I'm not the one to be questioned here." Avery shook her head. "You have a lot of explaining to do. Why didn't you tell me?"

Shelly's face was blank. "Tell you what, Ave?"

"That Ethan and Doctor Stella are siblings," Avery whispered.

"Didn't I send you the file and ask you to check it?" Shelly made a clown face.

They stopped whispering when they saw Doctor Stella approaching them. The doctor's face was flushed. She was growling at her brother, who was following her. "Oh my God, Ethan. I'm the OB here. Avery's fine, and she is not Patty. You need to calm down and thank me instead of nagging me like you're the boss of me."

Doctor Stella took Avery's hand. "Come, Avery. Let's go to my private space. I'll do a quick check on you and the baby. The Grumpy CEO here thinks I'm one of his staff and he can go on a power trip now."

Avery silently followed Doctor Stella. Just as they were a few steps from Ethan, the doctor paused and threw a pissed-off look at her brother. "Are you happy now, CEO?" she yelled at him, showing her hold on Avery's hand.

When the doctor and Avery were out of sight, Shelly approached Ethan. "Hi! I'm Shelly, Avery's best friend. Thanks for welcoming us into your home. I believe no one introduced us yet." She offered her hand.

Ethan reached out his hand. "Thank you for coming. How did you know Ste?"

"We're members of DIG at Yale. But unfortunately, we lost contact when she shifted to Obstetrics and Developmental Pedia," explained Shelly.

"I see. It's good you guys got the chance to reconnect. Where do you practice?"

"I own a DERMA clinic in Boston with my husband, Art." Shelly looked around for Art. "I'm sure he's somewhere here."

Ethan nodded. "You're the one attending our expo Ste told me about?"

Yes, thanks for the free pass, by the way," Shelly smiled.

"You're welcome. It's good to know Ste gets to be with the company of people she enjoys." Ethan's eyes darted toward where his sister had ushered Avery.

Shelly scanned him from head to toe. "Well, enough of chitchat, Mr. Hotshot. I came here because I want to see you in person. I need to know your intentions toward my best friend."

Ethan's face hardened. "Excuse me?"

Shelly maintained a poker face. "If Ste hasn't already told you, Ave came here to start anew, pregnant with no husband in the picture. Only her parents." She watched Ethan's face as she spoke.

"I didn't see any ring. Is she divorced?" Ethan's tone softened.

"She was engaged. She returned the ring just a couple of months ago. Even after finding out she was pregnant." The pride in Shelly's voice was unmistakable. "For what reason? It's her story to tell."

Ethan felt Shelly's protectiveness over Avery. The last sentence she uttered was a challenge. He knew his sister had already given him away to the intrusive woman vetting him. One brave friend was interrogating him right in his face in his own house. But he was never Ethan James, CEO, for no reason.

"And if I may ask, why are you telling me these things?" he asked Shelly grimly.

As expected, Shelly didn't back down. Instead, she scowled at him. She met Ethan's intimidation without blinking. "It's still fresh for Ave. I'm not sure if she's ready yet. But your portfolio came with a solid recommendation. And today, I'm giving the recommendation a significant consideration."

"Significant consideration, huh?" Ethan chuckled. "You're something! I wonder how you and Avery click. It seems odd."

Shelly was about to fight back with her sass, but Avery and Doctor Stella reappeared. "Come, both of you. Ella and Art have a sing-off in the entertainment room." The doctor couldn't hide the excitement in her voice.

When they entered the room, Ella was singing the lyrics of a song shown on a giant TV. Avery wasn't sure if the girl was reading the lyrics, but she seemed too familiar with it. Holding the microphone, Art was in awe of the eight-year-old in front of him. Ella was emotionally belting an adult song with her teeny, weeny, sweet voice.

🎵 *And take, take her to the moon for me. Take her like you promised me* 🎵

🎵 *Say you love her every time. Like how you told me the last time* 🎵

🎵 *Someday, we'll understand why I had to leave. But for now, I need you to set me free* 🎵

🎵 *So before I say goodbye, would you do one last thing for me? Be happy* 🎵

Suddenly, Ella stopped singing. She looked at her dad and reached for his hand. Ethan walked toward his daughter, sat on the floor, and pulled Ella onto his lap. Everyone except Art, Shelly, and Avery anxiously looked at the TV screen.

When the song lyrics faded, a charming blue-eyed woman appeared on the screen. Her gorgeous smile half hid the sadness in her eyes. Doctor Stella glanced at Shelly, then looked at Avery.

When the woman on the screen started talking, all eyes in the room focused on the TV.

"Hi, Ella, Princess. Happy eighth birthday!" The woman blew kisses, which Ethan animatedly caught by his hand and placed on Ella's cheek.

Shelly observed Avery, who was gazing at the father and daughter. The similarities between the woman and Ella made it an easy guess as to who she was.

"Princess, I'm sorry if Mommy couldn't be with you on your birthday. I know you know why, and you understand. Did you listen to our song? Please remind Daddy that Mommy meant what the song says. I love you and Daddy. Take care of each other." The woman stopped and looked up. It was apparent she was fighting her tears. After clearing her throat, she continued. "Ella, I wish you to continue growing kind, obedient, and happy. My greatest wish for you and Daddy is for you to be happy. Happy birthday, Princess! See you on your next birthday. Mwah!"

Chapter 39

A JOLLY HAPPY BIRTHDAY song followed the video. First, Shelly saw Avery wiping her tears. Then, she looked at Doctor Stella, who was watching Avery too. Even without Avery saying anything, her face and gestures said it all. She cared for Ella and, most probably, for Ethan, too.

Avery didn't notice the two pairs of eyes gawking at her. Instead, she was concentrating on the two people with whom she'd felt a special connection in just a short period of time. In her eyes, the father and daughter were two fragile souls getting love and strength from each other. She now understood what Doctor Stella told her when they were inside her home office.

"Ethan may appear a strong-willed leader, all power and stability, but inside, he's broken and fighting. It broke him when he lost Ella's mom eight years ago today. But Ethan never showed it. He needed to keep going for Ella. He'd been fighting and living for years now so he could continuously shower his daughter with love."

Avery somehow compared her situation with what Ethan had experienced. Would she be at least half the fighter for her little Bean, like Ethan had been to Ella?

"Since Ella was born, my brother only lived for her. He let no one get close to them like he had been to you, Ave. I've never seen my niece as happy as when she's around you. They're both captivated by your loving presence. This is new to both. But I know whatever is going on, Ethan will be on for the greatest challenge of his life. Please understand him; he didn't get the chance to grieve for his wife. So, when he comes to you, please give him a chance."

Avery discontinued her daze when Ethan lovingly covered Ella with his embrace. It compressed her heart when both looked each other in the eye. Their gaze toward each other spoke of a genuine commitment to love and care for one another. Ella may only be eight years old, but it seemed like her heart and mind breathed one that fit Ethan's perfectly.

Please understand him. He didn't get the chance to grieve for his wife. So, when he comes to you, please give him a chance. Doctor Stella's request replayed in her ears. She looked at Ethan again. Before, his hotness and Adonis-like charms had caused the butterflies in her stomach to fluff their wings, but now, in an instant, Avery felt differently.

She started seeing him in a different light, as a loving, responsible, and selfless father. She couldn't imagine how difficult it must have been for him when Ella was just a newborn. It might have terrified him. Being young, a first-time father, and brokenhearted. Like she is. It astounded her when the butterflies in her stomach suddenly merged with a loud, fast, and never-ending thud in her chest. It reminded her of a similar occurrence. When David asked her to be his girlfriend, she realized she had fallen head over heels in love with him that morning.

This can't happen. Why was she feeling this way? She'd just met him. This can't be.

At least with David, they'd spent multiple times together before she'd felt like that. She placed her hand above her heart, pressing and kneading her chest, hoping it would calm her. But then she saw Ethan staring at her face, his face wrinkled. When he started walking toward her, her chest felt intense. *Please stop, please.* Avery begged her heart to calm down before he could reach her, but it didn't listen. Instead, it acted as if it had its own mind, beating on its own.

Pretending not to see Ethan coming, she closed her eyes. "Are you alright?"

"Everything's good. I'm good." Avery's voice quivered.

Instead of facing him, she bowed her head. She wanted to hide her reddening face. But her hands were shaking, making it difficult for her to hide. How she wished Shelly could sense her situation and come to her rescue. The last thing she wanted was to be alone with the man who'd caused pandemonium in her heart in record time.

The one time she badly needed her best friend's protection, Shelly wasn't here. The heavens didn't listen to her plea. Instead, she heard footsteps leaving the room. Shelly and Doctor Stella were rushing everyone to help Ella open her gifts outside the entertainment room. When she looked up, Ethan was smiling at her, his eyes wide and friendly.

"Are you sure you're okay? Did you have a hard time breathing or something? I saw you massaging your chest." His hands were inside his pants' side pockets.

Why was he nice to her? He wasn't helping. "I'm fine. Don't worry about me. Thanks for your concern, though."

Avery took a few steps toward the door. She needed to get away from him. In her mind, nothing good would come out of whatever she felt for him, especially given both their situations. No man in his right mind would accept a woman in her state. And having learned what Ethan had gone through, she didn't think it would be his priority to be connected to someone like her.

Before she could reach the door, Ethan's hand grabbed her arm. Tight-lipped, she looked at the hand holding her.

"Avery, we need to talk. Please look at me." Ethan lifted her chin. "We should discuss this…" He gestured to himself and her.

"I don't understand what you mean." Then, stuttering, Avery moved her face away from his touch.

"You sure do. If you don't want to say anything, please listen to what I need to say. Please stay. Just hear me out, please."

Avery was reluctant to hear what he had to say. She was afraid that if she talked to him, he would feel what was happening inside her—the feelings she'd want to suppress. But when she saw his face, his earnestness hit her. She found herself guided by Ethan to the settee.

She wanted to avoid his gaze so much, but she looked straight at him, hoping it would conceal how she felt toward him. But it was torture mentally and emotionally. The more she looked at his face, the greater the pandemonium in her heart intensified.

"Patty was my wife. We met in pre-med. Six months after we were married, she got pregnant with Ella. We were happy and just waiting for Ella to complete our family." Ethan sighed aloud. "That's what I thought. I didn't know Patty had a medical pre-condition. She hid her heart problem from me. Patty pushed through with the pregnancy without asking me or getting my opinion about it. She knew she could die giving birth. I thought she was preparing me for Ella's arrival. Little did I know she was also preparing me for what could happen to her."

Avery's chest tightened, seeing the grief in Ethan's eyes. Without deliberation, she took his hand and squeezed it affectionately. An intense fleck of heat and ineffable sensation struck both of them. They looked into each other's eyes.

Ethan took the chance, caressed her cheek and the sides of her jaw, and traced her lips gradually. Avery strived to conceal the effect of his touch by avoiding his stare. But Ethan moved his face and made her look him in the eye.

"I know you felt it, too. Something is going on between us. A special connection happens whenever we are around each other."

Avery smiled and bit her lower lip. "I know. It's a confusing feeling and scary, too. It seems unreal because we just met. And you are, look at you, you're somebody..." She started fidgeting. "And I'm nobody, and... pregnant." She rubbed her forehead and turned her eyes to the floor.

Immediately, Ethan lifted her chin and cupped her face with both of his hands to make her face him. "Never say anything negative or feel bad about yourself. I'm not somebody, and you're not just a nobody. You're bewitchingly beautiful inside and out. You've captivated both Ella and me."

His words stunned her. "How?" she asked in a whisper.

Ethan smiled. "By just being you. And if you're saying being pregnant makes you a nobody, then my being a single dad to Ella would make me one, too."

"No, no. That's not what I mean." Avery removed Ethan's hands from her face and shook her head.

Ethan chuckled at her expression. "That's what it sounded like when you said it."

"But... ah! I don't know what to say." Avery covered her face with her hands.

"We don't need to identify everything right now. I want to let you know how I am right now. Just like you, I'm confused, too. I've never felt like this since Patty. But I'm sure of one thing..." Ethan took both of her hands and cupped them inside his. "Ave, you make Ella and me happy. And..."

"Excuse me..." Shelly coughed from the door.

Avery quickly pulled her hands away from Ethan's, her face reddening. Ethan didn't hide his dissatisfaction with Shelly's interruption.

"I'm sorry to bear the bad news, but Ave, we have to go. Your dad already gave a buzz. He's anxious you're not home yet." Shelly's eyes darted at Ethan. "Ste already put Ella to bed."

Avery stood up and glanced at Ethan, who was already standing beside her. "We have to go. Thank you for having us."

Ethan nodded. "I'll call you. We're not done talking about us." He slowly tucked the strand of hair behind her ear. The gesture didn't slip Shelly's observant stare.

"Let's go, Ave. Chop! Chop!" Shelly motioned for Avery to rush.

"Take your time, Ave. I'll walk you out."

Ethan glared back at Shelly as he held Avery's hand. Shelly fought Ethan's glare by giving him a piercing stare. Art was already waiting in the driver's seat when they reached the car. Shelly stood before the passenger's door and gawked at them.

As if Ethan didn't care, he kissed Avery on the forehead. "You have my name card, right? Call me once you're home."

Shelly's eyes rolled. "Ave, until his intentions are clear, you're not his. You're not obligated to call him. He should call you. You're not in a relationship unless he's committed."

Avery glared at her best friend, then smiled and nodded at Ethan. He opened the backseat door for her. She rushed to get in, stunned that Shelly gave Ethan an earful.

Ethan stuffed his hands in his pants pockets and sighed aloud, facing Shelly. He admired the woman's guts in saying what she said to his face.

Shelly wouldn't budge. She faced Ethan. "Just saying." Her mouth crookedly grinned as she got in the car. When the car drove away, Ethan remained still, astounded.

Chapter 40

UNTIL HIS INTENTIONS ARE clear, until he's committed, there's no relationship.

Shelly's words kept echoing in Avery's ears. Their ride back was quiet as Avery tried to remember what had transpired in her conversation with Ethan. Shelly was observing her from the rearview mirror.

She wasn't even sure if Ethan wanted a romantic relationship with her. She shook her head, took a deep breath, and sighed.

"That's it, Ave! Enough with your long breathing and loud sighing." Shelly faced her from the front passenger seat. "What did you guys talk about when we left the room?" Her voice was terrifying.

"Sweetheart, you almost gave me a heart attack!" Art said.

"Nothing—Nothing happened." Avery glanced at her best friend, closed her eyes, and leaned back in her seat.

"You know you can never lie to me. So, what's with him touching your hair? Holding your hand? And kissing your forehead? That didn't seem like nothing to me."

"Ethan got moves. I think he got it bad on you, Ave," Art butted in.

Avery slowly opened the window to her side. Her eyes were focused on the swarm of lights brightening the road at night. She sighed when she gazed up at the sky and saw the stars. "He said he feels it."

"What does he feel?" Shelly scrunched up her face. "Triple OMG Ave! This conversation is slower than a turtle."

"Our connection. Ethan said he feels a special and intense connection whenever we're around. That I captivated him and Ella." Avery glanced at Shelly and massaged her forehead. "I want to close my eyes right now. We should discuss this at home."

Shelly tapped Art's arms. "Hon, I think you're driving too slow."

"What?" Art checked the speedometer and shook his head. "No, Hon, I'm not." Shelly glared at her husband, exasperated. She looked at Avery from the rearview mirror. "You know what, Ave? I'm having a sleepover in your room tonight. We will analyze together what Ethan said word by word."

Art gawked at his wife, defenseless and begging. "What about me, Hon? I need you beside me!"

"So, you're telling me Ethan said you both can't deny something is going on between you guys?" Shelly's voice was loud, her eyes wide.

The best friends were both lying in Avery's bed. They were capping the night with face masks and "catch-up time," as Shelly called it.

"Yep, that's what he said. He told me he hadn't felt that way since Patty died."

"Patty?" Shelly tried moving her body to face Avery. "I assume Ella's mom, the woman in the video?"

Avery nodded. "She died giving birth to Ella. Ethan was clueless that she was sick." Avery's voice was thick.

"Ethan annoys me with his bossy vibe, you know." Shelly tapped her hand. "But I give it to him for raising Ella alone after his wife's death. He even made something of himself at a young age. Now it makes sense why Ste shifted from Derma to Obstetrics then." Shelly's tone softened.

Avery cleared her throat. "As I watched them, it gave me a glimpse of my future. Ethan and Ella could be me and little bean, you know? Just that David is alive and can be a present father if given a chance," she mumbled.

Immediately, Shelly removed her mask and faced Avery. "Except that dickhead is considered a living dead!"

Avery chuckled. "You know your ideas are out of this world! So why are you here in my bed and not in the guest room with your husband?"

Shelly started massaging her face. "You have no idea what I have to promise Art to sleep here tonight. So, you better make this night worthwhile." Pouting, Shelly asked, "but seriously, Ave. What did you say to Ethan?"

"I just agreed. That yeah… there might be something. But is that a love confession? Did we confess to each other? What are we now?" Avery moved and sat on the bed. "Triple OMG! I'm so freaking confused."

"Did you kiss? Like mouth to mouth, tongue and all?" asked Shelly.

Avery threw a pillow at her best friend. "I can't deal with you! No. We didn't!" Even with the mask on, she was sure her cheeks had turned pink.

"What's wrong with my question? I'm just trying to help you analyze the situation." Shelly shook her head.

"Sometimes I think you're a child hidden in a woman's body," Avery cackled.

"But Ave, in all seriousness. What did Ethan say when you acknowledged something was happening between you two? What is he going to do about it?" Shelly gave a half-smile.

"We didn't get to that part. I remembered a very nosy person came in and interrupted us." Avery rolled her eyes.

Shelly fake coughed and laughed. "I agree. My timing was not the best."

"He asked me to call him once we're home." She squeezed Shelly's hand.

"He should be the one calling you, Ave." Shelly's mouth twitched.

"But he doesn't have my number. I have his." Avery pouted her lips.

Shelly sighed and blew the strand of hair covering her face. "Why are you acting like a teenager? Trust me on this, Ave. If he wants to talk to you, he'll find a way."

Avery nodded silently. She wanted to call or send Ethan a message to tell him she was home safe, but she didn't want to look desperate to her best friend. As if Shelly could feel her agony, she took her phone from the bedside table and started typing. Once the sound of a message sent pinged, she put her phone in the space in between them.

"There! I sent Ste a message informing her we're home safe. If Ella's dad is as smart as he is hot, he should know what to do. Let's wait and see!" Shelly softly pinched Avery's arm.

They both kept quiet. Shelly sat still with her back leaned against the headboard. Avery did the same with the mask still on her face. Both silently counted the seconds from when Shelly sent Doctor Stella a message. When the phone chimed, they shouted in unison. "Triple OMG!"

With hands shaking, Shelly grabbed her phone. "It's Ste. She got the message."

Avery removed her mask, threw it in a bin, and gave a dismissive wave of her hand. She moved to face Shelly's side of the bed. "We better sleep. It's past my bedtime."

Shelly shrugged her shoulders coyly. "Wait! There's more!"

Avery sat on the bed in a swift motion. "What is it?" she asked.

"Ste gave my number to Ethan." Shelly scrunched her face.

She started counting. "One, two, three…" The ringing of her phone bewildered them both. Avery's face drained of color.

Shelly blinked her eyes several times and modulated her voice.

"Hello, this is Shelly. Who's this?" She looked at Avery. "Oh, hi, Ethan! Avery? Let me check if she's still awake. I'm afraid it's past her bedtime." Avery frowned and scowled at her best friend. Shelly chuckled. "Hello, Ethan. It's your lucky night. Ave is still awake."

When she passed the phone to Avery, Shelly quietly mouthed you owe me big time, to which Avery grinned.

"He…Hello…" Avery stuttered.

"Hi! I'm glad you got home safe. It worried me when you didn't call. Good thing Shelly texted Ste." Ethan paused with a loud sigh.

"Sorry… Um… I didn't get the chance to call you." Avery gave her best friend a pout when she felt Shelly's cheek beside hers and her ear pressed to the other side of the phone.

"It's okay. Shelly was right. I should be the one to call. When her text beat me to it, I was already asking Ste for your or Shelly's number. Can I ask for your number so I can call or message you directly the next time?" There was a long silence on Ethan's line.

"Sure. I'll text you my number once we end this call." Avery's cheeks blushed. Shelly mimicked Avery's blushing by pinching her cheeks.

"I won't take much of your bedtime. Is it okay if I call you tomorrow? I wanted to continue our talk a while back." Ethan sounded fruity.

"It's okay. We can continue our talk tomorrow." Avery choked when Shelly deliberately talked loudly with her mouth near the mouthpiece.

"Ave, please ask him. What is he going to do about the strange and intense connection you feel towards each other?" Shelly ran away, but the pillow Avery threw at her still hit her face.

"I'm sorry about that. Shelly can be annoying sometimes. Please don't mind what she said."

Ethan's tone turned husky. "Don't worry about it. Tomorrow, I will tell you what I plan to do about it, about us. Please text me your number. Good night."

"Um… Goodnight, Ethan." As soon as she hung up, Avery messaged him her phone number.

"Good night, Ethan. Please don't mind, Shelly. She's annoying sometimes." Shelly brought Avery's phone to her ear, imitating her, pretending to be talking to Ethan.

"Shells, stop it! What you said a while ago… it's so embarrassing!"

"Ave, I don't know what you're talking about. I mind my business here."

While holding Avery's phone in her hand, it chimed. "Lookie! Your Mr. Hotshot texted."

Avery tried taking her phone from Shelly's hand, but she got a good grip on it and started reading the message aloud. "Ave, thank you for giving me your number. I'll surely have a good night's sleep now that I've heard your voice. I look forward to tomorrow. I already miss you. Good night."

Avery grinned as she bit her nails. "That's my phone. You shouldn't read my messages." At speed, she grabbed her phone from Shelly's hand. Then, slowly, she leaned on the headboard. Shelly watched as Avery had her eyes glued to her phone.

"Hey, Miss Teen USA, stop reading the same thing. It might get deleted. Let's sleep. I need a beauty rest after all the shenanigans you put me through today."

Avery didn't spare a glance at her best friend. Instead, her grin turned into a soft giggle. Shelly hit a pillow against her arm. "You don't just like him. I think you're falling in love with him!"

Avery put her phone down as if the idea hit her and glimpsed at her best friend. She tried analyzing what Shelly had just said. Suddenly, her eyebrows rose, and she sniffled.

"What's wrong with me? I just recently left David. I can't explain how now… I'm feeling this strong…" Her right hand pointed to her heart. "Whatever, toward Ethan." She covered her face with both hands and bowed her head. "God, why am I feeling this way? Little Bean should be my priority, not another guy." When she lifted her head, a tear fell on her cheek.

Shelly moved toward Avery and hugged her. "Hey, there's no need to explain or make sense of it. It's your life, do what makes you happy."

"You think so? Should I let things be between Ethan and me?"

"Ave, let your past make you better, not bitter." Shelly's eyes twinkled.

Avery beamed. "Why are you so annoying and so lovable at the same time, Shells?"

"I may appear shallow and funny sometimes." Shelly grinned and pointed at her heart. "Deep inside this heart is learned from experience."

"That's why I love you, Shells!" Avery hugged back her best friend tighter.

"And I feel the same. Don't overthink what's happening. Sometimes for some people, it takes ten years to get that one year that will change their lives. Don't let this chance pass." Shelly pulled away from their hug and pointed at Avery's heart several times. "That swift feeling might be forever for you. Have faith, Ave."

To lighten the mood, Shelly started tickling Avery on her sides. When her best friend's face brightened, she pinched both of her cheeks softly. "Now, let's sleep. You wouldn't like to look like a zombie for Ella's hot dad tomorrow!"

Chapter 41

"SOMETIMES, FOR SOME PEOPLE, *it takes ten years to get that one year that will change their lives. So don't let this chance pass. The swift feeling you're having with Ethan might be forever for you."*

Avery watched as her best friend slept beside her. Could Shelly be right?

Though Shelly's personality always brought entertainment to any occasion, she was also the wisest she'd known, aside from her dad. Since they were little, she had always admired how Shelly looked at things—my ride-or-die. In the past months, she had been living up to being her protector.

When it came to Ethan, her best friend had been keeping her on her toes. She'd been her devil's advocate, the one who'd been vetting Mr. Hotshot since the day she told her about him. It had just been a few months since she'd moved, but so many things had already happened.

Avery sighed. Who would have thought Florida would also live up to its name? It had been giving her only sunshine in the past few months and some rainbows, too. She could say that it brought her some new people, special ones, like the man who had never left her mind since that day in the park. In record time, one extraordinary man had given her hope again. How could this be possible? She couldn't help but ask herself repeatedly.

She'd moved away to forget and begin again. It seemed Ethan and Ella had been doing a good job helping her. She realized it was not the people she had started forgetting but the pain. When she mentioned David to Shelly, she didn't feel the same heaviness and hurt. She even laughed when her best friend poked fun at David.

Did that mean she was moving on?

"What the hell, Ave? It's 2 AM. Why are you not sleeping? Go to sleep and dream in your sleep. We call daydreaming, daydreaming for a freaking reason!" Shelly blasted in her ear before going back to sleep.

Realizing the time, she yawned and dozed off as she looked forward to getting a call from Ethan. She felt excited to hear the voice of the man who'd been causing all things new and impossible in her heart and mind for a few months.

It had been unbelievable, but extraordinary months had passed since the day after Ella's birthday. It was the day Ethan fulfilled his promise of having the important talk with Avery. Though he was busy coming back and forth between Minnesota and Florida, they were able to form a dynamic. Ella and Avery spent more time together, especially when Ethan was in his office in Rochester. They'd been a familiar presence in each other's homes.

It had been the absolute best for Avery. She found an extended family in the loving company of Doctor Stella, Ella, and Ethan. She wouldn't forget the moment they sat and talked to each other about their lives. She still couldn't believe it had been five months since they had that talk. She didn't tire of remembering what Ethan had said and done.

"I meant it when I told you I felt this powerful connection between us, a special feeling toward you whenever I'm around you. And I know you feel it too." Ethan held her hand as they walked towards the park bench, where they first saw each other.

She couldn't refute what he said. Just him holding her hand made Avery feel the intense somersault of emotions in her chest that felt like exploding any minute. When they sat on the bench and Ethan faced her to caress her cheek to the corners of her lips, she couldn't help but close her eyes. She wanted to make sure what she felt wasn't just admiration for the gorgeous face with undeniable hot charms in front of her.

When Avery felt Ethan's soft lips gently touch hers, she lost it. She realized Shelly was right. There was no need to explain or make sense of it. Why give herself a hard time looking for a reason or counting the hours, days, and months since she'd ended things with David? Shouldn't she be thankful that after everything she'd been through, she got the once-in-a-lifetime second chance with Ethan?

Do what makes you happy, *she kept telling herself as she passionately kissed him back. Slowly, she put her arms around his neck. When they stopped gasping for air, she opened her eyes. Her eyes met his gaze. She felt his genuine devotion to her. His lips curved into his sweetest smile. When Avery felt sheepish and tried to remove her arms, he pulled her toward him with care. He put one arm around her waist. What he did next left her in awe. Ethan caressed her baby bump affectionately.* Shelly was right. She loved this man.

"Now that we have acknowledged what's going on between us, it's time we talk about our respective situations," Ethan whispered, then slowly brushed his lips over hers.

Avery shied her vision away from him by hiding her face on his chest. The overflowing happiness she felt halted. Her self-pity crawled into her. She was silent the whole time he told her. about his life after Patty died. All the while, she was staring at their hands clasped together—only a little of what he said registered in her.

How could I deserve this man? *she asked herself while Ethan poured his soul into her. How could she make him happy when she was not only bringing herself into his life? She was a package deal. How could she be thoughtless about it?*

Ethan interrupted her silent pity party when he kissed her forehead. "What's going on in that head of yours?" he asked.

"I admire you. You're so strong and loving for raising Ella alone. I wish I could be half as courageous as you." Avery gently touched her bump.

Ethan lifted her chin and cupped her face in his hands. "It wouldn't matter if your strength and courage were half or less. You have me. I'll be with you and the baby every step of the way. If I'm not around, we have Ste."

Avery gave a half-smile and slowly removed his hands from her face. "But I can't be selfish, Ethan. We are not your responsibility. It would be unfair to you to be burdened with us."

Ethan took her hand and gently kissed her knuckles. He fixed his eyes on her face. "Hey, where is that coming from? Do you think I came here to discuss these things with you without thinking about it? I'm a smart man with resources. I'm a man with plans, Ave."

"What do you mean?" she asked, gazing at him affectionately.

He tucked her stray hair behind her ear. "I didn't get to sleep last night. I thought of you... of us. Ella and the baby. The four of us. I didn't hide for eight years to be in a relationship I wouldn't want to last forever. I weighed up everything about your situation and mine. At first, I told myself it would not be possible; it would be hard. But there's only one answer: I couldn't imagine mine and Ella's lives without you."

She stroked the sides of his lips. Every word that came out of his mouth was hypnotizing her. How could he be so damned gorgeous, hot, and kind-hearted at the same time? *"What is it?" she asked.*

"I don't fucking care about you or my past. So what if it will not be easy? I've been living the hardest the last eight years, with only Ella by my side. I think it wouldn't hurt if we lived our hard lives together!" Ethan exclaimed.

Avery couldn't believe what she had heard. She gulped and unconsciously opened her mouth in amazement. Ethan grinned as he saw the shock on her face. He brushed her hair with his fingers. He planted soft kisses on her eyes, nose, cheeks, and lips in slow motion. She felt tears gradually fall from her eyes. She felt loved. Love no other man had ever made her feel.

When Ethan started kissing her tears away, she visualized the heavens handing from up above Cupid, who was holding all the romantic love wishes she had asked for since her first broken heart.

"I cannot promise that every day will be hearts and roses, for life's not perfect. But I will try not to make you shed sad tears," Ethan declared.

"Shelly told me not to overthink things, but I need to get this off my chest. What are we now?"

Ethan chuckled. "Your innocence is killing me, Ave! Should you be the one giving me your decision? I believe between us; I'd talked a lot and had laid all my cards on the table."

"Um… Okay," Avery muttered.

"Okay? Just, okay?" Ethan smiled. "Tell me about the baby's father and everything, good or bad. I need to know what kind of person I'll deal with." Ethan winked at her.

"Wait? What? Why will you deal with him?" Avery's face lost all color.

Ethan placed his right hand on her shoulder, pulled her body closer to his, and clasped his left hand with hers. "You are my woman now, Ave. I have to ensure you and the baby are always protected. Since the father is still living, I need to know who I must protect you from."

Avery almost choked. His woman? *She indeed liked the sound of it. She pulled her body slightly and faced him so she could look at his face. "Are you always this control freak and possessive?"*

Ethan cackled, "Only with the people I care about." He gave her another wink and flashed his gorgeous smile.

"What do you want to know about him?"

"Maybe his name, for starters," Ethan answered as he squeezed her hand. "Everything… I want to know everything."

"His name is David." Avery took a deep breath and leaned her head on his shoulder.

"I want to know anything that concerns your pregnancy and what happened between you and David. I wouldn't want to be left in the dark again. And we have to be honest with each other."

Chapter 42

"MOMMY PRETTY, MAMA STE is on the phone. She wants to talk to you."

Ella's voice stopped Avery from reminiscing. It had been a few days since Ethan had left for Minnesota, and Ella had stayed with her. It had been their normal since they agreed to be present in each other's lives. At first, her parents were worried about their relationship, knowing they had just met. But Ethan was Ethan—he didn't just win her heart, but also her parents. He even got a powerful ally in Shelly.

Avery couldn't ask for more. She gained a family. With Ethan came Ella and Doctor Stella. If not for Avery's wavering, Ethan would have wanted her to move in with them if he could have his way. But out of respect for her parents, she declined. She wouldn't want to make a similar situation with David before, moving in with a guy outside of marriage. But most of all, she wouldn't want to burden Ethan with her daily needs.

"Hi, Ste! What's up?"

"Ave! Ethan is killing me! Have you talked to him?" Doctor Stella was gasping for breath on the other line.

Avery wondered what Ethan had been bothering his sister about. "He called this morning to remind me about breakfast…" She smiled, remembering how Ethan kept telling her he loved and missed her and Ella. "You know him, commanding and all." *My man,* she whispered to herself.

"He asked me for your birth plan. Then he emailed it back to me with his demands. He even vetted my team for your delivery. And now he's asking me to email him back on how I will address his demands! Remind me now why I shouldn't ban him in the delivery room when you give birth." Frustration was evident in Doctor Stella's voice.

"You know your brother. I didn't know he had been going this length. I'm so sorry, Ste. But I promise I'll talk to him and tell him to get his ass off my birth plan." Avery chuckled.

Avery could hear Doctor Stella's loud breathing on the other line. "Do that, please. And for the love of God, tell him don't dare call any member of my team."

"I will. Don't worry. Ethan can be a pain, but he loves you so much. Bye, Ste. "I know. Kiss Ella for me. Bye, Ave."

A smile curved Avery's lip. She knew how protective Ethan was of her, especially with the pregnancy. She didn't expect he would be that overprotective. Ethan might frustrate Doctor Stella, but deep inside, Avery knew if there was someone who would understand him first, it would be his sister.

They both knew Ethan's reactions toward her pregnancy were the aftereffect of what happened to Patty. Since they had become a couple, Ethan ensured he missed none of Avery's prenatal checkups. He had his secretary fix his schedule to accommodate Avery's appointments. He didn't mind flying from Minnesota to Palm Coast to accompany her to her doctor's appointments.

"I wouldn't want to be left in the dark again. I will protect you and the baby." Ethan's words were music to her ears. But there were times she felt as if everything was just a dream. *So fleeting.* Any moment, she could be awakened from it. But Shelly kept assuring her Ethan was her life now. That she deserved all the happiness coming her way.

"Mommy Pretty, here's your juice and vitamins for the baby." Ella was all smiles as she held a glass of juice and her vitamins container.

She took the glass and the container from Ella's hands. "Thank you, Ella. The baby says thank you, too."

Ella watched as she took the vitamins and drank her juice. Once Avery was done, she motioned for the little girl to sit beside her. Ella eagerly sat and started caressing her pregnant belly affectionately. In return, she tucked Ella's loose hair behind her ears and kissed her forehead. She didn't just fall in love with Ethan; Ella had got into her heart first.

It was barely six months since the father and daughter had conquered her heart and completed her life. But the happiness the two were bringing into her life was beyond. There were times she pinched herself to ensure the contentment she was feeling was real and not just a dream.

Her parents and Shelly were the happiest for her. Doctor Stella was thankful her brother had found the happiness she'd been praying for him and her niece. For Avery, her family was Ethan and Ella. And her little bean would be one bundle of joy that would seal the completion of their family in a month.

Though Avery couldn't ask for anything more, one concern kept lingering at the back of her mind. Like Ethan told her, they would need to address it eventually. It was one topic where Ethan had proven he was a man who plans. But he didn't want to impose on Avery. So, instead, he told her to think it through and that whatever she decided on, he would be with her.

"Mommy Pretty, when will we know if our little bean is a boy or a girl?" Ella's buttoned-like eyes sparkled.

"When I give birth. Remember we wanted it to be a surprise?" Avery softly stroked Ella's chubby cheeks.

"I'm so excited to meet the baby! Daddy is happy, too. You make us happy! I love you, Mommy Pretty. I love the baby, too." Ella leaned her face onto Avery's chest as her hand was still caressing her belly.

Overwhelming emotion hit Avery. It was the first time Ella had said those three words. But, without a doubt, she felt the same way. She covered Ella's body with her arms. "I love you too, Ella. You may not have come from my tummy like our little bean, but I love you like my own." She kissed the little girl's hair and embraced her tighter.

"Daddy loves you too, very much." Ella's eyes twinkled, and her lips pouted. Then, suddenly, her cute little hands covered her mouth. She realized she'd blurted something she shouldn't.

"How did you know, Ella?" Avery chuckled.

Ella tried getting her perky composure back. "I just felt it." She immediately pulled away from Avery's embrace. "I want to play with Grandma outside. I'll be back."

Avery nodded, smiling. Ella, at eight years old, seemed mature for her age. Her maturity, kindness, obedience, and loving heart made Avery love her more with each day they spent together. She was Ethan's eyes, hands, and ears in making sure Mommy Pretty ate on time and took her vitamins whenever her dad wasn't around.

Time spent with Ella made her love Ethan more. All the good things about his daughter had been proof of how good a person and a father he was. Everything about the father-daughter team caused Avery's heart to curve deeper into the space it slowly devoted to them. Without her telling Ethan yet, she'd been considering what he'd been suggesting all along, informing her past about her present and, hopefully, her future.

"Ave, whether we like it or not, we will have to face David because of the baby. We might as well do it sooner than later. I don't want him getting between us in the future." These were Ethan's exact words to her after their last appointment with Doctor Stella.

Avery knew Ethan was right. Now, it was only more or less a month before the baby's birth. The time to talk to David needed much more attention than she wished.

She would never forget the conversation she'd had with Ethan about it. "Why do I need to talk to him? I made it clear the last time we saw each other, everything ended between us." Her voice crackled. She was almost in tears. The idea of her not deserving Ethan came back at that moment. "This is why I don't want to burden you with me and my situation." And the floodgates opened.

Immediately, Ethan buried her in his warm and protective arms. "Hey, we are talking about this to make things right, not to make you uncomfortable. I know in your heart that everything about him ended. But the situation then was different. I wasn't in the picture when you last talked to him. Possibly, the baby's presence hadn't sunk into him yet. But once the baby is born, I'm sure it will make a difference."

Just like the first time she'd cried before him, Ethan kissed away her tears lovingly. "I don't want his sorry ass looming over us, using the baby as an excuse. He needs to know you've moved on. And the baby is ours. He's just going to get borrowed time. Promise me you'll think about it, okay?" His eyes gazed at hers with affection. Their conversation ended with her nodding in agreement that she would consider it.

Ethan hadn't realized that not all her tears at that moment were sad tears. *The baby is ours.* His words made her heart want to explode out of her chest. But instead, it brought the warm emotion that took away all the doubts she may have had about their relationship.

Thinking about how she should accomplish the task of talking to David, she decided to call Shelly. But her phone rapidly chimed before she could dial Shelly's number.

Shells: *David is here at our house. He just came back yesterday. He said he came back in time for the baby's birth. I'm calm, but in my head, I already killed him 3x.* 

Shells: *What should I tell this dickhead?* 

Shells: *Is Ethan back in FL? I'll buy you time… I mean days. I'll ask Art to bring him camping for a week. Talk about it with Ethan before you decide on anything. Please don't reply to me right now.* 🙂

Chapter 43

AVERY READ SHELLY'S MESSAGES several times. *"I wouldn't want the shadow of his sorry ass looming over us, using the baby as an excuse."* Finally, Ethan's words dawned on her. He was right. David needed to know he was in the past. Her present and future were Ethan. Little Bean was hers, and he could only get borrowed time.

She sighed. Deep in her reflections, she hadn't realized her dad had been watching her all along from a distance.

"Everything alright, Muffin?"

Surprised, Avery looked in her dad's direction. From the look on his face, she knew he felt she was bothered. So, instead of answering, she gave him her "princess needs advice" smile. Immediately, her dad walked toward her and sat beside her.

"Your mom and Ella are busy wrapping gifts for the baby shower. I thought of checking on you and my munchkin." Her dad's voice was soothing.

When she saw her dad leaning back on the couch, she slowly rested her head on his chest. Warmth and comfort exuded when she felt her dad's hand slowly massaging her hair. He was the best dad she could have asked for. He came at the right time and at the right place. Always ready to comfort her and say the words she needed to hear. And this moment was not an exception.

Her dad cleared his throat. "What's bothering you?"

She took a deep breath. "David is back in Boston. He told Shelly he came in time for little Bean's birth." Slowly, she patted her bump.

Her dad sighed softly. "Okay… Did he contact you?"

Avery leaned closer to her dad's chest. Finally, he put his right hand on her shoulder and squeezed her hand with the other. It was his way of assuring her. He was signaling his readiness to listen.

"He didn't… not yet. Shelly asked Art to bring him camping to buy me time. She wants me to talk to Ethan first." Her speech was slow and monosyllabic.

"Have you talked to Ethan?" her dad inquired calmly.

She shook her head. "Not yet. I don't know what to say to him. I feel guilty bringing my past's baggage into his calm life." A long sigh followed as she closed her eyes

Her dad knew what she wanted to hear even without looking at each other's faces. "Do you want my suggestion?"

Silently, she nodded, not minding if her dad saw her gesture. She wanted to feel calm, hear the silence, and be comforted by her dad's wise words.

"Tell Ethan the truth. That's what he would want."

Avery turned her head away from her dad and looked at him inquisitively.

"He talked to me," her dad told her. "Ethan talked to me. He's worried that David didn't get a proper closure about your relationship. I couldn't blame the CEO." He laughed. "I have the prettiest, most charming, and kindhearted daughter. You are every man's dream, Muffin."

She smirked at her dad and pouted. "I'm not sure right now, Dad. I can be David's nightmare and Ethan's regret."

Jim Jackson shook his head. "I don't think so. Why do you regard yourself less? Where did my fearless daughter go?"

"I felt like I didn't stretch my understanding enough for David, especially since we have little Bean to consider. And now that I'm with Ethan, I feel guilty that I'm bringing all my life's drama to his present and future." Avery cupped her face with her hands in desperation.

Her dad pulled her for a hug and whispered in her ear, "Don't overthink things. Whatever makes you happy. I'll always be on your side. Never feel guilty feeling the happiness you deserve."

"Thank you, Dad. As unbelievable as it may seem, my connection to David will only be because of Little Bean. Ethan is my life now. I'll tell him that David is back."

"Hello, Ave! I'm in Charlotte now for my layover. Ste will pick me up at Daytona Airport. I'll see you at Ethan's house for the baby shower tomorrow."

Avery listened to Shelly's voice message. Her best friend and Doctor Stella had planned a baby shower for her at Ethan's house. The two would prepare everything with her parents and Ella joining them the next day. When she called

Ethan, she planned to tell him about David, but she didn't have the courage to discuss it. He was having a stressful day at work, and she didn't want to amplify the situation.

She hoped to see him at the baby shower, but he told her he might be unable to return that day. Instead, he needed to stay for another day to address an emergency. Since they'd been together, it would be the first time Ethan wouldn't be present at an important event in her life. She didn't want to say it, but there was longingness in her heart, knowing he wouldn't be around to celebrate with her.

Avery was surprised to wake up to an empty house on the morning of the baby shower. She had just read in a note left by her mom that everyone except Ella's nanny had already gone to Ethan's place. The note said the driver would come to pick them up an hour before the celebration. She knew it was Shelly's idea to leave her behind. She wouldn't want Avery hovering around during the preparations.

When she was about to start her breakfast, Ethan called her. The moment she heard his voice, she missed him more.

"Is the nanny staying with you right now?"

"Hello to you too. How are you? When are you coming home?" Avery's voice choked up.

She missed him so much.

"Are you alright, my love?" Ethan rattled, hearing the sadness in her voice from the other line.

"I'm okay. Don't worry about me. I miss you so much."

Ethan heard her sniffling. "I miss you too, my love. My staff and I will finish everything in a day or two. I can't wait to see and hold you."

"We will miss you at the baby shower later. When you come back, I need to tell you something. I can't say it over the phone." Avery sighed aloud.

"I'll be home before you know it. Promise me you won't worry about anything. Whatever it is you need to tell me, don't stress about it. Everything will be fine. I love you."

"I love you. Take your time for what you need to finish there. Ella is excellent. She has Mom and Dad wrapped around her fingers." Avery giggled.

"I love hearing you giggle. I have to go to a meeting now. Eat well. Take care of yourself and our little bean. I love you guys. Bye, my love!"

How she wished Ethan was just an hour away. She knew if that were the case, he wouldn't mind coming home daily. Unfortunately, his position on the board and the hospital HQ's out-of-state location restricted his ability to stay in Florida for more than a week. Ethan had filed for a month's leave from work after her due date. But work emergencies happen. It pushed the start of his work leave to a later date.

Just as she finished her breakfast, the nanny came with her vitamins. There was no denying it was Ethan who'd made the nanny stay with her. Even though he was away, he always made sure she was comfortable.

The fact that Ethan was so caring was one of his many good sides that still amazed her. Before, she never thought that someone's concern for her comfort could exist like Ethan's.

She was one lucky woman.

Avery gasped upon entrance to Ethan's house. Shelly and Doctor Stella had put much effort into preparing for the baby shower. She wouldn't want to make the event any bigger if it were her decision. She didn't want to burden anyone. But seeing how the house was transformed into a magnificent flower garden with a mixture of yellow, green, blue, and pink balloons elated her.

They'd placed a gigantic LED screen with the body of water in the background. On the front corner was a chair designed for royalty. A table for the cakes and gifts stood in the opposite corner. It was any pregnant woman's baby shower fantasy.

Though Avery couldn't help but think that Ethan might have had a hand in funding such an over-the-top event, if not on the decorations.

It was like a continuation of Ella's princess-themed birthday. The baby shower theme was for a queen, which confirmed that Ethan and Ella had influenced the event. Only the father-daughter duo called her their queen. And when Ella came out, she was in a colorful princess dress. She ran towards Avery and gave her a crown resembling the one on her head. Ella's smile reached her ears when her Mommy Pretty happily accepted the crown.

Slowly, the little girl guided her toward the big queen chair. Once seated, Ella helped her put the crown on her head. Avery asked to sit beside her, but Ella declined, to her surprise. "No, Mommy Pretty, the chair is for you only."

Avery felt thankful to see only a few chairs in front of her. At least they seemed to have listened to her request for close family and friends only. When the guests started coming and were seated by a group of ushers and usherettes in black dresses and ties, her parents came in together with Shelly and Doctor Stella. Everyone was all smiles and unable to hide the excitement on their faces. However, her dad's face looked more anxious than excited.

The emcee, who was part of the party planning team, started the program and led the flow of events. Everybody enjoyed the afternoon feast served at a long buffet table. Drinks were overflowing. Funny games, all baby-themed, were played. Ella even rendered a cute song and dance number. Avery felt ecstatic, witnessing her mom acting as Ella's cheerleader and her dad as her photographer. She felt happy that through her parents, Ella got to experience having grandparents since the James siblings had lost their parents a year before Ella was born.

When the time for gift-giving started, Avery saw how everyone, from her best friend and Ste, her parents, and Ella, turned cheery to anxious. All the gifts given were everything the baby needed. Because of some of her mom's superstitious beliefs, they hadn't got anything for the baby yet. Doctor Stella had made a gift registry to ensure everything the baby needed was on the list of options. At first, Avery was hesitant about the registry, but when Ethan insisted on buying everything himself, Avery opted for the registry.

Hearing all the best wishes for her safe delivery and seeing all the gifts given, she couldn't help but get teary-eyed. She caressed her protruding baby bump and whispered how lucky and loved her little bean was by everyone who came. After opening the last gift, Avery thanked all the guests. But Ethan's voice that came from the LED screen stopped her.

Ethan's gorgeous and smiling face was on the screen. It warmed her heart. It was thoughtful of him to be with them virtually. Shelly placed a chair at the center facing the screen and asked Avery to sit down.

"My love, this celebration will not be complete without my gift for you and our little bean. In the same way as, my life and Ella's wouldn't be complete without you. The day Ella met you and never stopped talking about her, Miss Pretty, I knew then that her life would never be the same without you. So, I have a confession to make. Since then, I had started imagining how Miss Pretty looked inspired by a seven-year-old's description."

Everyone watching laughed. Avery was over the moon with Ethan's words.

"But when I met you in the park that afternoon, I realized it wasn't just an interest I had gotten. You were bewitchingly beautiful inside and out. Even with all the colorful ribbons scattered in your hair." Ethan winked, followed by loud gasps and *ahs* from the guests. "You captivated not just my eyes but awakened my eight-year-old lonely heart. Since then, you own me, heart, mind, and soul."

Louder gasps and a succession of *ums* and *ohs* enveloped the air. Avery tried to hide her tears, but when she looked around, Shelly, Doctor Stella, and her mom were in tears, all smiling lovingly at her. Her dad gave her an emotional okay sign. When her eyes reached the nanny, Ella wasn't there, which worried her. She stood up and started gaping around, eager to find the little girl.

Ella suddenly came out from behind the balloon arc when she was about to voice her concern. The little girl was smiling, pushing a fancy baby stroller decorated with a basket full of more red roses than she had ever seen in her life.

Avery placed her right hand on her chest as she waved to Ella. Ella was her daughter in heart, mind, and soul.

When she was about to approach, her eyes grew, her mouth opened, and her body could not move. Behind Ella came Ethan, gorgeous in his most laid-back clothing. His face had the happiest smile she had seen on him. One hand held one big rose, while the other was inside his pants pocket. His eyes focused on hers.

They paused the affectionate gaze they had for each other when Ella shouted, "Mommy Pretty, I have 107 roses in Little Bean's stroller. Daddy's holding the 108th rose!"

Chapter 44

AVERY SMILED AT ELLA. She couldn't grasp what the little girl was trying to tell her. When Ella reached the spot beside her, she slowly entwined her tiny hand with hers. Together, they gazed at Ethan as he stepped toward them.

He stroked Ella's hair. In return, the little girl giddily clapped her hands as she looked at her dad and Avery. Ethan took a deep breath before handing Avery the one rose he was holding.

"Hi!" Ethan clasped both of Avery's hands with his.

"Hi to you too! You're here," Avery responded, grinning.

Ethan nodded. "I'm here. Sorry, I had to tell you I wasn't coming. It was part of the surprise. I wouldn't miss this for the world." He touched her face, with one hand still clasped in hers.

Avery smiled without removing her gaze from Ethan. "I miss you." Just like the first time they saw each other, she felt the intense beating of her heart. The feeling she only got when around him.

"Do you feel it, too?" Ethan asked, referring to the powerful connection between them. Avery nodded. "You make me feel this way all the time."

"Mommy Pretty, Dad has a gift for you!" Ella exclaimed.

"Does he now?" Avery touched Ella's hair.

Ethan pinched his nose. Avery noticed his hand shaking. "Princess, let Daddy breathe first, okay?"

"Give it, Daddy, give it!" Ella motioned for her dad to get something from his pants pocket.

Slowly, Ethan held back both of Avery's hands. It surprised Avery to feel both of his hands shaking. Then, when she looked at his face and tried to ask what was going on, he softly placed his two fingers on her lips.

"My love, when I said you have my heart, mind, and soul, I want it that way forever. When I said my life and Ella's wouldn't be complete without you, I meant I'm not letting you go." Ethan's voice croaked. "I'd love to feel this powerful connection and devotion when I'm around you daily for the rest of my life. I know for some, this affection we have for each other might seem too soon or hard to believe. But when I saw you the first time, my heart knew. We don't owe anyone an explanation. We're not responsible for anyone understanding how we feel for each other."

When a tear fell from Avery's eyes, Ethan wiped it affectionately. "I want to let you know you deserve all the love and happiness in the world. When I pursued you, I committed myself to love, protect, and care for you and our little bean. I love everything about you, and I won't stop. Though I can't promise you a perfect relationship, I'm committing to being honest. I want you to have my heart, mind, and soul forever. And I'm begging that you give me a chance to live my life loving you, little Bean, and Ella for the rest of our lives." Ethan's chest started heaving fast.

Avery gasped, her lips curving into a smile, her eyes welling up. Ethan tucked her hair behind her ear and slowly kissed each of her tears away. He slowly fell to one knee when he saw she had recovered from the shock. With his eyes gazing at hers, he brought out a small, red velvety box from his pants pocket. Once opened, the inside of the box revealed an oval-shaped diamond ring of just the perfect size. They heard loud gasps and whispers from the crowd in front of them.

"Avery, my love, will you marry me?"

At that moment, Avery couldn't see anything but Ethan's face. She could only hear his voice and the loud beating of her heart. Yet, she knew her answer all along.

"Yes. Yes. YES!" Avery answered with an ecstatic voice.

Ethan's face brightened, and his lips curved with a gorgeous smile. As he placed the ring on her finger, with her other hand Avery started tracing his eyes, nose, jaw, and lips. He slowly stood up and carefully pulled her into a tight embrace. Like he always did, Ethan planted kisses on her forehead, eyes, nose, cheeks, and lips. The kiss they shared started with their lips gentle, soft touching. It was an unhurried, sensual joining of their body and soul. It signified their total surrender to each other.

When they heard the loud clapping and whistles, both faced the crowd. Avery flashed her engagement ring to everyone. Before anyone could approach the newly engaged couple, Avery took Ella's hand and squeezed it. She stroked the little girl's hair and kissed her forehead. When Ella hugged her baby bump, she whispered, "I love you, Ella."

To Avery's surprise, Ella started sobbing and hugged her tighter. Then, worriedly, she cupped her face. "What's wrong, Princess?" she asked.

Ella answered in between sobs and tears. "I'm just so happy. I have a real mommy now. And Daddy got to find his queen. So little Bean will be my sibling. We're a complete family now."

"Oh, Ella. You're making me cry."

Ethan felt complete when he saw the emotional exchange between the two most important women in his life. Then, having wanted to cover both in his arms, he scooped Ella with his right arm and pulled Avery toward him with the other. The picture-perfect scene got another round of loud cheering and applause from the surrounding people.

He was over the moon, witnessing everyone's approval of his and Avery's engagement. The happy tears in his sister, Shelly, and his now future mother-in-law's eyes made him glad, too. The nod of approval from his future father-in-law made him confident, knowing he had all the affirmation from the people he needed it from.

His decision to disclose his plan to only Ella and Avery's dad was the right thing to do. It's a good thing little Ella could be trusted with secrets. The proposal was not the only secret he and Avery's dad had kept to themselves. Avery didn't know that he had come back from Boston to address an important issue.

Before he proposed to Avery, Ethan ensured he did what he thought was best for the woman he cared for. He promised to protect her, and he intended to keep that promise. He would never allow anyone, past or present, to hurt her again. But, as he always said, he was a man who plans. So he wouldn't let anything or anyone ruin the life he was committed to offering Avery.

But one thing was sure: he wouldn't keep Avery in the dark. He would tell her everything. But at the moment, he wanted to relish the woman in his arms who had agreed to be his wife. She'd accepted Ella wholeheartedly, even without seeing or knowing him first. Avery was the only woman his daughter felt sincerity and kindness from. She didn't pretend or lie about her situation. She was even willing to sacrifice her feelings for him to spare him and Ella from any difficulty once they became connected to her.

As her parents approached, Ethan released Avery from his arm. Doctor

Stella, still in tears, hugged her brother and niece. She couldn't contain her happiness. From a distance, Shelly was watching her best friend. The tears her eyes shed reflected the overflowing joy she was feeling for Avery. She prayed for the moment. A moment when Avery would be whole again. A time when a great man would shower her with the love and devotion she genuinely deserved.

After Avery's parents had expressed their love and support for the newly engaged couple, and Doctor Stella welcomed Avery into their family, Avery focused her attention on her best friend. With her signature-pouted lips and welled eyes, she motioned for Shelly to look at her engagement ring. Shelly ran toward her.

The tight hug and tears they shared spoke of their sister-best friend's love for each other. They conveyed the strongest and never-ending bond they shared without words, only happy tears and endless smiles.

Every piece of decor, every corner of the space they were in, all the laughter, and all the smiles said it all. Avery was one happy woman in love. Ethan was one happy man in love. And he would do everything to keep the woman he loved happy and protected all the time. He would ensure his new family was spared from the past pains.

After everyone left, Doctor Stella watched over the party planning staff to finish cleaning and called it a night. Avery tucked Ella into bed and went to join Ethan in his bedroom, the one he now shared with her whenever she stayed for the night. As always, he'd already run a bath while waiting for her. He placed her sleepwear on the bed.

Ethan was in his small office space, checking emails on his laptop. When he saw Avery walk in, he immediately stopped what he was doing and approached her with a kiss on her forehead as he caressed her pregnant belly.

"Are you tired, my love?"

"Happy tired!" Avery replied and pecked at his lips.

"That's a good way to be tired!" He winked at her. "I already ran a bath." Slowly, he guided her toward the bathroom. Avery followed when he motioned for her to let him take off her clothes and assisted her in getting into the tub. Once she was settled, he stripped off his clothes and joined her.

"I'm so pampered. I should be the one taking care of you." Avery peppered small kisses on Ethan's arms as they glided on her cheeks and jaw.

"I love doing this for you. And I will never tire of doing it."

"I have something to tell you." Avery's voice softened.

"What is?" Ethan asked as he washed her shoulders and arms.

Avery took a deep breath. "David is back."

Chapter 45

"I KNOW. I WENT TO Boston. We talked." Ethan shook his head. "No, I went to Boston to talk to him," he whispered.

Avery looked at Ethan's face over her shoulder. "What? How? When?" She placed her hand on his to stop him from washing her arm.

Ethan paused and embraced her from behind, resting his hands on her belly. He laid his chin on her left shoulder. "Don't be mad at me, my love."

"How? Were you in Boston the day you extended your trip?' Avery raised her brows.

"Yes. Art texted me, saying David was back and insisted on seeing you. He was begging Art to tell him where you are. Art felt I had to know. And I thank him for thinking that way instead of sending David here."

Avery felt a soft peck on her neck. "How did it go?" She clasped her hands with his.

"I met him in Shelly and Art's house. It surprised him. He didn't believe Art when he told him I existed." Ethan chuckled.

"Was he nice to you, at least? I mean, civil?"

"We had a staring match for about fifteen minutes, I think. Then Art broke the ice by introducing me to him. It was a funny introduction." Ethan's laughter filled the bathroom.

"Why? What did Art say?" Avery started massaging Ethan's arms.

"Um… Should we do a rain check on the storytelling?" He planted small kisses on Avery's left shoulder, all around her back, and on her other shoulder.

"Uh, ah… You can kiss me all you want, but you must tell me what happened."

"My love, we have to finish this bath, and I promise to continue my story later. I don't want you to catch a cold by staying too long in the water."

"Is that so?" Avery smirked, knowing he was trying to get out of it.

"Of course, I'll make sure I clean you up."

Avery's giggles overpowered the silence in the bathroom as Ethan teased her by peppering her back with tiny kisses.

The washing and cleaning that began in the bathtub ended in the bed. Though both of their bodies were spent after the pleasurable moment they passionately shared, sleep didn't come to them.

Knowing Ethan had met David was like a drug enough to keep Avery awake. To assure the love of his life that nothing or nobody from her past could get between them was a life goal that kept Ethan from sleeping.

Rested in bed with their bodies spooned together, Avery addressed the elephant in the room.

"I sometimes thought about her body when I was still in Boston. What she'd look like," she paused and cleared her throat. "The woman David cheated on me with. Was her body curvier? Was her skin smoother than mine?" She burst out a soft and long laugh.

"Hey, there will never be a body curvier… and no skin softer and smoother than yours." Ethan's hand softly stroked her right arm to the side of her waist and her pregnant belly.

She felt his kiss in her hair. "I hate him for that… making me doubt myself, sleeping at night feeling unworthy."

Ethan slowly moved her hair to her other side and placed his lips softly on her neck. Then, he took a deep breath and whispered in her ear, "Sometimes we have to meet someone who'll show us what love is not."

Avery felt his warm breathing when he whispered to her. She moved her right hand toward his face. Gradually, she traced his jaw and cheeks. "I even thought maybe he met someone perfect for him, even though he was committed to me. So I tried to find an excuse for what he did." She let out a long sigh.

"That's not true. When you're committed to somebody, you shouldn't be able to see perfection in someone else." Ethan carefully removed her hand from his face and planted tiny kisses on her knuckles. Avery giggled. "How are you so poetic, Mr. James? I love you so much."

"Me, poetic? I just speak from the heart, Mrs. James. And I love you more!"

"But what did you tell him?"

"I told him to back off civilly. I gave him a piece of my mind. To keep the story short, I told him, Avery Jackson is mine!" Ethan yawned aloud. "I think we should sleep now." He rubbed her belly affectionately. "It's past little Bean's bedtime."

Immediately, Avery caught his hand. "No, no. You can't sleep yet. We won't sleep unless you finish your story!"

"Let's save the rest of the story next time, my love. I'll end tonight with what I told him about our little bean." Ethan softly placed his hand on top of her belly. "I told him I'm a considerate man. I'll leave the decision to you whether you'll allow him into the baby's life. But whatever time he's given will be temporary. Little Bean is ours. My DNA doesn't need to be in this baby for him or her to be mine. I accept everything about you. I love all of you, including this life in your belly." He planted a kiss on her shoulder. "Now, sleep."

"Goodnight, Ethan. I love you!"

"I love you more. Goodnight, my love."

Ethan James. How could she sleep? After everything he said. What did she do to deserve him?

Avery woke up to the smell of bacon and blueberry. When she opened her eyes, she saw two sets of the infamous James eyes gazing at her. Ella held a small gift box, while Ethan had a food tray of bacon and waffles. The father-daughter duo was all smiling.

"Good morning, Mommy!" Ella pecked her cheek. "Morning, my love!" Ethan kissed her on the lips.

Avery noticed that Ella had called her simply Mommy and not Mommy Pretty. The grinning faces of the two confused her. What was going on? "Good morning, future husband, and good morning, our Princess! What's with breakfast in bed and with your bright smiles?"

"Ella has a welcome gift for you. And I brought you breakfast in bed to celebrate our first day of being engaged!"

"Oh my! I'm so lucky to have the sweetest family!"

Ethan placed the breakfast tray on the bed and brushed her morning hair with his fingers.

Ella excitedly handed her the gift box.

"Thank you, Ella, my daughter." Avery kissed the little girl on the cheek as she accepted her gift. "Should I open it now?" Ella nodded and motioned for her to read the card first.

"Dear Mommy,

Thank you for loving Dad and me. Welcome to our family! We're so happy to have you in our lives. Now I can call you Mommy for real! We love you!"

Avery couldn't hold her tears. No words could express the happiness she felt. Unable to say anything, she hugged Ella tight. Ethan moved toward them and enveloped them both in his arms.

"Dad, let go! I can't breathe. Mommy hasn't opened the gift yet," Ella yelped. "Oh, so sorry, Princess. Daddy's just so happy!"

When Avery opened the box, it revealed a white gold necklace with a crown-shaped pendant. "That's your queen crown, Mommy." Excitedly, Ella showed what was inside the pendant. It surprised Avery to see two small frames inside. One was with the little girl's picture wearing her princess crown, and the other was empty. When she looked at Ella to ask why the other frame had no picture, the little girl rubbed Avery's pregnant belly softly. "That's reserved for our little bean's picture."

Having heard what Ella said, Avery's floodgates opened. Her tears were unstoppable. She was a sobbing mess in the early morning. Finally, Ella started wiping her tears. "Why are you crying, Mommy? Didn't you like our gift? Did we make you sad?"

"No, Princess. Mommy is thrilled. These are happy tears!" Ethan smiled as he watched and listened to their conversation. After a few minutes, the three enjoyed breakfast in bed together. The sounds from Avery and Ethan's phones interrupted their laughter and conversation. Both got separate messages from Art and Shelly.

Art: Man, David is flying to FL today. He said he wanted to talk to Ave in person.

Shells: Ave. David is flying to FL to talk to you in person.

Chapter 46

"DAVID IS FLYING TO Florida to talk to you in person."

Avery's face dimmed. After reading Shelly's text, she had never felt the same anger she felt for David. Ethan's vision was immediately directed to Avery. He knew by the look on her face that she'd got the same message. After talking to David in Boston, he expected this action. He didn't expect the man to just accept everything he'd said.

"Shelly messaged you? I got the heads-up from Art. I guess we're going to have a visitor." Ethan winked at Avery.

"He's making a big mistake in coming here," Avery said.

"I know, my love. He does not know what he's coming into." Ethan's voice was soothing.

He asked Ella in a whisper to see her nanny outside the bedroom. He needed to be alone with Avery. The hell he cared about was coming to see them whenever. His concern was to ensure Avery wouldn't feel stressed by the drama the man in her past would inevitably bring.

"I don't understand why he has to come and see me. I made things clear to him the last time we talked." Avery's breathing was long and loud.

When she went to get out of bed, Ethan stopped her. He moved to the other side of the bed and pulled her toward his chest.

"Relax. You don't have to explain anything to me. You've done nothing wrong. David's coming to you; he's the one who should have problems right now."

Avery sighed, "But… What does he want now? What did he tell you when you talked to him?"

Ethan lifted her chin and kissed her softly on the lips. He cupped her face and cleared his throat. "He didn't believe me, I guess. I told him I was going to propose and marry you."

"Why wouldn't he believe you?" Avery's brow furrowed.

"One of Boston's smartest lawyers wasn't smart at all. He's still living in his imagination that you two are just on a break. I was right to think he still hadn't had his closure." Avery's mouth shivered. "What? Is he crazy?"

She felt Ethan's lips on hers. More prolonged and full of emotions. "He's still crazy for you, my love. But not as crazy as we are towards each other!"

Ethan tucked her hair at the back of her ears to fully visualize her face. Then, slowly, he started kissing each part. He started from her forehead, both of her eyelids, to her nose, cheeks, jaw, and down to her lips. When their lips touched, she opened her mouth to give him access. Together, they felt the intense heat and connection they always had for each other.

After minutes of their lips and tongues battling, they paused, both gasping for breath. Their eyes still gazed at each other. It was their love signal. He was hers, and she was his. No words were needed because their actions meant only one thing: They were tied together in heart, mind, and soul.

Avery softly touched Ethan's cheek. "I'm yours, forever. I have never felt this way or loved someone as much as I've had for you now."

Ethan smiled and placed her lower lip in between his softly. "I love you more than you'll ever know. Nothing or no one can ever change that. What we have is something I will protect and cherish all my life."

When Avery smiled, her face revealed her sass. "If David thinks differently, I'll put him in his place. Even if I have to break his heart again."

"Why are you so feisty now, huh? I think my lips and tongue energize you, Mrs. James!"

"I like the sound of my new name." Avery winked and bit her lower lip. "I think I need you to refill my energy again."

"Do you, now? It's your lucky morning. Finally, your husband-to-be is up to providing you with full service and add-ons. But unfortunately, I think our little bean is still asleep. So it's time we wake him up!"

Avery's laughter and giggles filled the room. Only their moans and screams of their names followed a few seconds later.

The day of the baby shower and engagement marked the beginning of Ethan's month-long leave from his work. He would be spending every day with Ella and Avery. For Avery, Ethan expressed his love for her by accepting little bean into their lives. She was so happy and blessed to worry much about David's coming.

But she wouldn't let her guard down. She'd put David in his place. She wouldn't hesitate to break his heart repeatedly if she had to.

"My love, don't you like chicken? You've been staring at it for a few minutes now." Ethan's voice awakened Avery.

"I'm sorry. I like it. Something just came to my mind." Avery's long sigh followed.

"Mommy, can we go to the park after your check-up with Mama Ste? Please!" Ella asked.

"Sure. Right, Daddy? We can go to the park after." Avery could tell she'd worried Ethan by the look on his face.

When Ella asked to leave the table, they agreed simultaneously. However, Ethan's brow creased and his abrupt movement toward Avery signaled his concern.

He stood beside where she was sitting at the table. His warm arms pulled her to his body. "Don't worry about him. Trust me. Everything will be fine. He's the least of our concerns. I don't want you stressing out, especially the days before you give birth." He lifted her chin so she could see him eye to eye. "Understood? I won't let him near you without me around."

Avery nodded. "I'm sorry if I made you worry. I'm not stressing out. Your wife was practicing her killer lines in her mind." Her devilish laugh followed.

"Is that so? Should I be worried I might have groomed a monster for a wife?" Ethan smirked as he cupped her face in his hands.

Before he could move his face toward her lips, Avery unhurriedly embedded small and soft kisses on both of his hands. "Thank you for loving me. For accepting the baby into your life. I love you so much."

Ethan bent down for his lips to reach hers. After a lingering kiss, he fixed her hair. "I love you more. And I'm thankful you came into our lives. You made our lives brighter. I thank God every day for you!"

"I still can't believe I met you, and soon we will be married!" Avery hugged Ethan's waist tight.

She felt Ethan's kiss on her hair. "We can decide the date now and start planning." His hand caressed her cheeks when she lifted her head to see his face. "By the time the baby is born, we can complete everything. What do you think?"

"That's not a bad idea. I can have time to lose my pregnancy weight."

"You believed me when I said you have the curviest body and the smoothest skin, right?" Ethan held her hand and started kissing it. "There's nothing for you to be conscious about your body, now or even after pregnancy."

Avery nodded. "That's why I love you. You always make me feel like I'm beautiful and all. Though I know I look like a train right now. With all my swollen feet and cheeks!"

"My love, you will always be beautiful in my eyes. Not just beautiful, bewitchingly beautiful!"

"Thank you! Now we have a doctor's appointment to go to."

"Everything looks fine. We're on the right track. All the lab tests came out with good results. We'll have to wait for our little bean to say hello," Doctor Stella announced the good news.

Ethan assisted Avery from the bed after the ultrasound was done. As he helped her sit opposite Doctor Stella, he grabbed the papers his sister had read a while back.

His eyes scanned the documents. "Don't you require a blood test for her PlGF, Ste?"

Doctor Stella's eyes widened. "No, Mr. James! Her systolic and diastolic blood pressure is excellent. Therefore, I would appreciate it if you would call me Doctor Stella inside my clinic."

"Sorry, Doctor. I didn't mean to offend you." Ethan frowned.

Avery rolled her eyes at Ethan. "Thank you, Doctor Stella. We have to go now. Ella is waiting with her nanny in the park."

Doctor Stella smiled at her. But the clinic's intercom rang before Avery could get up from her seat.

"Yes?" Doctor Stella answered.

"Doctor, Attorney David Thomas is here. He wants to join Ms. Avery. He said he's the father of her baby."

Chapter 47

AVERY'S FACE WHITENED, and her shoulders sank. Doctor Stella instantly stood up and signaled for Avery to relax. Ethan's face flushed, and his right hand fisted. Before he could walk toward the door, Avery took hold of his left arm.

"Ethan, please. Stay with me," Avery said.

Doctor Stella looked at Ethan. "Stay here, you guys. Let me talk to him."

Ethan brought Avery into his arms. He was throbbing with anger. How dare David come here to surprise Avery! He hadn't taken his word. Ethan had been nothing but nice to him! Avery felt Ethan's shuddering hands. Slowly, she pulled from his embrace and clasped his hands to hers.

"Don't worry about me. I just felt angry with him. I'm not stressing out. It hit me that he was too immature to come here without contacting me first. I don't even know how he got my schedule," Avery sighed aloud.

"The same reason I'm pissed off right now! What was he thinking coming here to surprise you? We're all professionals! For fuck's sake! I was expecting him to call or text you, at least!" Ethan bit his lip.

Avery kissed Ethan's knuckles to soothe him. "I knew I would have to talk to him, but I was hoping it was on my chosen day and time. Not here and not like this."

Ethan squeezed her hands. "We will make it your day and time of choosing, my love. Not here. If you give in to him now, he'll think he can intimidate you."

When the door opened and Doctor Stella came in, their eyes concentrated on her. She gave Avery a half-smile and handed her a name card.

"That's his. I asked him to leave and wait for your call. I told him I won't allow him to see you now since he's causing discomfort to my patient," Doctor Stella said.

"Did he leave?" Ethan asked.

Doctor Stella nodded. "I guess so. I saw him in the elevator and instructed the guard to call me if he wouldn't leave the premises."

Feeling relieved at her sister's declaration, Ethan hugged her. Doctor Stella was surprised by her brother's show of emotions, causing her almost to lose her footing. "Hey! Are you thanking me or trying to knock me down?"

"Thank you, my dear sister!" Ethan placed a kiss on Doctor Stella's forehead. "You have saved me from punching him!"

"What a sweet brother you are, huh! If you only knew how to hug, you could be perfect! You almost took the life out of me!"

Avery mouthed thank you to her future sister-in-law. Her smile was the brightest, seeing Ethan calm and happy. But deep inside, she knew the time would come. No Doctor Stella or anyone could stop David anymore. Though Ethan had promised to protect her from her past, David's insistence on being part of her present was a fight she needed to face and battle alone. So the sooner, the better, she uttered to herself.

"Are you sure about this?" Ethan asked as he kissed Avery's hand. She'd just shown him the message she was about to send David.

Avery pouted her lips. "I have to deal with this David situation, and I'd rather do it sooner than later." Ethan nodded, touched her cheek, and kissed her on the forehead. In return, Avery kissed him on the lips. "I should be the one asking you."

"About what, my love?" Ethan's brows raised.

"Are you sure you're okay with David coming here? We can meet him in a restaurant or at my parents'."

"This is your house, too. It's ours. I'd rather have him come here for your talk. You're my responsibility now. I don't want him bringing his toxicity to your parents. They've already had their share of him."

"But I don't want to burden you." Avery rested her face on Ethan's chest. Then, slowly, he lifted her face and placed his lips on hers. It was a soft but affirming show of affection.

"You'll never be a burden to me. I promise to care for you and the baby. Besides, he'll think twice before he intimidates you here in our home." Ethan teasingly touched the tip of her nose.

Avery smiled and placed a distance between them as she sent her message. Just after a few seconds, her phone chimed. She read the reply and shoved her phone into her dress pocket. "Done. He accepted and agreed to see me here.

I'll send him the address later."

Ethan winked. "Great!"

"Ethan James."

"Dr. James, this is from the community's front gate. A David Thomas is here to visit you, sir."

"Let him in. Thank you."

Avery looked at Ethan and smiled. Ethan walked toward her. He hugged her from behind and whispered in her ear, "He's here."

"I heard. You sound excited." Avery giggled.

Ethan brushed the hair from her neck and slowly kissed it softly. Avery's giggling became louder. "Ethan, you're tickling me!"

"I am not! I'm making sure you're fresh and smiling when our guest comes."

It took Ethan aback when Avery got out of his arms and faced him. She circled her arms around his neck and placed her lips on his. She whispered a moan as she bit his lower lip gently. When he slightly opened his mouth, Avery didn't hesitate. Her tongue took advantage of the access given to her. The distance caused by her pregnant belly didn't matter. She was taking the lead, and Ethan loved it.

The housekeeper's coughing interrupted their intimate moment. Avery pressed her face against Ethan's chest to hide. Ethan chuckled as he hugged her.

"Sir Ethan, Attorney Thomas is here."

When Ethan held his vision toward the voice, the housekeeper nodded and left immediately. His eyes caught David's face; one he wouldn't wish for himself. David's eyebrows were raised, face flushed. He had wrinkles on his forehead, and his jaw went slack.

"David! Welcome to our home." Ethan gestured for the Acme Picardy II sofa. David walked toward the couch without withdrawing his glare from Avery, whose face was still on Ethan's chest.

David's mouth opened when Avery lifted her face and cackled as she wiped her lipstick off Ethan's mouth. Then, with their hands held, Ethan and

Avery moved toward the living area and sat in front of him.

Avery graced him with a genuine smile, but David didn't conceal his discomfort as his eyes focused on their clasped hands. He unconsciously unbuttoned the neckline of his shirt. He bit his upper lip and blew his breath in dismay. When the housekeeper returned and placed a glass of water in front of him, David took the glass fast and drank it up.

"Thanks for accepting my invitation to come here," Avery said.

David nodded. Once he returned the glass to its coaster, he handed Avery the bouquet of roses he was holding. After thanking him, to his dismay, Avery just gave the flowers to the housekeeper. Then, without saying a word, he looked at Avery, turned to Ethan, cleared his throat, and looked at Avery again. "Can we talk in private?" he asked.

"We can talk here with Ethan. I want him beside me. I want him to hear whatever we say to each other." Avery squeezed Ethan's hand.

David sighed aloud, "Ave, please. I need to talk to you in private."

Avery shook her head. "No. We're engaged and soon to be married. What you say to me, you say to Ethan. We hide nothing from each other. We value honesty in our relationship," Avery said with eyes directed at David.

David frowned in disbelief. "You can't be engaged to someone else. You have my ring."

"I don't have your ring. I returned it to your mother before I left Boston. And last time I checked, I made it clear to you whatever relationship we had ended. If I counted it right, I ended it several times in different places too."

Exasperated, David raked his hair with his shaking hands. "What are you saying, Ave? Please don't make it hard. Let's fix this now. Let's fix us."

Avery twitched her lips and glared at David. "From what I recall, you have an excellent memory. That's why you aced all your law exams. But how can you forget the hospital in LA and my parents' home in Boston? Remember? In both places, I clarified that we're over!" Avery coldly enumerated.

"Ave… if this is about the woman in LA… she's gone for good. After getting the money, she took off with the baby. The PIs we hired are still looking for them. Even after my family offered to raise the baby and paid her, she ran away! I can't fail my parents again, please."

"I'm sorry to hear that. But it's not my issue to think about. If it wasn't clear to you, I'll make it clear here. We are done, David! There's nothing you can do to make me return to you."

Opposite, Ethan was calmly observing David. David raked his disheveled hair with both hands numerous times. His breathing became erratic from trying to conceal his frustration. "Why are you doing this, Ave? How can you get engaged to someone you just met?" David kept shaking his head.

"Huh!" Avery snickered. "That's like asking yourself how you can impregnate some random woman while you're engaged to be married to someone else. Don't you think so?"

David shook his head. "That's different. We're talking about you getting engaged to someone else while being pregnant with my child," his voice croaked.

Avery cleared her throat. "I'm trying to be considerate of you, but I'll be brutal since you asked for it. We're engaged and getting married because we love each other. I have never felt this way about anybody else in my entire life. He makes me happy, values my worth, and has been loving me in a way that made me realize you never really loved me. I can't live without him and will allow no one to stand between us, not even you!"

"This isn't what I expected to hear from you, Ave. But I'll do the same since you said you're being honest right now. If you wouldn't agree to fix us for the baby's sake, I have no choice but to fight for sole custody of the baby! I will not allow a stranger to raise my child!"

Avery protectively caressed her pregnant belly. She was trying so hard to calm herself. David's threat irked her. Ethan softly massaged her shoulder while his other hand fisted inside his pocket. He wanted so much to express a piece of his mind, but he'd promised Avery his silence.

"That was flattering but hypocritical to come from you! If you think you can threaten me, you're thinking very wrong! Bring it on! Tell me which court, and I'll come running!" Avery's words daggered at David.

Before David could say another word, the approaching presence of the housekeeper and another guest silenced him. Ethan's smile reached his ears. He stood up, shook the man's hand, and gestured for the guest to sit beside David.

"Let's spare everyone from threats and immature remarks here," Ethan calmly said. He gazed at Avery and stroked her cheek affectionately. "I wouldn't risk Avery's well-being and pregnancy with all the stress this unhealthy talking can bring." He looked David in the eye. "Since you mentioned the legalities of things, we will leave this matter to the expert." He moved his hand toward the latest guest.

"Attorney David Thomas, meet Attorney Grayson Bartlett, our family lawyer. I'm not sure if you had the chance to meet each other at Harvard when he was the head of the Family Law clinic. But I'm sure you'll have the chance to know each other well now. Anything you want to say to Avery or ask about the baby will be through Attorney Bartlett here," Ethan gradually said each word while glaring at David.

Ethan's declaration dazed Avery. She watched as Attorney Bartlett stood and extended his hand to David. Still in shock, David stood and reached out his hand. When Avery's eyes moved to Ethan, her heart skipped a beat. She saw a calm, confident, and amazingly gorgeous man inside and out.

"I will protect and cherish you." Ethan's endearing words echoed in her ears. He promised her and made true to his promise.

When Ethan reached out his hand to her, she took it with the sweetest smile curved on her lips. Then, in front of everyone in the room, she planted her lips on his. It was a kiss of overflowing gratitude and love. She didn't care if they had an audience. The hell she cared about Attorney Bartlett might think of her. And damn hell, she cared if David got a coronary.

Ethan gladly kissed Avery back with the same intense emotions. But, before everything got heated, Ethan paused. He fixed Avery's hair and rested his arm on her shoulder as he faced David's grimace.

"Oh, and we will inform you of any news about the baby through Attorney Bartlett too. The last time I checked, under Florida law, you don't have any legal rights to custody or time-sharing until the court establishes your paternity. So we will have to wait for the baby to be born, and of course, with the doctor's clearance for the procedure and through a court proceeding," Ethan added.

Avery couldn't stop looking at Ethan's face. Every word he said sounded like the profession of his love for her. How did she deserve this remarkable man? When Ethan removed his arm from her shoulder, she clasped his hand with hers.

As they were about to leave, Ethan gave his parting statement. "We will leave the discussion to you, gentlemen. My housekeeper will show you out once you're done. I'm sorry we can't stay. My family and I need to be somewhere."

Chapter 48

"MY FAMILY NEEDS TO be somewhere." Ethan's last words were a gut punch to David. The purpose was to mark what was his. A declaration of his love for Avery. It was a statement that she was not just loved but also family. Avery, Ella, and the baby were his family. The family he swore to protect, care for, and cherish for the rest of his life.

Ethan and Avery didn't look back. David was shocked as hell. He was in disbelief. Unable to grasp what had just happened. He remembered not believing Art when he told him about Ethan. Even after Ethan showed up in Boston, he was in denial. Never in a million years would he ever think that the Avery he'd known would do what the Avery he'd just seen just did. With his hands frozen on top of his hair, David kept asking himself where the naive and quiet Ave had gone.

What stunned him more was the list of conditions and demands enumerated to him by Attorney Bartlett. He came to Florida confident he could convince Avery. His goal was to show his sincere intentions toward her and their baby. Make her feel he deserved the last chance to work things out and fix what was broken. But what he saw hit him. HARD. It broke his heart and crushed his soul. How did it happen? The question kept wavering in his mind.

David left the James mansion full of questions. Though the law had his hands tied for the moment, he could never give up, and he wouldn't. The law may not have been in his favor, but his love for Avery and their child was beyond the rule of law. Ethan's words replayed in his mind. "Custody and time-sharing are possible after a paternity test through a court proceeding." He smirked. It seemed he'd underestimated Shelly's Mr. Hotshot. But he wasn't called Boston's Best for no reason.

Weeks passed, and Avery was due to give birth any day. Ethan never left her side. If Avery was both excited and scared, Ethan had his worries, too. Slowly, it got into him. He hated to admit it, but as the day of Avery's giving birth got close, his not-so-happy thoughts after Ella was born started resurfacing.

As a doctor, Ethan knew not all patients' situations were the same. But despite what he knew and his sister's assurance that Avery's pregnancy was all clear, Patty was his constant reminder. It was a fear he'd been silently fighting since he learned of Avery's pregnancy. So, for eight years, he'd buried all questions and anxiety about what happened to Patty when Ella was born.

With each passing day, Ethan had been getting flashbacks of what had occurred eight years ago. Though he was fighting the dark thoughts and memories inside him, Avery felt something had been bothering him for days.

"Hey, are you okay? You've been zoning out lately." Avery touched Ethan's hand, which hadn't moved since he held the fork when they'd started lunch.

Ethan smiled at her. "All is good, my love."

"Are you sure? What's bothering you?" Avery caressed his cheek and gently stroked his hair. "Is it about David? I think Attorney Bartlett gave him a good lecture when we left. He hasn't contacted me since then."

Ethan took her hand, slowly kissed her knuckles, and gazed at her. "I'm never bothered by Boston's Best," he chuckled. "You shouldn't be either. You surely put him in his place the last time."

Avery smiled back. But when Ethan took a deep and long breath, she knew it was time to put her sass on him.

"That's it! If it's not David, then what is it?" She pouted her lips and pulled her hand away from his grasp. "If you won't talk to me or tell me what's going on in your mind… better I take my leave now."

Avery's reaction surprised Ethan. It was the first time she'd shown irritation and walked out on him. When he followed her, Doctor Stella stopped him. "Leave her for now. She's right. You've seemed off lately. Do you want to talk about it? You're worried because Ave's due date is here. I'm her doctor. I can assure you they're going to be fine. It's you I'm worried about."

Ethan massaged his temples as he looked at his sister. "I'm getting flashbacks. I see myself the day Patty gave birth to Ella. You told me before to see a therapist to talk about Patty and what happened to her. But with raising Ella, finishing med school, and everything in between, I didn't realize eight years had already passed. I didn't get the chance to mourn. And since everything went so well, I thought I got through it with no therapy."

"Oh, Ethan." Doctor Stella stood up from her seat at the dining table and put her arms on her brother, who was sitting in the end chair. "You know you always have me, then and even now. I can call and have someone make a schedule for you."

"I know, Ste. You helped me a lot before and even now with Ave. Talking to someone now might not be the right time. Knowing she could give birth any minute, I don't want to be away from Ave. I want to be with her every step of the way. Not being with her during her delivery is a mistake I couldn't make for the second time." Not again, not with Ave.

Like when they were little, Doctor Stella planted a kiss on her brother's forehead whenever anything bothered him. "Whatever happened to Patty wasn't your fault. With or without you beside her, the inevitable would still have happened. Besides, she kept everything about her health and pregnancy complications from you."

Doctor Stella paused and stared at her brother while thinking. "I admire you for not using your position to get favors. But just this time, please make an exception. I'm sure you can call someone. Why don't you schedule a house call? I'll also check with my contacts to see if someone can make a house call to you. At least take the initial step. That way, you wouldn't have to leave the house or be away from Avery."

Ethan stood up and hugged his sister. "Thank you, Ste. I hope someday I can give back all the kindness and love you've given Ella and me."

"You owe me big time!" Doctor Stella tapped her brother's shoulder. "Now, talk to your wife before her hormones make it harder for you!" She pushed Ethan toward the door.

Once outside the dining room, Ethan prepared himself. He felt slightly nervous, remembering Avery's face when she left the table. When he didn't find her in the garden, he peeped into Ella's room, but no one was inside. On his way toward their bedroom, a crying Ella approached him.

"What happened, Princess?" He scooped Ella into his arms.

"Mommy is packing her clothes. She said she would stay with Grandpa and Grandma. Little Bean will stay there, too. But she said I couldn't come with them because I need to stay with you. I want to go where they go!" Ella explained in between sobs and tears.

Ethan felt a heaviness on his chest. "Why don't you join Mama Ste for dessert, and I'll talk to Mommy about it." Ella nodded and walked towards the dining room once he put her down. When he entered the bedroom, Avery was closing her luggage. She ignored his presence and continued taking her stuff from the vanity.

Ethan gently gripped Avery's hand to stop her. "My love. What are you doing?" He took her hand toward his lips.

Avery stopped, took a deep breath, and looked at him. "My dad is on his way. He's picking me up. I'm going back to my parents' house. Dad will clear his schedule from tomorrow. He'll bring me to the hospital when it's time."

He slowly brushed his hand over her face. "Why are you doing this, my love? I took a leave from work to be with you. We agreed you're staying here, and I'll always be with you."

"Ethan…" Avery looked up to stop her tears. "You don't have to do this for me. We're not your responsibility. I don't want to burden you or cause you any trouble. I'd rather stay away than let my giving birth trigger your trauma. I heard you and Ste."

Ethan stiffened. He leaned closer, pulled Avery's face towards his chest, and ran his hand through her hair. "My love, please don't do this. You don't have to worry about me. Ste and I planned about it. We'll have someone do a house call for my session while we wait for the baby. We settled everything."

A knock on the door paused their conversation. "Ma'am Avery, your dad is waiting for you in the living room." The housekeeper left after delivering the message.

Avery pulled away from Ethan's arms and placed a kiss on his lips. "Focus on yourself for now. I'll be fine with my parents. But, I wouldn't be able to sleep at night knowing my giving birth reminds you of what happened to Patty. You need to talk about it so it can be out of your system."

"I'm fine, Ave. You don't have to leave. I need you." Ethan wrapped his arms around her. He moved her hair to the other side, planting tiny kisses on her neck and shoulder.

"Ethan, please…" Avery held his chin and gazed at him. "My dad is waiting. I have to go." Then, slowly, she removed his arms. She held onto her luggage and was about to go when she felt Ethan's hand on hers.

"Ave, you can't go." Ethan's face was white.

"I'm not leaving you. I want to give you the time to work on…" Avery was unable to finish. Ethan scooped her in his arms and rushed outside.

Doctor Stella was stunned to see Ethan carrying Avery, his face pale. Likewise, Avery's dad was surprised. Immediately, Doctor Stella went into doctor mode and called the hospital; they all went to the garage while Ethan barked orders to the housekeeper and the nanny.

"Call the driver here. We'll get in the car where Ave's hospital bag is kept! Bring Ella with you in her grandpa's car."

"Ethan, what's going on? Where are you bringing me?" Avery yelled.

"My love, your water broke. We're going to the hospital!"

Chapter 49

ETHAN KISSED AVERY'S FOREHEAD as he put her down at the back of the SUV.

"How can my water break?" It baffled Avery. "I don't feel any contraction at all! Ethan, is the baby okay?"

"The baby will be fine. Relax. Ste is here. I love you!" Ethan softly brushed Avery's lips with his. Doctor Stella sat beside Avery as Ethan took the front passenger seat. Once everyone buckled up, they drove to the hospital.

Doctor Stella was monitoring Avery along the way. Not feeling any labor signs made Avery anxious. Ethan had performed many surgeries and witnessed others, but nothing could compare to his nervousness. His whole body was trembling. When he saw Avery's eyebrows pulled up, her mouth stretched and drawn back, and vertical wrinkles appearing between her eyebrows, his flashbacks came back. He started gasping for air.

"Ave, there's nothing you need to worry about. Normally, some can have their water broken even with no labor pains. Contractions can follow, or there could be no contractions at all. It would help if you calmed down, or your blood pressure would be a problem. We don't want that, remember?" Doctor Stella squeezed Avery's hand. "We're near the hospital. Everything is ready, and the team is waiting for you."

Avery nodded as she breathed in and out to relax. Doctor Stella's words gave her assurance. But when she glanced at Ethan, she couldn't help but point Doctor Stella in her brother's direction.

Ethan's face was white, and he was gasping for air.

"Ethan… take a deep breath." Doctor Stella started rubbing his shoulders softly. She guided him to relax and steady his breathing. Once Ethan's breathing normalized, she dialed a number. "Hey, it's Ste. Can you please meet me in the delivery room in five minutes? I need your help with Ethan. Thank you!"

When the car stopped at the hospital's emergency entrance, Doctor Stella's team was waiting for them with a stretcher in tow. Ethan was a nervous wreck, but he didn't allow anybody to touch Avery. Instead, he put her on the stretcher and never let go of her hand. Upon reaching the private delivery room set up for Avery, one nurse guided Ethan to an ensuite, where he changed into a scrub suit. When he returned, his sister was waiting for him with another doctor.

"Ethan, this is Dr. Robertson. He's the Psychiatry Head. I've known him since Harvard when I shifted to OB and Developmental Pedia. You guys can have your talk in the waiting room while we prepare Avery." She patted her brother on the shoulder when his face showed hesitation. "Don't worry; I'll call for you when Avery is ready."

Ethan shook the psychiatrist's hand and silently led the way toward the room. When Doctor Stella came to where Avery was, she gave her an assuring smile. Saying nothing, Avery knew, just like her, that the doctor was also worried about her brother.

"My psychiatrist friend is talking to him now. He'll be fine. I'll call him here when it's time. I need you to stay calm, Ave." When the doctor patted her hand, Avery squeezed hers in return. At that moment, Avery felt a family's genuine love coming from a sister. True love didn't need blood. Ethan and his family had accepted all of her, no questions asked, and no conditions were required to be met.

"Ave, since we have Premature Rupture of Membranes, we will have to do labor induction. There's nothing to worry about. It would be a normal step if the water broke with no contractions or signs of them," Doctor Stella explained.

"Will the baby be alright?" Avery asked.

"Yes. There's no reason for the baby not to be. I promise to take care of you both. Trust me." Doctor Stella smiled as she squeezed her hand.

"I need Ethan here, please."

"Of course, I'll call him." Doctor Stella excused herself as she removed her gloves. Once outside the room, she dialed her brother.

Ethan showed up in just a few minutes, followed by Dr. Robertson. Immediately, Ethan fixed Avery's hair away from her face and planted a kiss on her forehead.

"I'm here, my love. Everything's going to be fine." Then, after pressing his lips on hers, he looked at Dr. Robertson and introduced him to Avery. They exchanged courtesies, and the psychiatrist took his leave after.

"Do you feel better now?" Avery clasped her hand on Ethan's.

"Yes, I do. It's a start. I'll surely see Dr. Robertson again." Ethan slowly brushed his hand on her cheek. "Your dad and Ella just picked up your mom, but they'll be here soon. Ste will be back in a few minutes."

"Ave, we'll have to induce since you still don't have any contractions. But, it should help stimulate contractions so you or the baby won't get an infection," Doctor Stella explained.

Avery nodded and turned to face Ethan, seated on a chair beside her bed with his hands still clasped on hers. His eyes were closed, and he breathed in and out in succession. When she looked at Doctor Stella, she mouthed for an explanation about his state.

Doctor Stella smiled and mouthed everything was okay and gave a thumbs up. True enough, a few hours later, Avery started feeling the pain. However, she didn't show any discomfort as she had excellent tolerance for pain. Whether physical or emotional, she kept quiet through all the contractions that took hours before Doctor Stella announced it was time.

Avery's parents and Ella showed up for a bit and stayed in the waiting room. Ethan stayed with her amidst his erratic breathing. He was sweating profusely despite the VIP hospital room's high-end air-conditioning system. Without him knowing, Avery tried toning down her reaction over labor pains for him. Even in her uncomfortable state, she thought of him. She believed if she weren't loud, it would help ease Ethan's ongoing stress inside him.

When Doctor Stella announced it was time for Avery to push, her grasp on Ethan's hand became stronger. For the first time, Ethan opened his eyes and gazed at her. He couldn't tell her he was keeping his eyes closed to fight away the flashbacks of seeing himself in a hospital room eight years ago. As Dr. Robertson suggested, he needed to stay and watch Avery give birth. Hopefully, it would replace the flashbacks caused by his unfortunate experience with Patty.

While Avery was too occupied fighting each pain she felt in her body as she followed Doctor Stella's instructions, Ethan was also battling his. Ethan felt differently as Avery's grip got stronger and deeper into his arm. Slowly, his erratic breathing normalized. Avery's face showed her will to overcome all the pain. His flashbacks slowly faded as he gazed at her face and saw a smile curved on her lips while she endured the pain.

From that moment, Ethan could only see Avery. She bewitched him all over again. He saw the strong, selfless woman he bowed to as his only one for the rest of his life. Through Avery's face, he saw flashes of his future, their future. A bright and promising one, with the woman in front of him. Together with Ella, little Bean, and more, little Ethan, and little Avery.

Avery, the love of his life.

"You're doing great, my love. We're going to see our little bean in a short while." He pressed another kiss on her forehead. "I love you." He kept whispering the same words to her ear.

Little did he know, every word uttered was like a flash of light that gave Avery snippets of how her life would be. A future spent with a great and loving man who kept showing her how it was to be loved genuinely and unconditionally.

It was awe-inspiring that even at that moment, both only saw each other. Ethan and Avery's intense connection and amazing love for each other got them through the fears and pains they separately battled inside of them. Yet, their gazes at each other didn't waver through it all.

A loud cry was the only reason that caused their eyes to unlock.

"Congratulations! Our little bean is a bouncing baby boy! Great job, Ave!" Doctor Stella's voice of fulfillment echoed in the room.

Ethan's face was flushed, and his chest was heaving fast. He peppered Avery with soft kisses from her forehead to her lips. "You did great, my love. I love you more!" Without being asked, Ethan reached out his hand for her sister to hand him the scissors. But, of course, there was no freaking way he would allow anyone to cut the cord other than himself. With trembling hands, he accepted the scissors handed by his grinning sister. "Don't fuck it, CEO! Cut it well! Show us the best surgeon you are!" Doctor Stella teased him.

Ethan took a deep breath and gave Avery his most gorgeous smile. When Avery nodded, he carefully cut the cord. It was one of his proudest moments. He looked around when everyone inside clapped.

This boy is my son. It's not about the blood. DNA isn't needed. It's the feeling, Ethan told himself as he lovingly watched Avery holding the baby to her chest.

Family and friends filled Avery's room a few hours after giving birth. Everyone gave congratulations as waves of laughter filled the room. Avery was teary-eyed as she watched Ella sit down on Ethan's lap. He put the baby on top of Ella's small arms, making the little girl feel like she was holding the newborn.

The father-daughter smile was gorgeous. Doctor Stella couldn't help but capture the moment with her camera phone. Avery's parents were all smiles as they expressed eternal thanks to the doctor for taking good care of their daughter and grandson. Avery felt complete. Her tears spoke of her overflowing love and gratitude.

Ethan felt Avery's gaze on them. When he looked up at her eyes, he said I love you to her from afar. In return, she pretended to throw a kiss in his direction. Suddenly, the door burst open. A sobbing Shelly entered, followed by a sweating Art.

"Ave! Triple OMG! I'm sorry we're late!" Shelly screamed and grimaced at her husband." It was all Art's fault! God, I almost divorced him at the airport!" A loud laugh welcomed the two. Shelly, as always, provided entertainment as Art walked toward Ethan and the kids. "Congrats, man! Sorry, we're late. There was a mix-up in our flight." Ethan dismissed what Art said and thanked the couple for flying from Boston instead.

Shelly's eyes grew upon seeing the baby in blue in Ethan's arms. She immediately approached and took the baby from him. "Triple OMG! I've got a godson!" Then, to everyone's surprise, she slapped Art's arm. "I told you; little bean is a boy! Return all the pink onesies and socks you made me buy! I hate you right now!" Art whispered sorry and scratched his head. The adults in the room looked at each other and laughed in chorus.

When the visiting hours were over, everyone bid Ethan and Avery goodbye. Ella opted to join Shelly and Art in going home with Avery's parents. After everyone left, the nurse took the baby to the nursery.

Avery motioned for Ethan to join her in the bed. Once they settled on the bed, she stroked his face gently and kissed his lips. "Thank you for everything. I love you!"

Ethan held her hand and put it towards his lips. "I should be the one thanking you, my love. You helped me more today. Thank you for completing me."

Avery smiled. "While giving birth, my future with you flashed at me. It helped ease the pain and my fears."

"It was the same for me." Ethan faced her. He kissed her eyelids, nose, and cheeks down to her lips. "When I opened my eyes and looked at you, the flashbacks from eight years ago slowly disappeared. The scenes of us replaced it—our family. You, me, Ella, and little Bean together. Happy together."

Overflowing emotions filled Avery's heart, no words needed to be said. She cupped his face and pressed her lips gently on his. When their lips unlocked, Ethan remembered and asked, "What will we name him? He needs a real name soon. I'm dying to write his name on his birth certificate."

"I sort of thought of his first name, but for his middle name, I've been wanting to ask you…" Ethan's phone rang before Avery could finish what she was about to say.

"Let me take this call. It's Attorney Bartlett." He took the phone from his pants pocket. "James. Hello, Attorney. Thank you! Just a few hours ago. We got a boy! Ah… Um… Got you. Let me talk to her about it." Ethan looked into Avery's face and nodded. "We'll discuss it, and I'll get back to you ASAP. Thanks again!"

Avery's brow crinkled. "What did Attorney Bartlett say?"

Ethan cupped her face in his hands and placed a soft and long kiss on her lips. "David is back. He got the info you had given birth. He wanted to come and see the baby."

Chapter 50

AVERY NODDED WITH HER mouth open. What Ethan said made her realize David had someone watching her. In her heart, she was confident whatever the man in her past had broken had been put back together by the man in front of her. Though Avery wouldn't want to give David the time of day, she knew it wasn't possible. Meeting him was one reality she could never turn away from.

Ethan cupped her face and made her look into his eyes. "I know I was very vocal in saying I don't want David in our lives." He cleared his throat. "Heck! I don't want him near you ever!" He chuckled. "But putting myself in his shoes, I would surely want to see my child too." Ethan's loud sigh followed. "Though he had done shitty things and hurt you… he should see the baby. Our baby is his baby, too."

Slowly, Avery removed Ethan's hands from her face. She squeezed it and softly placed small kisses on his knuckles. "I still can't believe you are mine. Sometimes, I pinch myself when I am alone to ensure you and I are together." After kissing each knuckle, she enclosed his hands inside hers. She lifted her head and looked toward Ethan standing in front of her. "Little bean may have David's blood, but in my heart, you are his father, and he will grow up loving you just the way you are."

"In my heart and soul, he is my son. We are a family." Ethan twitched his face and laughed as he remembered something. "Do you know how I keep calm whenever I'm around Boston's Best?" Avery pouted, seeing Ethan's expression. He was grinning as if he were about to reveal a great secret. "I always remind myself I should thank him for being a shitty head and doing me a favor by driving you toward me!"

"Ethan!" Avery playfully slapped his arm.

"Ouch, my love!" He massaged his arm, pretending to be in pain. "Remind me not to have Shelly around you whenever she scolds Art like they were in the principal's office! You're getting her domineering tricks!"

Their eyes locked as they remembered the scene of Shelly hitting Art in front of an audience. It reminded them of how Art acted like a student reprimanded by a teacher.

Two days later, Doctor Stella gave Avery and the baby the clearance to go home. But before they were discharged, Avery and Ethan agreed for David to come and visit while the baby was still in the nursery. They were hoping they would not need to talk to him yet.

"Don't worry too much. David can't touch the baby from the glass. He wouldn't be stupid to take the baby and run away." Ethan's voice was calm. Avery was pacing inside her hospital room. He guided her toward the couch and gently formed circles on her shoulders once seated.

Avery took a deep breath. "I'm just worried. You know how crazy he is. Seeing the baby will make him crazier for sure."

"Of course, he will get crazy! But that's expected my love. Besides, who wouldn't go crazy seeing how cute little Bean is!" Ethan smiled as he tried to joke about it wanting to calm her.

Avery faced her side to see Ethan's smile. "By the way, Shelly insisted we choose a date for the wedding. She needs to fix her schedule at least a month in advance. She wanted to ensure she gets days off for a week."

"Haven't you told her about our little secret, Mrs. James?" Ethan's lips curved a half-smile.

Avery slowly shook her head. "I don't want to burst her bubble. She's been planning my bridal shower for so long. This will be her second time planning for me. But if you'll ask me, I'd rather we make it small, intimate. And it's not like we need it right now."

"I suggest you tell her as soon as possible before she discovers it herself. Her irritation toward Art preoccupied her. That's why she hadn't noticed your ring finger. I'm sure all hell will break loose once she finds out." Ethan smirked.

Avery nodded. "Yeah, I'm sure. Maybe I'll tell her when she comes to visit the baby tomorrow."

"I'm sure once you explain why we needed to do it, Shelly will understand. I'd rather face her wrath than allow little Bean to be born without having a name."

"You do not know how hot you are whenever you blurt words like that!" Avery chuckled.

Slowly, she brushed Ethan's hair with her fingers. In return, he gently touched the sides of her lips. "Are you trying to seduce me, Mrs. James?" Avery shook her head, laughing.

Gradually, her hands wrapped around his neck. Ethan grinned, "Okay." He stayed seated with her hands still around him. Their gaze intensified. When Avery placed her lips on his, he slightly opened his mouth. The moment their tongues touched, desire and passion encompassed them.

When their lips were untangled, they were both gasping for air. Ethan placed small kisses on each part of Avery's face. "From what I studied, pregnancy hormones can make one horny. But since the baby is out, I can't say it's the same hormones talking right now."

"Are you complaining? Can't it be that the woman you love just wants to love you back?" Avery giggled.

"Oh, no! Don't get me wrong! I'm not complaining. I am so enjoying this. It's just I know it's going to be torture. You know we can't make love right now for four to six weeks. But I'll be satisfied with this side of you any time of the day. I don't care what hormones are causing this!" Gently, he moved the hair away from her neck and planted his lips on her skin.

After a few minutes of sharing kisses and exploring each other's bodies, Avery got ready as Ethan packed all her stuff in her hospital bag. The nursery's viewing period was starting soon. They expected David to come with Attorney Bartlett. Once the viewing ended, they would check out and bring the baby home.

Once they got everything ready, they waited seated on the couch. Cuddling together in silence was something they both enjoyed. After just a few minutes of peace, their phones started ringing at the same time. It was Attorney Bartlett for Ethan and Shelly for Avery.

They looked at each other. Simultaneously receiving a call meant something or somebody might be the reason behind the rings. When Avery frowned, Ethan squeezed her knee. Ethan answered the call, and Avery opted to text Shelly instead.

Ethan's face was serious but calm. He listened more to what Attorney Bartlett was saying and only gave short acknowledging responses like okay and got it. When he ended the call, Avery's phone chimed.

Shells: *What's with the baby's name? David just called Art. He was furious about the baby's name. He mentioned filing a petition for paternity. Tell Ethan and your lawyer.*

Avery threw her phone on the coffee table. Despite her mood change, Ethan was calm and in control. He reached his hand for Avery to stand and said with a giggle, "Come here." He enveloped her in his arms when her body was close to his. "Don't worry about a thing, okay? He should be grateful you gave the baby a piece of him. Attorney Bartlett knows what to do. David was just upset we took ten steps ahead of him. He thought he could work his smart ass on us because he knows the law."

Avery lifted her head and faced Ethan. "You think so? I think I was generous when I decided on the baby's name. I was even expecting a token of gratitude through the lawyer."

Ethan laughed and pinched her nose. "You are one silly, silly girl! I think you're learning from Shelly. I should be worried!"

When Avery's phone chimed, they looked at each other. Ethan took her phone from the table. "Speaking of… it's Shelly!"

When Ethan pouted, Avery laughed. "Shelly surely has a sixth sense."

Shells: *I'm here at the nursery. I can't miss the show! I have to see with my own eyes what caused David's breakdown. Dang! I didn't see this coming! Ethan is one helluva of a genius! Seriously! Nathaniel Thomas James. I can't wait for the birth certificate! Just a question; how can little Bean use Ethan's last name when you aren't married yet?* 🙁

Chapter 51

AVERY BIT HER LIP and looked at Ethan. "Help! Shelly's asking now."

Ethan smiled. "Shelly would understand. It's David we have to be ready for. I don't think he will wait for the paternity petition result. I'm sure he would ask to meet you."

Avery nodded. "I thought maybe I shouldn't wait for him to ask. It might be better if I invite him now. Besides, I wouldn't know if he tried contacting me—I blocked his number."

Ethan pecked her nose. "That sounds good! Whatever you decide, I'll always be here to support you, my love."

Avery brushed her fingers over his cheeks. "Thank you for always making me feel my worth. For allowing me to make my own decisions."

The door burst open as Ethan put his arms around Avery's waist. Her face flushed. Shelly entered with Art holding her hand.

"Ave! What was Attorney Bartlett saying? What's with his evil smile when he told me I might have to ditch my epic bridal shower planned for my best friend?"

Without waiting for Avery's answer, Shelly untangled her hand from Art's and sat on the couch. Avery followed and sat beside her best friend. The two men gave each other an eye signal and walked out of the room together.

Avery slowly held Shelly's hand and squeezed it. "Shells… I'm sorry I didn't tell you." She cleared her throat. "Ethan and I married in the courthouse a few weeks ago." Shelly quietly faced her. "After the attorney explained everything to us, we decided. Ethan wouldn't want the baby to be born out of wedlock. I want little Bean to have a family…" Avery's voice croaked. "Ethan wanted him to know he belonged to a family from the moment he was born." Avery sniffed. She bowed her head and wiped the tears from her eyes.

When she lifted her head and looked at Shelly, she was surprised to see her best friend in tears. "Did Ethan say that? Did he mean what he said? He wanted my godson to have a family the moment he was born?" Shelly started wiping her tears with her hands.

Avery nodded. "Yes, Shells. David might see it as a revenge move or me not wanting him to have anything to do with the baby. But it's Ethan's way of showing how much he loves me. It's his way of expressing his complete acceptance of the baby."

Shelly hugged a startled Avery. After a few seconds, she pulled away and started wiping Avery's tears. "Ave, I'm so happy for you. I'm happy you found a good man in Ethan. A man whose genuine love is beyond. You deserve all the happiness coming your way!"

"Thank you, Shells! I love you!" Avery hugged her best friend back.

Shelly pulled away. "Forget the bridal shower! Instead, I'll plan the greatest baptismal celebration for my godson!"

Avery laughed hard, seeing the mood change in Shelly. "Triple OMG! I so love you! Mood swings and all!"

"I can't wait! You do not know how many significant themes there are now for baby celebrations! I can…" Shelly's face crunched when the door opened, and Art came in, his face pale, with a phone in his hand. "You have bad timing skills! Do you know that?" she scowled at her husband.

"I'm sorry, sweetheart." Art handed his phone to Shelly. "David wants to talk to you!" Shelly grabbed the phone. "What's going on, dickhead?"

David asked to meet with Avery when he called Shelly. He was a man on a mission. The day would not pass without him getting answers from Avery. From the last time he talked to her at Ethan's house, he had the feeling a chance to have a future with her had loosened from his grip. But he didn't want to give up. They were just engaged. Just like they were used to, anyone could still call off an engagement. The baby would connect them back. He'd never stopped loving Avery. Having a connection with another woman and impregnating the same would be his greatest life regret. He promised he would make Avery find it in her heart to take him back. He'd been asking for one last chance and vowed to live the rest of his life making it up to her. Knowing the Avery he'd fallen in love with, David thought it would be easy. She had the kindest and softest heart. Avery always found it in her heart to give reasons for his actions. There was never a time she didn't understand and forgive him. He needed to give her time. Giving birth to their baby was his last hope. The Avery he knew would not allow their baby not to have a family. That was why he took the next flight when his informant told him Art and Shelly had flown to Florida.

Making sure he was present the day their baby was born would give Avery the time to realize why they needed to be together. To give their child a family, to have them both as the father and the mother. His excitement at seeing his child was crushed, witnessing Avery's change of heart. He couldn't believe what he saw. A name he never expected was written on his son's hospital crib and wrist tag.

Nathaniel Thomas James.

It should be Nathaniel Thomas. Only Nathaniel Thomas, David whispered to himself. How dare Ethan give his name to my son! He wouldn't allow it. He couldn't take the situation sitting down. In his mind, he decided it was time to claim what was his: Avery and their son.

He was surprised to get a positive response when he asked to meet Avery through Shelly. He was expecting one big rejection. But just like the things that had transpired lately, Avery surprised him again. He knew Ethan, the guy he hated the most, and Shelly, but the most discomforting presence would surely be with Avery. It was not the ideal meeting he would wish for, but he couldn't back out.

When he entered Avery's hospital room, he saw Art and Shelly. Art nodded as Shelly signaled him to follow her toward a smaller area. Avery was inside. She was glowing. Motherhood looks good on her, David told himself. Avery smiled at him and motioned for him to take a seat.

When he took the chair opposite her, Shelly stayed and sat beside her best friend. "Take it or leave it. I'm staying. Sorry to disappoint you!" Shelly grimaced at him. David sighed in frustration.

He turned his attention to Avery when she said in a calm voice, "How are you, David?"

"I guess you know by now how I am," David exclaimed.

To his dismay, Avery smiled as if his intention of talking to her was nothing. He had to make her understand how he felt. "How could you give a stranger's name for my son to use? It should be Nathaniel Thomas only. Not Nathaniel Thomas James! You guys are not married yet, and he's already taking what's mine!"

"I beg your pardon?" Avery's eyes darted at David. Her calmness was gone.

It shocked David for a moment. "How could you do this to me, Ave? The baby is our son; he's ours. How could you allow a stranger you've known for a few months to dictate and manipulate your life?"

If looks could kill, Avery swore the inconsiderate man in front of her would have been six feet under by now. "Are you hearing yourself?" Avery took a deep breath. "For your information, I am my own person. I did nothing to owe you an explanation. You are here through the goodness of my heart. Out of consideration because of my son."

David calmed his tone, hearing Avery's angry voice. "Ave, he's our son. We're a family now. I'll forget you've met Ethan. Let's be together, be a family with our son, please."

Shelly was quietly listening. Though she would have wanted to put sense in David's thick skull, it wasn't her fight. So, instead, she was beside Avery for support. But she couldn't wait for her chance to make some sense come to him.

Avery's brows crossed. "There's no more us, David. You and I can never be together anymore. I feel nothing for you. I only respect you in consideration of your connection to my son. Ethan is my life now."

David's breathing was erratic and loud, his anger, hurt, and disappointment clear to see. "How can you trust a man you just met? To the point of giving his name to my son!"

"I trust Ethan not because he is a man but because he's worth it. I may have known him for a little time. But he's made me feel more loved and valued than you ever did. He's made me see, in a short period of time, how big of a disappointment you are." Avery's words were daggers shot at David. But he wouldn't let her say the last word.

"You're so naive, Ave. I'm always the bad guy. But you're not seeing how he's changed you. How can you make sure or trust he will not betray you?" David's hand fisted.

Shelly squeezed Avery's hand to calm her. "You don't trust that someone is never going to betray you. You trust you'll be able to handle it and walk away. And I'm glad about the way you hurt me because if ever I get betrayed again, it was you who prepared me to be stronger. I know how to handle it, and it will be easier for me to walk away."

Avery's sarcasm was evident. Unfortunately, David didn't see it coming. "Ave, what do I need to do for you to forgive me? How can you love another man in so little time, yet you can't forgive me now?" David's voice croaked.

Avery lifted her chin and looked him straight in the eye. "I forgave you even before I left Boston. I must forgive you, not for you, but for me. Because I realized when I forgive you, I give myself freedom. Freedom from all the self-blame, regrets, and pains. But forgiving you wouldn't mean going back to you or saying yes to what you want."

David cupped his face. His hands brushed his hair repeatedly. "I will file a paternity petition. I will ensure my son's name will never connect to that stranger's name. There's no reason for his name to be on my son's. Your lawyer should have told you that! I'll fight it!"

Avery sighed aloud. "You should thank me for permanently attaching your last name to my son's name as his middle name. It's my token of gratitude for bringing little bean into my life. It was a sign that he'd grow up knowing that you would be given a chance to spend time with him. If it were only me, there'd be no trace of you in his lifetime. But it was Ethan's insisting I gave the baby your name as his middle name. So, if there is anything you should be doing, you should thank the stranger who brought me back to life after you killed everything in me!"

David motioned for Avery to let him say another word, but she raised her hand in front of him. "I'm not yet done saying what I wanted to say! You should thank Ethan because after you betrayed me and caused me so much pain, he was there to accept everything about me. He came to make me live again. In a short time, he put back the pieces of my life you had broken. I'm sorry if I hurt you. But if you have any love left for me, you will let me continue living the life you failed to make me live. If you love the baby, you will accept what's best for him. Ethan giving the baby his name was also his way of confirming his genuine love for the baby and me."

David moved his hand to reach Avery's, but she pulled away. "Ave… if you give me the last chance I'm asking, I promise to make it up to you," he said.

Avery shook her head. "The chance of us being together again was long gone. If you sincerely want to make it up, give us peace. Focus on being a good father. We're not taking that away from you. But just like you, Ethan will always be in my and the baby's life. The name will stay. There's nothing you can do to make me change my mind. We want to ensure he has a family belonging to the moment he is born. It wouldn't change the fact that you're his birth father. But he's Ethan's son, too."

David's both hands fisted. "How can he be Ethan's son, too?"

Avery took a deep breath. "Ethan and I got married weeks ago. In our hearts and on paper, Nathaniel Thomas James is our son. We are a family."

A muscle in David's jaw twitched. The color drained out of his face as his mouth fell open.

Chapter 52

"**ETHAN AND I GOT** married weeks ago. In our hearts and on paper, Nathaniel Thomas James is our son. We are a family."

David couldn't believe the bomb Avery had just dropped. A muscle in his jaw twitched. The color drained out of his face as his mouth fell open. He came to win her back. What she declared broke the last thread of hope he'd been hanging on to.

It was twice the pain. First, he lost the woman he loved, the mother of his child. Second, the man who stole Avery's heart was claiming his son. The suffering was too intense. He couldn't find a word to describe it. If what he was feeling was death, he felt like dying repeatedly. If it was fate's revenge on him, he sure got the message.

For David, there was nothing more unbearable than realizing the one person you want to be with doesn't feel the same about you. Confirming the one great gift you once had in your life wasn't yours anymore was suffocating. Truth slapped in his face was like having his heart broken into a gazillion pieces. Only one question came to his mind. Was it this painful when he betrayed Avery?

Silence filled the room. Shelly kept rubbing Avery's back. Suddenly, a loud whimper echoed in the room. David broke down. All his remorse, resentment, sorrow, and desperation came out in sobs and tears. Shelly and Avery gaped at each other with wonder. The David in front of them wasn't the same as the one who cried to Avery in the hospital in LA. They were witnessing a defeated David.

Shelly's heart ached for the good friend she had in David. She believed the cheating David got what he deserved. Avery felt the heaviness and pain the man she once loved was suffering. She wasn't happy it was her words that had caused everything. But she wouldn't regret speaking her truth. If there was one thing she'd learned from it all, it was the importance of honesty.

Avery slowly moved near David's seat. If there was any space left in her heart for him, it was for all the beautiful memories they shared before all the cheating happened.

She patted David's back. "Even if we won't be together, we will always have a connection because of Nathaniel. So, please find it in your heart to accept the situation. I don't want to always fight with you. I want to replace all the hurt and bad memories with good ones for the baby's sake," Avery whispered to a still-sobbing David.

David answered with both hands covering his welled-up face, "I don't know how I can live without you, Ave! I never imagined my future without you!"

Avery removed her hand from his back and sighed aloud. "Live for your son. Plan a future that will make him look up to you. Make a life that will make him a son proud of his father."

Shelly stood up and grabbed the box of tissues from a distance. She took some from the box and sat beside David. Quietly she placed the tissue on his hand. At that moment, she allowed herself to be a friend to a lost and agonizing David. When she looked at Avery, they nodded and gave each other a half-smile. Then, with only their eyes talking, they agreed on one thing. Most of the time, regret comes at the end when it's too late.

"I don't know if I can. I don't even know where to start. Thinking you won't be with me is killing me…" David wiped his tears and looked at Avery.

Avery met his gaze. "Accept reality and forgive yourself, David. That should be a start. Eventually, you'll realize things will fall into place. Before I left for Florida, I realized I also needed to forgive myself and let go of all the blame and regrets. It was only after I found myself again. Sometimes, we are too focused on chasing after what we can't have; we don't see the goodness of what we have. To be free from the past, to be free from the pain, we must learn to let go."

After their talk, David left, saying nothing. Avery didn't press him for any reaction. She knew David needed time to absorb everything she had revealed. He needed to think things through. But she didn't let him leave without giving her word. She promised to contact him to spend time with the baby before he went to Boston.

Once Ethan got the discharge documents, he returned to the room to fetch Avery. Shelly and Art joined them in getting the baby from the nursery. In Ethan's house, Doctor Stella, Ella, and Avery's parents prepared a welcome lunch for the new parents and the baby.

When lunch was over, Shelly and Art stayed behind and joined Ethan and Avery for post-meal tea. Since Ethan was clueless about what had transpired between Avery and David, his vision interchanged between the two women. Avery knew Shelly wanted to say her piece. To everyone's surprise, Art broke the silence.

"I'll never go back to that situation, ever!" Art exclaimed and stood up. Then, he started pacing around the coffee table where the three others were still seated.

Shelly's forehead creased. "Hon, what's wrong? What situation?"

"David's situation. I will never cheat again!" Art replied. He sat beside his wife and took a deep breath. "The look on David's face when he broke down in front of you guys, I will never forget! I heard everything you guys said."

Shelly started rubbing her husband's back. "That's the most amazing thing you have said in your life, Hon. You should value the forgiveness and the chance I gave you."

Ethan bit his lower lip to hide his smile. Avery caressed his jaw. When her hand reached the side of Ethan's mouth, he held her hand and placed it on his lips. Art interrupted their gaze and display of affection towards each other when he spoke again.

"That… that gaze and the PDA!" He pointed at Avery and Ethan. "God! I would die seeing or imagining Shelly being like that with another man!" Art was flushed.

The new parents were speechless. Their eyes focused on Art. Shelly pouted, eyes gazing at her husband's face. Her hand moved from Art's back to his cheek. She started caressing Art's face, just like Avery did to Ethan. "Oh, Hon, you have no idea how handsome you are now!" Shelly's smile was up to her ears.

Avery and Ethan chuckled. When Ethan started placing small kisses on Avery's face, Shelly tapped the table. "And you, Doctor James!" The loud tap sound on the table startled everyone. All eyes turned to Shelly.

"What did I do now?" Ethan was confused.

"Be like Art. Remember to value your wife's trust and feelings. She chose you over David, even with the baby situation. Do you know how hard that is? I don't condone what he did to Ave, but when I saw him break down, realizing what he lost and confirming he doesn't have Ave's heart anymore…"

Shelly shook her head animatedly. "Triple OMG! If I had a second heart right then, I could have given it to that dickhead!"

Ethan nodded. Slowly, he brought Avery's hand to his heart. "I may seem arrogant most of the time, but I'm a faithful man. My heart is only for you, Ave. I've watched countless movies on cheating and infidelity. I know the consequences. I won't give myself any reason to look at someone else when I love someone."

Avery's lips curved into a big smile. She looked at Shelly proudly. Shelly twitched her face in return. Art quietly kissed Shelley's hand. When she kissed him on the cheek, he whispered something in Shelly's ears that caused her eyes to widen. When Shelly whispered back to Art, they both stood up. But before they could say goodbye, Art's phone rang.

Art motioned for everyone to be quiet when he answered the call. "David, dude. Ah… Okay. I'll ask him. I'll get back to you ASAP."

"What does he want?" Shelly asked.

"Ethan, man. David wants to meet us for a few drinks. He said it would be the three of us. Are you in?" Art stared at Ethan, waiting for his answer.

Avery looked at Shelly, then at Ethan. Ethan cupped Avery's face in his hands. "I should go."

Avery shook her head. "You should go with Attorney Bartlett. I don't want you going alone." Ethan pecked her lips softly. "I'm not going alone. Art is coming, too. Everything is going to be fine. I'll have to talk to him anyway. So, why not do it now?" Ethan shrugged his shoulders.

"Don't worry, Ave., I'll be with them." Art patted Avery's shoulder.

"Should I call and warn that dickhead?" asked Shelly.

Art waved his hand for Shelly to stop. "Hon, no need for that. Ethan and I are capable men." He pointed at Avery and Shelly. "You two should trust your husbands!"

Avery nodded as Shelly mouthed okay. As the two men were saying their goodbyes, Ethan's phone chimed.

Atty. Bartlett: *Atty. Thomas called me. He wants me to meet with him. I'll see him now. I will update you soon.*

Ethan sighed and looked at Art. "Looks like we're not the only ones invited. He also asked Attorney Bartlett to meet with him."

Chapter 53

SHELLY STAYED WITH AVERY as they both waited for the men to return from David's unexpected invitation. The drive to the Ocean Bar was enlightening for Ethan. Art's words of concern and encouragement confirmed to him why Shelly and Art were Avery's ride-or-die.

"Man, we should be thankful we're not in David's shoes right now. Not that I wished that for him. But it scared me. I witnessed how Ave was so in love with him before the cheating and how she tried to give him a chance. And when he was begging her to take him back." Art loosened a few buttons on his shirt. "I've never been so grateful for Shelly's forgiveness. But watching how the woman you love declares that she does not feel the same way about you anymore was scary. That you can't do anything about it because she's now more in love with someone else."

Art's face twitched. Ethan nodded. "I can't imagine how heartbroken he must have been. But David's smart. He should have seen the consequences of his actions. I still can't understand why he did what he did to Ave."

Art's animated voice and face suddenly turned serious. Ethan sighed. He felt embarrassed remembering that Art had cheated on Shelly once before their marriage. "I'm sorry, man. I didn't mean it for you to…"

Art dismissed the apology. "It's okay. I just remembered Shelly's face, then. It wasn't my proudest moment." When Ethan looked at the driver and reminded Art that someone beside him could hear them, Art smiled. He looked in the driver's direction and yelled. "You should learn from what you hear from us. So you won't make the same mistakes with your girlfriend or wife!"

The driver glanced at them through the rear-view mirror. "I'm sure, super-rich as you are, and with your position, you had your driver sign an NDA." Ethan laughed at what Art said.

Art took a deep breath. "I can't speak for David, but from my experience… I was so stupid. It just happened. I was amazed that a single woman could still fall for me despite knowing I was engaged. To this day, the hurt on Shelly's face still haunts me at night. Do you know I even prayed in different churches, promising if she forgives and accepts me back, I will live my life making it up to her? That explains my behavior towards her. Obeying and giving in to what Shelly wants is nothing compared to the pain I caused her." Art kept shaking his head. "If I have to kneel on her feet to make her happy, I'll do it, no questions asked. It wouldn't be enough to pay for my sins."

Through the silence inside the car, everyone felt Art's regret for cheating on Shelly. Ethan tapped Art on the shoulder. "I'm so glad you realized Shelly's importance before it was too late."

"Me too." Art nodded in agreement. He will always be grateful for still having Shelly in his life.

When they arrived at the Ocean Bar, Ethan saw from the entrance David and Attorney Bartlett seated in a booth talking seriously. He did not know what the meeting was about. But he came with only one goal in mind: to do everything for the sake of Avery and the baby. Even if it would mean talking and having a peaceful relationship with the man he didn't like the most.

Art saw the hesitation on Ethan's face. Though he wasn't a fan of David's misdeeds towards Avery, he knew he needed to step up as a friend who wanted nothing but peace and love for everyone. So, in his always cheerful tone, he cued Ethan. "Man, remember we're here for Ave and the baby. Let us be the bigger people."

Ethan nodded and laughed big when Art placed his fisted hand on top of his heart and blew a kiss on his fist, saying, "For the love of Ave!" Then, he motioned for them to proceed to where David was.

Art followed Ethan's lead. He clapped his hand and whispered, "Let's get this party started."

Except the meet-up wasn't a party as expected. It was, in Art's words, a man-to-man meeting. Attorney Bartlett has the copy of the birth registration form Avery and Ethan filled up and submitted in front of him. In front of David was a copy of his will. The first few minutes were ice cold. Nobody dared to say a word.

Art got his assignment. He spoke first to break the tension. "David, dude, you should have warned me. I should have brought a copy of my wedding vows!" Ethan and Attorney Bartlett gave a half-smile, but David has no reaction.

David just looked at Art, then at Ethan. "Why did you do it?"

Ethan's brows met. "Why what?" he asked back.

"How can you marry Avery and claim my son?" David brushed his hands through his hair repeatedly.

"Attorney Thomas, we should focus on the matter at hand…" Attorney Bartlett spoke. Ethan moved his hand toward Attorney Bartlett to let him know it was okay with him.

His eyes stayed on David, who was bowed down.

"Do you want the truth or me to say what your ego would like to hear?" Ethan asked.

David lifted his head, and his eyes darted to Ethan. "Of course, I want the truth, Hotshot!" Art gulped the beer in front of David in one shot. Attorney Bartlett was shaking his head.

Ethan was calm while David glared at him. "To do what you failed to do. I wanted Avery to feel protected by my love, not just for her but for everything about her, including the baby. I wanted her to be whole again. For her to see and believe she is worthy, cared for, and genuinely loved." Ethan took a deep breath, eyes not leaving David's glare.

David sighed aloud. "And you think I can't do the same?"

"Oh, I know you can do the same. But your time for doing things that matter has already passed. Not to forget your doing caused the woman I love to get hurt, broken, and lose her self-worth," Ethan answered calmly.

"You're such an arrogant prick! Do you know that?" David tapped his fingers on the table. His breathing turned erratic while his glare was still on Ethan.

Ethan took another deep breath. "If speaking my truth is arrogance, so be it. I'll gladly accept my title, arrogant prick."

Before David could spit out another word, Art interfered. "Hey, guys! We're all adults and educated here. There's no need for your sparing of words. No one's competing with anyone."

Art placed his arm on top of the table between Ethan and David. "Just like what the attorney said, let's stick to the matter. David, dude, please! Ethan, man!"

Attorney Bartlett coughed aloud to get their attention. When all three men focused on him, he looked at each one of them and started. "Well, Attorney Thomas called for me, and we discussed a few matters before you two arrived.

As the counsel representing the James couple…" David cleared his throat aloud, interrupting the lawyer from talking.

Art scowled at him. "Dude, please." David motioned, zipping his mouth.

"I offered to discuss the matter with my clients in a separate setting, but Attorney Thomas insisted Doctor James was on his way here. He insisted we discuss it now in your presence and with Art as a witness," Attorney Bartlett continued, but Art stopped him.

"Um, Attorney, so you know, I'm a software engineer. I'm not just plain Art. I played an important role in this meeting, but you seemed to look down on me." Art sighed, causing chuckles from both Ethan and David.

"I'm sorry, Engineer Art," Attorney Bartlett answered. "As I was saying, Attorney Thomas here has some propositions regarding the baby. The first is his willingness not to bring the matter of paternity into court if Doctor James issues his denial or decline in paternity. As I tried…"

"I'm sorry, but that will never happen. I won't deny or decline anything!" Ethan loudly declared, getting the attention of some patrons in the bar.

David answered with sarcasm. "It wouldn't be hard since you're not the father anyway."

Ethan's hand fisted on top of the table. The conversation that was filled with laughter a while back was now turning heated. Ethan glared at David. "Nathaniel may not have my genes, but it doesn't make me lesser than you as his birth father. Since Ave moved here, I have been with her and beside her during the pregnancy. The only thing that defines you is the blood that runs in his veins. But I willingly gave all the care, love, and time expected of a father. In my heart and soul, he's my son."

David banged their table and stood up. Before he could punch Ethan, Art grabbed his arms and blocked him. "Fucking arrogant asshole! Who do you think you are?"

"I am Avery's husband and Nathaniel's father." Ethan calmly stood from his chair and faced Attorney Bartlett. "Send me the bill. Whatever my wife and I discussed with you before the baby was born stays. Just let us know whenever and wherever the court hearing will be and we will be there."

Unhurriedly, Ethan walked away from the table and went toward his awaiting car. Once inside the vehicle, he received a message from Avery.

My Love: *What's going on there? Is everything okay? When are you coming home?*

After sending a reply, he put his phone inside his pocket. When the driver glanced at him in the mirror, he smiled. "Take me home to my family."

Shelly displayed a long face when Ethan arrived without Art. After Ethan told the best friends what had happened, Shelly became furious. Avery quietly listened to her best friend's rant. Then, without waiting for Shelly to finish what she was saying, Avery stood up and motioned to leave. Ethan stopped her by encircling his arm around her waist. "Where are you going, my love?" he asked.

"To the Ocean, Bar, to put a stop to all of David's bullshit!" she answered.

Ethan placed his lips on Avery's. Slowly, he planted small kisses from her neck to her ears. After kissing her ear, Ethan whispered, "Over my dead body. You won't get near Boston's Best until Attorney Bartlett figures things out."

Avery touched the sides of his lips and nodded. When Shelly took her bag and walked toward the door, she got the couple's attention. "Where are you going, Shells?" Avery asked.

Shelly looked at them with her lips in an upset pout. "It's time Art's lawyer gives David a piece of her freaking mind. Don't you think? Let me borrow your car and your driver. I'm too furious to drive! See you guys later!"

Dazed, Ethan nodded, speechless. Avery pressed her head on Ethan's chest to hide her laughter. In silence, their minds communicated. Shelly's arrival would bring havoc to David and Art.

Back in the bar, David's unstoppable speech listened to by Art, was already creating quite a show. Since Ethan and Attorney Bartlett had left, David gulped several glasses of beer. Art stayed to give him company. But his friend's drunkenness and loud voice had been causing them embarrassment.

When Art stood up and tried to make David stand for them to leave, David blocked his hand. Shelly's voice startled them before Art could grasp David's arms. Art's eyes widened, seeing his wife already standing between him and David. He was about to greet Shelly when she slammed the bag in her hand toward David's head out of nowhere.

"Freaking dickhead! What do you think you're doing?" Shelly whispered in David's ears.

Chapter 54

DAVID WAS INSTANTLY SOBERED by Shelly's whisper in his ear and her slamming her bag into his head.

Previously loud and talkative, David was now quiet. Art helped David leave his seat and walk toward Shelly's ride. Art slid into the backseat beside David as his wife took the passenger seat. Once buckled up, the couple looked at each other, exhausted.

Shelly sighed, "Where are you checked in?"

David just stared at her. Shelly then glared at her husband. Immediately, Art searched David's pockets. He smiled when he found a hotel room key and proudly handed it to his wife. As Shelly read the hotel name from the key card, she instructed Ethan's driver to take them there.

Inside David's hotel room, Art and Shelly helped him get into bed after making sure he drank hangover pills before dozing off. After an hour, Shelly sighed while the couple was resting in the adjacent living area.

"Freaking asshat! He's not in his right mind! Instead of resolving the issue, he's just creating more issues!" Shelly declared.

Art slowly massaged Shelly's tensed shoulders. "Relax, Hon; I don't want you to be stressed. You know that. But how long are we staying here?" he asked in a whisper.

Shelly glared at him. "We're staying here until we can put sense in that asshat's thick skull!"

"I'm not a fan of what he did to Ave, but I feel bad for him." Art started placing small kisses on his wife's neck and shoulders. "The more I witness what's happening to him, the more I appreciate your forgiveness and trust in me. I don't know how I would take it if I were in his shoes. Thank you, hon. I love you!" He placed his lips on Shelly's.

Shelly kissed back with the same passion. "Everything you just said… you should curve in your brain. Because this marriage we have is your last chance." She softly bit his lower lip.

Art's eyes were full of lust. He whispered in her ear, "Should we get a room?" Shelly smirked.

"Get a room, you guys!" David yelled as he stood at his room door, looking at the couple on the couch.

Shelly pulled from Art's arms and stood up with her finger pointed at David. "You dickhead! You haven't learned! What a circus you made today!"

Immediately, Shelly took a throw pillow on the couch and threw it toward a surprised David. Unprepared, it smacked him in the face. A loud curse came out of his mouth. Though he wanted to spit out more cursing words, he knew Shelly better than that. So, when she motioned for him to join Art on the couch, he followed without complaint.

Once he and Art were seated beside each other, Shelly took hers on the one-seater, facing them both. She was like a parent ready to make her children recite their confessions. But instead, Art cleared his throat and slouched. David did stretching motions on his shoulders and neck. They both avoided Shelly's scowl.

But when Shelly started talking, both men looked at her. They knew the woman very well. She should have their full attention. "What the fuck were you thinking?" she snarled at David.

"I'm just stressing my right as the father!" David replied with a firm but soft voice, not wanting to irate Shelly.

Shelly sighed aloud and blew a strand of her hair away from her face. "Don't you think the truth hasn't stressed it enough? We all know you're the father, dickhead! I know you're smart and one of the best in your field, but sometimes you must reason with your heart, not your smart brain."

Art clapped. He was in awe of his wife. "Dude, listen to my wife."

David's brows turned up. He was unable to decipher what Shelly's words meant. He tried to change the topic. "I'm hungry. Let's order room service. I'm sure you guys are hungry, too." He looked away from Shelly and started dialing for room service.

"Yeah, yeah. I know that's a lawyer tactic. You were ignoring it as a defense. Go ahead and order food. But we will not leave unless I soften your thick skull," Shelly smirked. The loud laugh of Art resounded in the room.

After they finished eating, David knew he had no reason to avoid the dreaded Shelly talk. Aside from the fact the woman was seated, waiting for him. So, when she called his name, he had no choice but to sit where she pointed at him.

When Art motioned to leave the room, Shelly called him to sit beside David. "I want you to hear everything. This applies to you, too," she told Art.

"I don't see any reason I should talk to you and not to Ave. This talk should be between me and her, Shells!" David announced.

"Well, suck it, Mr. Smarty Pants! I'm the only option you have right now!" Shelly snarled.

When David started brushing his hair with his hands in a frustrated motion, Shelly took one hand and held it. Art stiffened, looking at his wife's hand on David's. But when David bowed his head and his shoulders started shaking, Art was quick to rub David's back. The three of them muted for a few minutes. Only David's sobbing could be heard.

Shelly squeezed David's hand. "You might feel alone and hopeless for now. We all understand how you're feeling. All the thoughts in your mind are valid. But you should go with your heart and not with your mind. You may know all ways to fight the law or even circumvent it, no doubt about that. But you don't have enemies. There's no battle you need to fight."

David lifted his head and looked at Shelly. "It hurts. I'm starting to feel I lost her. And I'm losing both of them, Ave and the baby."

"You both lost… you've lost a woman that would never have given up on you. And Ave lost the woman she was before you broke her heart. But it doesn't mean you've lost your chances of being a good father and her as a mother. Instead, both of you gained the most important thing. You can win in that, though it has to be in your separate ways." Shelly slowly tapped David's hand.

"I tried thinking about it. I imagined letting Avery go, but I couldn't. How can I move from this?" David asked.

"I know. Letting go is the most difficult thing about losing someone you have loved; the way you never feel dies all at once. All you can do is wait and watch it fade away, one day at a time. But, while waiting, you can still be a good person, friend, and father." Shelly tapped David's hand for the last time.

David pulled his hand from Shelly's and slowly rubbed his chest. "It hurts so much seeing her with that arrogant prick… I've never felt this pain before. I was that guy before. She was mine. How could she have loved him more?"

Art nodded his head.

Shelly looked between both men. "That's a good point, Attorney Thomas. Same questions we had when you guys cheated on us." She placed her hands on the sides of her hips. "But seriously, the hurting is a temporary thing. Time will push the pain further away. It will look smaller and simpler at a distance. One day, it might disappear entirely. Then you will look back at the way you survived it." She smiled at both men gazing at her. "When I survived my pain because of Art's cheating, it felt like a miracle. I realized the days don't ache like they used to," Shelly's voice croaked.

"Holy shit!" Art stood up and squeezed himself beside Shelly. He put his arms around her. "I'm so sorry, hon."

Shelly rested her head on his chest. "We're good now. I know how sorry you are."

David took a deep and loud breath. "I'm so happy for you guys."

"Dude, fix your ass. You're stressing my wife!" Art scowled at David.

"David, I know you're a good person… we know. Ave and Ethan are, too. They aren't taking the baby away from you. They're willing to give you all the rights except in the paper. But don't take it against them. They were just both thinking about what was best for the baby. Ethan didn't want him to be born out of wedlock. He just wanted to assure Ave and make the baby feel that he was welcomed and belonged to a family from the moment he was born," Shelly explained.

"It's easier said than done," David answered.

"Think about it. Open your heart and mind to possibilities. It's not about you anymore. It's about your son. And it will do him good to have two admirable and loving fathers. Talk to Ave and Ethan." Shelly pointed to David's heart. "Heart talk." Then she softly slapped his forehead. "Not mind talk." David nodded when Shelly stood up, followed by Art. "We love you, don't forget that." She blew him a kiss and took her bag as she walked toward the door. Art hugged a sitting David and kissed the top of his head. "I love you, dude!" Art said as he ran toward the door where Shelly was waiting.

"I hope your words got into him," Ethan said to Shelly after hearing what happened in David's hotel room. Avery clasped her hand with Ethan's and nodded.

"Our home is open whenever he wishes to see the baby as long as he tells us in advance. He will always be his father and Ethan, too," Avery said softly.

Ethan glanced at Art and Shelly, then at Avery. "If he wants to, you can text him to come now while you are here. So he can have his moment with the baby before Nathan sleeps for the night."

"Are you sure? Are you okay with that?" Avery asked.

"That's a good idea, Dr. James!" Shelly was ecstatic. "Then you guys can have your real talk," she added.

Art waved his phone. "I'll text him now!"

Ethan and Avery looked at each other, and both nodded. Shelly smiled and mouthed for Art to send the message. Once done, Art placed his phone on the table where all four gathered.

When Art's phone dinged, all four were directed toward it.

Art: *Dude, Ethan asked if you'd like to spend time with the baby before his goodnight sleep. Just no freak show, okay?"*

David: *I would love to! I promise to behave, dude.*

Chapter 55

DAVID WAS STILL THINKING about everything Shelly had said when he received Art's message. He had to read it several times to believe he'd correctly read it. Then, he recollected how shitty his day had been.

It had started with excitement, learning Avery had given birth. First, he'd rushed to the hospital, wanting to behold both mother and son the soonest. Then, realizing he wouldn't get the chance to see the mother of his child, he settled for a glimpse of his baby, hoping to hold him. But seeing the name had made him flip.

When Avery had agreed to see and talk to him, he'd seen it as an opportunity. But the opportunity had turned into a disaster. Avery was firm and bold. He couldn't persuade her. But when he broke down, he'd felt behind the firmness and boldness. Avery was still the kind and caring woman he knew. The same Ave he'd fallen in love with. And it tripled the pain he was feeling due to his broken heart.

He'd left the hospital unable to hold his son. The child had his blood but not his name. He'd resorted to meeting Ethan, the arrogant prick in his life. His demand and threat didn't sway the guy. It irked him more. Seeing the man who now owned the heart of the woman he once had calm and unchanged was dreadful. Hearing the truth he uttered was like a knife cutting his wrongdoings.

Before, his fear was only losing Avery. But after seeing the baby from behind the glass window, he felt his son was so near yet so far. Finally, he realized losing Avery and the baby was like losing his life. He just wanted to drink all his sorrows and regrets. Then there was Art and Shelly. The two people he looked up to. After everything, David hoped his and Avery's story would be saved, like their two best friends.

In the back of his mind, David knew Art was different. Art had learned his lesson the first time, but he hadn't. Everything was coming back at him. In ways he never thought. In unexplainable pain, he never knew existed. He could only ask himself: was it time to throw in the towel?

Art's presence lightened the drive to Ethan's house. David was surprised to see Art waiting for him outside his hotel. Sending Art in Ethan's car with his driver was an olive branch. As expected, his best friend was sweet-talking him on their way. Little did he know David was a ball of nerves. He kept on telling himself he was coming for the baby. When they arrived, Shelly greeted them by the door. She warned David not to mess up his chance of holding his baby for the first time. They led him toward a room with the name Nathaniel Thomas intricately written. Upon entering the door, his heart stopped.

With his back facing them, Ethan slowly danced and hummed while he cradled the baby in his arms. Shelly saw David pause outside the door; his eyes fixated on the man inside. She squeezed David's hand, reminding him to calm himself. After a few seconds, Shelly coughed softly to get Ethan's attention.

Ethan slowly turned around to face them. He smiled at them and pointed at the baby. "He's still awake, but I don't want him to interrupt Ave's sleep. That's why I came here when I saw on the baby monitor that he was awake."

Shelly nodded and motioned for Ethan to acknowledge David. When he looked at David, he nodded at him. "Do you want to hold him now?"

He pointed at the side of the door. "There's a hand sanitizer by the door for you guys. If you would like to take your turns holding the baby."

Art shook his head and grasped Shelly's hand. "We'll leave you guys. I want my wife to have a drink with me at the minibar."

Immediately, the couple left without waiting for either man to answer.

David couldn't think of a word to say. Ethan took the lead and pointed the sanitizer at David after he gestured for him to sit on the reclined lazy boy.

"It's best if you remove your top. Since it's your first time holding him, skin-to-skin touch is strongly suggested for him to feel you," Ethan explained.

David nodded, quietly removed his shirt, and placed it on the side. Once he was rested, Ethan slowly placed the baby on his chest. He showed him how and where to put his hands and arms. When he was sure both were settled, he told David to take his time with the baby and quietly walked outside the room.

When David confirmed Ethan was out of earshot, he let his tears flow. His eyes gazed at one of the two most beautiful babies he'd ever seen. He remembered the other he'd once held in LA. When the baby's eyes met his, David smiled. "Hi! Welcome to the world! I'm your dad."

David couldn't describe the feeling. His chest felt like it was going to explode because of the overflowing love in his heart. At that moment, he felt like a switch had turned. He couldn't think of other things except how he was willing to do anything to love and protect the baby in his arms—the flesh of his flesh.

"Sorry, I'm late." He placed a soft kiss on the baby's forehead.

After a few hours, Ethan returned with Shelly to check on David and the baby. They smiled at each other, seeing the father and son sleeping. Shelly couldn't help but take a picture of the scene using her phone camera. David's eyes opened when he heard the camera click. He saw Shelly standing in front of him with a phone in her hand. Ethan was busy clearing the baby's stuff from the changing table.

David cleared his throat. "Sorry, I fell asleep too."

Shelly chuckled. Ethan stopped what he was doing, looked him in the eye, and answered, "That's good. You needed it."

He walked toward David. "Do you mind if I take him and place him in his bed? It's better if he gets used to sleeping in his bed during his sleeping hours."

David nodded and allowed Ethan to take the baby from his arms. He watched as Ethan carefully placed the baby in his crib. Ethan affectionately brushed the baby's hair with his fingers. He checked the diaper and kissed his tiny hands before he walked toward the door.

When Ethan stopped at the door, he looked at David again. "Would you like to have a coffee with Art and me at the boathouse?"

Before David could answer, Shelly picked up his shirt and handed it to him. "Put on your shirt and go… have coffee with them. I'll watch over my godson. Don't worry. I want to practice anyway."

Though adamant, David put on his shirt and followed Ethan.

While the three men had their coffee break, they watched several boats passing through. The lights from each boat and the night sky made a spectacular sight. The water was calm and relaxing.

Art knew the timing was right. "Guys, you can have the talk you should have. Don't mind me. Pretend I'm not here. I'm staying for security, nothing else." Both men laughed. Ethan was the first one to talk. "How did it feel? Were you scared to hold him the first time?"

David smiled. "It was scary but gratifying. Thank you. You were right about the skin-to-skin."

Ethan smiled as he sipped his coffee. After placing his cup on top of the table, he reached out his hand to a surprised David. "Thank you for coming. I'm sorry if it's only now that you got the chance to hold the baby."

Art stiffened in his seat. His eyes moved from Ethan to David. He was getting his arms ready for an altercation. But, instead, he stared at David, trying to get through, saying nothing. Don't mess this up. Art kept repeating the words in his mind as if he was talking to David telepathically.

"I should be the one thanking you," David answered, accepting Ethan's hand.

The relief on Art's face earned a chuckle from both men. Then, Ethan started the conversation again. "I know it's difficult, but we have to talk for the sake of the two people we love."

"I know." David nodded.

"I'm sorry if our action conveyed the wrong message. I couldn't blame you for thinking it the other way, though. If I were in your shoes, I'd surely do the same. But to clarify and assure you, we're not taking away your rights as his father. I'm not taking it away from you. I'm not replacing you. We want him to know and feel he belongs to a family. You will always be his father. Nothing can ever change that. But, in my way, I will love, care and protect him the best I can. I hope you won't hold that against me," Ethan explained.

David slowly rubbed his knees. "I understand. My mind flipped when I read the name. But I guess nothing matters now except his security, comfort, and happiness. I should have thanked you instead of saying everything I said in the bar earlier today. I was so focused on my selfish ideas."

"It was understandable," Ethan answered. "I also hope you understand everything I do is for my family."

"Objectively, I knew your actions were coming from a good place. But emotionally, I was in denial. I let my regrets and frustrations take the best of me. I allowed my ego to rule over me." David shook his head multiple times.

"I can feel bromance!" Art shouted. "But I have to say this, you both almost gave me a heart attack! I'm here only two days, but I felt I had aged ten years more."

Ethan's shoulder shook in laughter. "We should go over the document

Attorney Bartlett prepared. You can add or remove whichever you don't feel like. We'll be willing to meet you halfway. Believe me. Avery and I want you to be part of the baby's life. We can all be there for him at the same time."

"It will be good for the baby to have two admirable and loving fathers." Shelly's words played back in David's mind.

"I agree with that. We can do it while I'm still here. Hopefully, the baptism too?" David looked at Ethan.

"Did I hear baptism?" Shelly asked as she sprinted toward them. "Ave is feeding him now." She glared at Ethan's questioning face as she sat beside Art. "My uterus may still be a virgin, Doctor James, but I wouldn't leave my godson if Ave weren't there."

When David's phone chimed, Shelly remembered something. She tapped David on the shoulder. "By the way, I sent your picture with the baby I took to Mama T."

David read his message and sighed.

Mom: *I'm crying happy tears at seeing my grandson. When will you bring him here? We can't wait to hold him. What name did you give him?*

Chapter 56

Mama T: *Our dear Avery, how are you and the baby? Shelly sent us a picture of David with our grandson. Thank you from the bottom of our hearts. I can't wait to see and hold him. We love you both!*

AS DAVID READ HIS mother's message, Avery also read Mama T's message to her while feeding the baby in the nursery. A baby was truly a blessing. Though both first saw the baby as their connection, reading the messages they received reminded them of this. They weren't the only ones with whom the sweet bundle of joy connected. They also needed to consider their families whether they admitted it or not.

Mama T's message reminded Avery of a promise. She promised David's mother a lifetime connection. When they talked the last time, the woman she considered a mother had been nothing but apologetic, understanding, and loving toward her and her situation. She promised that whatever the circumstances between her and David may be, his parents, especially his mother, would not be deprived of any connection with her grandchild.

Avery felt sorry that with all the recent events, she'd only focused on her feelings and disregarded David. She forgot that just like her parents, another set of grandparents in Boston had been waiting in anticipation of her son's coming. It glinted in her mind; one reason for breaking up with David then took a toll on her. Their parents had formed a strong bond. It also shattered their hearts when they separated.

Mama T painfully told her about the worry and longing she felt for the situation of David's baby in LA. Though she had the chance to persuade and beg Avery to stay, she didn't. She only asked for the opportunity to be a part of the baby's life. Focused on herself, she forgot about it. She wouldn't have thought of it if Shelly didn't send the picture. Nathaniel Thomas was not a string; she and David could push and pull toward their own goals.

Remembering what David had told her about the baby in LA, Avery knew she couldn't break Mama T's heart for a second time. She may not be getting back with David, but she had the power to keep a grandchild's connection with his grandparents.

"Are you okay?" Ethan's voice woke Avery from her thoughts. Quietly, he sat on the armrest of the chair where she was seated. Their son reminded him of when Ella was still a baby. He felt a pinch of sadness remembering a baby Ella in his arms instead of her mother's. Watching Avery feed the baby gave him a feeling of a man's undying love for his wife and child.

"Mama T messaged me. She saw a picture of David and the baby," Avery said instead of answering Ethan's question.

Ethan squeezed her shoulder. "She messaged David too." "How was your talk? What did he say?" she asked.

"It was good. We were cool, thank God! First, he'll go over the document with Attorney Bartlett. Then he'll tell us if he has any requests or suggestions." Ethan slid a finger inside the baby's fisted hand.

Avery smiled and touched Ethan's cheek.

"I'm glad. I was thinking of inviting David's parents to come for a visit. They can stay at my parents' house. So they get the chance to see and hold the baby. But unfortunately, I don't think we'll have the time to go to Boston soon."

"Sounds like a good plan. But I think it's best to make them come for an important occasion, like a baptism, maybe?" Ethan smiled as his eyes locked with hers.

Avery smiled back with a grin. She imagined Shelly screaming at the top of her lungs when she asked her to plan the event.

The sprawling lawn facing the boathouse was a magnificent sight. Shelly lived to her promise of giving her godson a baptismal celebration for the books. A garland arch made of blue, silver, and yellow balloons adorned the made-up stage at the center of the lawn. It was an eye-catching view added with the water as the backdrop. The theme of the event, Thomas's Book of Blessings, written on a prominent book symbol, was plastered on the stage.

The whole decor made everyone's eyes pop. Around the lawn were life-size standees of book pages. Each page represented the blessings in the life of baby Thomas. There was a page for his grandparents, Doctor Stella, Shelly, and Art. A separate page for his Papa David, James Family, big sister Ella, Daddy Ethan, and Mommy Ave.

When Art entered, he couldn't help but shout how proud he was of Shelly's party-planning skills. "My wife is a fucking genius!"

Ella was busy staffing the cake and souvenir booth. As expected, she held the name tags for the people identified as the blessings in baby Thomas's life. She proudly wore the Big Sister tag. She cheerfully placed grandpa and grandma tags on David and Avery's parents. While the guests were arriving, she made sure Ethan, Avery, and David got to wear their tags. When all the guests settled at their tables, the event host took hold of the microphone and announced the celebrant's entrance.

Mama T and Avery's mom were both in tears when a smiling baby, Thomas, carried by Avery wearing the mom tag, entered the venue. Walking on both of her sides were Ethan with Dad and David with Papa tags, respectively. On the side were Doctor Stella, Shelly, and Art, all beaming with smiles. To some, the group of people who entered may have seemed unconventional. But they were a family for the people they loved and who loved them.

Games, dancing, and singing filled the program. One celebration highlight was when Big Sister Ella recited a special letter she had written for her new baby brother. It made everyone in the crowd cry or teary-eyed.

My Dear Baby Brother Thomas,

Everyone thought Mommy's beauty enchanted me first. They didn't know it was you who attracted me when you were still in her belly at the airport. The first time I felt your kick, I knew you'd be strong and healthy. I promise to love and protect you forever. I'll ensure you get your toy trains, robots, and cars so you won't break my dolls and Barbies' heads. When you're sad or crying, I'll sing you a song when you don't have Mommy, Daddy, or Uncle David around. I love you, Baby Thomas. Thanks for being my brother.

Love,

Your Big Sister Ella

Everyone clapped. Avery was in tears. Ethan was a proud dad. David felt assured knowing Avery's family welcomed and loved his son. David watched from a distance when the host called for the guests to take their pictures with the baby in the photo booth. It was just a month after he, Ethan, and Avery sat with Attorney Bartlett. They discussed and agreed on how they would handle the baby's situation.

It was a peaceful discussion, far from the ones they'd had before. From the night he held Thomas for the first time to the present, they'd indeed come a long way. A mature, amicable, and loving relationship, he could have said. He would never forget how Ethan and Avery surprised him that day.

"We would love to have his nickname be Thomas instead of Nathan. In that way, your last name will be his everyday name spoken by everyone," Avery announced with a smile.

"Avery's parents agreed to accompany Thomas on holidays or events you wish to have him with you in Boston. That way, they can stay with you and your parents," Ethan added.

"You are welcome to attend any event or celebration concerning Thomas, whether at home, school, or community-related events, anytime and any day. His emergency contacts will include your name aside from Doctor and Mrs. James'. Every legal document about him will show your name and Ethan's as his father. The three of you will jointly decide his attendance on all holidays, birthdays, etc.," Attorney Bartlett said.

"We are not obligating you for monthly support. Instead, we opened an account for Thomas in which you are free to put money into your own accord. That account will be for his college education and trust fund."

Ethan explained it wasn't to offend him, which he believed. A tap on his shoulder interrupted his reverie of the day. A smiling Ethan handed him a glass of red.

"We have a handsome son to raise over there, eh." Ethan pointed to a cooing Thomas in Doctor Stella's arms.

David nodded. "You're damn right! He should be one hell of a perfect son since he has both of us!" His statement earned a laugh from Ethan.

When the host called for the baby's immediate family, Ella came running to them. She took each of their hands with hers, each on her side, and they all walked toward the photo booth. Once all the guests had left, the grandparents bid goodbye. Shelly and Avery watched Ella open the gifts for a sleeping Thomas. Art, David, and Ethan were in the boathouse for their coffee.

Suddenly, Doctor Stella came running to her brother. "Whoa! What's the rush?" Ethan asked.

"I got the call!" Doctor Stella gasped. "I'll be the team lead of Doctors Without Borders to Thailand." She pressed her chest. "Thailand is my dream location! Can't you believe it?" Her smile went up to her ears.

Ethan stood and hugged her sister tight. "I'm so happy for you, Ste! It's time you follow your heart. Ella and I will be fine. We're not alone anymore."

"I know! I'm so excited!" Doctor Stella exclaimed. "Congrats, Ste!" Art saluted.

"When do you leave?" David asked.

"In a week. We're collaborating with a group from Lawyers Without Borders," answered Doctor Stella.

David raised his glass. "I guess we're leaving for the same assignment. I'm leading the lawyers' group."

EPILOGUE

IT WAS A PLEASANT sunny morning. The park outside the family clinic building was enchanting. The view from the parking lot was a sight to behold. Giant domes of pink peonies and babies' breath surrounded a makeshift altar. The altar was placed in front of a gigantic wall of white lilies and roses. Silver ornamented chairs were arranged left and right facing it. In the background, a fifteen-man orchestra played instrumentals of prelude favorites live as the guests arrived at their seats.

After thirty minutes of anticipation, the music changed. The atmosphere in the space turned into a quiet excitement when the groom in his all-white tux walked into the altar after his best man, Art. His smile was contagious. The feeling of pride and happiness showed on his face. It was an intimate event. In his toddler tux resembling the groom's, three-year-old Thomas entered, holding the rings and the coins. Ella followed him, pretty button-eyed in her classy princess dress of pink and purple satin. Slowly, she threw flower petals along her way.

Camera flashes focused more on the entrance when Doctor Stella entered with a bouquet in her hands. Being the only bridesmaid, she wore a satin gown resembling Ella's princess dress colors.

Art excitedly grinned when Shelly entered in her classy and sexy matron of honor dress. Once the entourage settled in their places, the orchestra started playing the instrumental of Shania Twain's song, 'From This Moment'.

Everyone stood up when the makeshift door at the opposite end of the altar closed. Standing in waiting in the middle of the aisle carpeted in red was the father of the bride. Everyone's faces showed intense anticipation as they all wished to see the bride from the other side of the door. The groom's eyes glistened. Finally, when the door opened, all eyes were on the most radiating bride, slowly walking toward her teary-eyed father.

The guests were in awe of her beauty. She was wearing a simple but elegant cream gown. Lace sparkling with Swarovski crystals made the top part. It was made of satin from the waist that overflowed on the floor. Everyone gasped in admiration at the bride, slowly walking toward her father. Standing beside each other, she reached for her father's hand. Both emanated happiness when they started walking toward the altar.

David's eyes were focused on the bride walking. He agreed with all the guests. The bride was the prettiest he'd ever seen her. Her gorgeous smile and aura were pure happiness. Yet, she focused her eyes on only one person. Reality flashed to him when she passed by where he was standing; *she was once mine*. He had long accepted Avery was the one that got away.

Avery never thought she would still get to walk down the aisle. She had reasons of her own. One, they already got married three years ago. Though she couldn't wear a wedding gown, the reason behind the very intimate union was all that mattered to her. Second, when she gave birth to Thomas, it seemed a perfect reason for her to focus on her family life. But her husband wouldn't let it go.

A month ago, Ethan proposed again while walking in the same park. There was no audience, no elaborate party. Just the two of them, walking hand in hand. He told her she deserved all the happiness in the world and the world itself. He would love to give her the best wedding. In between their sobs and tears, she said yes.

Little did she know, even before Ethan proposed in the park, all the preparations were already in motion, thanks to her ever-prepared best friend and loving sister-in-law. When Ste came back from Thailand four months back, she had no idea that both women had secretly started preparations for their wedding. Everyone was successful in keeping her off the loop. She thought all the while all the preparations were for Ethan's birthday. But she couldn't complain. Everything happening on her special day was a pleasant surprise. A moment she would forever remember.

"You realize David the dickhead had been eye fucking you since the ceremony started?" Shelly whispered to Doctor Stella, who was standing beside her.

Doctor Stella sighed, "He can eye fuck me all he wants, but he can't have me! A man whore like him, not to forget a cheater, will always be a red flag to me."

"Good thing he didn't hit on you in Thailand?" Shelly looked the doctor in the eye.

"He tried, but I didn't give him a chance. I don't get attracted to someone like him." Doctor Stella glanced toward Art and David, who had Thomas on his lap. Then, she whispered to Shelly, "Once a cheater, always a cheater!"

Shelly pretended as if Doctor Stella had struck her in the chest. "Ouch! I believe David falls into that category. But, as with Art, he hasn't shown any signs. If ever he will, I'll cut him while he's sleeping and feed all of him to the pigs!" Both ladies chuckled as they looked toward David and Art's side. Before Shelly could say another word, Ella interrupted them.

"Mama Ste, Auntie Shelly, please be quiet. Mommy and Daddy are going to say their vows now." Ella placed her pointer finger on her lips.

"I'm sorry, Princess," Doctor Stella whispered.

They all focused their vision on the altar. Avery and Ethan's gazes were locked on each other. When Shelly looked at Doctor Stella, a smile curved on both their lips. Happiness and love illuminated the couple who were about to say their vows.

Ethan cleared his throat. "Avery, my love, I give you my solemn promise to be your faithful friend, partner, and lover in sickness and health. I will hold your hand forever, whether in good or bad times. It will be my lifetime commitment never to give you a reason to doubt. I will do my best to make you feel you are enough every day. Even on bad days or when you yell too loud or cry too softly. When you feel as if you're going to crumble, or when your hair tangles as you lay in bed. You are and will always be enough. My mind, body, and heart will cherish only you for as long as we both live." A lone tear fell from Ethan's eye.

Affectionately, Avery wiped the tear on Ethan's cheek with her thumb. "Ethan, my gorgeous man. I give you my solemn vow to be your faithful friend, partner, and lover in sickness and health. I will never let go of your hand forever, whether at good times or bad. It will be my lifetime commitment to trust and respect you. Though there'll be times I will not be a diamond, just glass. Every day of our lives, I will thank you for making me feel my worth and believe I am enough. You have been my miracle in the depths of despair. I thank God for giving you to me. You made me realize it's not about the one who promises, for anyone can promise anything and leave. It's about the one who stands by the promise." Avery's voice croaked as tears slowly fell on her cheeks. "You brought me back to laugh in the places I have cried to change my life's sad and painful narrative. My mind, body, and heart will cherish only you for as long as we shall live."

As Ethan lovingly wiped Avery's tears, the pastor loudly pronounced them husband and wife. When the groom was instructed to kiss his bride, he slowly placed soft kisses on Avery's eyelids, nose, and cheeks. When his lips touched hers, they shared a long and passionate kiss, which earned loud clapping and whistles from the guests.

It delighted everyone watching the couple. Art squeezed David's shoulder and smiled at him. When David smiled back, Art's words replayed in his mind. *"Accept the wedding invitation and attend. Close that chapter of your life."* For the last time, he looked at Avery. She may have forgiven him and moved on, but David knew he couldn't forgive himself, for hurting her would always be the greatest regret of his life.

BONUS 1 | CHANGING THE NARRATIVE

TWO YEARS, **AVERY WHISPERED** to herself. That's how long it was since she stepped last at the same Charlotte airport. Of course, it was years ago, but she remembered everything like it was yesterday.

In the same cafe, her parents were sipping their favorite coffee. She smiled, seeing the sparkle in their eyes. Their excitement showed as they giggled, watching people walking back and forth from the table where they were sitting.

When Avery looked around, everything seemed the same but felt different. She knew why. The last time she was here, she was broken. Her life was at a crossroads. Her heart was in pain, moving away to let go. It was the same with her parents. They felt her pain, yet they stood beside her. If someone had told her two years ago, she'd be standing in the same spot unbroken, happy and grateful, she wouldn't have believed it. Instead, she would have broken down in tears and wallowed in self-pity and hopelessness.

But honestly, life is a never-ending mystery. Her heart was overflowing with joy. She didn't realize tears were slowly falling down her cheeks. As she wiped her tears, a pair of small hands planted on her leg.

"Thomas!" Ella's voice boomed.

"Ella, Princess, stop running!" Ethan's was louder.

When Avery looked behind her, a screaming Thomas was clenching her leg. Then, with a chuckle, Ella ran toward them. Ethan followed with a baby bag on his shoulder. Avery's smile said it all. Though everything seemed the same but felt different, the reason was in front of her: her family.

My family, she repeated to herself as she scooped two-year-old Thomas in her arms. When Ella reached them, she hugged her on her other arm and kissed her hair. All three of them grinned and giggled.

The moment Ethan reached them, he pecked Avery on the lips. Then, gently, he wiped a lone tear on her cheek with his thumb. "What happened, my love?" Avery shook her head and brushed her lips softly over Ethan's.

"I'm just so happy. I can't believe my life has changed since the last time I was here. Tears of joy!" Ethan caressed her cheek. "You deserve all the happiness in the world."

When Avery mouthed thank you, he kissed her on the forehead. Thomas and Ella's giggles stopped their moment. Avery took the baby bag from her husband as the other took the little boy from her arm. "How was the diaper change?" she chuckled at Ethan.

"It was a success!" Ethan rolled his eyes. "I wouldn't miss it for the world!" he remarked.

Ella pouted. "I helped Dad. He's not as good as you, Mom."

The couple laughed at Ella's statement. "Well, thanks for the compliment, Princess!" Ethan reacted. When Thomas pointed to where his grandparents were and started babbling and clapping, they all walked towards the cafe.

"Are you guys sure you don't want to stay here with the kids and your parents?" Mama T asked as Avery and Ethan said goodbye.

Avery shook her head. "Ethan has a timeshare and hasn't used it for a while. We're going to use it for some alone time."

Mama T nodded. "Thank you for bringing Thomas to us. We thought we might not see our grandson this time since David is still in Thailand."

"We wouldn't do that to you guys. Your grandson needs you. It's also a good time for you guys to bond together. But are you sure it's fine for Ella to stay? We can take her and just leave the nanny with Thomas and our parents," Ethan asked.

"Of course, it's fine! We love Ella. Besides, I don't think she will leave her brother and her grandparents." Mama T tapped Ethan on the shoulder. "Go, you guys. Enjoy Boston, and don't worry about the kids. They're in expert hands! You can have the car and the driver for yourselves for as many days as you want to."

Avery hugged Mama T. "I don't think we need it downtown. We'll send him back once we get to the hotel and call him whenever we need a ride. But I don't think so."

"Okay then. See you again. Enjoy your alone time, and we will enjoy our time here, too." Mama T waved goodbye as the couple got in the car.

On their drive, Avery noticed the route they were taking was different. "We're going to the Four Seasons on Boylston Street," she told the driver.

Ethan took her hand and kissed it. "We need to stop by somewhere."

Avery's eyes widened when the car parked in front of a familiar building. A smile formed on her lips. She faced Ethan, looking for an answer.

Ethan winked at her. "Art texted me to pick up something for Shelly. I realized we had brought nothing for them. And I assumed you would want to taste the coffee and pastries here. I won't let you miss the chance, my love!"

When Ethan got out of the car and opened her door, she felt her heart pounding. Seeing the cafe signage gave her mixed emotions. It wasn't just a place for her favorite coffee and pastries. The small building witnessed almost all the significant events in her Boston life. The moment she took Ethan's hand and stood in front of the cafe, everything flashed back to her. Both happy and sad moments.

She saw her eight-year-old self meeting Shelly for the first time. Their mothers shared a table on that busy Monday afternoon. Everything clicked from then. Both their mothers realized their little girls attended the same class in school. All four women formed a long, tested, and unbreakable friendship.

It was their go-to place. The four corners of the small box space heard all their secrets and giggles together from when they were in grade school to college. It was her and Shelly's safe and happy place. But it was also their crying place. They shared all their heartaches, problems, and tears in the same spot. The cafe stood their friendship as she and Shelly's friendship stood the test of time.

She sauntered when Ethan placed his hand on her shoulder and motioned for them to get inside. When they entered the door and saw her favorite spot, she remembered her talk with Mama T the last time. The memory was enough to bring back another moment in her life, her life with David.

It did not surprise her when Ethan told her to pick a booth as he went toward the counter to order. For sure, her husband already got info from her best friend about what her favorite drink and pastry were. After placing her jacket on the chair at her favorite table, she walked toward the picture board. Like before, her eyes darted to the spot where her and David's engagement picture was pinned.

Her lip curved into a small smile. She placed her palm on her chest. The feeling she was having was so much different from the last time. There was no pain, no more aches. "You look so young there," Ethan whispered as she felt his arms wrapped around her waist from behind. Slowly, Avery covered his arms with hers. She held him tight. "Did I?" she asked while slowly tracing Ethan's face with her fingers.

"You do. But you look more beautiful now than in that picture." She felt Ethan's lips on the crook of her neck. Immediately, she faced him and placed a soft kiss on his lips.

Ethan moaned. "I so much enjoy what we're doing right now. But I don't think the next scene in my mind is good for public viewing." They both laughed and walked toward their table. Once they were seated, the server brought their order.

Before the server could leave, Ethan asked for their picture to be taken using his phone camera. From behind, he embraced Avery as they flashed their radiant smiles at the camera. When the server asked if they wanted their picture printed and pinned on the board, they both said yes. Via Bluetooth, the server helped them send the picture to the cafe's printer.

Avery couldn't help but grin as they both enjoyed their coffee. Ethan gazed at her in wonder. "What?" she asked. "Why are you staring at me like that, Dr. James?" She giggled, awaiting his answer.

Ethan held her hand and brought it to his lips without removing his gaze. "I'm thinking, how else can I make you this happy? You deserve all the love and joy in this world."

Avery's eyes glistened. She clasped her fingers on his. "You always make me happy. You unbroke and completed me. Being here brought back memories, happy and sad. But right now, having you here made me feel so thankful. We are together, our family… our life now. It's a testament. Even though my past was painful and heartbreaking, hope never left me. My past didn't define my present and will surely never define our future."

Ethan started tracing her face from her eyebrows, nose, cheeks, jaw, and lips. Avery kissed his knuckles when his fingers reached the side of her mouth. When their eyes locked, they both whispered I love you to each other. Suddenly, the server they didn't realize was standing near their booth cleared his throat. Avery chuckled when Ethan smirked. They got two copies of their printed picture. One for the board and one for them to keep. Once they were done with their coffee, hands held, they walked back to the picture board.

Ethan gave the picture and the pin to Avery. "Do the honors, Mrs. James." He brushed his lips over hers. Without thinking twice, Avery hand-pinned their picture on top of hers and David's engagement photo. With Ethan's chin on her neck, she whispered, "That's the best spot! To remind me that even though my past was not what I expected it to be, my present and future are and will never be like my past. That's because I have you, and I'm with you!"

BONUS 2 | TURNING THE PAGE

"ARE YOU SURE ABOUT this?" Avery's brows crinkled. "I'd love a getaway with our family, but I don't want you spending so much money. You didn't have to fly everyone and rent an entire house for a month-long vacation." She gently brushed Ethan's hair with her fingers.

Ethan looked at her, smiling. He took her hand and placed it on his lips. "I won't mind spending money on my family. You know I wouldn't allow my work to keep me from you guys for over three days. If not for my presence needed in LA for a month, I wouldn't go there. But I must be there, so I'd rather bring you guys with me."

Avery's heart melted. Ethan always fulfilled his promise. He never allowed his work to impede spending time with her and the kids. For that, she was grateful. It was always his idea to bring them wherever he went away for work if it was beyond a day or two. *"I wouldn't give you any reason to doubt me or our relationship."* A smile formed on her lips as she remembered his words.

"What is that smile about?" Ethan pulled her body closer to his. When he lifted her chin and placed his lips on hers, she placed her arms around his neck.

"I just remembered something." She distanced her face a breath away from him and grinned. When Ethan's forehead creased, she pecked his lips and softly bit his lower lip.

Ethan cupped her face. "Someone's being a temptress right now!" He traced her lips. "What did you remember, my love?" Slowly, he started placing soft kisses on her forehead. "What did this beautiful mind of yours remember?"

Avery giggled louder. "The vow in our wedding."

Ethan smiled and placed a soft kiss on her nose. "My vow or yours?" he asked. "Yours." Avery traced his lips.

Ethan's eyes grew big. "Was there something I promised in my vow that I failed to do?"

"No, you're amazing every day. You always live up to your promise. Sometimes, I still can't believe what someone like me did to deserve someone like you." Avery placed her lips on his gently and for a longer time.

"My life's mission is always to please and make you happy, my love." He kissed her back.

Avery slowly brushed her fingers through his hair. "And I thank you for that. I thank God every day for giving me you and our family."

Ethan slowly nuzzled her cheeks. When he lifted her chin, Avery saw his deep love for her in his gaze. Every day, she wished Ethan also would saw through her.

"I wish the time will come when you see how worthy you are. You realize you're not just someone, but you are somebody special. I always wish you feel you're enough and deserving of my love and everyone who genuinely loves you, as I do."

Avery rested her head on Ethan's shoulder. "I feel your love all the time. Even the kids, my parents, and our friends. It's just sometimes I feel I'm unworthy of it all."

"That's expected because of what you've been through in the past. But it wasn't your fault. Your self-worth shouldn't suffer because of someone's wrongdoing. Remember, one will never be good enough for the wrong person. When people do not see your value, they're not for you. That's what happened, then. But for me, you're enough. You will always be," Ethan explained as his arm clung to her waist while the other hand massaged her back.

"I love you," Avery whispered in his ear.

Ethan kissed her hair and whispered, "I love you more."

The house Ethan rented for them to stay in for a month was a thirty-minute drive to the hospital, where he was required to work for a month. But Avery and her parents' jaws dropped when they arrived in what he called their short-term vacation house.

They entered a seventeen-acre estate overlooking the Pacific Ocean. It was a six-bedroom, seven-bathroom villa masterpiece that provided panoramic sunrise-to-sunset ocean views through its floor-to-ceiling glass doors and windows. It was a Malibu beach haven in all its perfection.

"Do you like it?" Ethan asked a wide-eyed Avery.

Avery looked around and laughed, seeing her parents' mouths open in shock. When she saw Ethan gazing at her, waiting for her verdict, she made a serious face. "What came to your mind? Why here?" Ethan scratched his head. "I thought you would love the ocean view and all-day access to a private beach and pool."

He sighed, "I should have asked for your input. I'm sorry. We can find another place if you…"

Avery pressed her lips to his. "Are you kidding me? I love it! We will love it here!" Ethan's lips curved out his signature gorgeous smile. His wife's reaction was priceless. He always wanted to make her happy and enjoy the finest things in life.

"But this must be so expensive! We could have gotten a smaller one," Avery exclaimed.

A soft brush of her husband's lips on hers was enough to remind Avery that money shouldn't concern her. "I invited Shelly and Art. They'll be arriving tomorrow."

"Really?" Avery showered her husband's face with soft kisses. "You're full of joyful surprises! If Shelly and Art join us, there'll be no dull moment. One month will be a breeze."

"That's what I thought." Ethan chuckled as he walked toward the ocean view. Before Avery followed, she felt small hands hugging her leg while another pair hugged her waist from behind.

"Whose hands are these around me?" she asked loudly.

Cackles echoed around her. When she lifted Thomas, Ella held her other hand and guided her toward Ethan. "Mom, can Thomas and I swim in the kiddie pool?" Ella asked with her button-sized puppy dog eyes.

When they stood beside Ethan, his arms opened for Thomas, who eagerly flew his little body to his. Avery looked Ethan in the eye. When he nodded, Avery smiled.

"Okay, you can swim since Dad, and I can watch you now. But you can never swim without adult supervision." Ella nodded with a smile plastered on her face. "But you both need to change into your swim clothes first. Let's leave Dad and Thomas here while I help you change."

Ella pulled Avery's hand before she could turn around. Immediately, she removed her clothes to reveal her swimsuit already worn. When Avery pointed at Thomas, Ella took off her brother's clothes and revealed his cute swim trunk from the inside. Avery and Ethan looked at each other, surprised.

"I'm sorry if I didn't ask permission. When we arrived, I saw you busy talking. So, Nanny and I brought Thomas into the changing room and put on our swim clothes. I thought it could save time," Ella explained.

"I'm Spidey! Look, Spidey, Dad!" Thomas happily pointed at the Spiderman logo in his swim trunk.

The couple couldn't help it; Ethan guffawed, and Avery tittered. Avery tucked a loose strand of Ella's hair and whispered a thank you in her ear. Realizing she wasn't in trouble; Ella took the deep breath she had been holding since.

"Okay, we're about to leave for the airport, but we'll go there. Don't worry; I'll handle everything once we arrive." Ethan sighed as he ended the call and instructed the driver to go to Cedar Sinai instead.

Avery squeezed his hand. "Is everything alright? What did Art say?"

Ethan smiled at her. "Nothing to worry about. After landing, Shelly had just gotten faint spells and vomited several times. They're on their way to the hospital, and we'll meet them there."

"Shelly doesn't get sick." Avery's face turned pale.

"Hey, she'll be alright." Ethan pulled her toward him. "I'll make sure she's taken care of well."

Avery's breathing seemed to stop for a few seconds when the driver pulled the car up outside the hospital entrance. When Ethan mentioned the hospital, she hadn't realized they'd be going to the same place where she'd last stepped foot several years back.

Ethan felt the coldness in his wife's hand when they walked hand in hand inside. "Trust me, my love. Shelly will be fine. They're just taking precautions." He placed Avery's hand on his lips, earning a smile from her.

After talking to the front desk, they walked toward the familiar hospital wing. As luck would have it, Ethan led her to the room she never thought she'd ever set foot in again—Room 606.

Once the door opened, Shelly and Art's eyes darted in their direction. Ethan stopped by the door to check the doctor's name in charge as Avery marched toward her best friend's bed.

"Shells! What happened? How are you feeling?" she asked.

Instead of answering her question, Shelly was smirking. "What a reunion, right? Who would have thought we'd be in this room again?" She smiled at Avery.

Art cupped his wife's hands. "I only want the best doctors to check on you, babe. Besides, the circumstances weren't the same as the last."

"Should I thank you, babe?" Shelly rolled her eyes at Art.

Avery waved her hand to stop her best friend. "Don't worry about it, Shells! We all moved on. But seriously, what happened? Since I can remember, you never get sick," she asked.

Art stood up from his seat and gave it to Avery. She hugged Shelly first and sat down. "It's been days since I've been a little under the weather, but while on our flight, I vomited several times and had some faint spells. They took some tests, and hopefully, I will get discharged soon. I'm so dying to see our Malibu haven!" Shelly grinned.

Avery's eyes twinkled. "You guys will love it there! The kids love it! Mine and my parents' jaws dropped. Literally!"

Shelly's laugh echoed in the room. "I find it funny your Mr. Hotshot still surprises you in the richness department!"

"You know the both of us! We're lucky to have lived a good and financially stable life since we met. But Ethan's..." Avery shrugged her shoulders and rolled her eyes. "I still find it unbelievable most of the time."

Shelly nodded. "I know. You're one lucky girl. And I'm one lucky best friend to enjoy the perks!"

Silence replaced their loud laughter when Avery's eyes roamed around the room's four corners. Shelly broke the silence. "It looks the same as I remembered it."

"I didn't see it from the inside before. I just remembered the door and the room number." Avery pouted her lip as she shook her head several times. "And the scene I saw from the outside of that door." She chuckled and pointed at the half-glass, half-wood door.

Shelly sighed aloud and took Avery's hand, squeezing it. "Funny how life makes a joke sometimes, right?"

"So true," Avery replied as she squeezed back her best friend's hand.

The moment their eyes locked, they clasped each other's hands and giggled like when they were teenagers. Shelly, always the entertainer, blew the strands of hair away from her face. She looked up at the ceiling and raised her right hand. "Yes, Lord! Please tell us what you want us to know. Is this a Deja vu, a coincidence, or an affirmation of something good coming our way?"

Avery's shoulders were shaking hard from laughing as she watched her best friend. Shelly never fails to entertain her.

"What's going on?" Art's voice cut Shelly from her antics.

"What did we miss?" Ethan asked.

Both women looked at each other and answered their husbands in chorus. "Nothing." Before either of the men could say anything, a man in a white doctor's coat came in, followed by a nurse.

"Hello, everyone. I'm Doctor Germain." Art immediately shook the doctor's hand and introduced himself. When the doctor looked in Ethan's direction, he nodded as he mentioned having a doctor-to-doctor conversation with him a few minutes ago. Ethan, in return, introduced Avery.

Shelly pulled Avery's hand while the doctor was checking on the chart. "He's the same doctor who checked on you last time," she mouthed. Avery nodded and smiled.

When Doctor Germain needed the space where Avery was, Ethan offered his hand to his wife. Standing beside each other, he hugged her waist with his left hand to pull Avery closer to him. "Does Shelly know Doctor Germain?" he asked in a whisper.

Avery brushed her lips over Ethan's cheek and whispered back in his ear. "The three of us met him years ago."

"How? Here?" Ethan asked as he placed a soft kiss between his wife's ear and cheek.

"Yes, here." Avery nodded. "Remember the LA hospital story I told you?" she asked in a soft voice.

Ethan's eyes grew, looking at the doctor and back at her. "Really?" his mouth opened.

Avery nodded with a huge grin. "Really."

He pulled her toward his body more and kissed the top of her hair. "Small world." Ethan softly chuckled as he placed a kiss on her forehead. "I'm glad it's me with you right now," he added.

Avery placed her lips on Ethan's, soft and slow. "Me too," she responded. It felt like they were the only ones in the room. At that moment, they were back in their happy love bubble. Before things got heated between them, Art's loud voice burst their bubble.

"Yes! Yes! Yes!" Art was shouting between kisses on Shelly's face and raising his fisted hand in the air.

"What happened?" Avery asked with widened eyes.

"Ave!" Shelly was rubbing her belly in tears, eyes focused on her best friend. "Art and I are pregnant!"

BONUS 3 | HEALING AND LETTING GO

"CONGRATULATIONS! YOU HAVE A baby girl!"

Doctor Stella's voice echoed in the room. Tears and a big smile plastered Avery's face. For her, it was a hundred percent ultimate friendship experience. Seeing tears and smiles on Shelly and Art's faces was beyond. After Art cut the cord, loud clapping and endless words of congratulations surrounded the new parents.

Avery couldn't contain her heart's happiness. It was a surreal occasion to witness such a big milestone in her best friend's life. She was sure Shelly would be hands-on and a caring mother like she cared for Ella and Thomas. Art's presence and care would make a perfect team as loving parents to their newborn daughter.

"Happy tears?" Ethan's whisper in Avery's ear caused her body to shiver. They'd been together for almost four years, and everything about her husband excited her the way it did since they first met in the park.

Ethan's arms slowly wrapped around her waist from behind. Avery felt a kiss in her hair. She couldn't help it. One hand softly traced his jaw while the other clasped his hand around her waist. "She's beautiful! The baby's got Shelly's eyes and Art's lips. I'm so happy for my best friend!"

"She sure is beautiful. We all are happy for them!" Ethan placed small kisses between her ear and cheek. "I can feel the joy radiating through your body. Maybe tonight we can try for a baby too? Look how beautiful Ella and Thomas are. We surely can make another gorgeous one!"

Avery giggled. "Ethan, you're tickling me!" she whispered.

A few days after the hospital released Shelly and the baby, all four were doing final touches in the baby's room. Ethan was helping Art in putting up the crib. Avery was putting the decorations she bought for her goddaughter while Shelly relaxed the baby in a rocking chair. It had been six months since the new parents moved to Florida and purchased the house next to Ethan's. When Shelly looked around and locked eyes with Avery, they both smiled.

Living beside each other and nurturing their friendship with their own families were other friendship goals checked off their list. As the four of them exchanged banters, an almost-four-year-old Thomas came running with Ella holding on to him.

"Papa is here! He has pink balloons for my girlfriend!" Thomas' words earned chuckles from the men and surprised stares from the women in the room.

"About time, dude!" Art yelled at David, who entered the room with the balloons and flowers.

"So sorry I wasn't able to catch a flight a few days earlier." David hugged Avery as he handed her the flowers and balloons. When Shelly reached, he kissed her forehead and caressed the baby's hair.

"Thanks for coming!" Shelly mouthed.

David scooped Thomas in his arms and walked toward the guys fixing the crib. "I thought you wouldn't need any help with small stuff like this, Engineer Art!"

Art rolled his eyes at David. "Screw you, dude! I don't know why I agreed to buy this complicated piece of shi—"

"Art!" Shelly's voice halted her husband from finishing his statement. "The kids are here!" she added.

Ethan and David laughed, seeing Art's pale face as he gestured a sorry to his wife. "Is that pink bed for my girlfriend?" Thomas asked.

All three men eyed each other, speechless at the boy's question. Shelly pointed Avery toward the little boy, hinting at her best friend to say something.

Avery shook her head and looked in her son's direction. "Thomas, who said something about a girlfriend? Where did you hear about girlfriends? You're too young for that."

The little boy wriggled for David to put him down. "I told myself! Like in the toy story." He moved toward Shelly. He put his pointer finger on the baby's palm. A smile formed on his lips when the baby clamped it inside her small hand. "See! She's my girlfriend, and I'm her boyfriend!"

Art snickered. He stood up and passed the screw to David. "Dude, you better work on my blessing now. I leave this crib in your and Ethan's hands. Both of you better build this crib." He made a thumbs-up sign on the little boy. "Right, Thomas?"

Thomas nodded and gave a thumbs-up sign back. "I'm going to marry her when she turns twenty!"

Shelly and Ella laughed. Avery waved her hands toward the little boy. "Shush right there, lover boy! You haven't started school and are already considering marrying."

"Thomas got moves, huh!" Art blurted. "It astounds me that he talks straight like an adult at his age. I know the heart and smartness he got from Avery and Ethan. I'm curious where he got those sloppy lover boy tricks!" He pointed a finger at David, which earned laughter from everyone and an F sign from David.

"That was an exceptional dinner, Ave! Thanks to your cooking skills and Ethan's handsomeness!" Art exclaimed while rubbing his stomach. Avery smirked as Ethan bowed proudly.

After enjoying their dinner, they all agreed to dessert and tea at the boathouse. Avery looked around. Shelly was fascinated as she watched what was happening in their house over the baby monitor. It showed Ella sitting on the rocking chair with the baby in her arms while the nanny assisted her. On the floor, Thomas was playing with his Legos.

Avery looked over the men when she heard them discussing the improvements and additions Art wanted for their new house. When she looked back to Shelly, they locked eyes as she pouted her mouth toward the guys. They both nodded, silently agreeing they'd all come a long way.

Shelly being Shelly, she beamed and shifted on the seat beside Avery. "Who would have thought?" she murmured.

"I know." Avery gently grabbed her best friend's hand.

"I guess the saying was true. When you forgive, you heal. When you let go, you grow. Look at us now!" Shelly snickered.

Avery nodded. "Yeah. I guess it's right."

"Doesn't it feel like we're able to heal from all the misery of the past because the damage it inflicted felt like it never existed?" Shelly asked.

Avery closed her eyes for a few seconds. When she opened them, she glanced at David. Quickly, her visions shifted toward Ethan. She gazed at her husband with profound gratitude and love.

"No, Shells. I think healing doesn't mean the damage never existed. We're healed because the damage no longer controls our lives."

Shelly nodded and looked at the baby monitor again. When she saw Thomas peppering her newborn with kisses, she placed the monitor in front of Avery. Her best friend's eyes widened, knowing what her son was doing could irritate the calm baby. Unable to contain whatever she wanted to say, she turned on the monitor's speaker.

"What are you doing, Thomas? You might make her cry with all those kisses!"

Thomas paused. He placed his arms over his chest, sighed, and answered aloud. "I'm just marking my territory!"

Avery remembered the little boy's statement from one time he saw Ethan placing soft kisses on her eyes, nose, cheeks, and lips. When Thomas asked what his dad was doing to her mom, Ethan gave the same reasoning as a joke.

The men in the room were all eyes on the monitor with shocked faces. Avery's face paled. Shelly broke the silence. "Um… we may have a problem with my favorite godson. I mean… I love him to death, but I think him getting Ethan's possessiveness and David's manwhore moves..." She shook her head multiple times. "It doesn't seem like an excellent combination."

"And my daughter is not a territory! You little…" Art paused, seeing the adults in the room scowling at him. "You little godson of mine!" he said instead.

"What's wrong with Thomas ending with your daughter?" David yelled back at Art, laughing.

"Yeah! Thomas is a good catch!" Ethan added in chuckles.

Avery tapped her forehead in frustration. "You guys, this isn't funny! The boy needs to have a father-son talk; don't you think?" She glared at both Ethan and David.

"Well, I wouldn't mind them ending up together. Just thinking about the inheritance Thomas will get from a lawyer father and a doctor dad… It wouldn't be bad at all!" Shelly was laughing as she made a peace sign to Avery.

"Shells!" Avery squealed in exasperation.

BONUS 4 | TRUE LOVE IS NEVER LATE

"THIS IS HAPPENING!" AVERY whispered to herself, looking at the third stick lined with the other two she placed on the side of their bathroom's marble sink. It had been two months since Shelly gave birth to her and Art's beautiful daughter, Steffi. It seemed like heaven had finally granted Ethan's wish that night.

Her heart was beating loudly. It felt like happiness and excitement would burst out of every cell of her body. Getting pregnant after four years of being married to Ethan was another dream come true. Though Ella and Thomas completed their family, the precious life inside her was beyond. She couldn't ask for more.

In tears, Avery stared at herself in the mirror. She was truly one blessed woman. The Avery she was looking at was very different from the one she'd seen before Ella, Ethan, and Thomas had come into her life. The one she saw in the mirror now was a complete woman. One whose man constantly reminded her she was enough.

"Are you practicing for a role in a drama or what?" Shelly's voice startled her.

"What the…" Avery massaged her chest. "You almost gave me a heart attack!"

"I'm baking and realized I ran out of vanilla extract. I don't want to take anything from your kitchen without your permission. Besides, Ethan permitted me to come here."

Shelly lifted Avery's chin and studied her face. "What's going on? Your husband said you'd been acting weird since yesterday…"

Shelly stopped staring at Avery's face and looked around. Her eyes widened when she saw the sticks lined up in the sink. "OMG! Triple shit!"

Without another word, she enveloped Avery in her arms. Their eyes welled with tears. Though they didn't talk much about it, both women knew how everyone in the family had been praying for Ethan's wish to be granted.

Shelly's excitement for her best friend showed in her trembling hands as she wiped the tears from Avery's cheeks. When their eyes met, the crying turned to giggles. "We need to plan the best pregnancy reveal for Ethan!"

Avery almost choked on her laughter at hearing her best friend's party-planning mind in action. "Do we need to do that?"

Shelly nodded. "Of course! Hotshot waited for four years. He earned it!" Immediately, she grabbed all the sticks and placed them in Avery's hand. "Hide them. We should tell Ste. My chest will burst if I don't tell her about this now!"

"I should get Ste to check me to confirm. What do you think?"

"Right! Let's go to her now." Shelly started pacing inside the bathroom. When she stopped, she looked at Avery. "What do we tell your husband? He's downstairs."

"What did you tell him before you came here?" asked Avery.

"That I need vanilla extract." Shelly nodded multiple times as if she had made the most incredible plan. "Let's tell him we both ran out of the vanilla extract, and we'll run to the grocery store. Give me the sticks. I'll hide it for you." She grabbed the sticks from Avery's hand.

Both women smoothed their dresses and looked in the mirror to make sure there was no trace of crying on their faces. They were relieved to see Ethan busily teaching Thomas how to ride his bike in the driveway. When they informed him of their last-minute grocery run, it didn't raise any suspicion because it had been like that since they became neighbors.

After kissing Ethan and Thomas goodbye and Shelly running back from informing Art about their plan, the best friends excitedly drove away. It surprised Doctor Stella to see the two ladies power walk inside her clinic. She didn't waste any second when they informed her about her sister-in-law's pregnancy.

Doctor Stella gave Avery a full pregnancy check-up. When all the tests confirmed she was three months pregnant, all three happily cried together. Shelly and Doctor Stella were unstoppable in their over-the-top planning ideas. Ultimately, they all agreed to do the revelation during their regular Sunday dinner at Shelly's house.

"My love, did you notice something with Ste?" Ethan placed his chin on Avery's shoulder while she was brushing her hair in front of the vanity.

"What do you mean?" Avery's forehead creased.

Ethan started placing soft kisses on her neck. "First, she came a day early for our Sunday dinner, which she was always late to since." His lips moved to the back of Avery's ear. "Second, she brought new clothes for Ella and Thomas, specifically for tonight's dinner."

"And what's unusual about that? Shouldn't you thank her for coming early and remembering the kids?" Avery started giggling, feeling Ethan's hands inside her lace top.

"Yeah, I think I should thank her." He lingered his hand under Avery's breast, which caused her to gasp.

"Except that, I think you three… Ste, Shelly, and you are hiding something."

Avery cleared her throat and placed a kiss on Ethan's jaw. "What could we be hiding?

"Tell me, Mrs. James. What could you guys hide from Art and me?" Ethan smiled when a moan came from Avery as he softly pinched her nipple.

Avery closed her eyes. "I don't know what you're talking about, Dr. James."

"We promised no secrets, my love. You know I can keep a secret even from Art." Ethan's hands gently cupped Avery's mounds at the same time.

Avery started panting with her eyes still closed. She knew her husband was trying to get a confession out of her. But she promised Shelly and her sister-in-law she wouldn't spoil the surprise. But with her pregnancy hormones, she couldn't help but enjoy Ethan's way.

"I know… I haven't forgotten our promises to each other. But… why did you mention Art?" Avery couldn't hold another gasp when Ethan's other hand moved down her thigh.

"Tell Shelly to stop torturing her husband. The man thinks his wife is pregnant again. He's going crazy about it because Steffi is just three months old." Ethan softly blew on her neck, causing a louder gasp from Avery. "He's afraid Shelly is planning revenge on him because he initiated having sex with her earlier than six weeks after she gave birth."

Avery's panting, gasps, and moans were getting louder. "Why would Art think Shells is pregnant?"

Ethan's hand was now between her thighs.

"He found three pregnancy test sticks in their bathroom. All positive."

Avery's moans turned into a choking sound, followed by uncontrollable coughing. "Art found what?" she asked.

"Positive pregnancy test sticks. He has a feeling Shelly is up to something. He's expecting her revenge on him tonight during our dinner." Ethan didn't notice Avery's expression since his lips were busy ravaging her neck while one hand was kneading one of her mounds and the other was in her center.

Before Avery could think of what to say next, Ethan's lascivious acts raced through her to complete ecstasy. Her whole body was always enjoying the feeling of helplessness, leaving all the pregnancy's secret worries behind. Shelly's house might be a few steps from theirs, but with what they were lovingly sharing at that moment, they both knew they would arrive late. And they couldn't care less.

During dinner, Ethan and Art exchanged secret glances. Their wives and Doctor Stella were acting weird. After dessert, all three took Ella and Thomas inside the baby's room. Both men agreed in silence that the ladies had planned something. When Ella and Thomas came out wearing statement shirts, the two men confirmed what Art had been thinking.

Ella's shirt had *I'm so excited!* written on it. While Thomas's shirt said, *I can't wait!* When the three ladies returned to the dining room with a gift box, Ethan winked at Art. Art blinked back with an I told you so expression written all over his face.

Ethan cleared his throat; his eyes darted to the gift box Shelly was holding. "What's the occasion, Shells?"

"Oh, this?" Shelly looked at Art and smiled. "I have a special gift for my husband. But I want you to do the honors and open the gift box for him."

When Shelly handed the box to Ethan, his lips curved into a big smile. He gave Art a thumbs-up sign. "I got you, dude!" He wanted to ease Art from the torture his wife was giving him.

Immediately, Ethan removed the ribbon tied to the box. When he lifted the cover, it revealed the three positive pregnancy sticks taped on a bond paper showing a bold "CONGRATULATIONS, DADDY!" written on it. He stood up, walked toward Art, and shook his hand.

"Congratulations, dude!" Ethan said to Art as he handed him the box.

Art's hands were trembling when he pulled out the paper. He even mouthed sorry for a giggling Shelly. The moment he lifted the paper from the box, it revealed a tiny onesie. Art's eyes grew. "Wait! What?" he yelled as he looked at Shelly, then at Avery. When both women nodded, he called Ethan, who was about to sit back. "Ethan, man! Look at this!"

Ethan turned around with his brows raised. "Look for yourself!" Art waved his hand for Ethan to see what was inside the box.

The giddy faces of the women and Art's changed expression made him bolt toward the box. Ethan's eyes went around. He blinked three times and looked at what was inside the box again. He looked at Avery. When her eyes turned glossy, she started nodding. Ethan sprinted to her and brushed her hair back away from her face.

"Is it true?" he asked Avery.

Avery nodded, her eyes glistening. Ethan drew in a long breath and blew out his cheeks. He chuckled, and Avery giggled louder. He slowly took both of her hands and clasped them in his. Gently, he pressed his lips to her forehead, eyelids, nose, cheeks, and down to her lips. His lips planted the gentlest and softest kiss on her lips. Avery felt nothing but genuine affection.

With his shoulders shaking, Ethan whispered Thank you, and I love you in her ear. When she lifted her head and looked at his face, she remembered her dad's words, *"One day, you'll find someone who will show you why it never worked out with someone else. And that someone will prove to you that true love is never late."*

PLAYLIST

This is the list of the music I listened to while writing the book.

Before It Sinks In
Take Her to the Moon
Moira dela Torre

What If I Never Get Over You
Ryan Hurd

I'm Never Getting Over You
Gone West

It's Time to Go
You're Losing Me
Taylor Swift

Healing
Keep on Hoping
Riley Clemmons

God Took His Time on You
Casey Barnes

Vow to Be Yours
Leanna Crawford

From This Moment On
Shania Twain

Best Friend for Life
Grace Leer

You can also listen to the playlist "Before It's Too Late" on Spotify

About the Author

EastCoastPinay captivates readers with her evocative storytelling and heartwarming romance narratives. Her latest book delves into themes of resilience, self-love, and finding love after heartbreak, offering a poignant journey of healing and hope. Despite being a newcomer in the storytelling realm, EastCoastPinay has garnered a loyal following on Wattpad, continuing to stir the hearts of her audience with her compelling narratives. With a Bachelor's degree in Secondary Education, EastCoastPinay's passion for women's empowerment shines through her work, transporting readers to new worlds and immersing them in the highs and lows of love, loss, and relationships. In addition to writing, she finds joy in reading novels, crafting heartfelt poetry, and indulging in the timeless allure of romance and contemporary literature.